THE UNEXPECTED EARL

PHILIPPA JANE KEYWORTH

ISBN (eBook): 978-1-9998652-3-8

ISBN (Print): 978-1-9998652-5-2

ALSO BY
PHILIPPA JANE KEYWORTH

LADIES OF WORTH SERIES

Fool Me Twice

A Dangerous Deal

Lord of Worth

Duke of Disguise

REGENCY ROMANCES

The Widow's Redeemer

The Unexpected Earl

MULTI-AUTHOR SERIES

Finding Miss Giles

FANTASY

The Edict

Dedicated to Feebie

That most lovable Hound
That most loyal Friend

CHAPTER ONE

BLACK HOOVES STRUCK THE COBBLESTONES IN rapid succession, the sound echoing into the London night. Torchlight caught the well-polished flanks of the pair pulling the carriage, their ebony coats stained even darker with sweat and their heads bobbing up and down as they made quick work of the streets. On either side of the travelling carriage, the Town houses climbed high into the midnight, an avenue of sleeping giants. Tucked away inside the buildings, the owners were either entertaining guests or else enjoying a breath of quiet before the bustling London Season truly began.

On went the carriage. The houses and squares disappeared into darkness while bright lights illuminated the destination ahead.

The driver headed towards the lights as fast as the cobbled streets would allow. The autumn had begun mild, but tonight was proof of the progression towards deep winter. The horses' breath escaped in plumes from their nostrils. The heavy greatcoat that the driver had donned in place of his summer livery warded off the majority of the cold, but fingers of icy air still managed to find their way around his neck. Blast it! How could he have forgotten his woolen scarf on a night like this?

The occupants of the carriage fared slightly better. Protected from the cold wind, two gentlemen sat across from each other on the cushioned seats, both in evening attire. One lounged comfortably, but the taller, darker of the two kept his arms crossed over his chest and threw frequent glances out of the window.

"Curse it all, Courtenay! How long does it take to get to Almack's?"

The ill-natured question only served to make the other gentleman smile, his rounded cheeks bulging on either side of his mouth. "Oh, you are in a sour mood tonight, Wolversley."

The taller man scowled in return. "You would be too if you had travelled all the way from Sussex only to have your best friend cart you off to the most boring charade of polite Society."

"You're lucky there is no one to hear you say so. I declare, if one of the patronesses heard your description of their hallowed rooms, your voucher would be revoked!"

A jolt on the near side of the carriage upset the occupants for a moment until the vehicle settled into its regular motion again.

"Besides," Courtenay continued after repositioning himself, "how can you be in a bad mood? You have been away from Society all this time, not even bothering to come back to Town for Viscount Beauford's ball, and now you are back to civilization and dinner parties and masquerades and all things marvelous, and you're miserable! I tell you, I do not understand you."

That last bit was a barefaced lie. Lord Courtenay understood his old university friend very well—which is exactly why he had refrained from telling him that their destination for the evening was not, in fact, Almack's. They were en route to a private ball, the sort of event that Wolversley rarely attended, preferring his estate and account books to most kinds of social engagements. Part of Courtenay did not blame him. After all, it was not an easy thing to mix with your peers when you had a past like Earl Wolversley's.

"You make a mistake in thinking my misery is connected to being in London. Rather it's connected to you whisking me away from a large bottle of Burgundy I had at home. It could have kept me far better company than you will this evening."

"Oh, a dagger to the heart! I am so hurt." Courtenay's lips gave an affected pout. "But in truth, you did surprise me. I half thought you'd refuse to come out, even at *my* invitation."

Wolversley snorted, muttering something about rather being under the table at home, and then finally mustered up some kind of civility. "I suppose I *am* pleased to see you again. My sister, though pleasant company, is somewhat exhausting when she assumes I am her sole entertainment on the estate."

"Ah, the lovely Selina, I wish I could see her again." Courtenay's eyes went misty in the dim light of the carriage and his tone turned wistful.

"I expect you do," said Wolversley dryly, "but I shall not let you near her until she is out and until some of that naïvety is rubbed off. You are far too much of a scoundrel for her company at present."

"Well, no matter, we shall have plenty of schoolroom misses where we're going."

"Almack's? It's all rather staid don't you think? Hardly the place for you to make young chits swoon."

"Ah, well...that is the thing...." Courtenay looked down at his black silk breeches moulded tightly over his podgy thighs and below those to his astonishingly elegant feet encased in evening pumps. The thing was—although he was dressed in the requisite uniform of Almack's, one of the most exclusive assembly rooms in London, he had never intended to go there.

Now came the sticky part.

"I actually thought we could take advantage of an invitation I received. It's to a somewhat better place than Almack's." He was trying his best to seem nonchalant while revealing his deception. "It's a coming-out ball. I know your distaste for this kind of thing, but it will be a splendid evening. I was assured by the father of the debutante that his wife was sparing no expense. All the beauties of Society will be present, and I daresay one might even catch your eye, despite your habitual insistence on prolonging your bachelorhood."

Wolversley's anger had been growing steadily as Courtenay unfolded their new plans for the evening, and due to that last comment, he was positively seething. "You ass! How dare you lie to me?"

"It's for your own good, my friend, I promise." Courtenay shifted a little farther away from the Earl who looked ready to round on him. "You know, since you've been away from Town, there have been plenty of young bachelors trying to usurp your place as the most eligible gentleman this side of thirty. I had to take it upon myself to hold that position until you came back."

Wolversley's lips curved up into a crooked smile, "You did, did you?" If there had been more light in the carriage, Courtenay would have seen Wolversley's pale gray eyes begin to dance.

"Yes, because I am a dear, dear friend."

"And a dear, dear liar." Wolversley sighed. "How on earth could you be deemed an eligible bachelor with your estate teetering precariously between dun territory and utter ruin?"

Courtenay could hear the Earl's anger turning to amusement, and he took advantage of his friend's improved temper. "Ah, it's all about wording it right, my good man." He leaned forward and waggled his finger under the Earl's nose. "But since I am a faithful friend who cannot help but see to your best interests, I will allow you to reclaim your position. You need to come out into Society again somewhat, reclaim at least a semblance of a figure in the best circles, if only to ensure you can someday get yourself betrothed and all that."

Wolversley grimaced, but his face was obscured by the shadows in the carriage. He had been betrothed once. He did not have any intention of finding himself in that position again.

"Besides," continued Courtenay, "I have it on good authority that Jonny Odd is attending Almack's tonight."

Wolversley grimaced again. Courtenay was adept at stirring up unpleasant memories. The two of them—or rather, the three of them—had attended university during the same period. Jonny Odd had never liked the Earl, making him the object of many of his taunts and practical jokes. Graduation and the intervening years had done nothing to improve their acquaintance. The man was an ass and Wolversley quite agreed with Courtenay that he was best avoided.

"So, I thought the ball the better invitation of the two. And of course, if you should manage to find a little amusement there to entice you back into Society, then all the better."

Before the Earl could question Courtenay about their actual destination, their journey was over. The horses ceased their spanking trot, the hoof beats slowed from two to four beats, and the carriage came to a dignified halt.

"Ah, we are arrived. Excellent." Courtenay peered out of the window at the Palladian Town house lit up by hanging lanterns.

Outside, the driver relinquished his tight hold on the reins, giving the slack back to his horses. He pulled the collar of his greatcoat up about his ears and blew on his hands. The groom was not long in performing his duties, and soon the steps were down. The door swung wide, and Lord Courtenay's elegant foot and shapely calf descended, followed by his rather larger upper half.

Courtenay's countenance was now lit by the lanterns held by the servants either side of the door. His avid consumption of wine showed in his pinkish face, and he had a rosy tint to the end of his nose. That being said, it could not be denied that Lord Courtenay was a good-looking man with a good-natured face. As he reached the ground, he swung round to await his friend.

"A coming-out ball, you said?" Wolversley called, descending the carriage steps. He glanced up at the house, not waiting to listen to Courtenay's response. He was too intent on stifling the unpleasant memories that his friend had dredged up. As he caught sight of the building, however, a sickly feeling began to invade his body. He glanced up and down the street, trying to ascertain if they were in fact standing where he suspected—and feared—they might be.

"It is indeed, and in honour of a beautiful young girl I'm told." Courtenay slapped a hand on the Earl's athletic shoulders, ignoring the unsettled look that had painted itself across his face. "I am jolly glad you're back in Town. It's been dashed dull without you, believe it or not. Despite your moods, you do make a man much better company than these jumped-up young scamps running about the clubs and balls these days."

Wolversley neither felt umbrage at the insult nor gratitude at the compliment. It was all quite lost on him as he kept looking up at the house, determined to believe he was anywhere other than where his mind told him he must be.

"Where are we exactly?" he managed at last.

"Wiltshire Square."

Wolversley cursed.

"I say!" exclaimed Courtenay, looking around uncomfortably. "Bad form, old man."

Fortunately, there were no ladies in earshot, but two young bucks who had just alighted from a nearby carriage ceased their jocular conversation to raise eyebrows at Wolversley's uncouth remark. One of them looked the Earl up and down and snorted unfavourably.

The Earl, who took no pleasure in being so brazenly measured, felt a stab of annoyance as the young man's appraising gaze fell fearfully short of impressed. It was not just the crude language the Earl had used that caused his disdain; it was the Earl's jacket. Wolversley could feel the young man's eyes on his shoulders and lapels as his lips curled up in scorn.

Wolversley had been in the country too long. His jacket was outdated—he had known that when he had put it on this evening, having already seen several gentlemen walking the streets of Town in far more modish creations. He enjoyed a well-cut jacket, though he would not claim the careful eye of a dandy where his appearance was concerned, but his extended trip to the country had left him no opportunity to ensure that his wardrobe was full of the current fashions, nor to cut his hair for that matter. The luxuriously dark lengths were tickling his collar, unlike Courtenay's sandy locks which were swept up into a form of the Brutus, a style far too ostentatious to be attractive. Wolversley looked back to the young men. Those scrutinizing eyes that would not forgive his outdated clothing were one reason he disliked Society gatherings so much, and yet, thanks to the cajoling—and chicanery—of a particular friend, he was back.

The Earl glared at the young buck who did not approve of him, but it seemed that he had already forgotten the Earl's existence as he turned to go up the stairs to the house. Wolversley looked back at his friend. His jacket was a very minor problem compared to the one presented by his location.

He knew exactly where he was. He knew exactly whose

house this was. And if his exacting knowledge was correct, he was in quite a deal of hot water.

Courtenay, having missed most of this unvoiced exchange thanks to a beautiful young woman stepping out of a carriage four spaces down—waved his hand at their waiting vehicle and ordered his driver to come back later.

The driver tipped his hat and then took this last chance to pull his collar up. After his neck was protected as well as it could be from the elements, he whipped up the horses and returned the way they had come.

The Earl stared at the departing carriage, his only method of retreat disappearing into the foggy London evening. Several more people emerged from carriages and chairs along the length of the street. Mothers and fathers shepherded young daughters past the two men towards the open door of the house.

Courtenay smiled at his friend. "Shall we go in?"

"A moment." Wolversley held up a hand. "It would perhaps be best for me to know who the hosts of this ball are, seeing as I am arriving on their doorstep uninvited." He struggled to maintain an even tone.

"Oh, well, the funny thing is, someone I was talking to the other day seemed to think you might know them. It is the delightful Miss Annabelle we are welcoming into the affectionate arms of Society this evening, but the family name is Rotherham."

Wolversley cursed again, this time under his breath. "You should have told me where you were taking me this evening."

"Oh, I know, I know—my deception was inexcusable. But it can hardly be helped, and besides we are here now."

"Courtenay?" Another male voice entered the conversation. The gentleman walking towards them presented a fine sight, his long legs encased in some very fine and very tight silk breeches, his stockings showing off a set of fine calves and his evening jacket, made of superfine, mirroring his form with a closeness some might think impossible. The subtlety and taste of his clothes denoted his status as a dandy, and the fine cut indicated he was a man of considerable fortune. His countenance gave nothing of his age away with its high cheekbones, well-cut jaw, and lack of wrinkles. He could have been anywhere between one-and-twenty and thirty years of age.

"I say, is it Highsmith?"

"Yes, Courtenay, how'd you do?" The gentleman was upon the two now and bowed to both.

Courtenay presented the Earl. "A fine friend, Wolversley, and quite the ladies' man!" He winked at Highsmith. "I can vouch for him."

Wolversley hardly cared. He was far too distracted by the confirmation of his fears. This was the Rotherham house, the house he had avoided since their taking it. The family he had avoided for six years. He was hardly in the mood to make new acquaintances. He mumbled a perfunctory greeting to Highsmith and was so distracted that, before he knew it, Courtenay had taken his arm and led him into the house he so much wanted to flee.

They walked through the crowded hallway, discarding their coats and hats and, in Courtenay's case, a cane. All the while the colour was draining from Wolversley's face. Courtenay reached the top of the stairs beside Highsmith, oblivious to the Earl's deteriorating state of calm. Wolversley drew level with them at the end of the landing where a small set of stairs led down to a ballroom. The high ceilings of the large room had filled with the heat from the energetic crowd of people, and below, the guests were dressed in their finest gowns or breeches and eagerly chatting to their neighbours.

"I say, a splendid affair, just as I was told it would be." Courtenay turned to Wolversley for agreement, but his look of pleasure was soon changed to one of slight concern. "You're looking a trifle peaked." The concern turned to funning as he nudged his friend's arm. "Perhaps a glimpse of our beautiful debutante will restore your colour. Come, it's high time we greeted our hostess."

Courtenay descended the stairs and left Wolversley to do the same. The Earl did so with a mind full of foreboding and a set of particularly unsure feet. Courtenay's earlier words concerning Wolversley finding a betrothed were about to become shockingly true.

WHEN JULIA ROTHERHAM caught sight of Lucius Wolversley at her sister's coming-out ball, her jaw shot downwards, her fan fell to the floor, and her feet stumbled backwards in an unladylike fashion. She blinked, but rather than the Earl's presence being a trick of the mind, as it so often had been, he remained. She felt her fan pressed back into her hand by one of the servants, but her gaze could not be shaken from the man who had just entered the ballroom. He had not seen her yet, and she prayed that it would remain that way. If only the priceless crystal chandelier would fall down and break a hole in the ballroom floor through which she could be swallowed.

At any moment, according to decorum, he would come to greet the hostess, her mother, the woman next to whom Julia was standing. She absolutely could *not* speak to him. Why on earth was he here? Had he been invited? How dare he invade her home in this manner!

Julia's wide green eyes flashed around the room, in the hopes that Peter Highsmith, who had greeted her mother just before Lord Courtenay, was still in the vicinity. Surely, he would lend her his arm and support her through this nightmare? They were friends, after all, despite the proposal he had offered and she had declined last year. Where was he? It was no use, thought Julia. He had already dissolved into the crowds.

The shock Julia felt at once again seeing the dark hair and cool eyes of Earl Wolversley gave way to sheer panic. He was closing in on her. She glanced about again. How could she escape speaking to him?

Her darting eyes found a path through the crowd. Perhaps if she ran now.... She looked back at her mother and father and knew in an instant she could not run. It was quite simply the most scandalous thing for a lady to do in the midst of a ball, and her mother would not forgive her for it.

The middle-aged woman, dressed in dark blue, began sending her eldest daughter excited looks. Julia could sense that her mother had spotted Earl Wolversley, and her panic increased.

No, she could not run, but if she managed an athletic leap, she might dive under the seats lined up against the wall just to the side of her. A whisper of reason told her that this plan was also no good. Even if she managed to fit through the chair legs, she would most probably upset the occupants of said chairs, not to mention that it would be far more improper than merely running away.

Botheration! Why was it so difficult to form a devious, last-minute departure plan in the midst of a ball? One would think that, owing to the large amount of people, it would be easy to dissolve into the melee. Not for Julia Rotherham it seemed. There was a spacious gap between the Rotherham welcoming party and their guests, and her mother's watchful eyes would catch and put a stop to her flight in seconds. Julia glanced again at the chairs next to her and huffed in frustration.

In mere seconds she would come face to face with the man who had broken her heart six years ago, and not one decent plan of escape would materialise in her mind. Fiddlesticks! If only she had worn a better dress. She had not wanted to steal attention from her sister this evening—as if she *could* steal attention from her golden haired, Greek goddess of a younger sister—but the determination not to do so had led her to wear a plain evening gown with very little decoration and a rather high neckline. If only she had taken up her mama's offer to buy her a new dress. She could have chosen a ravishing one. She would have had it made up in green silk to pick up her eyes and set off her rich brown hair. She would have asked Madame Trouleux to cut it daringly low. Oh, the preparations she would have made if she had known that Lucius Wolversley would be in attendance. She would have looked so enchanting that Earl Wolversley would have fallen on his knees and begged for her to take him back.

Ridiculous! She reprimanded herself silently. Her daydreams were even more foolish than her plan of running through a crowded ballroom or diving under a set of chairs. She closed her eyes and shook her head a little just to be sure she had rid herself of the ludicrous notions her panicked mind was manufacturing.

She opened her eyes again to see a much larger hand taking hold of her own. Before she could look up, she felt the briefest press of lips on her silk glove.

"Your servant, Miss Rotherham."

After presenting her hand with a perfunctory kiss, the face before her rose steadily, its eyes intentionally evading her own. Her hand froze into position, and it was just as well that the Earl's larger hand let go of it, for she would not—could not— have made the conscious effort to take it back.

After the first jolt of recognition, her lips became an uncompromising line and her eyes widened with anger. It took all her will power to keep her from laying a stinging slap across Earl Wolversley's falsely smiling face. Fortunately for him, the gentleman had turned back to her mother almost immediately after greeting her, thus avoiding the blow to the cheek that he richly deserved.

How dare he! She cast a look of fury in his direction. She could still feel the heat of his fingers where they had touched her silk gloves. She clenched her hand, pressing all her fingertips savagely into her palm, obliterating the sensation of his hand holding hers.

She watched his face as he spoke to her mother. It still contained many of the features of the youth that she remembered, and yet now she could see small lines at the side of his mouth and eyes. The latter were still the pale, engaging gray they had always been, but now they seemed less open, with a sharpness she had never seen. His face also seemed stiff and guarded. He appeared old—well, not old, but certainly aged. She remembered the boyish side of his character with the mischievous tendencies that she had found so amusing in youth, but now he looked world-worn. If she had been on good terms with him, she might even have accused him of being in the sulks. Then again, she was fairly sure her own face did not hold any affability at this present moment, and besides, she was most certainly *not* on good terms with this man.

He glanced at her then, as if to include her in the conversation he was having with her mother. She stared back at him as though she were a statue, wondering what had paralysed her, wondering why she could not react. Then realisation struck— the one thing that was missing from his face was a recognition of their past. There was no spark or knowing look when his eyes met hers. There was only the presence of controlled bad flavour underlying a false smile of civility. Julia could not but wonder if it was really an act or—heaven forbid!—had he really forgotten?

She certainly had not forgotten. It was not every day that an engaged girl was thrown over. It was not every day that a betrothed young man tasted the sinful fruits the world had to offer and developed a decided preference for them over his intended. A saint turned rake. Well, that was a slight stretch— he had never been, exactly, a saint, and she did not have any proof that he was a rake, just a suspicion.

All those years ago she had been in love and had thought herself loved in return. In the end it had all been for nothing, leaving her with a deep, aching loss which time had only been able to numb but not completely heal. Now he was here and she had no idea what to say. She was, in fact, for the first time in her extremely talkative life, completely lost for words. There were no words large enough or furious enough to express what she was feeling. Nor were there any words subtle enough to convey the cutting remarks that wanted to fly through the air like knives at this very public occasion. And since the right words were not available to her, Julia could only stare, her mouth poised to open but refusing to do more.

Mrs. Rotherham, seeing her daughter's verbal ineptitude, fanned her pink face in an attempt at charm and then leapt into the conversational void as Julia still remained silent. "Do not mind my eldest, my lord. I suppose you will remember her." She fanned herself slightly faster as she glided over the allusion to Julia and Wolversley's youthful betrothal. "She was a shy girl always."

Julia could hear her mother's voice babbling away and, despite her frozen state, she was sensible of the fact that her mother was telling outrageous lies. If Wolversley remembered their first meeting, he would most certainly know the truth that she was not now, nor had ever been, a shy girl.

She had been introduced to the Earl when he was still in shortcoats at a garden party. Much to her mother's distress, Julia had run amok, engaging in rowdy horseplay with Wolversley and another neighbour's son. The real gem in this memory was when Julia dared Wolversley to paddle in the lake, and then called him a coward when he refused. There was a supposed man-eating fish lurking in the algae-infested waters. Julia had then decided to brave the beastly deep herself in order to prove Wolversley's cowardice. Annoyed by such slurs being cast upon his character, Wolversley had raced ahead of Julia and knocked into her as he ran past. This rude bump she had taken to heart, and when they both finally stood in the shallow waters, Julia discreetly put a neat foot behind Wolversley's right leg and gave him a sturdy kick. He landed on his backside in the muddy shallows and promptly pulled her down after him. It had ended in a quarrelling match, a bout of splashing, and finally a fit of the giggles.

Whilst Julia dallied in the waters of nostalgia, her mother continued to talk to the Earl, asking after his family. "I was sad to hear of your uncle's passing, though it is some years ago now—so sorry that your family has suffered so much loss, first with your parents and now your guardian." Mrs. Rotherham's most winning trait, as anyone of her acquaintance would tell you, was her compassionate heart. Her soft brown eyes grew wide with sympathy. "I suppose you miss him greatly."

The object of said sympathy, however, did not seem to receive it in an appreciative light. His eyelids narrowed, the muscles at the corner of his mouth twitched, and his lips compressed themselves into a firm line. It seemed that his uncle, the guardian of his deceased father's estate until Wolversley had come of age, was someone he did not care to discuss.

Mrs. Rotherham did not notice the displeasure manifesting itself in Wolversley's manner. She carried on, assuming it was grief that kept Wolversley from speaking. "How have you been getting on since?"

Wolversley, seemingly pleased that the topic had changed, spoke again, but his conversation was now stilted and abrupt. "Well enough, thank you, Mrs. Rotherham."

"And your poor, dear sister, Lady Selina. How is she?"

"Well, I thank you, and much grown since you last saw her, I am sure."

"Does she accompany you for the Season?"

"As simple observation can show you, madam, she does not."

This curt remark, unlike Wolversley's previous change of countenance, did not go unnoticed by Mrs. Rotherham. But once again, she simply attributed his abrupt manner to grief at the references to his departed uncle. Knowing that gentlemen in general disliked showing sensibility of any kind, especially in public, she smiled and accepted that the conversation was coming to an end. A queue of guests was forming behind the Earl and, not wanting to be disagreeable to them or detain the Earl against his will, Mrs. Rotherham decided it best to release him.

"Well, it has been a pleasure to renew our acquaintance." Her voice softened. "I am sure you are also pleased to re-acquaint yourself with my daughter."

Julia, still frozen with shock and unable to deliver the set-down she so desired, cringed inwardly at her mother's mention of her.

"Indeed," responded the Earl flatly.

Julia did not miss the slight.

"I do hope you enjoy the ball, Wolversley!" said Julia's father, who had hitherto been caught up with another guest and was just now turning to shake hands with the Earl. "I am sure you remember most of the faces—a good many of our neighbours from Sussex are in attendance." Mr. Rotherham's good-natured voice seemed to soften Wolversley's reserve, at least for the moment.

"Good to see you again, Mr. Rotherham. I must apologise for not calling previously, and also for darkening your doors at such an event without an invitation. My friend, Lord Courtenay, insisted that I come along with him. I only arrived back in

Town today." Wolversley's guarded tones had changed to honest ones as he conversed with the country squire.

"Think nothing of it. It's just jolly good to see you again, my lad." Mr. Rotherham pumped his guest's hand with genuine warmth. "It's been too long since we've had you under our roof."

At this comment Wolversley's clouded countenance cleared a little.

"Thank you, sir."

"Yes, indeed!" Julia's mother would not let the chance slip by, especially as the Earl's mood had become affable once again. As her daughter shot her a despairing look, knowing what was about to take place, Mrs. Rotherham proceeded on her motherly course. "So much dancing to be done this evening." She lifted her eyebrows helpfully at her daughter, but Julia only shot venomous looks back.

Oh, goodness! Julia felt sick. How was this happening? How could he simply barge back into her life again? It was true she was situated in the busy hub of London at the start of the Season—certainly not the place and time to avoid seeing another member of the ton—but still! This was *her* social circle, *her* life, *her* part of the world—and he was like a bull, coming in and crashing everything about. She felt the crushing misery of six years ago come bubbling back to the surface.

"Indeed," said Wolversley, once again without much enthusiasm. He bowed with ingrained courtesy and took his leave of his host and hostess.

Julia stared after him like a lost pup, completely ignoring the guests who attempted to greet her. It was a letter—that is how he had broken their engagement. One single sheet of paper, that's all it was, and that insignificant object had broken her heart. She forced her eyes away from his shoulders melting into the crowd and turned her attention to the boards on the floor.

"Daughter, you do not look yourself," Mr. Rotherham whispered in Julia's ear. "I think you had best go and find some refreshment, my child."

Julia grasped for an excuse to explain away her pale face, but one look at her father told her she did not have to. She nodded and left the greeting line.

Mr. Rotherham turned back to his wife. "Now, my dear, that was a little hard on poor Julia."

"What was?"

"You know very well what I mean, my dear, and although I admire your knowledge of the marriage mart and your match-making ways, that was not one of your finest moments."

Mrs. Rotherham coloured at her husband's reprimand. She fluttered her fan for a few moments before speaking. "It's all very well her wanting to be unmarried now, but the years are passing faster than she knows. I simply thought that perhaps, since he has come tonight and since so much time has passed since the...unfortunate event, there may still be hope for them."

Mr. Rotherham, who knew the anxiety his wife suffered over their eldest daughter's future, could understand her path of logic, but he could hardly concur with it. He sighed. "Do you remember how low our Julia was after Wolversley cried off? That same look she used to wear was on her face again just now. I doubt there is any hope for them until her heart is mended."

"It's been six years, George!"

"Yes, and just imagine if it were you and I."

Mrs. Rotherham smiled at that. "Well, I don't believe you would have been foolish enough to cry off."

"And suffer your wrath? I think not!" He let out a prac-tised cough and shook his head.

"George!" She swatted his shoulder with her fan. "Behave

yourself. We have guests to greet, and you will paint an awful picture of me if you carry on so."

"Your wish is my command, O Wrathful One!" Mr. Rotherham grinned mischievously at his wife, winked, and then nodded to signal that the next guest could approach.

CHAPTER TWO

"...now he was vexing her mind..."

DESPITE THE LOUDNESS OF THE CROWD, Julia felt as though the ball guests were all far away, voices muffled by several doors and walls. She failed to focus on any of the faces. In fact, several people may have spoken to her whilst she traversed the room without her either realizing or replying. Politeness was never her forte.

Then, out of the blur, something did come into focus, sharp and clear, and she headed straight for it. The punch table! Lifting a full glass of the colourful beverage, she proceeded to drink it down in seconds.

"Another!" she demanded.

The footman looked a little scandalized, but at a quelling look from Julia, another full glass appeared in her hand as if by magic. She repeated this most soothing of occupations several times before she felt quite able to cope. After the fourth glass, she was feeling quite well if not entirely splendid. She smiled in a haphazard way and swayed a little, bumping against the table.

Unfortunately, one of the evils of being a trifle disguised, Julia was finding, was the inability to control where one's thoughts might wander off to. In her case, the very thing that she had begun drinking in order to forget was now the only thing that consumed her mind.

There had been nothing in his eyes to suggest he had ever harboured feelings for her. In fact, he had appeared as though he had not even remembered her. In contrast to his calm ignorance, *her* heart had been freshly exposed. The years that separated their betrothal from the present day had been stripped away, and the feelings which had faded but never fully died had bloomed again with full force. Oh, how much did she want to deliver him a set-down! To sharpen her words so they pierced and cut where she directed them. Thinking back to the greeting line, she half wished she *had* slapped his face. That would have been a short-lived pleasure, but a pleasure nonetheless.

She turned, wobbling a little, to spy on the crowds. She must find more positive things to focus on, she decided. Her sister could be seen a little way away, surrounded by several over-excited misses fresh out of the schoolroom and an equal number of youths. The latter group were panting like hounds after the scent of a fox. Blinded by over-tall shirt collars, they flourished embroidered handkerchiefs and flexed stockinged calf muscles. Julia was sure, from the knowledge she had gathered during her five Seasons, that one of the gentlemen's stockings had been helped into their attractive shape with a little more than just his own legs.

The scene which was being enacted before her was the same one that had so enraptured her upon her first coming out—the excitement, the anxieties, the joys. Although, in Julia's case, the pall of her broken engagement had always detracted a little bit from the experience. Perhaps that was why she had never found a suitable partner, one that would last her more than a dance or two. She shook her head in defiance—she would *not* wallow in that misery any longer!—and continued to stare at the group.

Annabelle Rotherham, younger than her sister by a good five years, was looking radiant. She exuded all the qualities and attributes which Julia lacked. She was taller, though Julia could not be considered small, with beautiful golden hair, a pretty set of manners, and a soft femininity to all her actions and words. Brown-haired Julia was notoriously good at showing no manners, as her mother liked to remind her, and though she was not unfeminine, she always felt lacking in the grace her younger sister so naturally displayed.

Julia mused upon their differences, wondering briefly if she had ever been as lovely at that age, then smiling ruefully as she conceded that she had not. Annabelle in a newly-made white dress, her fair tresses falling simply about her face, was a vision of the goddess Aphrodite. Even surrounded by so many other fresh girls, she stood out as a diamond of the first water...a diamond who did not know quite how to work her fan just yet. Despite Julia's current state, she could clearly see Annabelle's unwitting signals to one of her beaux. The young gentleman in question had a gleam in his eye and nodded slightly, accepting her fan's request to speak with him in private. Oblivious to the enthusiastic youth's expectations, Annabelle was reveling in all the attentions she was receiving. And so she should, thought Julia. It is *her* night.

"Your sister is looking delightful this evening."

The sickly sweet voice was one that Julia knew well. She turned and saw Miss Lily Merriweather had come upon her from the side—a sneak attack from the preening young woman who had a propensity for insulting her.

"And you are looking...well, what an unusual cut of dress. I am sure I have not seen one in that low-waisted style in such a long time. You are most brave to wear it—I declare, I am quite jealous of your bravery!"

And there it was, the insult Julia knew was coming. As Miss Merriweather finished her snide remarks, Julia was quick to shut her fan and even quicker to quell her desire to clock Lily Merriweather over the head with it. Taking a breath she replied in equal tones, "Oh, thank you for your compliment, Miss Merriweather. How delightful that you accepted the invitation to my sister's ball." Thankfully, Miss Merriweather did not notice the slight slur to Julia's words. She rarely noticed anyone other than herself.

Julia could see Miss Merriweather's mother standing a few feet away with another woman. How this quiet and retiring woman had ever managed to produce such an obnoxious child Julia had yet to find out.

"I am sure it must be ever so hard for you," continued Miss Merriweather, "having such a beautiful sister quite eclipsing you now she is out in Society." She placed a patronizing hand on Julia's arm. Julia's skin began to crawl. "Then again, I am sure you will find a match of your own before *too* long."

No, she was not sure—not even Julia was sure of that— and the only reason Miss Merriweather had mentioned it was to subtly hint at the opposite.

Julia's hackles could not help rising at this pretty upstart. After all, had not Miss Merriweather's own fortune and ambition failed her when she was launched into society last Season and unsuccessful in securing a husband?

"Peter Highsmith is still a dear man," said Julia—just that, and nothing more. She did not have to. Lily Merriweather had been furious when Julia had unwittingly attracted the gentleman with well-lined pockets that Lily had set her cap at. The best part was, Julia had not even married him.

Miss Merriweather's eyes narrowed. "Oh, he is, I suppose.

But there are others more eligible than he. Have you seen Earl Wolversley is come back to Town and is here tonight? He is most handsome though I have only seen him from afar."

Julia's gaze turned frosty, and she was seized with a moment of inner panic. What did she mean by mentioning Wolversley? What was she insinuating? Their betrothal had been private—thank the Lord!—only known of by immediate family. Mrs. Rotherham had wanted it that way, in order to give Julia the experience of her first Season in London without the whole world knowing she was engaged. And the jilting had been private too—no one but Annabelle, her mother, and her father had known the reason for her broken heart.

The only person from whom Miss Merriweather could have heard about Julia's disappointment was...Wolversley! Julia gasped. He would not have dared to spread the story, would he? She narrowed her eyes at this odious woman with the delicate features and the sharp tongue. The punch was making Julia lose all the inhibitions of politeness, and whether Miss Merriweather knew her secret or not, she was still deserving of a forceful set-down....

"Oh, Julia!" Annabelle came bursting into the tête-à-tête. "This is all too delightful! And, oh,"—Annabelle caught sight of her sister's companion—"Miss Merriweather." The young woman curtseyed rapidly to Miss Merriweather but immediately turned back to her older sister. "I am quite overwhelmed with partners. I declare I would be dancing forever if I said yes to everyone who asked me." Like her sister Annabelle not only had a fortune to bring to any match but she was also a rare beauty, and that was not a combination often found. It was no surprise she was in demand.

"You must make sure you have some refreshment or you may faint in this heat." The words came out of Julia's mouth before she remembered that her mothering of her younger sister was never well received.

"I can take care of myself perfectly well!" snapped the debutante, metamorphosing from Greek goddess to petulant child in seconds.

Miss Merriweather, disgusted that her place as centre of the conversation had been usurped by the pretty Miss Annabelle, flapped her fan impatiently. "Well, you sisters clearly wish to speak only to each other, so I will take my leave." She barely curtseyed and flounced away into the crowds.

The comical display of pique from the Society belle made both sisters forget their enmity and look at each other with expressions of wide-eyed amusement. Annabelle was unaware of the offer Julia had received from Mr. Highsmith and was thus also unaware of the source of the rivalry between her sister and Miss Merriweather. But she had seen the two at odds in the past and had always sided, as any good sister should, with her own kin.

Annabelle was not the only one oblivious to what had passed between Julia and Peter Highsmith. Thankfully, the rejected gentleman was a good enough friend to keep quiet about the matter, and in this way, Julia had kept the offer secret from her mother. Who knew what bricks would come tumbling off the Rotherham house if Julia's mother ever found out that such an eligible suitor had been declined!

After Miss Merriweather's back had completely disappeared into the crowds, Annabelle giggled. "As much as I would love to stay and speak *only with you* my sister, it *is* my coming-out ball and I am engaged to dance!" The beautiful young miss, all remnants of temper gone, dropped a quick kiss on her sister's cheek and departed.

Left to her own devices, Julia briefly closed her eyes in the middle of the crowded room. The longer she stood there, the more the punch took over her senses. There was only one thing to do. She stepped unsteadily over to the side of the room, where the footman who served the punch was becoming accustomed to, though not approving of, her presence. He refilled her punch glass yet again and handed it back to her.

Peering over the rim of the glass, Julia was about to take a sip when she was horrified to see Wolversley bearing down upon her. She swivelled back round quickly, almost spilling her fifth glass of punch as she banged it down unceremoniously upon the table. Her hands reached for the table on either side of the glass and pressed upon it for support.

"Are you well, Miss Rotherham?" asked the footman, clearly more bewildered than ever by her behaviour.

Julia waved away his concern. She was far too preoccupied at this moment to allay a servant's concern. She had a few seconds before the Earl was upon her. What had his face been like? Very unexceptional, at least she thought so, though her mind was not at its sharpest. Perhaps he had come to fall down on his knees and beg her forgiveness. No, indeed, that would be too perfect. Besides, she was not sure whether she even wanted him to fall to the floor in front of her. She was left no more time for thinking. She turned as she heard his voice.

WOLVERSLEY SAW JULIA turn towards him. She was leaning precariously to one side, but despite this laxity in her stance, her eyes held him firmly in their gaze. Invisible hands pulled him back but he fought against them. It had been so long, so many years, since he had seen her, and now her presence seemed to pull him towards her as if she were the ground and he an apple. What would happen when they collided? He stopped before her. A few seconds of nothing stretched by, and then, readying himself for the task at hand, he bowed.

"Miss Rotherham. May I engage you for the next dance?"

His voice sounded monotone, even to his own ears. He tried to gain her hand to kiss it but, unlike their earlier encounter in the receiving line, this time he failed.

"No!" She pulled her hand farther away when he reached for it again. "Please stop being ridiculous!" she cried, turning swiftly and regaining possession of her punch glass. She raised the cup and took what a doctor would call a draught of it.

Wolversley, finally hearing Julia speak, was taken aback by the abrupt reply. "I am not being ridiculous," he said, managing to keep his voice calm and collected. Strangely, the flustered state of the woman before him seemed to solidify his own self-possession. "Will you not dance with me?"

His gray eyes bestowed a condescending look upon her, as though her tempestuous reaction was childish and beneath him. Had he realised the sneer he was giving her, he might have tried to soften it, but it was his automatic and unconscious reaction when faced with rude treatment. In the years they had spent apart, he had become used to dealing with attitudes that were less than congenial toward him. Circumstances had not been kind to the Earl, and neither had many of his peers.

Julia's green eyes flashed dangerously. Her face contorted into a scowl before she unfurled her fan and looked about her. Wolversley could see that an excuse was on the tip of her tongue, and she was about to disappear into the crowds.

He cut in before she had the chance. "I simply wish to dance with you."

He did wish it. He had not seen her in six years. Six long years. Now she was here before him, and even her temper was not dampening his wish to dance with her. She was perplexing —and intriguing. The suddenness of their re-acquaintance had taken him by surprise, and evidently her as well.

"And I simply say, *no!* Do not lie to me, my lord. You have clearly succumbed to propriety's demand for you to partner me—your host's spinster daughter. In light of that, excuse me for not finding the offer flattering or leaping to accept it."

"You see straight through my manners." His mouth curved up on the right side into a half-smile of admiration for her wit. He had forgotten just how quick her wit could be. Despite the unladylike rebuff, he bowed in acknowledgment and then attempted to present what he thought was another olive branch. "We have not spoken for these six years—may I at least procure a little conversation from you?" Let her speak, just a little. How much in this moment he wished to hear her talk!

When he saw the look in her eyes, he knew he was flogging a dead horse. She had no intention of remaining in his company an instant longer than she must.

His own intentions were a little less clear to him. Why was he seeking her out? Was it guilt, or surprise at seeing her again? Or was it merely a curiosity—after so much self-discipline in avoiding her—to see for himself the woman she had turned into?

"You showed no such desire when you abruptly severed our acquaintance six years ago, my lord. It therefore seems odd that you should seek conversation now. What reason could you possibly have?" Her voice was less flustered; instead of the wildly changing pitch, there was a warning edge to it.

Wolversley set his jaw. It appeared her rudeness knew no bounds. He had assumed from her silence at the door that she could barely remember him and was embarrassed when he took her hand. Clearly, that was not the case. The more he tried to talk with her, the more he beheld the lack of manners and quick temper that had plagued her youth—and played a merry role in their many adventures together. Where time had clouded the extent of both these attributes in his mind, the present was rapidly bringing back the memory in full, rich colour.

Her parents' supervision had, when she was younger, kept her lack of manners somewhat in check. He was sure that even now, her father and mother's absence had a part to play in her cutting conversation. Her unpleasant allusion to their past had brought a shadow over his face, but the exhibition of her temper and rudeness was producing a smile he could not help.

If his courtliness was so repugnant to her, perhaps touching upon their past, as she seemed so keen to do, would lay flat her hackles. "I simply wish to converse with an old friend"—he finally let the smile transform his face—"and beautiful woman." He could not help that last part—it slipped out unbidden. He should have known that the honeyed compliment would be too far a step.

"My lord." She turned to face him. Her eyes held a resolve he could not remember seeing before. Her stance took on one of importance and quite suddenly she was no longer just the impetuous schoolroom miss he had seen when last they met. "Do me both the honour and the courtesy of ceasing these adulations with which you are smothering me. I am no great beauty. Even in my bloom I was merely pretty, as well you will remember. Nor have I ever, in these years apart, claimed your friendship."

Her fan snapped shut. "Enjoy the ball. There are plenty of beautiful women who may indeed wish to converse with you and could even be persuaded to accompany you onto the dance floor." She let the corners of her mouth pull upwards in something akin to a satisfied smile, but he perceived her eyes held nothing of mirth. "I have no expectation that our paths will cross again."

Wolversley watched Julia curtsey, the curls of her rich brown hair falling about her slender neck. He considered her as she walked from him, a thing he never recalled her doing before. Either he had lost his touch, he decided, or she was not the woman from his youth. His emotions were torn—half of his mind battled to poke fun at their meeting and her outrageous behaviour, while the other half was occupied with heaping curses upon himself.

He had been so unprepared, for he had never expected to see her again. Indeed, he had spent the last six years ensuring that tonight's meeting would never take place. That moment in the receiving line when he had taken her hand in his had almost completely overset him, but he had managed it. He'd had to—all the fault of that dashed fool, Courtenay!

But then, afterwards, he could have avoided her all evening. He could have stayed in the corners of the ballroom and departed without looking upon her face more than once. He could have maintained the silence of their six years of estrangement, a silence that the passing years had only made easier to keep. Why had he not?

Hell and curse it!

Wolversley turned to the footman who was still serving punch dutifully and asked for a glass of Burgundy. The servant, who clearly thought this particular beverage was completely out of his jurisdiction, conducted a hurried conference with another of the retainers and dispatched him on the task. Wolversley tapped his foot impatiently.

Here it was at last. Seconds after the glass met his fingers, the dark liquid had been half drained. Fortified by his favourite beverage, the Earl scanned the crowds for Julia but saw nothing of her.

What on earth had he been hoping to accomplish by speaking with her? Had he expected her to have forgotten him as easily as any debutante forgets her first beau? Or had he expected a friendly reception and a recounting of fond memories? Neither of these expectations was anything close to reality, he thought with chagrin. She remembered him certainly, but there was nothing approaching friendliness in her demeanour. Whether from a wounded heart or damaged pride, he could not tell, and whichever was the case, his attempt at re-acquaintance had resulted in a set-down.

Well, he supposed, she was probably right—they would not see each other again after tonight. At least, he thought nostalgically, she had not lost that most captivating and troublesome of her traits which he remembered so well—her impetuosity.

JULIA FELT HERSELF quivering with rage. How she had managed to control her temper while he flirted with her was quite beyond her comprehension. How dare he! Indeed, how dare he! After forming an attachment with her in his youth, after offering all those protestations of love, and after crying off from the engagement with only a letter! She had not realised she harboured such fury towards him, but this—her first encounter with him since that wretched day—had been her first opportunity to expend it.

He had not even alluded to it—to the engagement. Perhaps to him it had meant very little. Was it possible he barely remembered it? At the thought of such an enormity, she grew even angrier. It was unjust that he could forget a broken heart so easily while she was still nursing hers. But indeed, perhaps his heart had never been broken.

Julia managed to weave her way between the crowds, avoiding eye contact with every guest she passed. She did not want to be dragged into any conversations for, no matter the topic, she could not trust her tongue to play the gracious hostess. She caught sight of her fair-haired sister being escorted onto the dance floor by a dandyish youth. He bowed as the dance began, flourishing a large lace handkerchief in Annabelle's direction. This foppish gesture would have made Julia laugh had it been in any other circumstance. Now it just reminded her of the reason she did not wish to speak to any of the ball guests.

She desperately needed to be alone with her thoughts. She knew that if she could not calm her feelings, every porcelain object in the house was in danger of being shattered by her hands. Striding through the crowds, in a walking style that her mother had told her many times was unladylike in the extreme, she finally found herself at the door of a side room which had been set aside by her mother as the ladies' powder room.

Julia opened the door upon a bustling scene. At least six ladies were making use of the elegantly furnished room with its Chinoiserie décor. It was halfway through the evening now, and all these women were attending to their toilettes which were beginning to look tired. One of the Rotherhams' maids was re-pinning the hair of a lady whose dancing had been too exuberant, whilst another carried a needle and thread to a guest who had been lucky enough to procure a chair in the crowded room but unfortunate enough to rip her hemline.

Slipping into the room quietly, Julia hoped she would yet again evade conversation. She skirted two women who were talking in deep whispers, clearly about some scandalous happening in the ballroom. Just as Julia was about to pass by the chair in the centre of the room, the occupant having her hemline stitched reached out a hand to stop her.

"Ah, my dear,"—the Dowager Countess of Grasmere smiled kindly up at Julia—"your sister is looking beautiful tonight, is she not?"

This was exactly the small talk that Julia had been fearing. Worse, by no fault of her own, the Dowager Countess of Grasmere was a distant relation of Wolversley. Was she to have no peace?

The Dowager was waiting for an answer. The comparison of her sister's prospects against her own was something she knew would happen tonight. She did not resent her sister's beauty, but she did resent the pity others would shower upon her. She had borne it from Lily Merriweather—but that was before she had spoken to Earl Wolversley. Now she not only did not want to hear it, a small part of her wanted to scream.

"Yes, yes she is," Julia replied truthfully and with as much enthusiasm as she could muster.

"I am sure that you look quite pretty as well, my dear."

There was so much pity in that one remark that Julia, had she been her normal self, would have indulged in a bout of self-loathing. Thanks to a certain person's appearance, however, and to the fortifying effect of punch, she was not herself. In fact, it was becoming rather difficult to focus on her surroundings.

The elderly woman took Julia's hand and pressed a few fingers against her wrist. "Your mama has organised a wonderful ball, and all the young people are enjoying it so much. Why, I even danced myself, as you can see." She fanned her arm wide to show off the maid and the torn hem.

Julia stared and managed to nod. She remembered tearing her own hem at a country dance many years ago by dancing too rambunctiously with a certain someone.... Fiddlesticks! There was no end to Earl Wolversley's aggravating propensities —now he was vexing her mind and he was not even present!

"If I had a daughter of my own, I would be quite envious of dear Miss Annabelle." The Dowager shifted a little, arranging her skirts to make the maid's task easier. "I suppose it is hard for you still being unmarried."

And there it was! The sole reason Julia had avoided conversation with the roomful of guests this evening. Of course, the Dowager was oblivious of Julia's youthful betrothal to her relative. There was no malice in the comment, just that same pity Julia loathed.

The old lady started patting Julia's hand, but although the

gesture was made with the best of intentions, Julia could not appreciate the kindness. That face of pity was one Julia had seen far too many times before, and she abhorred it just as much this evening as she had the first time she had received it.

Perhaps she was being cruel. Her abhorrence was not directed towards the Countess herself—after all, Julia knew for a fact that the Dowager Countess of Grasmere was one of the few women in Society who intended kindness to everyone. But no matter who wore the face or spoke the words, Julia was tired of them.

"You suppose correctly!" she said to the Countess, in a tone that brooked no reply. She stalked over to the only unoccupied seat, a cushioned bench in the bow of the window, turned her back on the bustling room behind her, and stared out of the recently cleaned pane.

High in the heavens hung a small host of discernible stars, each one a piercing contrast to the navy blue backdrop in which it lay. The moon was bright tonight, though not quite full, and enough of its surface reflected light down from the heavens to make the neighbouring London buildings visible to Julia. Her gaze lingered on the rooflines of the other buildings and traced the lines of the architecture across the façades. Though fog hung in the air about the street below, it was thinner this evening and failed to obscure the view as it so often did.

What she would give to be able to leave this ball! She thought about pleading a headache and retiring to her room, but she knew that Annabelle—not to mention her mother— would see through that subterfuge and be cross beyond words. If she went back out into the ballroom, she knew she would see Wolversley again. A worse event she could not imagine.

The anger that had filled her earlier had come and gone like a flash of lightning and now her heart was overcast by more pensive storm clouds. She began to worry that she had acted childishly, or worse, missishly. It was true he deserved a thrashing, but without a riding crop to hand she had had to be content with a set-down. That set-down, she could see now, had probably lost her the high ground. At least, she thought grimly, he would not now wish to pursue any further acquaintance with her.

Her mother's voice sounded in her head. "Julia, you should be happy to receive attentions from any gentleman! After all, you are not exactly a new prospect in the ever growing marriage mart, are you? Do you not wish to be happily settled?"

And as much as she loathed her mother's incessant emphasis on her marital state, Julia knew she was right. She could not very well live here for the whole of her insipid life. She loved her father and her mother dearly, but a daughter was not supposed to stay at home forever. Perhaps she could become a companion to Annabelle, for her younger sister was bound to marry some inordinately rich gentleman who would spend most of his time on his estate and provide her with far too many babies for her to supervise on her own.

Julia sighed against the pane of glass, sending streaks of mist shooting across her view. She must return to the ball before her mother missed her or her sister thought herself snubbed. Though Annabelle so often played the confident younger sister, she was a sensitive child. If she suspected Julia was envious of all the attention being heaped upon her, then Annabelle would be angry and cease to enjoy her ball.

Julia stayed a little longer at the window, staring up at the abundance of heavenly darkness and willing herself to be calm. In the stillness of the world outside she was lost for a few moments. But all the while she felt the persistent tug of her obligations, and slipping from the cushioned seat, she turned to leave the night behind and re-enter the glowing ballroom.

CHAPTER THREE

Peter Highsmith caught sight of the brown-haired Miss Rotherham as he was dancing the last few steps of a country reel. He bowed to his fair partner, the daughter of a wealthy merchant, and led her from the dance floor back to her parents. With the pleasantries taken care of, the gentleman turned on his heel, a large grin on his face, and headed straight for the vivacious Miss Rotherham.

Julia was walking determinedly past the punch table and he saw her pick up a glass of the stuff.

"Jules?"

She appeared to hear him, but she was having a little trouble focusing, her vision moving along with the dancers in the background instead of latching onto his face. "Oh, it's you!" she said finally, in a happy tone that made Highsmith feel exceedingly welcome.

The son of a wealthy landowner, Peter Highsmith had entered Society well in his youth. Immediately accepted and befriended by his peers, he had wasted no time in falling in love several times over. He had a knack for doing so, his deep brown eyes always finding another to become the apple of them and quickly persuading that particular apple to return the affection. His most recent paragon, however, had declined his regard.

Miss Rotherham had captured his attention last Season, and unlike the other women that had taken his eye, he had foreseen a longer future with this lady. Unfortunately, she had not seen the same thing, being quite certain that his affection for her was not enough to hold his attention for a lifetime. Thanks to the help of various opera singers and theatre girls, Highsmith's spirits had righted themselves after this rebuff and he had settled into a firm and fast friendship with Miss Rotherham—although, every so often, the thought of matrimony still resurfaced in his mind.

As he came upon his paragon this evening, his smile displayed a set of particularly splendid teeth, an attribute that had melted many hearts before.

"Ah, good evening, Jules."

She gave a lopsided smile and then spoke in severe tones. "You must not call me that." Her attempt to swat him playfully went terribly awry. She missed entirely and dashed the contents of his recently procured drink all over the floor.

Highsmith shook the drops off his hand and looked down at his sodden clothing with a rueful grin. "Oh, I am so sorry. I should call you *Miss* Jules, no doubt." A few of the surrounding guests began to stare. "Though, I would take it as a genuine kindness if you would not upset my drinks in the future. This is a new waistcoat I've had made, and now it's quite ruined!" He spread his hands wide, taking in the stained waistcoat. A dandy through and through, the destruction of his clothing really was abhorrent to him. It was a sign of true regard that Highsmith could still take Julia's hand and proffer a kiss to the air directly above it.

"Well," replied Julia, retracting her hand with humorous disdain, as though it were priceless and he an undeserving cad, "I should be more careful of your drinks, I am sure, if you did not call me Jules." She straightened her silk gloves. "It's far too intimate in public, and so I have told you." She wagged a finger at him, but the movement was unsteady and her words slurred together.

"You are too cruel! Do you not know I believe us quite intimate enough for such an endearing nickname? I have heard your family call you it on occasion." Highsmith produced another charming smile.

"I dare say you do think us intimate, and I dare say you're right—though dreadfully presumptuous, especially as I happen to know from your own mouth that you are *intimate* with a number of other ladies of rather less quality than I. But you know very well that if Mama were to hear you, she should have something sharp to say."

He could tell that Julia was trying her hardest to maintain a stern face, although a smile kept threatening to break through her defences. "That I cannot argue with, and as we both know, your mother is always right. I shall submit at this public event and call you by your proper name."

He inclined his head as though that began the conversation afresh. "Miss Julia Rotherham, although you have a proclivity for alarming acts and shocking sayings, I have not before recalled a clumsiness in your actions. I am at a loss, therefore, to understand why you seem to be so unbalanced this evening."

"Oh, dreadfully sorry, old boy!" Julia blurted out, in the voice of a haughty old man. Her uncontrollable excitement did not stop there. She whipped the handkerchief out of Highsmith's pocket and began to dab at the damp patch on his waistcoat.

Highsmith was alarmed at this. As much as he might enjoy

the situation, the proximity of her hands to his person was worth a pretty penny to the scandalmongers among the guests. As Julia's dear friend, therefore, he gently took hold of her wrist to make her desist from dabbing at him. Leaning back on one of his long legs, he cocked his head to the side to get a good look at her. "Oh, dash it all! You're foxed aren't you?"

"Now, now, Mr. Peter, language please! I am a lady after all." She had taken on the tones of an elderly dowager now, trying to peer down her nose at him—in vain since he was more than a head taller than her.

"You're no lady at the moment," he said in a low tone, releasing her wrist.

She dropped his handkerchief to the floor, and pulled another much smaller one from her own reticule to dab the wine which had splashed onto the elbow of one of her gloves. Highsmith was just bending down to recover his own handkerchief, when he spotted something bright drop from her reticule and roll towards him on the ballroom floor.

Highsmith's look of reproof changed to one of interest as he retrieved both his linen handkerchief and the small trinket found near it. He looked up. She was still dabbing, unwittingly, at her stained glove. He would restore it to her later, but right now there were more pressing matters.

Highsmith stood up straight, took Julia's right hand, and placed it firmly in the crook of his arm. He then walked her steadily towards the supper room, his strong hold ensuring she remained vertical.

Upon entering the supper room, Julia spoke up in protest. "But I am not hungry, Mr. Peter." Her head bobbed about wildly. The punch, though it had not impaired her flavour, was clearly working its way through her system.

"Well, perhaps if you eat something it will soak up some of your...spirits." He looked about the table. "Bread, bread, my kingdom for some bread."

"Speak up, Mr. Peter! Mumbling is quite rude, you know." Julia was speaking rather more loudly than she realised, and several scandalized glances came their way, directed from a group of mothers who sat partaking of white soup.

"Hush, Julia!" said Highsmith. "What on earth has put you in this mood? Getting foxed at your own sister's coming-out ball is really too much."

"You wish to know? Well, I shall tell you what—no, I shall tell you *who* has put me in this mood. It was that dreadful Lucius Wolverly, no, Wolfery, no, Worlvereselly." The name, alas, was too hard to pronounce. Her brows crinkled in confusion as she tried to string the syllables together.

"Oh, him! Yes, I met him briefly." Highsmith pulled out a vacant chair and placed her in it before carrying on. "Fine fellow, if somewhat quiet, and, I have to be honest, I did not care for the cut of his jacket. But, my dear Jules, why become three sheets to the wind?"

She did not reply, nor did she look him in the eye. It did not take long for Highsmith to concoct an answer to his own question.

"Ah! Lovelorn for a handsome Earl, are we? I should have known you would set your sights higher than my humble station." He sighed in a way that would have made any sober person feel sorry for him. "But becoming foxed is not exactly the way to attract him. You should know that by now. You are a seasoned Seasoner, my dear."

Julia cast an evil glare up at him, both for his alluding to her age and for his atrocious assumption that she wished to attract Lucius Wolversley! Her look, though meant to instil fear into her friend, seemed to do the opposite. He smiled back at her, a little sourly, as though he had struck upon a secret he wished to put back in the dark.

"Don't be ridiculous, Peter! I don't love him. I...I loathe him...." She pushed the words out with some effort before collapsing back into the chair. "He's odious!"

"Never mind that now," said Highsmith. He began to ply her with bread and a little ham in the hopes of sobering her. After a quarter of an hour of sitting and eating, she felt rather more herself, although she was still under intense scrutiny from the mothers across the room. Highsmith sent one of the servants to fetch some orgeat lemonade, and as Julia drank her fill of the cooling liquid, a salute from the door of the supper room captured both their attentions.

"Halloo!"

"Courtenay!" returned Highsmith.

Hugh Courtenay swaggered towards the two seated at the table. He half-waved a ring-clustered hand and smiled, his pale blue eyes displaying his pleasure beneath their hooded lids.

Highsmith rose and executed a neat bow. "How do you find the ball?" He stepped aside from the table just enough to leave Julia in the background and out of the conversation.

"Splendid! Just splendid!" Courtenay returned the bow.

"Wasn't it Earl Wolversley that you walked in with?" asked Highsmith casually. Julia, though seated a few steps away, could hear the conversation quite clearly and was tempted, for a moment, to transfer her irritation from Wolversley to Highsmith and present him with a smart slap.

"Yes, of course!" replied Courtenay. "I introduced you to him, remember? Isn't it grand that he's back in circulation again?"

"Very," Highsmith replied, his face looking a little too smug for Julia's peace of mind. "Though I do not know much of him."

The comment was leading, and it worked. The peacock,

without realizing he was being coaxed, carried on. "Well, I'm very glad to have him back. Been a trifle dull at White's without him, and one knows, though one would never tell him, that his gray eyes attract the dem' ladies like no other."

"So it would seem," said Highsmith, his voice pregnant with meaning. The back of Julia's hand began to twitch again, and it was with great effort that she restrained herself.

"I'm surprised you haven't met him before," said Courtenay, "considering you spend most of your time in Town. Then again, Wolversley is forever disappearing from polite society. He has been gone from Town this past month—but I've got him back for now, and I don't intend to let him escape for a good long while. Hang all of that business he supposedly has on his estates—I tell him that's what a steward is for!"

Courtenay threw his head back and succumbed to a bout of laughter. His face was horizontal and gaining a very good view of the ceiling for a full minute before he straightened himself up again, his double chin bulging over his starched cravat.

Highsmith continued to pursue the subject. "So, I gathered he is an Earl. Where exactly does his estate lie?"

"West Sussex. Not a bad part of the country by all accounts. I've visited there half a dozen times, and it is a well-run sort of place with exceptional pastures on the farm. The shooting is fine too. Wolversley is a brilliant shot. I will tell you now, Highsmith, it takes all my will power not to be jealous of the chap." Courtenay proceeded to prattle on about more particulars of the estate while Highsmith turned to Julia and made a face which said, "You should have told me."

Julia rewarded her friend with a scowl whilst inwardly cursing. Highsmith had just ascertained that the Earl's home county was her own, and he was clearly drawing his own conclusions from that knowledge. He would be snooping even further if she did nothing.

Rising to her feet a little unsteadily, Julia came forward and leant her hand upon Highsmith's arm. "Mr. Highsmith?" The eyes she cast up at the fair-haired gentleman were as innocent as a lamb's. "Are you going to be so good as to introduce me to your friend?"

Highsmith recognised her intention to silence his questioning and gave a grin. "Ah, I do apologise, my poor Miss Rotherham. Lord Courtenay, may I present Miss Rotherham, eldest daughter of our hosts this evening." He backed away slightly to allow the two to see each other properly.

"Indeed? I know your father. It was he who had a hand in inviting me this evening." With a flourish of his rings, Courtenay grasped her hand and laid a rather ravenous kiss upon it. "And may I say, you are a beauty just like your sister." His plump lips curved into a satisfied smile.

"Oh, I would not say that to her, if I were you." A third man's voice broke in on the conversation.

After six years, Julia could still recognise Wolversley's smooth voice the moment he spoke. The Earl came up behind Courtenay and took his own place in the gathering.

"Speak of the devil and he will appear." Courtenay's smile changed to a grin, and he nodded his head towards the newcomer. He moved back a little to allow Wolversley access to the inner circle, and the dark-haired Earl came to stand beside the fair-haired Highsmith. "But Wolversley, why do you warn me not to say to Miss Rotherham what is only the truth?"

Courtenay's syrupy words were well-practised, but Julia, as Highsmith had said earlier, was a seasoned Seasoner. She would have written off Courtenay's flattery entirely, but the appearance of the loathsome Earl put an idea into her head.

"No. Trust me, old friend," said Wolversley with a gleam in his eyes, "she would rather hear lies."

Julia fumed inwardly at the Earl's audacity, at his

presumption of knowing what she would and would not like to hear from other gentlemen. Worse than that, she could see that look in his eyes, and she remembered exactly what it meant—he was having amusement at her expense. Well, that simply was not allowed! "Oh! Lord Courtenay, I beg you, pay no attention to the Earl. We knew each other as children, and I am afraid he still thinks me an angel of eight and quite as stupid! But really,"—she arched an eyebrow at Wolversley—"are you not the fool, my lord, to assume a lady does not find pleasure in compliments?"

"Yes, man, that is a trifle dim!" Courtenay exclaimed.

"Exactly my feelings," Julia corroborated. "He even thinks I cannot dance like a lady!" She attempted a giggle, though it was more like hissing from behind her open fan, and cast a flirtatious glance at Courtenay. Both Highsmith and Wolversley could see their portly friend lapping up the attention like a basset hound.

"I am shocked—shocked I tell you, Miss Rotherham! My only suggestion is that we prove him wrong. Let us dance and show him." There was that ring-clad hand again and—much to the other gentlemen's surprise and aggravation—Julia took it with enthusiasm. Courtenay and Julia left the supper room side by side, gliding off in search of the ballroom and an exuberant dance.

CHAPTER FOUR

"Memories came flooding back..."

HIGHSMITH HAD WATCHED THE PAST FEW exchanges silently and with a growing frown knitting his brows together. Julia was acting dashed odd and at complete variance with the character he had come to know. First she was getting in her cups, next she was taking compliments from a complete peacock, and now she was off to dance with the same preposterously dressed gentleman whom she had only met five minutes since!

Something was afoot that he had no knowledge of, but Peter Highsmith was determined to sound out the matter to his own satisfaction.

"Well." Highsmith's voice, though not cold, had lost its cordiality. He turned upon Wolversley much as a watchdog would turn upon an intruder. "Miss Rotherham does have a habit of doing things suddenly."

"Yes, quite," Wolversley replied in a clipped tone.

If Highsmith had been hoping for Wolversley to give anything away, he was doomed to see his dreams unfulfilled.

The gentleman was a closed book, and he seemed to have no intention of opening, especially where Julia was concerned.

"Perhaps we should find some chairs?" Wolversley pulled a snuffbox from his pocket. There was a mother of pearl design on the box, and Wolversley's initials were beautifully intertwined in silver upon its lid.

Highsmith eyed the Earl as he took his blend and could not help noticing that the aristocrat's gaze still followed the wake of the departed couple. "In a moment. First, tell me how you come to know the Rotherham family?" Highsmith's cordiality had returned, though it was somewhat forced, and his polite questions now had an agenda.

Wolversley's eyebrows rose. "My connection with the Rotherhams?" He replaced his snuffbox. "We are from the same part of the country."

"Neighbours? How delightful. I expect you know the family well then?"

"That would not be my description."

"Oh, oh I see." Highsmith put on a remorseful face, as though he had stumbled upon a great secret and wished to put it back in the box from whence it came. The bait worked.

"And what is *your* connection with the family?" demanded Wolversley.

Highsmith could not help feeling rather smug upon hearing Wolversley's question. It was not as though the Earl had asked anything unusual, but his tone had turned cold and his words had snapped like a whip. Highsmith knew it; there had been some kind of flirtation between Julia and this Society recluse. This jealous question of Wolversley's proved it.

He had hardly ever seen Wolversley in Society. Of course, he had heard his name, but he had never met the man. He had understood the Earl to always be away from Town. It was curious, really, for a man with such a prestigious title not to desire the distractions afforded by London.

This whole affair was becoming more interesting by the second!

"Oh, just a friend of the family," Highsmith replied. "I met the charming Miss Rotherham in her first Season and was quite simply captivated. She's a rather spontaneous woman, and, although you do not know her well, you can imagine that her spontaneity never leaves me bored. Quite charming!"

"I would describe her as amusing rather than charming."

"Would you? An interesting perception for someone who does not know the family well." Highsmith let the silence linger after his words, but Wolversley refused to pick up the thread of conversation.

"Well then," said Highsmith. "Shall we forget those chairs and see if we can do a little dancing too? Perhaps we can seek out *amusing* partners of our own?"

WOLVERSLEY CONSENTED, MUCH against his will, and followed Highsmith to the ballroom. They navigated the crowds easily enough. Being a head taller than the majority of the ball-goers was somewhat of an advantage for both gentlemen.

Coming near the edge of the dance floor, they found a space amidst the throng, settling between two groups of younger ball attendees whose spirited conversation and laughter was almost deafening. Wolversley winced in annoyance, but his companion decided to make the most of being surrounded by very young and very loud females. In such an opportune position, it would be thoughtless of Highsmith not to raise his quizzing glass and survey the beauties on parade.

Wolversley, unlike his companion, avoided the groups in their immediate vicinity and instead looked farther afield. He caught sight of wallflowers whose retiring frames intertwined together around the sides of the room. The mamas of those individuals stood behind them, growling in their deep-coloured silks and every now and then ruthlessly pushing their dear, sweet girls into the paths of eligible men.

Yes, everything in Town was as Wolversley had left it. The young, arrogant bucks who cared more for the cut of their coat than anything else, the pretty debutantes, the artful mothers, the shrinking wallflowers—everything was the same. Everything, that was, except Miss Rotherham.

It was true; they were neighbours and should have seen each other over the years—would have, if it were not for Wolversley's unceasing care to avoid the Rotherham family. When they had been in the country, Wolversley had been in Town; when they had been in Town, Wolversley had retired to his country seat to manage his estate. Only once had their paths almost crossed, a little over three years ago, but thankfully the only view he had been afforded was one of their carriage passing his.

Over time, it had become a matter of habit to avoid them, a habit that became so deeply ingrained in his subconscious that he barely had to think of it to carry it out. That is what had left him staggering when the carriage pulled up to the door this evening, trying desperately to come to terms with where he was and who he was about to meet again before he saw them—before he saw her.

His eyes instinctively searched for the subject of his thoughts. He let them wander across the dance floor and alight on Julia and her partner. He saw them come together after their turn in the centre of the quadrille. Courtenay's head was lowered for a moment whilst he whispered some joke in Julia's ear.

"Do you see anything you admire?" asked Highsmith. He

had diverted his attention from the bevy of beautiful debutantes to follow the line of Wolversley's gaze.

Wolversley's eyes narrowed. "Not particularly. There were no beauties last Season that I recall, and my few months sojourn in the country has done nothing to improve the waters." He regretted his unkind words as soon as he had uttered them, but tonight was not exactly turning out as he had anticipated, and his temper was bearing the brunt of those mislaid plans.

"I believe Courtenay's dancing with an old favourite." Beneath Highsmith's cheery exterior there lurked a coldness, and Wolversley could not help thinking the words were baited. How much did this Peter Highsmith know?

"Indeed?" Wolversley put on his well-practised mask of detachment, the mask he had worn for years, the mask which had helped him appear immovable amidst fallen circumstances and treacherous relations.

"Oh yes, quite a beauty. Do you not think so?" Highsmith smiled enigmatically at the Earl before casting his gaze carelessly back towards the couple. "I certainly did."

Wolversley's brows gained some noticeable height and, like a waking lion, stretching and making ready to stand, he turned with some purpose to face Highsmith.

The man who was about to be interrogated took on a crooked smile. He slipped a cheeky wink to the Earl and waited for a response.

Ever since he had seen Julia tonight, Wolversley had been thinking of what he had been doing in the years apart from her, but suddenly a question loomed large in his mind—what had *Julia* been doing all these years?

"What are you two wagging your bone-boxes about?" Freddy Rotherham's high-pitched voice sailed over the music. The young would-be dandy pranced toward them, leaving a boisterous group of youngsters behind. With his brightly patterned waistcoat, high shirt points, and painstakingly styled hair, he paused and preened.

"Your sister, in point of fact," said Highsmith, smiling at the younger man.

"Oh, yes? Have you had to listen to Highsmith moping over her again?" Freddy said flippantly, turning to Wolversley without an introduction. "Oh, I say, Wolversley! Didn't realise it was you, old man! How d'you do?"

"Well, I thank you. Though I am fortunate, I see, for I have had no moping from Mr. Highsmith, only reminiscing."

"How unusual of you, Highsmith. You disappoint me." Freddy grinned and nudged the older man with his elbow, a gesture of familiarity noted by the Earl.

"Alas! I cannot keep up with all the changeable emotions I am supposed to feel as a snubbed suitor. The more I remember courting your sister the less I can mope. How can I when she is still so captivating?"

"Urgh!" replied the unimpressed brother. "Enough of that gushing talk, Highsmith. It makes me positively nauseated." He turned to Wolversley whom he remembered as a childhood acquaintance who once had a fancy for his sister, nothing more. "Oh, it was ugly, trust me, Wolversley. He would not stop sending her flowers and poetry. I could have sworn a proposal was on its way, but then I guess you realised what you were letting yourself in for, eh?"

The young lad nudged Highsmith again who coughed a little at his rudeness and frowned reprimandingly at him.

"I say, still soft about the whole thing, are you?" The young man was incorrigible.

Wolversley's question of what Julia had been doing since he had last seen her was being answered. He looked with some curiosity at Highsmith, seeing the man in a new light. He understood now the prying questions the man had put to him —this fellow still had feelings for Miss Rotherham, and someone must have drawn a connection for him between the lady in question and Wolversley.

Young Freddy began chattering on about some famous bout that had taken place at Jackson's earlier that week and, following that, begged Highsmith to tell him how he folded his cravat so expertly. Had Wolversley been in different circumstances, he would have listened with some interest to the description of the bout, but now he had Highsmith's apparent affections towards Miss Rotherham to think upon.

The two almost-husbands of Julia Rotherham in one room for an evening—it should have been diverting, amusing even, but Wolversley felt no such amusement. Clearly, Julia had not wanted for suitors since their betrothal had been broken off. If she had had a bruised heart, surely she would not have begun fresh flirtations. So was the indignation she had shown earlier really just injured pride? He did not know what else it could be—his private jilting of her had clearly not hindered her expectations. He should have been content with that knowledge, but as it was, he was not, and this evening was rapidly turning into something far, far more complex than a mere coming-out ball.

DESPITE COURTENAY'S GARISH appearance, the overpowering scent of his perfume, and the false flattery he was intent on dousing Julia with, she was finding he could dance with a high degree of agility. She even found him funny, though rather than laughing at the poor jokes the peer told, she found his vibrant personality and dress a joke in itself.

Whilst amusing herself at her partner's faults and enjoying his company on the dance floor, Julia was also occupied in another task. She had quite a talent for doing two things at once, whether it was scolding her sister while darning a dress, or keeping time in a dance while keeping an eye on an old lover. She laughed beautifully and looked merry, and every now and then cast a pair of venomous eyes in the direction of Wolversley who, in his irritating fashion, never caught sight of them.

Courtenay finished the dance as he had started, with an exotic bow, and then led his partner back to the pair of gentlemen now standing beside the dance floor.

"Still not managed to get partners of your own? Shame on you," chided Courtenay.

"No," said Highsmith, "we have been remiss in our attentions to the unengaged young ladies. However, we have managed to be properly introduced to each other—have we not, my lord?"

Wolversley made no reply.

Julia looked nervously between the two gentlemen. What had Highsmith learned? There was a look of knowing in his eyes which had been absent before. She did all she could to calm the butterflies stirring inside her. Soon they would be raising a storm in her stomach.

"Being properly introduced is always an asset," said Courtenay, responding to Highsmith's comment but keeping his eyes on Julia. "Although I fear our introduction was rather lacking since I did nothing but make my partner laugh at inconsequential jokes on the dance floor. I beg your forgiveness, Miss Rotherham." He bent over her hand theatrically. Julia gave him a quizzical look.

"You must tell me, Highsmith," continued Courtenay, "how I can gain a better introduction to Miss Rotherham. I know barely anything about her!"

"Certainly." Highsmith smiled. "Wolversley and I simply started by finding out how each of us was connected to the people we saw before us on the dance floor."

Wolversley's jaw began to clench.

"Well, that is a jolly idea!" said Courtenay. He turned back to Julia. "You mentioned earlier a mutual acquaintance of ours, Miss Rotherham."

"Yes?"

"How d'you know my friend Wolversley, here? You spoke of childhood before."

"Him?" She did not bother to look at the Earl, though he stood in the circle. "Neighbours in our home county, though I have not seen him these six years together!"

"No! What a horrid neighbour you are, Wolversley. More so for knowing this beauty dwelt next door whenever I visited and never deigning to introduce me. Just horrid."

"I try." Wolversley sipped from his glass, keeping an intent eye on Julia.

"Oh, he is just terrible! Was he always like that?"

Julia, who now felt more sober than she had an hour ago, was losing the serenity she had been enjoying. She could feel the Earl's eyes upon her, and the situation she had instigated with breathless amusement was rapidly becoming suffocating.

"Oh, I could not tell you what he's like, my lord. I certainly have no idea." Julia bestowed a cold look on the Earl, one which not even Courtenay could ignore. There was an awkward pause. No one knew quite what to say.

"Well,"—Courtenay finally spoke—"shall we dance again, Miss Rotherham?"

"Oh, no, I don't think so, Courtenay. I'll have this next dance, thank you." The purposeful authority in Highsmith's voice outdid any argument Julia's previous partner could make. He had gathered as much information as he needed to make an educated guess as to Wolversley and Julia's past, and more than that, he could see how worn she now looked. Stepping forward, he took a grateful Julia by the arm and manoeuvered her onto the dance floor.

They were soon out of earshot.

"Thank you, Peter." Julia clung heavily to her savior.

"I may not have been able to understand your heart, Jules, but I can most certainly understand your moods. I felt a swift exit would not go amiss."

They moved away from each other as they joined the separate lines of dancers. Julia smiled in response to Highsmith's words—it was all she could do now they faced each other at a distance, but it was all she needed to do to tell a friend she was indebted to him. When the dance finally drew to a close after half an hour and Julia's tired feet were once again walking in step with Highsmith's, he asked her how she fared.

"Not well, dear Peter." She smiled wanly. "Tonight was rather unexpected and I am so tired. I shall retire early, but if you call upon us tomorrow, I shall tell you all. You have been such a friend to me this evening."

He nodded and released her to the crowds. She found her father and mother, bade them a good night on the pretext of a headache, and disappeared from the ballroom.

Julia should have gone straight to bed, and later she would regret she had not. As it was, instead of seeking the solitude of her bedchamber, she made her way to her father's library which was safely shut off from the guests. She was falling into a depressed mood and just wished that the ball would be over and that Lucius Wolversley would disappear from her life. She had managed to face him earlier, but she did not feel she had the strength to do so again. Her resolve was hard put to continue keeping up the unaffected façade.

That is why she had come to the library. The room was a fortress of dark mahogany panels, interspersed with the sombre colour of burgundy. A fire blazed merrily in the hearth, shedding its light across the richly coloured Axminster carpet. Candles flickered in wall holders and upon various tables, bathing the room in a warm, welcoming glow.

She loved this room. She loved the books that lined the shelves, the gold lettering on the spines that winked at her, the rich warmth of the mahogany's colour, the comfortable winged armchair by the fire belonging to her father but often commandeered by her. The smell of the books, the dust the maid had missed, and the sweet wood from the fire—all of it she breathed in, and the anxiety she had been feeling ebbed slowly away. Half an hour later she was curled up in her father's chair by the hearth, a book in her hand and her mind in another world. She had tucked her ball gown about her knees to keep herself warm, and with the ball two sets of doors away, the only sound to break her paradise was the intermittent turning of pages.

"Miss Rotherham."

Julia jumped in her chair at the sudden interruption and was thankful she was not close enough to the fire to catch her skirts in it.

"Who on earth?" she cried after her initial jolt of surprise. She snapped her book shut and swung round in her chair to see the door. The look in her eyes changed from alarm to fury as she saw who had entered her sanctum.

Wolversley was standing right there, calmly watching her, as though it were the most normal thing in the world for them to be alone together. The serenity she had felt growing inside her this past half hour was dashed to pieces. She felt as exposed as if he had come upon her in only her shift. Her cheeks flamed red—embarrassment turning to anger—as she leapt up from her chair. "This is the outside of enough! What are you doing in here?"

"I came to talk to you." Wolversley paused to pick up a book from a nearby end table. The leaves opened in his hands and he spent a few moments casually flicking through the volume before placing it back upon the surface from whence it came. "It took me some time to find you. Then I remembered." A shadowy smile flickered across his mouth. "There was only one room you used to run to when you were...."

She stared at him, her arms folded across her heaving bosom, her silk skirts crumpled from sitting upon them, and her face, which had looked so brilliantly defiant before him earlier, tired and drawn. "When I was what?"

"Upset." His face was indecipherable.

The anger she wanted to display was too taxing. His appearance now was even worse than his appearance at the receiving line. She felt more vulnerable now than she had this whole evening, a target for whatever arrows the Earl was about to send her way.

"I am surprised you remember that." She dropped her hands from her chest and attempted to pin a large brown curl back into place. She must look a mess, and that just made all of this worse, especially when he looked so composed. "You should not be here alone with me."

Her words were prudent, but she made no attempt to leave the room. She could not help looking at him as she had done long ago, comparing him to the younger self she had known. She could see the strength he still held in his shoulders, his dark hair still tousled as it had been before, and the gray eyes, those eyes which had felt as though they could pierce her very body when he had loved her—*if* he had loved her. She could not take anymore. Her eyes hardened. "Get out."

"Julia, please."

"My name is Miss Rotherham. If you can remember my past habits you can certainly remember my proper title." She threw the words back at him, tempted to throw her book along with them.

"My apologies, Miss Rotherham." His voice was calm though his eyes betrayed his annoyance. "I just came to say—"

"No!" Julia's hand shot out in a command for him to cease. "My lord, please"—she paused, raking in a breath, her green eyes willing back tears—"please, just leave." She turned away.

It took Julia some time to realise he had gone. She was too fearful, too proud, to turn around and show him her tear-stained face, and when she finally did he had disappeared as silently as he had come. The room had felt empty before, but never this desolate. Why must he cause her such pain? Why must he seek her out when he had been the one to discard her? She could not forgive him.

Her heart had been laid bare this evening, and all she could think to do was curl back up in the winged armchair and read. It was some hours later when a servant woke her and she was sent to bed. The ball was still going on below, though half the guests had already left.

Now, lying in bed she could not sleep. Memories came flooding back as she stared silently into the darkness, memories from six years ago—of a youthful love, of promises given, of a future that had once shone so brightly.

CHAPTER FIVE

"...harsh realities..."

THE MORNING BROUGHT WITH IT THE harsh realities of Julia's punch consumption the previous evening.

Her middle-aged maid wore a face of condemnation as she placed the ewer of hot water upon the table and went to open the curtains. "Well, it serves you right for enjoying yourself a little too much. I hear the punch was a favourite of yours?"

"Lucy, wherever did you hear such a pack of lies?" Julia lay in bed rubbing her temples rhythmically. She had shut her eyes tightly against the severe morning light, and the mess of bedclothes rested atop her like a mountain.

"Mr. Rotherham told me, miss. You know how he sees everything." Lucy did not try to hide her smugness, nor did she try and speak quietly for her mistress' benefit. "So's I know why it is you feel ill and, like I says, you brought it upon your own head, miss. You spare no thought to the future."

Julia was sure that at any moment her skull would crack from the high, nagging pitch of Lucy's voice—or from the horrid brightness coming in through the window. She groaned and rolled over before realizing her stomach had a preference for staying in a stationary position this morning. She rolled back. "Well," she said, sighing and tentatively cracking one eye open. When her skull remained intact she continued. "Well, yes, fine! Perhaps I did enjoy some of Cook's punch, but I do not see that I should be rebuked for it." Both her eyes opened into two thin slits, and she grinned weakly at the bustling mother hen.

"It's no good you looking at me like that, miss, for you must get out of bed and dress and eat breakfast."

"Oh!" Julia cried, draping an arm across her forehead. "Do not say the word *breakfast* to me, I beg of you."

Lucy's hard face fell into a reluctant smile before finding its way back to a look of reproof.

"It's no use, Lucy—I saw you smile." Julia, it seemed, had miraculously recovered from her fit of melodrama and was now grinning mischievously at her maid.

"You saw nothing! Now, you need to be up, for Mrs. Rotherham insists you be ready to sit with her for the morning callers."

"I wonder why she wants me for the morning callers," Julia mumbled, knowing full well that her mother wanted her elder daughter available whenever there was the possibility of an unmarried gentleman setting foot over the Rotherham threshold.

At the thought of unmarried gentlemen, Julia's mind suddenly recalled the events of last night, and she thought with a measure of anxiety about Wolversley's unexpected reappearance in her life. It was most vexing. She moaned again, an achy feeling creeping over her body. "Sleep would be a far better use of my time."

"Not today," Lucy replied in her matter-of-fact manner, walking back and forth across the room, picking up garments, and grumbling under her breath. Lucy had joined the Rotherham household when Julia was just a baby, and her longstanding service allowed her a freedom of speech with which her mistress was only too familiar. Although Julia was adamant that she herself was a grown woman now, Lucy refused to award her that status.

With the clothing all tidied, Lucy left the room to attend to some of her other duties. Julia sighed in relief. The silence was an immediate balm to her aching head though her nausea was still present. Lucy's rapid movements had made everything worse, and now all Julia wanted to do was to sleep away the sickness she felt. It was quiet in the room—delightfully soundless. The punch victim drifted slowly to sleep, finally at peace.

"Up you get, miss!"

Gasping with fright, Julia sat bolt upright, nearly hitting her head on the canopy of the bed. Her head swung round and she saw Lucy smiling wickedly at her.

It was immediately after this that Julia's much put upon stomach unburdened itself. Thankfully, a chamber pot was near to hand.

Lucy, exhibiting not one ounce of remorse, helped Julia out of bed. "I was worried you might have fallen back to sleep, miss," she said with a twinkle in her eyes, "but I see you are as bright-eyed as a hare on a March morning."

Julia shot her an evil look before relenting and allowing herself to be walked unsteadily towards the washstand. She gave a soft little moan, her stomach cramping as she bent nearer to the water.

"Now, now, miss." Lucy stroked her back gently and pulled her hair away from her face. "You'll feel much better once you're washed and dressed." It was always a miracle when Lucy decided to show compassion, and Julia appreciated those rare moments.

The old maid helped her mistress wash away the feelings of sickness. She dressed her in a lightly-patterned muslin gown, and a high-necked chemisette poured frills from beneath Julia's chin.

Julia sat down at her dressing table. One glance in the mirror showed the greenish tinge to her countenance, but she had to admit—Lucy's choice of dress was rather strategic. It highlighted her slender neck, and with Lucy pinning her hair higher than usual upon her head, the tresses which escaped the careful hands softened the harshness of the shadows beneath Julia's eyes and the ill pallor of her countenance.

As the rhythmic pulling and twisting and tightening of her hair carried on, Julia fell into a trance-like state, allowing herself to be the babe Lucy still saw her as. She saw with a stab of annoyance half an hour later that Lucy had been right—she was feeling a lot better already.

ONLY JULIA'S FATHER was in the breakfast room when she entered. He had several letters opened and spread out before him which he had rejected in favour of ale and ham. Dressed in a double-breasted coat reminiscent of fashions a decade past, a style which Mr. Rotherham solemnly refused to give up, he ate sedately in the quiet room. Julia disturbed this peace by coming in with a groan. She picked up a piece of toast and began pointing it at her father who leaned back in his chair to observe the scene his eldest daughter was about to make.

"Now, Papa, it is no good you smiling at me in that way. It was quite cruel of you to tell Lucy that I had...had..."

"Overindulged," Mr. Rotherham offered.

"Yes." Julia slid onto a chair and sighed. "She read me a fine sermon, not forgetting to make sure I knew it was all my own doing."

Mr. Rotherham nodded sympathetically as he chewed a particularly delicious mouthful of ham. "I am a bad father," he replied after swallowing. "But you are a bad daughter. I may not have eyes on you at all times—more's the pity considering the trouble your temper can get you into—but I did see you several times during the course of the evening. And in many of those moments you seemed to have had difficulty...balancing."

Julia blew a curl out of her face. "I know." Her tone was resigned. "It was thoughtless of me, and on Annabelle's coming-out ball as well. I do not know what came over me." She nibbled the bit of toast that had been her accusatory pointer a minute ago.

"Do you not?" asked her father, carrying on with his meal.

Julia did not respond. She took her breakfast in amicable silence and though she could only stomach a bland meal of butter and toast, she did feel far better afterwards. When she rose from her chair, she paused with two fingers still resting lightly on the tablecloth.

"I am sorry, Papa."

He put down his fork and reached across to pat her hand but said nothing.

Satisfied, Julia nodded. "Mama is in her rooms?"

"Yes. I believe she is breakfasting."

Julia turned to leave. She must go to her mother before the callers began to arrive. It was only polite to be at home to visitors the afternoon after a ball you had hosted. To be quite honest though, Julia could not see the sense in it. In her current state she did not wish to see anyone, so why on earth would other ball-goers think differently? Propriety really was a burden at times.

As she walked up the stairs she thought of what would happen if she fell asleep in the midst of a morning call. It was a little too likely, but the thought did make her smile as she walked up the stairs. She stifled a yawn and pushed away the returning nausea. If only she were still in bed. Lucy was positively beastly in her efficiency!

Once she had reached the first floor of their London home, she headed for her mother's rooms. She knew her mama would want her suitably employed during the calling hours. After all, as Mrs. Rotherham was always telling her daughters, an eligible girl was far more attractive to a potential suitor if she were displaying some sort of accomplishment. Would it be embroidery? Drawing? Tinkering on the spinet? Oh, the joys that awaited the tired Julia! It was then that she remembered the promised visit of Peter Highsmith. At least *he* would not demand a display of accomplishment. She entered her mama's room and braced herself, ready to receive instructions.

When the ringing of the door was heard, Julia had already been placed on a sofa and posed by her mother. But no matter how much Mrs. Rotherham had urged her, the defiant daughter refused to replace her novel with the embroidery the woman held out. She had been obedient to her mother's demands to attend her during the calls, but she was most certainly not going to embroider after finding out her mother had let Annabelle stay in bed. The fact that Julia had been allowed exactly the same privilege after her own coming-out ball was simply not the point. If she should be up today, Annabelle should be too, and so, no matter the coaxing, the embroidery was adamantly refused.

"Very well!" Her mother eventually gave up, seating herself on the sofa adjacent to the one her eldest daughter occupied. She huffed a little before settling to look at her embroidery hoop. Her eyes creased at the corners in well-known wrinkles as she attempted to decipher the half-finished work.

"Mama, you and I know that embroidery does not stand a chance. Why not leave it before you damage it irreparably?"

Mrs. Rotherham shot her daughter a glare, her eyebrows raised menacingly. "And what exactly are you saying, my child? You doubt my embroidering ability?"

"Well, yes," replied Julia flatly. "We both know how that cushion for Papa's library chair ended—it was a rather patchy and knotty affair."

"The cheek! Your father said he adored it."

"Yes, but...." Julia was saved from being the instigator of a future marital argument when the maid came in to announce Mr. Highsmith. The servant bobbed a curtsey before retreating, and soon afterwards the gentleman in question was admitted.

His long legs carried him into the room with very little effort. He was looking splendid in a blue jacket, cream coloured pantaloons, and a pair of gleaming hessians with little tassels hanging off the front.

He bowed his fair head low and then, beaming a genial smile up at the two women, offered his salutations. "Good morning, ladies! Ah, I see no Miss Annabelle this morning?" He slipped a mischievous wink to Julia but turned back to her mother. "No doubt she is over-tired after such a triumphant entry into Society!"

Mrs. Rotherham glowed at that compliment, the vexing embroidery forgotten for the moment. "Well, that is most kind of you to say, Mr. Highsmith. I will admit, I was rather pleased with how the evening ran." Mrs. Rotherham rubbed her hands together with some satisfaction before she picked up the hoop again. "And, I trust you enjoyed yourself, Mr. Highsmith."

"Madam, I could not have had a more agreeable evening."

She smiled appreciatively once again and gestured for the gentleman to sit down. Highsmith took a chair beside Julia's sofa, and with them so closely and comfortably installed, Mrs. Rotherham feigned some complaint about a draft and moved off to a chair against the far wall to continue her stitching. There was no harm in giving an eligible bachelor and her daughter a little room.

After waiting to see that the lady of the house was otherwise employed, Highsmith leant forward.

"Now, dear lady, I am sure that you must have felt ill this morning? Am I right in assuming the ill effects of your alcohol consumption?"

"Oh, you are a horrible tease," replied Julia without the least discomposure. She flicked a stray embroidery thread from her lap.

"Yes, I am." He paused. "And I fear I shall have to tease you some more before I depart. You made me a promise last night, and I am come to redeem it."

"Must you?" Julia recollected which story she had promised to share, but she was in no mood to recount her dealings with Lucius Wolversley. She had awoken at an unearthly hour, feeling wretchedly ill and remembering afresh the man who had broken her heart six years ago. She would rather embroider every morning for a month than talk about the Earl who had come upon her so unexpectedly at her sister's ball.

"Yes." Highsmith's voice became gentler. "You are unhappy, my dear—I can see it in your eyes, and you would be better to tell a friend. You yourself told me last night that I have been a good friend to you—let me continue to be so now." His handsome face leaned in to her, his soft brown eyes comfortingly sweet.

She did not reply. He waited a few minutes and then, realizing she had no intention of telling him what she had promised, took a different route.

"In truth, Mrs. Rotherham," he called, turning to his hostess, "other than thanking you for a delightful evening yesterday, I had another design in calling today."

"You did?" Mrs. Rotherham was brought out of her pleasant recollections of the ball and away from the thread which had knotted under her unskilled hands.

"Yes, I came to see Miss Rotherham for, as I was enjoying your eldest daughter's company last night, she dropped something which I wish to return."

"Oh, my eldest daughter is forever losing things—the housekeeper found a reticule beneath a pile of books in the library just last week." Mrs. Rotherham was shaking her head, though her gaze was directed once again towards the embroidery, her interest in her daughter's carelessness clearly fading.

"Well, Mr. Highsmith, and what, pray tell, did my scatterbrained self misplace last night?" Julia cocked her head to one side in curiosity and addressed Mr. Highsmith with a flicker of defiance in her eyes. What was he planning? "Come now, I grow impatient—what is it?"

"Yes, yes—I know patience is not one of your virtues." He stopped and looked at her strangely. "Would you be so kind as to please stop looking at me like some inquisitive owl?"

Julia gaped. She had been attempting to disguise her tiredness from last night by opening her eyes wider than usual. Now she felt ridiculous. "I am not an owl, you odious man! Now where is my lost item?"

"Julia, my dear, stop insulting Mr. Highsmith. I am sure you are grateful that he had the wit to pick up whatever it is!" Mrs. Rotherham apologised for her daughter's behaviour. "But now my curiosity is piqued," she said in calmer tones, peering over at the couple. "What is this object?"

"Alas, it is not something I can freely speak of. A trinket or keepsake, I suppose, but perhaps not something Miss Rotherham will want made public."

Now he was being thoroughly exasperating! Despite his attempt at seriousness, Julia could see the corners of his mouth twitching. It was all a game to him. She would not tell him what he wished and so he was making up some scandalous falsehood to get her into her mother's black books. The worst of it was his charming countenance, which had won over so many ladies before, would not fail to do the same with Julia's mother. How dare he blackmail her!

But Mrs. Rotherham was in an indulgent mood. "Something I do not know about, I see," she said, and instead of demanding an explanation, she smiled and went back to untangling her embroidery. If Julia had glanced over at her mother, she would have seen her thoughts as plain as day—the faint flicker of hope that perhaps her daughter and Mr. Highsmith were courting.

It had been so long since her eldest daughter had let a suitor woo her, not in fact, since she had been but seventeen. Unfortunately, no good had come of Lucius Wolversley's affections. The betrothal was broken off soon after his uncle died, and he had not renewed his attentions in the intervening years. Since then, Julia had shown little interest in the eligible young men Mrs. Rotherham had pushed her way. It had all been most exasperating, especially since Mrs. Rotherham had never caused *her* mother any such trouble, marrying the first eligible gentleman she saw.

This morning, however, Mr. Highsmith's mention of a trinket and her daughter's spirited reaction were leading Mrs. Rotherham to some rather desirable conclusions. She had watched Highsmith court her daughter last Season and he was back at her side again now. Yes, there was certainly something afoot, and like any good mother, Mrs. Rotherham knew when to turn a blind eye and let love bloom. She smiled at the two and made a show of turning away to find more thread in the sewing basket at her feet.

Julia, who had read her mother's thoughts, was now even more furious with Highsmith. She scowled at the handsome countenance which was grinning so largely at her from the neighbouring chair. "Now you have sufficiently raised my mother's hopes that we are having a romantic tête-à-tête, I demand that you produce the cause of all this vexation —*if* you can. For you know, I believe this trinket nonsense is just that—a piece of nonsense. You are merely inventing irritations so that I will tell you more about last night."

"If that is how you feel, I shall keep your trinket. It will now be my treasure instead of yours whilst I interrogate you about the ball as you so candidly prophesied I would."

"For goodness sake! What is the blasted thing?" Julia flinched as the curse left her lips, but a sideways glance at her mother confirmed that she had not heard her daughter's rude language.

"So very unladylike! Before I hand it back, I shall use it to bargain. Content me with answering this question: what is your true connection to the Earl?"

"To whom?" Her attempt at indifference was an insult to herself as well as to Highsmith, and it only took a look from him for her to relent. "Oh, very well! I suppose since you are such a dear friend and since you'll keep what I say in confidence...."

"Silent as the grave, my dear." Highsmith tapped a long forefinger knowingly to his lips.

"Thank you." She took a breath. "Well, you probably would not believe it, but I was very much...very much in love once." She paused again. "A long time ago. We were betrothed —though considering how he acted last night I do not think that he ever loved me. It has taken me years to realise and admit it, but he could not have." She was talking more to herself than to him, until a sympathetic sound from her listener dragged her back to the present. "Last night was the first time I have seen him in six years."

"And, what happened six years ago?" He spoke gently, the joking manner of his earlier words having vanished entirely.

"Well, he...he cried off." Julia could not help her cheeks flushing red. It was so shaming no matter how she dressed it up. She played with the tassels of a cushion, unable to look her friend in the eye.

"I see." Highsmith's eyes flooded with sympathy at her admission. He moved his hand to cover hers and gave it a sympathetic squeeze. "Did he give a reason?"

She felt his voice radiate both concern and anger. Her hand felt warm and safe under his. A few lone tears ran down the length of her cheek. She pulled a small handkerchief from where she had placed it between the leaves of her book and wiped them away. "Oh, Peter, you are just so kind. You have no idea how I wish I could love you!"

He laughed. "I had no idea someone could insult and compliment simultaneously."

"Sorry, but you know what I mean."

He nodded. "And now it makes sense why you...why you refused me when I offered."

She nodded. For the first time, perhaps in her entire life, she felt a little shy. Highsmith was a dear friend and she was used to brushing off his past attentions in laughter, but now she remembered how cast down he had been at her rejection. A nagging feeling came into the back of her mind that he would never have treated her so. Whatever his faults in the petticoat line might be, he would not have offered her the insult of engaging himself to her and then crying off.

The feeling of shyness did not last long. The emotion never had suited Julia. "In answer to your question, no, he did not give a reason, at least nothing of note. When I saw him at the ball last night, I had not seen him for six years, not since he had revealed by letter that he no longer wished to marry me. Then without warning he simply appears at my sister's coming-out ball and everything is ruined." She felt several more hot, angry tears course down her cheeks, and again she wiped them away. "Well, I suppose not everything is ruined—that would be rather dramatic wouldn't it?" She half smiled.

"Oh, my dear, I am so sorry." Highsmith patted her hand. "If I had but known, I would have whisked you away from him immediately last night and danced with you all evening, whatever the dowagers would have said!" He smiled jovially, but his hand was still firmly over hers.

"That would have been lovely! He came to try to speak to me a few times, and he even alluded to our engagement as though it were nothing. I was so furious, Peter, I could have struck him!"

"And I would have cheered you on! That fool needs to be taught a lesson. It's dashed awful to desert a maiden, and even moreso without a reason."

Julia did not mention that she thought the reason was him finding other enjoyments at university and in Town. There was no need to make it worse.

"I tell you what, he seemed a little put out last night when you swanned off with Courtenay—well, *I* was a little put-out, truth be told, when you snubbed me for that peacock. Courtenay's an all right chap but an outrageous dresser. I was taken aback when you agreed to dance with him, but it makes much more sense now."

"I highly doubt that the Earl was put out, Peter. He was the one who broke off the engagement. I doubt very much that he feels anything towards me. He was so cold when I spoke to him, as though I were absolutely nothing to him."

"Why did he come then? He must have known that it was your sister's coming-out ball."

"Lord Courtenay brought him. Perhaps it made no difference to him whose ball it was. Or perhaps he did not know. I cannot be sure." The thought made Julia cringe—had he really not known that by attending the ball he would be walking into his past?

"Whether he knew it or not, there was a definite look of irritation on the man's face when you were flirting with Courtenay."

"Me? Flirting?"

"And don't you deny it, you sly minx. I shall withhold my judgment, however, for it is just the sort of thing that Wolversley deserves."

The arrival of Annabelle Rotherham into the room, closely followed by her elder brother Freddy, precluded further conversation, though Julia's thoughts clung to Highsmith's last words. Annabelle collapsed on the sofa beside her sister with a sigh, not of exhaustion, but of pure, unadulterated happiness. Freddy came striding into the room, having spent several hours with his valet to perfect his hair and cravat, and was now perusing the results in the looking glass on the far wall.

"Morning, Highsmith," he offered without looking over his shoulder.

"Oh, yes, good morning, Mr. Highsmith," added Annabelle in sunny tones. "And how did you enjoy my ball last evening? I thought it was marvelous," she carried on without catching breath. "There were simply hundreds of people, and everyone said I was pretty and I danced with twenty gentlemen, I daresay. 'Tis no wonder I am thoroughly exhausted this morning."

"Exhausted but well-rested." Julia shot a look at her mother.

Mrs. Rotherham ignored it. "Children, you say good morning to my guest but not to your own mother."

The rebuked son and daughter sung half-hearted greetings to their mother before Freddy turned upon Annabelle. "You say *you're* exhausted. I am sure I was in bed a good four hours after you. Old Herring found a right smart place for me and the boys to go. We were playing at faro until early morning, though I was horribly beat by a gentleman I hadn't seen before. He was a bang-up player—Sylvester was his name. Terribly good at keeping a straight face. I swore that he would have all my allowance and father's fortune if I carried on till morning, which I very nearly did. So, I am sure I am far more tired than you, Belle."

"Well, you scarcely danced," accused Annabelle, "and I hardly think cards counts as exertion. You were either sitting down all evening or else you were looking in the mirror at your mathematical cravat, or whatever it is!"

Freddy looked scandalized at the careless remark about the most sacred object of his attire. "Fine! If you wish to be so missish about it, I shall not bother to introduce you to Sylvester. He was asking me all about the family last night, and he said he would be delighted to make the acquaintance of my sisters when I told him I had two. He was most interested in you, Jules, but he wishes to meet you too, Belle—but as you are going on so, I shall just not bother."

"Oh, you are heartless!" cried Annabelle, suddenly anxious that she would lose the chance to meet another eligible suitor.

Freddy smirked. "I invited him to ride out with me in Hyde Park on Friday. You should come, Highsmith. And you too, Jules."

"And me!" squealed Annabelle.

"Now, now, my children," said Mrs. Rotherham, raising her hand slightly. "Enough of this snapping. It is most inelegant in front of our guest."

"Oh, Highsmith don't mind, do you?"

"Not at all. In fact, I am sure it is time I left."

At that moment the bell rang downstairs announcing another caller.

Whilst her brother and sister descended into another squabble, Julia spoke in low tones to Highsmith. "Was that trinket you spoke of a falsehood? If so, I shall be utterly enraged with you."

"Oh, I'm glad you reminded me of that." Highsmith pulled a handkerchief from his pocket and carefully plucked apart the corners. In the folds of the soft fabric lay an object whose sight set Julia's heart aching.

"My pearl."

"It dropped out of your reticule when you were retrieving your handkerchief last night."

"Of course." Her voice was soft and far away, her eyes remembering some past time and place. She picked up the freshwater pearl from his hand and gazed at it a moment before putting it in between the leaves of her book. The book could only half close at an odd angle, but she had nowhere else to hide it.

"I am sorry for ruining your waistcoat." She smiled wanly.

"'Tis quite all right. Now I have a wonderful excuse to visit my tailor for another. 'Til Friday then." He kissed her hand.

Just then, the door of the morning room was opened by the butler, and the guest who had rung below a few moments earlier was announced.

"Lord Wolversley, Mrs. Rotherham." The butler bowed.

"Oh, indeed?" The lady of the house who had been busily creating another enormous knot in her stitchery looked up at the interruption with pleasure. "Do send him in."

WOLVERSLEY TOOK A deep breath and stepped into the room as the butler announced him. He could see a knot of young people gathered around the two sofas, while the lady of the house sat in a chair farther off.

Freddy Rotherham swung round to greet him in his offhand manner. "Ah, Wolversley, good chap, tell me what you think of my cravat this morning? I'm rather pleased with it. It's the Oriental style, y'know? The dem' thing took me two hours at least!"

The rest of the room turned to greet the newcomer. Wolversley noted that out of all of the family only Julia omitted a "good morning." That fellow Highsmith who had shadowed her steps at the ball was here as well. Wolversley could see him eyeing her with concern. The Earl watched with annoyance as Highsmith pressed her hand in his before standing to take his leave.

"Wolversley's here," said Highsmith, "and that is my cue, I think." He turned to his hostess. "I will see your daughters and son on the day after tomorrow for the promised ride." He bowed to Mrs. Rotherham, thanked her again for the splendid ball, and told Annabelle she had already broken at least a dozen hearts. The girl blushed with pleasure. Then he took his leave, nodding his head curtly to the Earl without offering a farewell.

Wolversley was not oblivious to this snub, but it did not bother him in the least. Apparently, his intrusion had annoyed Highsmith as much as Highsmith's presence had annoyed him. Good! The Earl watched Highsmith exit and then paid his addresses to his hostess. "Good morning, Mrs. Rotherham. I was remiss in not calling on you before the ball, so I am come to you now."

"How lovely!" exclaimed Mrs. Rotherham. A skilled observer might note that her words were actually referring to her eldest daughter's ability to attract two potential suitors to the house in one morning. "My children you know—Miss Rotherham, Mr. Frederick Rotherham, and Miss Annabelle Rotherham."

The Earl bowed to each in turn, though it was only with Julia that he attempted to make eye contact. This she refused him, keeping her angry green eyes directed furiously at the rug by his feet.

Clearing his throat, Freddy Rotherham gestured with an air of ostentation at his neck. "More important than all this pleasantry nonsense—your opinion, if you please."

Wolversley's face fell into a smile at the young fop. "I am hardly the man to ask, Freddy. Have you seen the state of my jacket?"

At these words Julia looked up, involuntarily, from the floor.

Wolversley saw his opening and pursued it. "And now that I have attracted your attention, Miss Rotherham,"—he turned his gray eyes upon her—"it is my turn to ask a question on apparel. Give me your opinion of my jacket, if you so please." He would not let her get away from him again. They must set things straight, and the first step was to gain the conversation which she had so adamantly denied him last night.

"I am sure I do not know." She toyed with the book in her hands, refusing to look him directly in the eye. Was she nervous? Angry?

Whatever emotion it was, it made her clumsy. She nearly dropped the book she was holding, and a trinket that had been wedged between the pages fell to the ground and hopped a few steps across the floor towards the Earl.

"Botheration!" Julia snapped, laying the book aside and bending down to pick up her treasure. She was too late, however. Wolversley had already procured the object. He was in the midst of handing it back to her when he caught a closer look at it and drew back his hand to inspect it further.

No one was watching the two of them. Another bout of bickering had struck up between the two youngest Rotherhams. Their mother's nerves, already on edge due to the rebellious embroidery, were strained even further as she tried to stop the quarrel.

Wolversley looked at the trinket in his hand—a pearl. A single pearl. "Is this...?"

"It is nothing of consequence. Now hand it over." Without waiting for him to comply, Julia snatched it from his hands, and fell back onto the sofa with a resounding thump.

Wolversley stared at Julia intently. When they had been little more than boy and girl, one of Julia's mother's necklaces had broken during an evening soirée. The beads had scattered everywhere, and the next morning Julia and Wolversley, who had been too young to attend the evening's entertainment, had found a single forgotten pearl beneath the chaise lounge. Wolversley had given it to Julia as a token of his affection, an affection which at that time had barely budded. She had kept the pearl, kept it for quite some time. When they were betrothed, he had joked that he would get it set into a ring for her—an idea she had loved. That was six years ago, and here they were, the pearl still in her possession.

Julia looked haughtily away, presenting Wolversley with a fine view of her profile. He continued to stare. The pearl was confirmation—a sign that he had been right to come. He needed to speak to her privately, to say all of the things which had before remained unsaid. He had resolved to do it last night in the library, but she had been too fragile, and he could not bring himself to force his words upon her. Now it was different. Now he could speak.

But Julia, as if sensing that he had something important to say, forestalled him, using her own words like a shield to keep him at bay. "The coat—you wanted my opinion? Well, you shall have it." She rose from her seat rapidly, and then, strolling across the room, began circling him much as a hawk does its prey.

"Julia—" He needed to do it now, whilst the other Rotherhams were occupied with their tiff.

She raised a hand to silence him and continued to appraise his attire with her eyes.

"Please, forget the coat. I wish to—"

"No." Again she refused him speech. "Here is my verdict," she said in a commanding voice.

He could see the stubborn glint in her eyes and knew that any protest was useless. "Very well. Go on." He had a feeling he was not going to like what she was about to say.

"The shoulders are too wide for you, the middle fits you ill, and the buttons are nothing to speak of." She paused, as if deciding something. "It is certainly not as fine as Mr. Highsmith's attire. That smart blue coat of his shows him off to every advantage."

"Indeed?" Wolversley fought hard to make his tone expressionless. "I shall certainly have to observe him more closely." He knew she was baiting him...and watching him eagerly to see if the bait had done its work.

Try as he might, he could not hide his emotion completely. He felt his mouth harden into lines of dissatisfaction and his nostrils flare with annoyance. She was determined to be odious —he could see it in her eyes. Did he blame her?

"Truth be told, my lord, your coat is an appalling specimen. Do you not think so, Freddy?" Julia pulled her brother into the conversation purposefully.

"Well," started Freddy, leaving off the argument he was having with Annabelle about a flirtation of hers, "it is a little old-fashioned—too long and the turn-backs are rather large— but Jules, aren't you being a little hard on poor Wolversley?"

Julia threw a daring look at the Earl. "Am I being too hard?"

Wolversley knew that the question's motivation was far more multi-faceted than it first appeared. He had no intention of answering and instead continued schooling his countenance into submission whilst his adversary continued her goading.

"If you want my advice, for you have clearly been out of Town for some time, you need to take a leaf from Mr. Highsmith's book of fashionable attire. His dress is all that is agreeable in a gentleman."

"Indeed?" Wolversley pulled his snuffbox from his jacket pocket and proceeded to take some. The action was cathartic, the movements second-nature, the blend soothing—anything to calm his growing irritation.

Mrs. Rotherham chimed in at this point, "Mr. Highsmith does dress very elegantly. Those brass buttons on the coat he wore this morning were very modish. I am sure he could catch any young lady's eye."

"One present young lady, if you ask me—or rather, one present *old* lady." Annabelle's comment contained obvious notes of jealousy.

"You horrid child!" Julia snapped.

Wolversley watched the interchange, absorbing the inferences. Was Highsmith paying court to Julia? Was this something he had missed last night? Thinking back over the ball, he remembered how Highsmith had been by Julia's side most of the evening, how he had praised her and declared himself a snubbed courtier, how they had danced together. He had been here this morning too and had omitted a morning salutation to the Earl. Was it because Wolversley had formerly been Julia's betrothed? Had she told Highsmith of their connection?

"Oi!" Freddy Rotherham's dandified appearance was shattered by the boisterous exclamation. "You can't go at Belle like that. Everyone knows you and Highsmith are on a close footing."

"Now, now, my children," said Mrs. Rotherham, herding

her offspring into order. "Let us not speak of such things before our guest. It is hardly polite conversation, and I am sure your father would not approve." She turned the topic of conversation, marveling at how all the bachelors in London were suddenly at her spinster daughter's heels. "Tell me, my lord, how long are you to stay in Town?"

"It depends, ma'am. I am engaged for several days on business here. I was considering prolonging my stay beyond that to enjoy some of the Season—however, circumstances have changed, and I may need to return to the country earlier than expected."

Wolversley kept a pleasant tone with his hostess, but inside a bitter sadness began to fill him. He spoke of circumstances and intimated that they were business related, but in reality the circumstances were personal. In reality, the circumstances were Julia.

He had come here today to explain himself, to say the words he had not been able to say in the library last night. But Julia had made it abundantly clear that her relationship with Peter Highsmith surpassed the bounds of friendship. It would be better for him to say nothing.

He had hurt her—hurt her deeply, that he could tell. She had been crying when he had left her in the library last night, and he was the cause. Would it not be better now for his past actions to remain in the dark in order to spare Julia any more upset? Would it not be best if he disappeared from her life again?

His only regret would be that he had not gained some insight into Highsmith's character before he left. He would like to have known what kind of man he was, the man who bade fair to join Julia Rotherham on the road to the altar. But if he stayed, it would only bring trouble and pain back from the past—and it was becoming increasingly obvious that Julia wanted him gone.

"Well, you mustn't go before Friday," said Freddy Rotherham, once again affecting his disinterested and dandified accent. "We're riding out in the morning—just to Hyde Park, but it'll be a good run. You'll come, I hope?"

"I am sure the Earl has far more pressing engagements than a ride in the park!" Julia burst out.

Wolversley's lips pressed into a line. Was the prospect of his company really so horrifying to her? "I would not like to intrude."

"Nonsense!" cried Freddy, his feigned disinterest evaporating into youthful enthusiasm. "If you don't come, I shall beat down the door of your lodgings and drag you out myself!"

"I do not think everyone in your party is quite as eager for my company—"

"Oh, ignore Julia! She is always missish when it comes to her riding. Complains people can't keep up."

"I see. Well, I would not like to be counted among them...." Wolversley fumbled with how best to escape the engagement.

"Then prove it!" challenged Freddy. "At least Highsmith's man enough to ride against Julia and that mare of hers."

Wolversley did not appreciate his plans being thwarted in this manner, but that last comment made him pause. Highsmith would be there? That changed matters. Perhaps one ride would be enough to set Wolversley's mind at rest where Julia Rotherham was concerned. If he could gain a little deeper knowledge of Highsmith's character, find him worthy of Julia's affections, he could leave London in peace.

Another thought bubbled up in his mind—that there was *another* reason to go on this ride. He looked at Julia, formidable in her displeasure and yet still beautiful, vulnerable, and—even after all these years—very desirable. He remembered the pearl she had dropped. There was no mistaking it. What possible reason could she have for keeping it still?

He clenched his jaw. No. The time for asking that question was past. She had revealed all too bluntly where her affections now lay. To evaluate Highsmith's worthiness—that must be his sole object if he ventured into Hyde Park on horseback.

"Well, what will it be, Wolversley?" Freddy was determined to lock him into the arrangement. "It'll make an even six if you do come, since Highsmith and my friend Sylvester have already said yes."

The Earl made no further protest and instead bowed graciously to the sister at Freddy's side. "I shall endeavor to keep pace, Miss Rotherham."

Julia folded her arms and scowled. "See that you do, my lord. See that you do."

CHAPTER SIX

"...he would not be refused."

FRIDAY MORNING CAME TO THE ROTHERHAM household swiftly that week. Instead of dreading its arrival, Julia had been looking forward to it with an almost devilish glee. The fury she had felt when Wolversley had unexpectedly invaded her home, twice, in two days, had crystallised into something else—a clear and definable plan for revenge. If Lucius Wolversley was so intent upon settling back into her life, she could at least make sure that he would not be settling comfortably. If Highsmith had been right and her flirtation with Courtenay had vexed him, then that flirtation would be just the beginning. The more she planned, the more her thirst for revenge grew, and though it did not eliminate her pain, it was rapidly eclipsing it.

Julia was familiar with Highsmith's haunts, and she had crossed paths with him yesterday whilst shopping in Town, eager to tell him of her plan. As a gentleman he should have been shocked, but Julia was delighted to see him react with a high degree of enthusiasm. Help her mete out a just recompense upon the Earl who had jilted her? Peter Highsmith would be delighted!

With her ally firmly brought into the ranks, Julia descended the stairs of the Rotherham household on Friday morning with the air of an empress. Today she would be prepared for Wolversley's appearance and, even better, she would be able to defend herself against the pain he caused her.

She entered the morning room to find it all but empty. Crossing over to the window, she observed the street from her vantage point. There was no sign yet of the three gentlemen who had engaged to join the Rotherham siblings this morning. The third man she knew nothing of, save that he was a new friend of her brother's—no doubt a dandified drip. He would not be capable of keeping pace with her, however, so she had no fear of having to put up with his company. It was the anticipation of the other two that kept her pressing her nose to the window.

A few minutes passed and she grew impatient, leaving the window to sit down on one of the old-fashioned, heavily brocaded sofas with their gold floral patterns. She fiddled with the tassels on a cushion and let the plan she had developed for today's ride parade through her mind. It seemed she had left the window just a moment too soon, for before long, Highsmith came into the morning room, closely followed by Freddy, Wolversley, and Freddy's friend Sylvester.

With barely a nod to the other gentlemen, Julia whisked Highsmith away to the alcove by the window. She did not think he would be having second thoughts about the plan that they were about to set in motion, but she wanted to be sure all the same.

Wolversley was not blind to the private tryst being enjoyed by the two lovers. He cursed inwardly at being fool enough to be trapped into this outing. What had he been thinking? He should simply have left the past where it was, in the realm of silence, and left London when he could. With distance the pain of the past grew fainter, but because of his foolish decision to stay in the presence of Julia, he was destined to be confronted by it all day.

The only thing he could do now, apart from regretting decisions already made, was to turn his back on the two whispering individuals and attempt to distract himself by speaking to Freddy's new friend, the pale-skinned Sylvester.

"You have been in Town the entire Season?" As Wolversley looked at the man he realised he was not simply pale; his face was powdered, and there was the faintest hint of rouge on his cheeks.

"Alas, no," replied the gentleman, his voice full of over-expressed sentiment. "I have but recently come from Somerset, but I do hope to make my stay a long one."

"I should hope not!" Freddy Rotherham joined in, his voice filled with mock-horror. "My roll of soft won't be happy at all. This man has won more from me at cards than any other gamester, I tell you, Wolversley."

"You game?" Wolversley's tone turned noticeably cooler.

"I dabble, my lord, merely dabble." Sylvester turned to Freddy with an affected smile. "And if I cease to press your pockets so hard, Mr. Rotherham, perhaps you will be good enough to introduce me to your elder sister?"

Wolversley leant back on one of his long legs and lapsed into silence. His gray eyes flicked over Sylvester's long, thin face with its sharp features. No, he decided, he did not like this fellow at all.

"Certainly, I shall," replied Freddy. "How could I not be tempted by that offer? I'm firmly in dun territory, can't even afford the new hessians I wish to purchase—they have golden tassels, you know." Freddy nudged Sylvester.

"They sound immensely modish," replied Sylvester, ignoring the nudge. "I would be glad of an introduction today."

"Yes, but I don't know how far you'll get in that quarter. My sister is incredibly hard to pry away from Highsmith at present. Those two are as thick as thieves." Freddy looked over at the couple who stood conversing in low whispers.

"They are?" Sylvester's sharp black eyes followed Freddy's gaze.

Wolversley could see a look of disappointment flash across Sylvester's powdered face. It was the briefest display of emotion, almost immediately banished, but his perceptive eyes still caught it. It appeared Julia really had no shortage of potential suitors.

"Ah, I see I am too late," Sylvester stated. "The lady's attentions are already fixed."

The Earl clenched his jaw, his teeth grinding against each other. He did not know which was more irritating—Highsmith's presumption in cornering Julia in private or Sylvester's pretension in thinking that Julia would have ever considered him.

"'Fraid so, old boy," said Freddy, oblivious to Wolversley's discomfiture.

"But your younger sister is joining us today?" continued Sylvester. "Perhaps I can leave Miss Rotherham to Mr. Highsmith if I am allowed an introduction to Miss..."

"Annabelle." Freddy finished for Sylvester. "Why, certainly I can introduce you two."

"Delightful," replied the rouged Sylvester. "I am excited to make her acquaintance."

Wolversley mused that Sylvester's dashed hopes where

Miss Rotherham were concerned had been rather rapidly repaired by the promise of Miss Annabelle's acquaintance.

"Excellent. I'll make the introductions, and you'll ease up on me at the tables." Freddy's voice was exuberant. "He's a slap-up fellow, Wolversley," he said to the Earl, nudging Sylvester again.

A flash of irritation showed on Sylvester's face, but he quickly controlled it. He straightened his black jacket and brushed a hand down the matching black breeches. Licking his thin lips, he then curled them back to reveal a smile of slightly crooked teeth.

"I only wish you'd teach me how to tie my cravat like that," carried on Freddy, eyeing Sylvester's starched concoction with some envy. The parallel lines of the Gordian knot perfectly framed the thin, angular face of the wearer.

It was at this point in the conversation that Julia interrupted. "Are we to ride this morning or merely stand here talking nonsense?" Her imperious tones rang across the gathering as she finally separated herself from Highsmith and walked through the circle of men as though she were Princess Charlotte herself.

"We're still waiting for Belle," replied Freddy, but their wait was not to be much longer for the young lady in question entered the room on the tail of his comment. Freddy seized on the opportunity to introduce both of his sisters to his new friend. Wolversley could tell by Julia's face that she was not overly impressed with the powdered dandy. She quickly turned from him and, leaving Annabelle to enjoy the compliments of her new acquaintance, faced the Earl whom up until now she had been studiously ignoring.

"Good morning, my lord. How delightfully horrid to see you."

Wolversley watched as she looked his attire up and down. He was dressed for riding in a pair of top boots and buckskin breeches which—he thought—fit his muscular legs particularly well. He wore a jacket, newly acquired and of the finest cut, and carried a riding whip.

"Surely not completely horrid. I am sporting a new jacket quite up to snuff with Mr. Highsmith's, I am sure."

"So I see," she replied, looking coldly down her nose at him. It was true. His jacket was a well-fitting display of immaculate taste, but he knew she would never admit as much to him.

"Not quite the standard you were hoping for? Well, I am sure if you divert your eyes back to your favourite, you will find his jacket will more than make up for the damage mine has done to them." Wolversley could not refrain from letting his displeasure show.

Instead of being dismayed by his icy words and clenched jaw, Julia looked positively delighted. "You must be out of sorts this morning." Beneath the sunny tones of her statement, he could hear her triumph. "Now I must leave you," she said, gathering the skirt of her habit over one arm, "for I have had my horse ordered and must go to the stables. Perhaps your temper will improve on our ride."

Wolversley watched her depart with a growing sense of annoyance. If this short conversation was any indicator, the ride could only serve to worsen his temper. Curse it all! He should not have come. And now it was too late.

As Julia flounced down to the stables, she replayed the conversation with Wolversley over and over in her head. How absolutely marvelous that he should be so put out! Flirting with Highsmith had been an excellent idea—now on to the next part of the plan.

As Julia mounted her mare Sheba, she exchanged a few

words with the faithful groom James, a retainer who had been in the Rotherham household since she was a child.

"She's feelin' a might fresh this mornin', miss, though I'm sure you can 'andle 'er."

"She feels perfect, James," replied Julia, an impish smile directed at the stocky man with speckles of gray in his brown hair. She took the whip from him, an action which Sheba took objection to by hopping sideways. Her rider, however, was not in the least shaken. She was used to her mare, an agile Thoroughbred cross Welsh with a set of exceptionally fine legs in the habit of doing what they oughtn't do. Headstrong Sheba usually gave Julia a very interesting ride, and that was exactly what she was counting on today.

The other riders were soon suitably horsed, and the party set off down the cobbled street away from the Rotherham house. Julia struck out in front, followed by the rest of the party.

Sylvester, who rode a very docile hired hack, fell in beside Highsmith, who was mounted on a heavy chestnut called Rufus which belonged to the Rotherham stables.

"I have been delighted to meet the Rotherhams," said Sylvester to his companion. "You have known the family long?"

"A few years." Highsmith spoke loud enough for the whole party to hear, although one particular Earl was his intended audience. "I have spent much of my time in the delightful Miss Rotherham's company."

"So I see," replied Sylvester maintaining his quiet, silky tones. "And a woman of fortune, I hear. How very agreeable for you."

The truth of the statement was unquestionable, but it was an odd thing to say.

"Then we are equally suited," Highsmith replied, alluding to his own inheritance.

"And the younger sister, Miss Annabelle, she is quite unattached?"

"You will have to ask Miss Annabelle, for I am no expert regarding her heart, I can assure you. It is quite a different sister whose heart I am making my study."

"Quite, quite," hissed Sylvester in self-deprecating tones.

"Mr. Highsmith?" Julia turned in her saddle and called for her lovelorn swain. He was doing a marvelous job singing her praises in front of the whole party.

"Yes, Miss Rotherham? I am at your service."

It was all rather theatrical, and Julia was enjoying every minute of it. "Come and keep me company at the head of our cavalcade."

"Your wish is my command." Highsmith swept his hat from his head and performed the lowest bow his horse's neck would allow. He replaced his hat on his head and then headed to the front, leaving Sylvester to fall in beside Annabelle and begin flattering her outrageously.

Before much longer they had reached the park. Julia nudged Sheba into a high-stepping trot, and Highsmith, riding by her side, followed suit. Behind them rode the Earl, making idle conversation with Freddy Rotherham about the correct way to take snuff. Sylvester and Annabelle rode at the back, quite unheeded by the rest of the party.

"Ready?" asked Julia, sitting deep and preparing to canter.

"Are you sure about this, Jules? It could be risky." Highsmith tried to keep his voice low, but he had to speak up to be heard above the clatter of hooves.

"Nonsense! If there's any way to cause him pain, it's to show how much you care for me. And besides, it will only be a small tumble." She gathered up her reins. "Now let's go!" Sheba leapt forward into a canter, Highsmith a little way behind. They were only going at this pace for a few moments before the plan was put into action.

Julia collided with the ground. Mud and grass slid beneath her, smearing across the skirts of her habit. Lucy would have her head when she saw the stains, thought Julia, relieved that the moment of impact had not been more painful.

But the speed with which Julia fell from Sheba charged her body with enough momentum to turn her over for a second landing. This time she hit the ground awkwardly, landing on her right arm. A searing pain tore through her shoulder.

Sheba, shocked by her mistress' unexpected dismount, spooked, jumping sideways to avoid the fallen rider. Thankfully, Julia had had the forethought to take her foot from the stirrup, and the mare, without any ties to her owner, made a swift getaway across the common whilst the rest of the party looked on in horror.

Annabelle let out a shriek, inciting her usually placid mount to attempt a getaway of its own. Sylvester, even paler than usual beneath his powder, slid awkwardly from his horse, fearful that the docile beast would begin rearing at any moment. Snorting, the gelding pulled his head down and started munching on the grass.

Freddy Rotherham was far more sensible than his younger sister and her escort. He halted his horse and looked in the direction of Sheba's rapidly shrinking tail. "I'll get the beast!" he shouted over to Wolversley. "Annabelle, would you close your mouth and get that horse under control?"

It was the most firmness he had exhibited since the London Season started—for in truth, the youth was far more at home in country pursuits than he was in emulating dandies in Town. He tore off after the escaped mare, leaving Wolversley and Highsmith to attend to the fallen.

Julia had by this point ceased her tumbling. She lay still on the ground. The cold, damp earth pressed against her cheek, the pungent smell creeping up her nostrils. Flashing lights passed before her vision, forcing her to close her eyes. She could hear the beats of scattering hooves, her brother's yell, muffled and incomprehensible.

"Miss Rotherham? Miss Rotherham?" She recognised Highsmith's voice. The plan had been for her to lie still until he could come to her aid. Julia was lying still, but if truth be told, it was not by choice.

Highsmith leaned over her and put a reassuring hand on her uninjured shoulder. "That was a little more dramatic than I would have liked, Jules, dear. It actually looked rather painful."

Julia cracked open her eyes, taking in Highsmith's blurred form. She attempted a chuckle, but her chest was still winded from the fall and nothing came out but a wheeze. After a few minutes she gained her breath. "I think it was a little more spectacular than even I intended." She struggled to sit up, but the pain in her shoulder grew sharper and she fell back.

"Is she all right?" asked a deep voice from behind Highsmith's bent form.

Highsmith had tossed his reins to Wolversley as soon as the accident had happened in order to rush to the fallen, and now Wolversley, saddled with two beasts, could not get close to Julia.

"Sylvester! Do something useful!" barked the Earl, tossing the reins of the two horses to the gentleman who was looking more and more frayed by the minute.

Unencumbered, Wolversley knelt beside Julia on the ground, with no care for his buckskin breeches. "How is she?"

"She's conscious," said Highsmith, shouldered out of the way by his rival and falling back a step or two.

Julia had closed her eyes once more against the pain. She could feel Wolversley's presence at her side and she could hear his voice, but she could not see the anxiety in his eyes. Someone laid a hand on her forehead and then took hold of the arm she was clutching protectively.

"She landed heavily on this arm."

"Ouch!" Julia's eyes snapped open. The Earl was right there above her, his face so close to her own. "Let go of my arm! I am being well looked after by Peter."

"You may have broken something." He carried on ignoring her. She could not pull her arm away because of the pain, and he would not relinquish it until he was satisfied it was unscathed.

"Where has Peter gone?" Julia looked around longingly.

A grim look overtook Wolversley's face. Relinquishing his premier position, he moved back and begrudgingly allowed Highsmith to resume his care of the unhorsed damsel.

Freddy Rotherham was trotting back, leading a traumatised Sheba lathered in sweat. "That was rather unfortunate," he called out.

"I've never seen Julia fall before," said Annabelle, riding over to peer down at her sister now that her mare had calmed.

"I know," replied Freddy. "Jules has always had a fine seat. I can't think what happened."

Wolversley made no comment, although if he remembered past days, he would likely have agreed with the younger Rotherhams. He barked at Sylvester to hand over the reins and took back the two mounts from the nervous dandy.

Highsmith smiled down at Julia and whispered, "Oh yes! That worked like a charm, you sly damsel of distress. He is most put out."

"Superb!" said Julia faintly.

"Here you are, Jules." Highsmith placed his arm beneath her own, drawing her up to a sitting position. She finally opened her eyes fully, able to focus as the pain in her shoulder changed from sharp to throbbing.

"Give her this." Wolversley was back, this time offering a flask. When Highsmith tried to thank him he had already turned away with his horses in order to take Sheba from Freddy Rotherham.

Julia felt the first few drops of brandy burn a course down her throat and spluttered.

"Good, Jules, just a little more," Highsmith encouraged her. "It might have been pretend, but it's still a shock to have a fall."

As more of the strong liquid dropped down her throat, she felt warmth flood her body. "You had best take it away, Peter, or I'll finish the whole flask."

That drew a chuckle from her temporary nurse. "She's all right," he called to the others. "But I think it best if I take her home to rest. The rest of you can carry on if you wish."

"I do not think that is advisable," said an anxious Sylvester.

"I agree," said Wolversley.

Julia sat up in her own strength and looked for the audience of her charade. She saw Wolversley gliding his hand over Sheba's neck and shoulder, calming the horse with his touch. There were no agitated movements, no frustration leaking through his reserve. Highsmith had said the fall had worked—but if it had, it did not seem to have affected him deeply.

"Shall we depart?" asked the Earl.

Wolversley's voice was passionless, and Julia began to wonder if he even cared at all.

Her shock and the throbbing in her shoulder, combined with the realisation that perhaps he did not care, sent a tear rolling down her cheek. She tried to brush it away, frustration overtaking her sadness. He would not see her cry. She could never show him that weakness—never.

"All right, Jules," said Highsmith. "It is high time I got you home. I think you're a little more hurt than you let on, you vixen." Highsmith winked as he looked down at her, though she saw that past the cheery exterior, he was worried.

"Put your arm about me. That's it." He raised her from the grass and stood upright, holding her small frame easily within his arms. The sodden ground sucked at his boots as he made his way back to the waiting horse.

Wolversley led the horses over to the couple. "Can she not walk?" he demanded. Despite the fact that Julia's eyes were now open, Wolversley spoke over her as though she did not exist.

"Just bruised, I think, though it's never nice to have a fall. She will be better when we get her home."

Wolversley eyed the arm Julia still clung to. "She needs that arm checked." Again, he refused to make eye contact with Julia. In fact, the Earl was not even bothering to look Highsmith in the eyes. He had turned to the horses and focused on the mare, laying the empty stirrup over her neck to keep it from banging into her side. "This one will need leading home."

"Yes," replied Highsmith coldly. "I shall take Miss Rotherham on my own horse." He walked over to Rufus.

"You will need to mount and then have her handed up to you," said the Earl, ignoring the unfriendly tones of Julia's beau.

It was true. Freddy was still on his horse with no intention of dismounting to help. Sylvester was as white as a sheet and could barely stand himself. That left Wolversley. If Highsmith were to have Julia lifted up to him after he mounted, it would be Wolversley who would have to do the lifting.

"Perhaps I can get her up myself," replied Highsmith.

"Yes, I am quite all right now. It really was nothing, just a little tumble. I feel quite myself again." Julia's voice babbled on. She was realizing, as Highsmith had, that she would have to be put into Wolversley's arms to be handed up, and the thought filled her with dread. "I can stand by myself, and you can lift me up, Peter."

The Earl said nothing. He merely watched as Highsmith attempted to put Julia down. Julia seemed fine for a moment, then a lightheadedness came over her, and she fell back towards Highsmith. He caught her up in his arms again. She winced as her shoulder was squeezed too tightly and the throbbing increased.

"Hmm, perhaps not, my dear." Highsmith looked down at Julia apologetically. "I'm afraid we shall have to take his help."

Before Julia could protest, she found herself being passed over into Wolversley's arms.

"Easy, my dear." Highsmith spoke into her ear as he released her to the Earl.

Once she was solely in Wolversley's arms, she was assailed by the smell of him. She could discern the faint scent of soap from his morning bath, the fresh smell intermingled with musty traces of horse and leather. All those smells threw her with some force back in time, to when they were young, when they had loved each other, when they had kissed. She looked up at him, careful not to let him see her do so. His jaw line was just as strong as it had been then. His arms were holding her as though she were a child, and his dark hair, ruffled by his rapid movements, lay slightly damp against the sides of his face.

"I'm ready," said Highsmith. He had mounted once again on the heavy chestnut and was waiting with open arms for his charge.

Wolversley passed the invalid over carefully. He lifted her up, his crisp cravat scratching her chin a little, until Highsmith could get his hands about her waist. She felt the Earl's hands retract from her upper body and slip down to her hips, hoisting her onto the pommel of the saddle. The feel of those strong hands about her brought memories of desire flooding back so strongly that she felt her stomach turn over. She blushed and stole another look at him, but he was not looking at her. His hard gray eyes had refrained from looking at her the entire time she spent in his arms, and they were not giving in now.

Safely, though rather uncomfortably, seated upon the pommel of Highsmith's saddle, Julia watched all the other riders remount, and then they began to walk in the direction of the Rotherham house. For Julia, the beginning of the journey was spent wondering at the details of what had happened now that she felt more lucid. She came to no conclusions and, if anything, she felt more confused by the Earl's reappearance than ever. He had decided to see her again by coming on this ride and yet had seemed as stony as ever when she fell from her horse. Did he care, or did he not?

The latter half of the journey was spent pondering why damsels ever let knights save them by taking them away on their horses. She would much rather wait until a second horse was procured, even if that meant being a little singed by the dragon, as it was extremely uncomfortable being seated on the pommel of the knight's saddle. All in all, she was now quite certain from her own experience that being a damsel in distress was a hard lot in life.

"AND NOT A scratch! Well, my dear, you are very fortunate. I am sure James must have been feeding your mare oats again."

"I concur, Mrs. Rotherham," said her husband from across the other side of the morning room. "I shall have him soundly whipped for doing so."

"Oh, Papa! You must do no such thing." Julia's condescending command carried with it a tone of worry.

Her father had been expecting the protest, however, for he knew exactly who asked James to stuff Sheba full of oats for a more exciting ride. "Perhaps you're right, my child.

Besides, I have never known a few oats to set you on your ears before. Alas, my teaching was clearly lacking if you could not sit a high spirited canter as Annabelle recounts it." Mr. Rotherham was standing beside Wolversley with his back to the fireplace. Beneath his gray-streaked brows he was eyeing his eldest daughter with a look of provoking inquisitiveness.

The young witness of whom Mr. Rotherham spoke was seated on the sofa, looking very pretty in the blue habit which set off her cornflower blue eyes. The exciting ride had done nothing to disrupt her toilette, and her golden hair was still tucked artfully beneath her hat. She had, however, lost her ardent admirer, Sylvester, who had quit them, quite shaken, upon their return to the house.

"It was awfully dramatic!" Annabelle said in awed tones, her eyes widening. "Mr. Highsmith, you were a knight in shining armour! He rushed straight over to her, you know, Papa."

"It was rather unexpected," said Highsmith, who sat beside Julia on the sofa. He was as cheery-faced as ever, his handsome countenance a balm to the tensions filling the room. "My waistcoat is a little muddy, which is a crying shame, but all is well with Miss Rotherham apart from a minor bump."

Julia, who was sipping tea with her uninjured arm, could not agree with her accomplice. A minor bump was not her description for the continued throbbing in her injured shoulder. It was taking all of her will power to school a look of calm serenity onto her heart-shaped face. Wolversley was still here, and the charade must go on. "Not the ride I had anticipated, but nonetheless, most enjoyable." Julia smiled sweetly at Highsmith in the sickening way that lovers do when they are in the first throes of that affliction.

"Yes, shipshape as ever, eh, Jules?" Freddy Rotherham

rounded the sofa and placed a heavy hand upon her injured shoulder, squeezing it tightly.

Julia gasped, dropping her cup and saucer. The tea splashed across her skirts, the pale brown splattering her green habit. Fortunately, none of the dishes broke—the saucer landed on her lap and the cup was saved by the rug which cushioned its swift descent.

"Oh, steady on, Jules." Freddy pulled back his hand from her shoulder.

Julia dabbed a hand at the wet skirts, trying to keep the tears of pain that had started in her eyes from brimming over onto her cheeks. Thankfully, the riding habit absorbed the spill in a much neater fashion than a muslin dress would. She would never be more thankful for her mother's laxity in allowing them to stay in their riding wear for tea. When she had finished dabbing the spill, she looked up to see that all the eyes in the room, including a pair of remarkably enigmatic gray ones, were upon her.

"How dreadfully clumsy of me!" Julia smiled, picking up the cup and saucer and placing them upon the table. She did not want Wolversley to see her in pain. That kind of vulnerability was not an option.

Her father skirted the tea table and murmured for only her to hear. "Are you quite all right, my child? Are you sure you injured nothing in the fall?"

Julia looked up into those understanding brown eyes and felt a sickness in her stomach at the lie she was about to tell. Her gaze dropped to the outdated skirts of his frock coat. "I'm quite all right, sir. Freddy just surprised me, that's all." She had done it—she had let a little poison slip onto her tongue, all for the benefit of that man across the room who watched her even now.

Mr. Rotherham inclined his head a little and then wandered off across the room to catch his son in some inconsequential conversation before calling Highsmith over as well. Mrs. Rotherham drew Annabelle into conversation, and they began to ask Wolversley about their common acquaintances in the country and how his sister Selina did.

It left Julia quite alone, and before she realised she was doing it, she drew her unhindered hand up to her injured shoulder and prodded it a little, wincing as she did so. She had thought herself safe with the others all engaged in their conversations, but she soon found that the Earl had managed to extricate himself when Mrs. Rotherham and Annabelle turned the subject to the fashions of the latest dresses.

"You never could lie quite as well as I could," said Wolversley. His words were laced with humour, but the gaze he directed down at her was piercing.

Julia looked up at him with as much condescension as she could muster. "I am sure I do not know what you mean, my lord." She dabbed elegantly at her skirts again with a handkerchief.

Wolversley's lips pursed a little and he cocked his head to the side. "The best horsewoman in West Sussex falling off her horse at a canter, landing on her shoulder so awkwardly, and claiming no pain." He pulled his snuffbox from his pocket and took a pinch. "Whatever will you come up with next?"

"I do not appreciate the direction of this conversation, my lord."

"You do not appreciate most of what I say, let alone my presence."

Julia rose at that, casting him a look of derision before walking to the window. She pretended to look out into the street, but she knew very well he had followed her.

"You need a doctor to look at that shoulder."

"And you need to mind where you put your nose. I will be quite well looked after by Mr. Highsmith and my family."

"Mr. Highsmith?" he paused as if he meant to ask a question but thought better of it. "He is much in your company."

"Yes," she replied flatly. She turned back to look at the room, glancing from person to person before looking at the Earl, as though a decision had been made in her mind. "I expect an offer from him very shortly, my lord, and I do not expect he will jilt me. *His* heart at least is constant."

It was as though a stinging blow had been dealt across Wolversley's face. Julia watched the colour drain from it and the countenance of calm he wore crumble away for the first time. His upper lip twitched, and for the briefest of moments, Julia thought she could see something broken in the depths of those gray eyes, as though a grief kept buried was springing up to the surface before being pressed down again by the afflicted.

"I understand." He bowed stiffly. "You will see no more of me from this day on."

The words spoken, he walked away with a look somewhere between humiliation and pain on his face. Julia saw him take his leave of her mama and her siblings. He bowed courteously to Highsmith, and though she tried, she did not hear the words that passed between them.

Julia then watched him speak to her father. As Wolversley spoke, her father glanced towards her, and she wondered what the object of their discussion could possibly be. After a few more minutes of conversation, her father nodded and accepted Wolversley's farewell.

Julia watched him depart from her life as suddenly as he had arrived, a week ago at Annabelle's ball. She had hoped for a feeling of joy, of relief when he departed, but instead her heart felt more exposed, more abandoned than ever.

"And so he goes from Town again." Her father's voice sounded beside her. "Pleasant to see the fellow, though he's a more sombre version of himself than the character who graced the threshold of our house in youth."

Julia was choking back tears, and her father was quite aware of it.

"I remember a young girl who was quite in love with him once, a long time ago, before he broke her heart, and I can't help but think that his appearance the other night was an omen."

"An omen of what?" Julia's whispered exasperation was directed towards the window where she had turned to cry without the audience of the morning room to see her.

"It is of no matter now. I don't think we shall see him again. His farewell was one to last a lifetime, not a few months." Mr. Rotherham paused. "Julia, I cannot help thinking to myself that you have not been yourself these past days." He placed a hand upon her arm, rubbing it gently. "And perhaps, when hurt, we humans do the most unhelpful of things, things we may later regret. It would do you well to think upon this, my child. For the moment, you must go upstairs and lie down. The physician will be here within the hour to take a look at your shoulder."

"Physician?" Julia rubbed the tears from her face and looked inquiringly at her father.

"Courtesy of Wolversley. I do not know what possessed him to think you needed one,"—he eyed his daughter knowingly—"but he would not be refused."

CHAPTER SEVEN

"You have left me no choice."

I T WAS LATE. THE CANDLES FLICKERED a little, as though complaining of the hour. Julia Rotherham lay in bed, her rich brown hair strewn in curls across the covers. Her arm and shoulder had been smeared with basilicum ointment and wrapped in linen. Lucy had wanted to use the family recipe for the ointment, but the physician had brought his own and would brook no argument—in accordance with the instructions of the peer who had engaged his services. The peculiar smell of the ointment was a familiar one to Julia, whose buoyant childhood had contained all manner of bruises and scrapes that needed tending, and with the pungent scent in her nostrils, Julia fell into a restless sleep.

While the Rotherhams' eldest daughter was drifting into unconsciousness, the underbelly of London was beginning to come awake. Catcalls and bawdy yells echoed down gin-soaked alleys. Painted ladies came out for the night, dressed in whatever rags they could find, their faces smeared with rouge and powder. Gentlemen of all walks of life left their homes intent on finding entertainment in the city.

White's was one particular establishment that these gentlemen could frequent, an establishment that catered to the upper class. A gentlemen's club that lay claim to a genteel reputation, White's had flung open its doors over a hundred years ago with the express purpose of attracting a clientele bent upon discussing moral and intellectual thought. Now, although there was still opportunity for such discussions to take place, they were the exception rather than the rule. At this hour of the night, its frequenters could make little claim to genteel pursuits. The small hours were ones for drinking, gaming, and filling the famous betting book.

On this particular evening, the tables, which had started with reasonable stakes, were now trifling with gentlemen's fortunes. The players were either lounging in various states of intoxication or standing about the tables in small groups talking and joking with one another. Dandies, with their extravagant shirt collars, discussed the latest fashion in cravat tying. Corinthians, with their perfectly cut coats, discussed how best to handle the reins. Scattered around the outskirts of the room, a few less fashionable gentlemen in garish waistcoats, old-fashioned queue wigs, or bright silk breeches guffawed at each other's jokes.

Each man present had a drink in hand. Earl Wolversley preferred an inexpensive vintage of Burgundy, and since he refused to hazard the smallest particle of his fortune at the gaming table, he had more than enough to waste on that particular beverage on his last night in London. He slouched to one side in a winged chair, with one leg stretched forward and one hand idly playing with his drinking glass. The swirling red liquid threatened to jump overboard and splash onto his evening attire, but he did not seem to care.

His clothing, like his riding wear, was once again of the

finest cut—another new contribution from his tailor in the last week to replace his outdated evening wear—but he had let it deteriorate over the course of the evening in a manner that any dandy would deplore. His jacket hung open unbuttoned, and his cravat had wilted underneath the pressure of his chin as he sat slumped in his chair. After the way his afternoon had gone, a crumpled cravat was the least of his cares.

Wolversley's drink-soaked eyes roamed the room, observing the gaming tables, examining the players, deciding from their body language who was winning and who would be drawing on personal safes, banks, or even disgruntled relatives in the morning.

Lord Menders groaned. He could not help himself from throwing down his cards and crying out, "You're just too bloody sly, Foulett. No point in even bothering!"

Wolversley caught sight of Foulett's smug smile before it was masked with a decidedly false expression of apology. The whole scene disgusted him. He turned his attention to Courtenay who sat a few tables over.

Unlike Lord Menders, Courtenay had actually won a few hands this evening. But after this unprecedented start, it seemed his luck was beginning to run dry. He valiantly sustained a few heavy losses, putting him neatly back into the financial position he had started in. One more round went by before he laid down his cards. That final hand had lost him yet another roll of soft and, unsure how he would pay for a carriage home, he resigned his position and swaggered over to Wolversley.

"Still planning to leave Town tomorrow?" Courtenay asked his friend. His fair hair was pushed up off his forehead in the large Brutus style he always wore, and his evening wear was in far finer condition than the Earl's.

Wolversley grunted and took another swig from his glass.

Courtenay shook his head at his friend, a comrade since

their days at university together. He wrapped his fingers around the slender neck of the bottle of Burgundy that had been keeping Wolversley company. Raising it for inspection, his face soon took on a look of disgust. "Really, Wolversley, why do you bother with this cheap stuff?"

The Earl snatched the bottle back, scowling up at his friend, and poured himself another glass.

Courtenay shifted uncomfortably. He gestured to a passing waiter, ordered another bottle of "poison" for his friend, requested a glass of brandy for himself, and then collapsed into a matching chair. "By the by, did you hear about the bet?"

"No, but I expect you will tell me about it, no matter how boring I find the tale." The Earl sighed over this unwelcome hardship. He wanted to be gone from London, from the Season, from everyone. The worst was that he had not been given the chance to explain himself. And there was no way on God's green earth that he would be in Town when the engagement was announced. He could not bear it.

"Oh, what a face you put on! As a human, you must have been created with a propensity for curiosity about other people's lives. Most people would enjoy hearing the private information I am about to dispense."

Wolversley rolled his eyes at Courtenay who, adopting a grin, continued to vend his gossip. "You must be interested in this tidbit. After all, it involves a certain golden-haired Cyprian whom I have heard you mention with admiration more than once." The bait did its work.

"Found another backer, has she?"

"Indeed. It would seem the darling Mrs. Thompson, cast off by Lord Cornell, is now warming Jonny Odd's bed and everybody is taking bets on how long it will last."

"That fool of a man? Ridiculous! Even if he is in line for a dukedom, she's selling herself a little low, don't you think?"

"I knew that would be your assessment." Courtenay's usual smile faltered a little. Perhaps, with Wolversley in this mood, it had been unwise to speak of Jonathan Oldsburg-Windlesham. The heir to the dukedom was well known in Town; however, it was not from the capital that Wolversley knew Windlesham. It was easy to remember the cruel taunts Windlesham and his pack of cronies had flung in the cloisters at Oxford, always finding their mark in the young Earl. Wolversley's circumstances had made him the perfect target for derision in a world of moneyed bluebloods. And Windlesham, that rat-like excuse for a man, had refused to relinquish his taunts even now in adulthood.

The Earl, whose silence had borne heavily upon his friend, finally spoke again. "She's actually very beautiful, that Mrs. Thompson. I had the joy of meeting her once. What does she want with an ass like Jonny Odd?" The beginning of his speech carried a tone of admiration—the end came with bitterness.

Courtenay braced himself before saying it. "Money."

Wolversley smiled a cold, bitter smile much lacking in mirth. "Can't hold it against her. It's what she was born to latch onto."

"Yes, I suppose so." Seeing that Wolversley's sullen mood was beyond salvation, Courtenay allowed his eyes and mind to drift off to the gaming tables once again. The players were gradually dwindling, casualties of either the advancing hour or their empty pockets. Courtenay's concentrating forehead displayed deep furrows, and for once he looked his age.

It was ironic, thought Wolversley, that Courtenay had urged *him* to find a bride, considering that Courtenay was the older of the two and certainly in need of a handsome dowry to shore up his ever-precarious estate. Wolversley himself had not thought of marriage ever since....

"What do you make of Highsmith?" asked the Earl suddenly.

Courtenay looked across at him, slightly surprised. "Who?"

Wolversley's eyes flashed over his glass. "Highsmith—the man you introduced me to the other night. He's courting Miss Rotherham." He poured the last of the Burgundy into his glass.

"Ah, the delightful Miss Rotherham! As fine a figure as any and a face quite sparkling with wit—can't fathom why she hasn't been snapped up yet. Although maybe Highsmith's the man to do just that. She was throwing him doe-eyed looks every time I saw them together at the ball. A lucky man, and quite the fortune he will have coming to him, too." Courtenay sounded almost envious.

"Yes," said Wolversley, his gray eyes unreadable. "With his boyish face, one might think he was still in the midst of tutoring if not for his superior stature. But what do you make of him besides being lucky?"

"He is a good fellow, I suppose." Courtenay pressed his fingertips together. "Though snapping up a girl with such a fortune when he has a perfectly good fortune of his own almost places him on my bad side."

Knowing that Courtenay simply did not have a bad side, Wolversley let his mouth dip into a smile. "So you have not... heard anything untoward about the fellow?"

Courtenay wrinkled his nose in thought. "No."

"Ah," said Wolversley, a feeling of almost disappointment coming over him. But was that not what he wished? To know that Julia would be well taken care of by an honourable man?

"Hold on a moment," said Courtenay, his voice brightening. "I *have* heard something about Highsmith recently. I don't know why I didn't think of it earlier. It's rather amusing."

Wolversley's grip tightened around his glass. He knew enough about his friend Courtenay to know what sort of things he found amusing. Whatever came next would not be to Highsmith's credit.

"Well, the other night he was at the theatre, and as one does, he visited backstage." Courtenay's tone suggested this ungenteel activity was somehow a sacred tradition.

Wolversley inhaled sharply. He was no prude, as his friends knew, but the sacred tradition Courtenay described was not one he was accustomed to participating in.

Courtenay carried on. "He had an understanding with one of the opera girls, y'know. A pretty, dark little thing she was...."

Noticing the warning look in his friend's eye, Courtenay adjusted his tack. "Well, that's not important. As the story goes, Highsmith went to find his ladybird, and, seeing her from behind in her dressing gown with a feather in her hair, he went over to say hallo. His greeting was rather lover-like—and was not exactly what the girl was expecting, given that she was not in fact his *amore*. She screamed blue murder and a heavy came in. Highsmith tried his hardest to explain the situation, but unfortunately, it was Joey the Bull he was talking to."

Courtenay paused to snort down a laugh. Wolversley, despite the comedic nature of the situation being described, could not find the incident as amusing as his friend. "Go on," he commanded.

"Well, needless to say, Highsmith was thrown, quite literally, out of the theatre. He landed, according to onlookers, unceremoniously in the gutter and ripped one of his best waistcoats as well!"

Wolversley remembered Julia's endless compliments upon Highsmith's attire and noted with satisfaction that a waistcoat of his had met its demise. "What a lobcock!"

"Just so! There was already a wild hullabaloo in the room

when the Bull arrived, and to think of Highsmith trying to explain himself? Joey's ears have been beaten to a pulp in all those fistfights. I thought the whole of London knew the Bull was almost deaf."

"Apparently not."

The morose state of his companion contrasted sharply with Courtenay's levity. The story had done nothing to lighten the Earl's spirits. If anything, they were darker than ever.

Wolversley's mind was swirling around the events like the Burgundy swirling in his glass. His earlier plan to quit London was now balancing on the cliff edge of uncertainty. Before, he had assumed that Julia had found a worthy partner to spend her life with and that his own presence was only hindering her plans. It would only hurt her further to dredge up the past that he was so desperate to explain. Her future was with another.

Had he not heard this story, he would have been not exactly happy but at least content to leave her to Highsmith's affections. But now everything had changed. Highsmith, it seemed, was a proven rake, dallying with opera singers at night even while he courted Julia Rotherham by day.

Protective instincts towards the woman he had once promised to marry flared up inside of Wolversley. Did she know? Bright, hot anger flashed to life within him.

He could not leave London now, not bearing this knowledge. The truth had been laid bare, and now the path before him lay littered with complications. Had he not come to White's tonight, he would not have heard this tale from his friend. Had he made his way home to Sussex, he would have assumed Highsmith virtuous. Perhaps it was fate. He studied his half-filled glass. What should he do?

Courtenay, neither realizing the seriousness of his friend's thoughts nor the revelation he had just made, carried on talking. Wolversley answered simple ayes and nays as Courtenay kept the conversation afloat, time slipping by unheeded. By a quarter to three, the majority of the men present had slipped off to less reputable establishments, desiring entertainments of a more carnal nature. The only ones left were either those too stretched to afford anything but a drowning of their sorrows, or those whose advanced years would send them home before too long.

Growing restless, Courtenay shifted in his seat, bringing his bulk forward and making ready to vacate his chair. "Are you for bed, Wolversley? Or game for more of what the evening has to offer?"

Wolversley was still pondering the conundrum that Courtenay's story had given him. He knew he needed to take action, but in what form, he was not sure.

"I think I need my bed." He rose, discarding his empty glass on the table.

"Yes," replied Courtenay, rising himself and smoothing the creases in his large waistcoat. "Go home to an empty bed. You're good for nothing else, you sour pup! Leave the London beauties to me." Courtenay slipped a saucy sideways smile at Wolversley, one which was not returned by his friend.

Wolversley's frugal youth had forced him to forgo these types of pleasures enjoyed by the majority of the gentlemen in Town, and now he was older—wiser, perhaps—carnal plea-sures pursued in the night held no appeal. A wife would be the only one to warm his marriage bed, and with this week's events, he could think of nothing further from his grasp. He would leave such activities for his friend to pursue.

The pair sauntered from the room, picking up their coats and hats from a bleary-eyed servant at the door. As the sleepy man sank back into his button-back hall chair, the two men walked out into the London evening.

"Ah, yes!" cried Courtenay, inhaling a great lungful of air

and glancing left and right down the lamp-lit street. "The night is young! Have you ever found that the air at three in the morning smells exceedingly better than at any other time during the day?" He strode lightly forward, observing the antics of a group of young revelers farther down the darkened street.

"That's because"—Wolversley yawned—"it's fresher. After all, it is morning, you dunce!"

"No, no, I shall let none of your gloomy talk spoil my mood! I have an enjoyable night ahead of me—many places to call in at, many ladies to see. *Adieu, mon ami!* Until the morrow!" He bowed theatrically, letting loose a flourish of his bejewelled hand before striding off in the direction of somewhat darker haunts.

Wolversley watched after him, waiting for him to be gone from sight and earshot before straightening himself up and pulling at a collar half-heartedly. He presented a sorry figure, his evening attire well and truly wilted. "My good man, a hackney if you please." He flicked a half-crown into the doorman's hand.

"Right away, my lord." The servant tugged his forelock, grinning at the prospect of a few extra drinks with his friends later. He tucked the precious tip inside a coat pocket before raising his fingers to his lips and letting loose a whistle that would have deafened a dog. A cabby responded within a few seconds, and the reason why the prestigious White's establishment had employed this servant became immediately obvious.

"Before I leave...." Wolversley turned back to the servant just as the sad looking horse pulling the hackney came to a welcome stop. "I don't suppose you know if a Mr. Highsmith is in the habit of frequenting this establishment?" His words came out with a surprising amount of sober clarity.

"A Mr. Highsmith?" The Londoner scratched his head. "I couldn't say, my lord, couldn't say."

"And now?" Another half-crown exchanged hands.

"I think maybe he does, my lord, maybe he does. Fair locks, has he?"

"That's him. A fine pair of beady eyes you have there. I knew you were a sharp one."

The doorman became bashful.

"And I'd thank you if you would let me know when he stops by again." The Earl passed the doorman his card and a final monetary encouragement.

"Yes, my lord. Thank'ee, my lord."

Wolversley nodded briskly. He turned on his heel and launched himself into the hackney. Landing on the seat he fell into a thought-filled silence that any stranger could have mistaken for sleep.

DAWN BROKE OVER the rooftops of London, golden shards fracturing over the tiled roofs and falling down upon the pools of water that scattered the streets. Bakers were already awake, kneading their dough and heating their ovens, the smell of fresh bread wafting through the streets and mingling with the previous evening's revelry, for in some cases the revelers themselves had not yet made it home. Those, like the baker, with jobs that required early starts, were already struggling awake and beginning their tasks for the day whilst others, like the hackney drivers, were still resting their weary limbs.

The genteel classes, who woke when it suited them, were largely still abed. Amongst the few who had risen early was Earl Wolversley, whose late evening had not kept him from waking to attend to certain business. He sat at a walnut writing desk, drafting a letter to his steward informing him of his change in plans. By eight o'clock, he had finished the letter. He laid his quill upon the table and passed a hand over his eyes to shade them from the morning light pouring in his dressing room window. The headache that he had been warding off all morning was beginning to gain ground, throbbing behind his temples. He would happily blame it upon not having broken his fast yet, but truth be told, it was probably more due to the stresses and worries that would not let his mind alone.

He blotted and sanded the sheets destined for his steward and, after sealing them, wrote the direction. His sister was long overdue a letter too, and now that he was no longer leaving London early as planned, he could not afford to ignore her frequent writing. After all, if his steward were to receive a letter and not Selina, there would be hell to pay. He pulled open a drawer and rummaged for fresh paper, but for once, his walnut writing desk did not appear to be well stocked. He was on the verge of calling for his butler when his fingertips brushed against something familiar that gave him pause.

He pulled the tattered letter from the far recesses of the drawer, bringing it out into the light. The flamboyant script across its front sent him falling back into his chair with a resigned thump. He felt the discoloured, over-soft edges of the correspondence, both results of its overhandling. His finger traced the letters of his own name.

How many letters had Julia written? How many had he ignored? It had been too hard to unlock the past when he had vowed he would not fetter her future.

He toyed with the seal, almost at the point of breaking it —then he sighed and placed the letter back in the drawer with all the others from her that remained unopened. He had taken them out and put them back unopened so many times before for a reason, and though that reason might no longer exist, he could not bring himself to walk over old pastures again. What was lost was irretrievable. He knew that now—she had made it clear. So why reopen old wounds? He shut the drawer with unnecessary firmness and turned the key, locking away his past.

A search in the bottom drawer of the desk revealed the fresh paper he had been searching for in the first place. "*Dear Selina,*" —he had not written to her in an age—"*I sincerely hope my letter finds you well and of course behaving well.*" Though she had a golden heart, she was inclined to be mischievous, especially in his absence. "*You will no doubt have many stories to tell me which will prove otherwise....*" With that winning look, which she had spent far too much time perfecting, she could influence him however she wished.

"*I have news from London.*" He must word this carefully. "*I happened, quite by chance, upon some old acquaintances. You will remember them, no doubt, the Rotherham family who reside in our neighbourhood in Sussex. We visited them many times before you went away to finishing school. I believe we shall soon hear of an engagement in that family.*" He paused, the pen poised over the letter long enough for a drop of ink to gather on the nib. It deposited itself in an unseemly splotch on the page.

"Curse it!" Reaching for his blotter, he tried vainly to make the best of it.

"*I hope you are seeing to the dogs while I am away. Fergus will not tolerate being cooped up inside all day, as well you know. In regards to your constant nagging, you ungrateful sister, I shall arrange a trip for you to come to London on the condition that you shall not be going out to balls or the like, since you are not out in Society yet (and I refuse to launch you until I deem you are ready). So you see, your nagging has gotten you nowhere, for you will be just as bored here as in the country—it will only be noisier and more confining. Be it on your own head!*"

Wolversley smiled as he wrote the severe words. "*I have written to our steward, Mr. Platt. He will see that everything is arranged for your journey, and I shall look to see you on Wednesday next."*

He ended with love and a few brotherly, yet in his eyes quite reasonable, commands. He sealed the finished letters, placing them in a neat pile upon his desk before calling his butler. The tinkling of the bell brought forth a ruddy-faced fellow who would have been more at home in a field than the dressing room of an Earl. His weathered face and wild white hair contrasted enormously with the perfectly-arranged livery.

"My lord?"

"Send these to the post, Fitz." Wolversley gestured carelessly to the letters as he rose. "Then bring me the invitations I have received since being in Town, and bring me the accounts as well." He had already been over the accounts twice this week, but the discreet butler made no comment on that fact. He might look like a wild man, but he was as conscientious and respectful as any servant should be.

"Oh, and Fitz, fetch me up a bottle of Burgundy as well."

This did not bode well, but Fitz would never question his master's commands. For Fitz knew that questioning always got one into hot water and that mere statements of fact were far more effective.

"My lord, it is ten o'clock." The butler's face was deadpan.

"I dashed well know what time it is, Fitz. What of it?" There was a note of warning in Wolversley's tone and eye.

Fitz had been in the service of the Earl's family since Wolversley's father had held the title. Rather than back down as any other servant would, he remained bravely where he was for a few moments longer.

"See here, Fitz,"—Wolversley softened his tone—"just fetch it for me. I shall hear your lectures another day."

The wild-looking Fitz looked his master in the eye and, seeing the unhappiness there, nodded and scurried off through a small servants' door. Ten minutes later the Earl was sitting with his second glass of Burgundy in hand, the accounts book forgotten on his desk, one pile of invitations sitting before him and another pile of crumpled invitations lying on the floor just over his shoulder. He must find one event, at least one, which he knew that Highsmith would attend.

Another gilt invitation to some chit's coming-out ball sailed through the air. As the collection in his hands grew smaller, and the pile behind him grew larger, he was beginning to lose hope. Moments before he was going to give up there was a scratching at the door.

Fitz's white hair shot round the door followed by his ambiguous countenance. "Sorry to disturb you, my lord, but there is a message just arrived for you."

The Earl sighed, "Yes, bring it in. Who did the messenger say it was from?"

"A Mr. Smith, I believe. It is only the one sheet, my lord. The boy did not say to what it referred."

"Let me have it." Wolversley plucked the single sheet of paper from the tray.

He's here.

That was all. Nothing more. But Wolversley knew exactly who it was from and what it meant.

"Excellent. I shall be dining out for breakfast, Fitz."

"Yes, my lord. And will you be wanting me to take away the Burgundy, my lord?"

"Yes, yes."

"Very good, my lord." Fitz removed the bottle and glass with a certain degree of satisfaction.

Wolversley was already gone from the dressing room. He could always order more Burgundy where he was going— although, as he reflected on the enormity of what he was going to do, he realised he would rather order coffee on his arrival.

WOLVERSLEY'S CARRIAGE DREW up outside White's at a quarter to eleven. Usually, weather permitting, he would have walked to the club, but this morning he could not be late. White's, that most noble of establishments, had already welcomed a number of respectable and titled gentlemen, the large majority wishing to breakfast or meet acquaintances. The minority, one to be precise, had another intention entirely. Wolversley entered the coffee room, immediately ordering that most precious of dark liquids and taking a seat at one of the scattered tables. From there he would search out his quarry.

Peter Highsmith, fresh-faced and full of laughter, was sitting betwixt the young Freddy Rotherham and the faint-hearted Mr. Sylvester. Highsmith was looking as young and boyish as ever and, if Wolversley did not know any better, he would have said the man was still waiting to come of age.

Though not of colossal fortune, Highsmith possessed a generous income, capable of supporting him in some style. Without the rank of a Viscount or a Baron, he might not be at the top of the list for maidens on the lookout for husbands, but he had charm and friendly character that could not be frowned upon by any lady. Still, that easy smile was grating upon Wolversley this morning as he thought of Highsmith's relationship with Julia.

His scrutiny of the one he had come to confront was cut short when Courtenay entered the coffee room and saluted him. His friend was dressed in a blue jacket with brass buttons, yellow pantaloons, and shiny hessians pulled taut against his large calves. He met Wolversley with a smile and seated himself comfortably beside him.

"Are you not the worse for wear because of your cheap drink, my friend?"

"Are you not the worse for your expensive drink?" countered the Earl, the flicker of a smile came and went across his face. He was not here to make jokes; he was here to fight for Julia's future happiness.

"Very well then, my attempts at reforming your taste in wine vintages will cease. But why are you still here? I thought you were to leave London?"

"I had unfinished business." He did not pause to allow Courtenay to ask what the business was about. "And yourself? Are you to breakfast here this morning? I thought you refused any breakfast except the ones concocted by your French cook —what's his name?"

"Bertrand." Courtenay's eyes lit up. "Oh, he truly is the most divine cook, Wolversley."

The Earl refrained from saying that the cook's divinity was obvious from a cursory glance at Courtenay's waistline.

"But alas, no! I am to visit Howard and Gibbs but wanted to pop in and see who was about."

The mention of these moneylenders to the fashionable caused Wolversley to sit up in his chair. "I thought you didn't lose anything last night?"

"I didn't. But I most certainly lost the night before— cursed Foulett." Courtenay's mouth turned sour. "I felt my luck was high last night—if I had won I should have paid off my creditors, the cheeky upstarts."

"I can lend you the blunt if you need it," stated Wolversley, a little concern showing in his gray eyes.

"No, no," Courtenay brushed off the offer, shaking his fair head. "Wouldn't think of it. Besides, you know I always end up shipshape. You keep those carefully saved pennies of yours."

"It seems to me that the most rational thing for you to do would be to give up gambling."

Courtenay's eyes narrowed, but he continued to smile. "Aye, I'm certain it seems that way to you. In fact, I would be willing to bet on the fact you think so." He chuckled. "If I decided to cease gambling, I daresay I'd be the only man in London who doesn't besides you."

"Yes."

"Tempting. Next you'll be telling me to give up women too, since they are quite as much a gamble as gambling itself."

"I have not said I have given up women."

"Have you not?"

No, Wolversley had not. He had given up one woman in particular, and he had given her up to Peter Highsmith to be exact. Or at least he thought he had, but now he was here, pursuing him, wishing to confront him.

Courtenay snorted. "I may be a fool about money, but you are a fool about women."

"What?" Wolversley looked up, a little surprised at this. "What do you mean?"

"I would not insult you by explaining." Courtenay winked in a knowing way, rising as he did so. "I shall see you at the Merriweathers' ball?"

Wolversley did not know what to make of his friend's words. He must be referring to one of those invitations that had been tossed over the Earl's shoulder. "You will see me... depending upon the outcome of certain circumstances." His gaze reverted to his quarry once again.

"Suit your sour self." Courtenay swept him a bow and left the coffee room without further ado.

With no distractions, Wolversley examined the gathered trio. Highsmith and Freddy Rotherham were laughing at some joke, but beside them, Sylvester seemed out of place with his sharp countenance and dark eyes. Those black spheres did not contain the same jollity of his companions, and his indeterminate age, due to his powder and rouge, only separated him further from those with whom he sat. He was wearing black again, as though attending a funeral, and Wolversley saw he still exuded his affected air. The Earl disliked it. He had heard nothing of this Sylvester since his return to London. When he had asked Courtenay about him a day since, he had not known of whom the Earl had spoken. Something was odd about the man.

Wolversley's view was obscured for a few minutes as a group of gentlemen quitted their table and walked between the hunter and his quarry. When the room had again settled, Wolversley took the opportunity to pull a copy of *The Times* across the table and create a meaningful rustle as he opened the pages.

HIGHSMITH, RESPONDING TO a comment by Freddy Rotherham, glanced in the direction of the rustling newspaper and took in the sight of Wolversley. What was that fellow doing here? Hadn't Julia said just yesterday that Wolversley intended to quit Town immediately? Yet here he was.

"Wolversley? Wolversley, dear fellow?" Highsmith put on a false smile as he hailed the Earl, beckoning the gentleman over whilst pulling an empty chair up to their table.

Wolversley, dropping the broadsheet a fraction, seemed to look surprised. "Good morning," he said, inclining his head to the men. He laid down the paper and rose, careful to skirt an empty table with a scattering of chairs as he came towards them.

A waiter, seeing the move, carried Wolversley's steaming pot of coffee over to the new table. The bittersweet scent of the drink drifted upwards, a welcome smell to all the gentlemen.

"Highsmith. Rotherham." Wolversley nodded to each gentleman in turn. "Sylvester, I trust you are recovered from yesterday?"

"Quite, thank you," replied Freddy's friend. Highsmith noted that the words clung to the man's tongue as though sticky with syrup. "I am no horseman, unlike you, my lord. I could hardly hold my head up this morning. My home affords no good riding country, and on my recent sojourn in Bath I could find no suitable hack to improve my inadequacies."

"A shame," said Wolversley curtly. Highsmith sensed that Wolversley did not approve of Sylvester or his affectations. But then, it was unlikely that he approved of Highsmith either, especially after yesterday!

"Indeed." The man with the powdered face sniffed. "If only I could master a horse completely as all of you gentlemen seem able to do."

"Far too much flattery, Sylvester, but I shan't be turning it down." Freddy Rotherham smugly plucked at a jacket cuff. "I rather think I have a seat for anything thrown at me. I say, Sylvester, are you for gaming tonight? I hear Dufrey's will be packed to the rafters. He has a nice new girl dealing some of the games."

"At your service, Rotherham, though I hope this time you may be the lucky one, not I, or your fortune will suffer." The comment was spoken with a sharp tone, but Freddy Rotherham paid no heed.

While those two gentlemen carried on their preparations for the evening ahead, Highsmith turned to the Earl.

"So, Wolversley, what brings you to White's? I see you partake of no breakfast." He gestured with his fork at the hearty meal laid out before him, his plate heaped high with meat and eggs.

"I came in the hope of meeting a few acquaintances." The Earl did not specify whom, but he picked up the cup of coffee before him and sipped the rich brew. "You came for breakfast?"

"Indeed." Highsmith speared another slice of beef. "I am

just come from calling on dear Miss Rotherham. On my visit I gained her brother and we were met here by Sylvester—Freddy's new bosom-beau."

"Miss Rotherham is well, I trust?" Wolversley seemed to be growing impatient with all this small talk.

"She is in high spirits in spite of her fall. She declared the physician who attended her a horrible wretch, but she is much better for the ointment he provided."

Wolversley snorted but made no comment.

Highsmith decided to lay it on thickly, knowing that Julia would approve. "She is such a marvelous young woman—crashes to the ground one day and up and about the next. I was deliriously happy when I found her at home to callers. Those green eyes are hard to keep away from."

Freddy Rotherham spluttered into his tankard of ale at this outrageous adoration of his elder sister and began to laugh.

In spite of this distraction, Highsmith carried on. "Yes, I confess myself quite within her powers once again."

"I'd say!" offered Freddy. "You two'll be leg-shackled soon enough, I don't doubt. You've been doting on her far too long, and it seems like she's finally come round this past week or so. Been acting quite peculiar whenever she's around you. Extremely coy she's been. The sooner you bring it all above board the better, in my opinion."

Wolversley remained silent, though Sylvester was not long in offering his customarily sweet words. "Miss Rotherham and you? I am to congratulate you then?"

Highsmith just smiled and made to tap his nose with the flat of his knife.

Sylvester smiled at Freddy Rotherham, his thin lips curling back and the rouge on his cheeks standing out as the lean flesh bunched together. "That means of the Rotherham beauties, I shall have to content myself with your younger sister."

"Yes, leave the elder to me." Highsmith was well aware of the lengths to which this falsehood was going, but something had to be done. Wolversley was still here, threatening her happiness. He had to reinforce the lie. And perhaps he and Julia*could* make a go of things, if only this wretched Earl would leave Town as he had stated.

"To the future nuptials of Highsmith and Miss Rotherham!" Sylvester raised his coffee theatrically.

A chair jerked back as Wolversley rose abruptly. He leant towards Highsmith, speaking close to his ear.

"I need to talk with you privately."

Highsmith observed the rigidity of his body and the clenching of his jaw. What this was about he knew not, but that clipped tone was not hard to translate.

Refusing to answer straight away, Highsmith raised his tankard with Sylvester and, crossing his fingers beneath the table, took a draught of ale. It was only after this that he turned back to the Earl. In the aristocrat's face he saw an expression of such anger that for a moment he felt incapable of meeting it. When he remembered what this man had done to Julia, however, he found himself smiling, as if to sway his opponent.

"Now," said the Earl with a voice of quiet thunder.

Highsmith wiped a linen napkin across his mouth, discarded it on the table and then rose. "Yes, of course. Gentlemen, if you'll excuse us a moment." He nodded to the other two, not taking his eyes off Wolversley, and then walked with the Earl to a quiet corner of the breakfast room.

The other two gentlemen gaped after them.

"What's to-do with them?" asked Sylvester.

"Lord knows!" replied Freddy. "Something to do with my sister, no doubt. Used to be close to that Wolversley and is about to be engaged to Highsmith. I had an inkling something might upset. No notion why they're bothering so much over her." And that was all the thought that Freddy Rotherham gave to the situation before returning to planning his evening.

Over on the other side of the room, a far more intense conversation was taking place.

"Well, what's the bother, Wolversley? A trifle out of bounds to be barking orders at me like that."

Wolversley paced towards the large bay window, which was occupied by an exquisitely dressed gentleman, and then turned back towards Highsmith, his countenance dark and troubled. "I know it may not be my place...." He paused, rubbing a hand along his jaw. "It concerns your relationship with Miss Rotherham."

The change upon Highsmith's face was instantaneous. "You're quite right. My relationship with that lady does not concern you in the slightest."

"It may not,"—Wolversley's voice was suddenly harsher— "but you shall hear me out nonetheless. My friendship with the Rotherham family is of a far longer standing than yours, and I would not be doing my duty by them if I did not speak up."

"As I recall, you have never done your duty by that family." Highsmith sniffed, an unusual coldness overcoming his countenance. His chin came up. "Your duty was most lacking in regard to the lady I am currently addressing."

They could have been on a hillside, swords in hand, line drawn, and death the only satisfaction. Highsmith's hand would not falter, and his blows would be as brutal as necessary. The woman he felt strong affection for had been hurt, far more than he could know or fathom, and indignant anger rose within him, shouting for release.

"You know exactly to what I refer, Lord Wolversley."

The Earl halted as if stunned by darts carrying some debilitating poison.

"I am in Miss Rotherham's confidence," carried on Highsmith, believing correctly that his words had found their mark. "It has taken that good lady's most vehement persuasion to stop me from causing you harm. Were it legal, I would have half a mind to call you out. As it is, I shall content myself with naming you to your face the dog you are."

"Insult me all you will,"—Wolversley's voice was a low growl—"but there is something I must say to save Miss Rotherham from the hurt you will cause her."

"How could I possibly hurt the woman I love?" As the words came out, Highsmith shuddered to realise that they might, in fact, be true. "Some men are honourable in their dealings with women."

"Unfortunately, neither you nor I can claim that honour." Wolversley had regained his footing. He began to parry the attack. "It has come to my attention that you have been consorting with opera girls, and even retaining one as your particular mistress. If it were not for the longstanding acquaintance I have with the family, I would say nothing. Miss Rotherham deserves honesty, if nothing else." The Earl winced as he said the last part, as if he realised the irony in his own statement.

Highsmith bridled. "What I do in my leisure hours is, once again, none of your concern. It would do you good to remember we are not friends, my lord, and this kind of address is more than unwelcome in my quarter. I shall not tolerate it again. And as for my relationship with Miss Rotherham, I do not intend to relinquish it but shall instead pursue it further. I advise you not to stand in the way of her happiness a second time."

Highsmith's eyes smouldered. There—let him feel the guilt of his actions six years ago. He straightened as though he were the victor in the fight, making his salute before wiping his blood-stained blade and sheathing it.

Wolversley, who had lost this exchange, spoke in a voice

turned deadly. "You have left me no choice. Good day." Ignoring the stares of a few curious patrons and the confusion which had overtaken Sylvester and Freddy Rotherham, the Earl strode out of the establishment.

Highsmith exhaled slowly. Who did that fellow think he was, lecturing him about his enjoyment of the opera? Miss Rotherham deserves honesty? She had received little enough of that from Wolversley! Highsmith reflected on what he had said, that he would not relinquish his relationship with Miss Rotherham. Once again he was struck by the kernel of truth that had lain in his own words—perhaps he *would* pursue his relationship with Julia despite last year's setback.

CHAPTER EIGHT

"...teetering edge of destruction."

U NLIKE THE EXCITING ENCOUNTER AT WHITE'S, the morning in the Rotherham household had been largely uneventful. Julia had woken with her shoulder well on the road to recovery, and she realised now how that injury had distracted her from the other pressing matters of yesterday. As the physical pain slowly ebbed away, she felt a far deeper emotional ache reveal itself. It had begun as something intangible, but as the morning wore on, an ache took over her chest, a sick feeling rose in her stomach, and the space between her temples began to throb with sharp pains.

The anxiety had been budding since Wolversley had left her yesterday, but it was not until she had told Highsmith of the Earl's intention to leave London, that the flower of despair had fully unfolded. The admission that she had succeeded in her mission, that she really had driven him away, was the door that opened the floodgates. She thought she would have been relieved at his departure—it was what she had wanted from the start—but instead, feelings of grief threatened to overwhelm her. Emotions from six years ago came back to her in full force, and as the pressure built, the headache threatened to take over her head and her vision.

What was her heart thinking? It complained, it groaned, it wept. She had driven him away, and now she must live with the consequences. One moment she wanted the painful memories to go, and the next she was drowning in their bitter-sweetness. In this mood of confusion and low spirits, she had gone to breakfast.

Upon entering the room, she found her mother and sister hard at work planning a trip to the modiste, and she was more than thankful when she realised she was not invited. Barely touching her food, she used the first opportunity that presented itself to slip from the room and retreat to her father's library, a place she could feel safe.

Julia shut the door behind her, giving orders to the servants she was not to be disturbed, and then drifted deeper into the sunlit room. The mahogany panelling between the numerous bookcases, though dark in itself, was illuminated by the late morning light. The housemaid had just been in to clean, and there were still plumes of dust swirling upwards from the furniture and shelves. Sunlight caught the particles as they descended back upon the books from whence they came.

Walking through the room to one end of the large book-cases, Julia inhaled the familiar smell of paper, leather, and dust. She ran her fingers over the spines in her customary fash-ion, before picking up the book she had last discarded upon an octagonal marquetry table. Seating herself beside the fireplace, she leant back until the wings of the chair obscured the rest of the room from view and then opened the book in her lap. As she attempted the first few words of the chapter, a large tear dropped down her face, falling on the pale muslin of her dress. The droplet shocked her. She knew she was feeling low, but she did not wish to cry. She had shed too many tears over that man before, and she refused to do so again—but even as the thought came, so did more tears. She drew her knees up to herself, and, like a child rather than a grown woman of four-and-twenty, she sobbed, the book quite forgotten.

There was a point at which she thought the tears would never stop, but she was wrong. They slowed with time, her eyes feeling sore and puffy and her headache intensifying. Finally, when all her tears had gone, she dropped her feet to the floor and sat there for time immeasurable, staring into nothing, thinking, thinking, and thinking. She thought about nothing and everything until it became too much and she wanted to cry again. After the latter half of the morning had passed by, she rose from the chair and crossed over to the tall sash window.

Outside, the sun was high, dropping its golden hair upon London, and the inhabitants had responded to the promise of fair weather by leaving their homes to step out into the streets. Some walked in pairs or threes, like Julia's mother and Annabelle, eager to partake in some shopping. Others were off to fulfil their engagements, at the park or the gardens.

Past the ladies and gentleman, Julia could see others, less discernible to the eye at first, but as she focused on them, the genteel classes faded away. There were street urchins, grubby from the gutters and alleyways, scurrying about past the rich pickings. Then she caught sight of a woman selling flowers.

She was young and fair, though the harsh realities of life had left her with a tanned face and a patched old dress. Julia watched as she hopped and skipped and danced towards individuals on the path, curtseying flamboyantly and offering them a posy. On her way back from a successful sale, she met with a man about the same age. He wore a worn-out old frock coat, and his long brown hair was loosely tied with a ribbon at his neck. He planted a kiss on her lips and together they looked over the woman's takings for the morning. He dropped several more posies into her box and then disappeared again with a farewell wave.

It was simple and beautiful, and it made Julia turn away.

Perhaps her father had been right, and she really had been foolish. How could she regret sending him away? But wouldn't she have regretted *not* doing so? Her own shortcomings, her impetuosity, were staring her in the face and she sighed inwardly. She had never had much luck controlling herself or her temper. Her intrinsic nature was always running away with her. She sighed again.

The anger which had burned so brightly was fading with the onset of a depressive night. She longed to be rid of these low thoughts. She longed for the days before Wolversley's unexpected return, the days when she had moaned freely of her boredom and her inability to do embroidery, the days when she exclaimed about wishing to visit Jackson's when her brother came back with stories of the boxing club at dinner.

She had succeeded in not showing Wolversley how deep her scar ran, she had succeeded in parading her pretend feelings for Highsmith in front of him—but somehow, it all felt like a failure. Oh, dash her feelings! Was she to be forever a moping miss? Enough of this! She could not stand it any longer. He was gone, she was alone, and now she must go on.

Perhaps she could find a boring country squire to marry, or maybe even Peter? He did seem to still care for her and, as far as she knew, she was the only woman he had ever proposed marriage to. The thought made her lips part into the tiniest of smiles. She could never marry Peter—he was too much like a brother now. She must get on with herself. She had a sister to tutor in the ways of Society, and a silly brother to goad and scold simultaneously.

She let the curtain fall back against the window, ready to leave the library. Her feelings had had a brief jaunt out into the open, and now they were locked back in the solitude of her soul. She was ready to begin a new life as the calm, sensible Julia. She would be the epitome of the mild-mannered woman, never having a cross word, willing to do as Society expected, and accepting court from older gentlemen with impoverished fortunes. Of course, the only thing standing in the way of this new and improved plan of hers was...the old one. She was currently being courted by Highsmith. Wolversley believed that there was some level of understanding between them—which meant that everyone else did too. How to get out of that pickle?

There was no more time for her to think around that problem. A knock on the door signalled the end to her prolonged solitude, and the end to her newfound calm. "What is it?" she snapped. Why could she not be left alone to reason through this problem?

Lucy, wearing a face of some displeasure and holding out a note as though it were contaminated by smallpox, entered the room.

"Lucy, I ordered no interruptions."

"I am well aware of that, miss, but this note arrived for you." She had apparently forgotten her curtsey and deposited the note in her mistress' hand with a sniff.

Honestly, she was becoming far too much. She had scolded Julia already this morning for her stained riding habit and for the fall, and now she was determined to act as though she were Julia's aunt, or even her mother! It was beyond cheek, but even Julia's hot temper was not bold enough to challenge the formidable Lucy.

"Very well!" Julia accepted the note.

"You are looking rather peaked, miss."

The blunt comment drew a look of shock from Julia.

"Your eyes are puffy. Perhaps we can use some paste on them. I made a batch up for your mother when the alum arrived last week. The egg whites and rose water can only do good." Lucy's censorious tone had softened ever so slightly.

Julia realised the effects of her crying had not yet worn off. She muttered a hurried reply and turned her embarrassed attention to the note, but Lucy did not leave.

"It was delivered by a young man from White's Gentlemen's Club." The severity in the maid's voice returned.

"I see." Julia refused to acknowledge the servant's critical eye.

"I do not condone messages of this clandestine nature. I am sure your mother would have something to say about it."

"She has something to say about everything." Julia voiced her opinion under her breath. "Then neither of us will mention it to her," she said more loudly.

"I do not like this above half, miss."

"Lucy! I do not care about what you like, but you will do as you're told and hold your tongue."

Lucy, ever stalwart, did not seem too abashed by this harsh treatment. "Do you wish to reply to the"—she added an ominous pause—"note?"

"I do not yet know whether it solicits a reply, Lucy. That will be all."

"Very well, miss, but if you need to reply, I shall be the one to take it and save it from the other servants' gossiping tongues." Lucy departed from the room, once again omitting her curtsey.

Julia felt she had been too hard on her, but she was happy to perceive that her firmness had resulted in a discreet Lucy. Finally at leisure to look at the note, she recognised the hand immediately—all she could think was how atrocious Peter's writing was. She unfolded it to find a cryptically addressed and signed missive:

· · ·

JR,

Couldn't wait to let you know. Wolversley confronted me (on a matter I shall not include—suffice it to say it involved a woman), and did so with your interests in mind. I think we have succeeded in green-eyeing him, but he has not left Town, and I believe he will soon be paying you another visit. Be on your guard for an attack. I shall endeavor to defend.

Your conspirator in arms,

PH

P.S. Burn after reading. I can already hear your mother coming.

Shocked by the letter's content, Julia's trembling fingers let the sheet of paper flutter to the floor. She snatched it up and read it again, feeling her recent plans crumble and disintegrate before her.

At the same time, a tiny and utterly confusing wave of relief washed over her—he had not left her!—but this wave was more than equaled by the realisation she would have to see him again. What on earth was he still doing in Town? And why was he confronting Highsmith? Oh, the mess! Even Julia's quick-witted mind could not think of a way out of this. The idea of meeting him again was so dreadful. What would he say? What would she do?

AFTER SILK GLOVES had been lost and found, servants had been reprimanded, and screaming matches had been quelled, the Rotherham family had finally entered their carriage and were on their way to that most detestable of locations. By this point, Julia honestly felt as though God were intent on smiting her. Why else would she have had to suffer the torments of the last few days and now be seated in a carriage on her way to the London home of the Merriweathers for a second coming-out ball for Miss Lily Merriweather? As if one coming-out ball were not enough, she must have another this Season simply to make sure no one had passed her by on the marriage mart. It was most disagreeable and Julia was becoming rather put out that her prayers were going unanswered.

Lucy had chosen Julia's dress this evening, an occurrence which was rare—not from any lack of attempt by the maid but more from the stubbornness of the mistress. But Julia had not been paying a great deal of attention earlier whilst Lucy had been dressing her hair, which meant that when she had looked up, she had been very pleasantly surprised. Her rich brown curls were delightfully wild, trapped by three bands of green silk. Despite her features being fairly regular with nothing of the remarkable in them, Julia did look pretty tonight. She had complimented Lucy on the dressing of her hair, and the maid had taken advantage of her mistress' good favour by choosing her dress for her.

At first, Julia had protested. It was a dress of her mother's ordering, in a deeper green silk than she liked and with a hemline design bordering on garish. Lucy could be stubborn too, however. She would take no protests and insisted her mistress at least try the dress.

After Lucy had laced the silk top at the back and let the skirts drop over the shift, Julia looked in the mirror and found herself quite transformed. The merely pretty Miss Rotherham was now quite striking and quite beautiful in the unusual green. The cut of the skirt was narrower than Julia's other ball gowns, accentuating her height. Julia noticed with a spark of humour that Lucy had dressed her hair in the same colour silk as the dress itself. The sly old maid had already known.

Even Annabelle, who was sitting at a looking glass across

the room, had halted her toilette for a moment. "My, Julia! I should not like you dressing like that all the time or I should be quite outshone!"

Annabelle herself was looking divine in a pale blue ball gown. She had a fine white and gold threaded shawl draped across her shoulders. A comb adorned with beautiful blue jewels was set in her hair, and her fair curls, inherited from her mother's side, cascaded in large ringlets down the nape of her neck. She was altogether lovely to behold and she was aware of the fact.

The rest of the Rotherham family were also attending the private ball this evening, and after getting ready, they had all squeezed into the narrow Town carriage to make the event just in time. As they travelled through the foggy streets of London, Mrs. Rotherham's Circassian turban caught the passing lamplight with its silver lamé, and Julia watched her bird of paradise plume flicking backwards and forwards with the carriage's motion.

Annabelle was chattering excitedly about all the gentlemen she would be dancing with this evening. She had had many callers this past week, all asking to engage her for a dance at the upcoming ball. Even Sylvester had shown his pale face, gaining an acceptance to a dance from Annabelle with such triumph you would have thought he had won a vast fortune. Annabelle would not cease going on about how charming and flattering her new beau was, forcing Freddy to rebuff her in brotherly irritation.

Julia stared out into the night, wondering if tonight would be the night that Wolversley appeared. It had been several days since Highsmith had warned her of the Earl's intentions, and she had had enough sense to realise he would not make a morning call with the purpose of confronting her. So she had waited, knowing he would choose a public engagement, but she had not seen him at any of the small soirées the Rotherhams had attended. Perhaps tonight would be the night. She shivered at the thought—she was still no closer to knowing what he might do when he did come upon her.

Out of the window she spied a flag that fluttered listlessly in the evening breeze. The murky light which hung above the rooftops threatened a turn in the good weather London had been enjoying, and even in the carriage Julia could feel the humidity which hung close in the air. The sky looked sinister behind the restless flag, an odd colour of green she had never seen before in the heavens. The sight went in step with the disquiet in her stomach. She pulled at the edge of an off-kilter glove and smoothed a finger over an eyebrow.

Annabelle asked her mother and Julia for the tenth time whether she looked pretty. Julia rolled her eyes, but her heart softened towards her sister. She knew, as one's age lengthened, one was apt to forget the time it takes to grow comfortable with oneself. The lengths to which one would go in order to feel accepted knew no bounds in youth—at least, until that one moment when reason breaks through, as a beam of sunlight from cloudy heavens breaks through a storm-filled sky, bringing a sudden feeling of contentment with oneself. From then on, though one might find a way to be discontented with a certain attribute or action, by and large, one felt a sense of security—a security which Annabelle had not yet attained.

Julia spent the next few moments assuring her sister she was quite as pretty as anything in her new dress.

"Oh, wonderful!" Annabelle sighed in reply to the flattery. "Although I find Miss Merriweather a little missish, I do love a ball!"

"Yes," replied Julia, not sure that an entire night of dancing could ever make up for Lily Merriweather. "Though I am afraid we shall have to greet her, and *that* I am not likely to recover from."

Annabelle grinned wickedly across at her sister. "She really is rather awful to you."

"She is only jealous, my dearests," Mrs. Rotherham said. "And as much as I agree with you two, it would have been most ungracious to decline the invitation after her attendance at your coming-out ball, Annabelle. Do be careful of your tongues, girls. Nasty talk breeds bitterness."

Julia obeyed her mother. She was, after all, vexingly right.

Upon arrival, the young woman so disliked by the Rotherham ladies was there to greet them.

"I hear you and Mr. Highsmith are quite as acquainted as ever after your little topple in the park," said Miss Merriweather after Julia had made her curtsey.

So London's gossip chain was still in full working order, thought Julia. Stupendous!

Miss Merriweather dropped her eyelids coyly. "I have personally been told, by several gentlemen of my acquaintance, that I have a fine seat and would not fall for anything!"

"Hmm," was all Julia offered in reply, ignoring her pink-faced rival to gaze with far more interest around the crowded entrance hall.

But Miss Merriweather refused to be ignored. "Out of all the gentlemen in London, I swear it is Earl Wolversley that interests me most. Handsome, with a fortune, and titled—I am quite determined to make him my beau before this evening is out!" Miss Merriweather's indiscreet comment was followed up by an irritating titter.

Thankful for the warning of his attendance, Julia curtseyed in a flourish of evening gown. "You are welcome to him!" she said, before making a most rapid escape, dissolving into the crowd like a grain of sugar in hot tea.

Had Miss Merriweather heard something about Julia and Wolversley as well, or was it no more than a lucky guess? Julia wove through the crowds, glancing behind herself in fear that she would see him bearing down upon her.

"Oh my, Julia! Would you slow down, please? Goodness, what is the matter? Was Lily Merriweather that horrid? I thought I would never catch up with you. What did she say?"

Julia had forgotten Annabelle was with her. "Nothing but a few irksome comments."

"Well, slow down then!" Annabelle took hold of Julia's arm and stopped her from the frantic movements she was barely conscious of.

A crowd of nearby gentlemen caught Annabelle's attention. "Oh!" she cried, releasing her hold on Julia. "Freddy has found Mr. Sylvester. Oh...oh, I say, that man is devastatingly handsome!"

Julia saw her brother, Highsmith, and Sylvester a short way from them. Despite his use of powder and rouge, a habit Julia found very old-fashioned and garish, she could not deny Sylvester was somewhat attractive. He had two very enigmatic eyes and a good set of shoulders beneath his coat. It was understandable that Annabelle was attracted to the man, but Julia could not help feeling an uneasiness towards him. Alongside his good looks there was a cold detachment in his black eyes that seemed abnormal, and the falseness of his affected air only made Julia trust him less. Her sister, however, felt no such anxiety, and to her delight the gentlemen were descending upon them.

"Remember to behave yourself, Annabelle," Julia whispered in the excited girl's ear.

"Do not steal the attention from me with that dress and I shall not have to misbehave!" Annabelle huffed in an unladylike fashion.

"Ladies! You are all looking as ravishing as ever!" Peter took up Julia's hand, hovering over it with his mouth, and gave her an impudent wink.

Freddy guffawed. "Oh, give it a rest, Highsmith, you charmer!"

Sylvester gave his good evening to both ladies, taking Annabelle's hand. "A veritable pleasure, Miss Annabelle, to be graced by such beauty this evening." He kissed her hand.

The young girl's eyes sparkled at the compliments, whilst Julia wryly wondered whether Sylvester would leave any face powder on her sister's gloves. As the sycophantic gentleman carried on, Julia rolled her eyes at Highsmith who returned a cheery grin.

"I believe I reserved this next dance with you," Sylvester said, "and I should die of disappointment if we should miss it. I have many sweet nothings to whisper into your ear, and I must do it where no others can hear." Sylvester flashed his dark eyes towards the others and then returned them to Annabelle, huge coaxing orbs seeking to hypnotize her.

Annabelle glowed. "Of course, Mr. Sylvester, I should be delighted to dance with you. And where else is better than the dance floor for a private tête-à-tête?"

Sylvester placed Annabelle's arm in his, and they began walking away before Julia could condemn any of that most inappropriate conversation. Her mouth had dropped open several inches from shock and continued to stay there as she heard him piling his "sweet nothings" at Annabelle's feet while she, like a grateful bird, swooped down and picked up every last crumb.

"He is a charmer!" said Freddy after the couple had left.

Julia's mouth snapped shut. Back in control of her faculties, she replied in a dark voice, "He is trouble." She began fanning herself against the mounting heat in the room.

Highsmith said nothing, though he was silently agreeing with Julia. That brief conversation between Annabelle and Sylvester was certainly past the bounds of propriety. Not even he, a proclaimed ladies' man, would speak so freely to a lady of quality in such a public setting.

"Sylvester trouble? Nonsense," said Julia's brother, quick to defend his newfound friend. "The chap's as sound as any, even lent me some blunt so I could purchase this jacket before my next allowance. What if he *does* like Belle? Can't think of a reason why it's a problem."

"We shall see," replied Julia, frowning. There was something not right about Sylvester's increasing and unrelenting attentions.

Annabelle's dance continued for the next half hour, and in between standing and talking with her parents and their acquaintances, Julia kept an eye on the dance floor. As soon as Annabelle was released back to her company, away from the other gentlemen and her parents, she began her reprimand.

"Really, Annabelle! To accept such flattery and improper conversation from a man you barely know! You must be more careful—people will talk, and you will end up attached where you do not wish to be."

"If I were more careful I expect I would have no dance partners." She shot her eyes pointedly at her sister who had yet to obtain a partner.

"That is not the point," said Julia, trying not to be embarrassed.

"I rather think it is. Besides, what if I should want to *attach* myself, as you call it?"

"That's far too sudden. Besides, your behaviour, it makes you look—" Julia halted before a table with a crystal punch bowl the size of a bathtub atop it. She turned on an already furious Annabelle. "It makes you look fast."

"Huh!" Annabelle threw up her hands. She disregarded her sister and helped herself liberally to the punch. "Better fast than unmarried at your age."

After the initial shock from the insult wore off, Julia

prayed for strength and the ability not to dash the contents of her own punch glass all over Annabelle. She breathed in deeply once, then twice, and then, feeling capable of facing her sister without shouting, she spoke. "Belle, I would not bother scolding and warning you if I did not care for you."

The pouting schoolgirl did not answer and was not given a chance.

"Ah, dear ladies, I find myself in need of some refreshment too." Highsmith had caught up with them, but his expression seemed to indicate that thirst was only a pretext.

Julia, reading the urgency in his eyes, turned to her sister with a tone completely changed. "Oh, I say, Annabelle," she whispered loudly. "I think you had best go to the ladies' powder room. Your jewelled comb has come loose in your hair."

"Oh no!" Annabelle's feelings of animosity disappeared, overwhelmed by care for her appearance. "But the dancing will begin again soon."

"Well, you had best hurry."

As Julia's sister scurried away, Highsmith leant in. "He is here! He arrived in the room just after you left us and has been watching you ever since. Now laugh!"

Julia did as she was commanded, though unable to suppress the sudden anxiety in her eyes. Her laughter came out high-pitched, and her eyes roved about the room trying to spy the Earl.

"But I cannot see him. Where is he?"

"S'all right—easy girl." Highsmith spoke to Julia as though she were a young filly. He took over the search but could not spot him either, the bobbing heads of so many people obscuring the Earl's face from view. He had been there a few moments ago, a glass of Burgundy already in hand, pretending to listen to frivolous chit-chat while his attention was in another quarter.

"Let me get to a higher vantage point," said Highsmith. "I'll find him." He moved into the crowds towards the stairs at the side of the room.

"The music is starting," Julia called to his retreating figure.

"Indeed it is!" Annabelle pranced past her sister, her hair newly pinned. "I shall have to find my partner for he has not been able to find me, else I shall have to dance with Mr. Sylvester again."

Irritated at her sister's folly, Julia reached out to seize her sister's arm, hold her fast, and rebuke her properly. Unfortunately, however, Annabelle had glided out of Julia's reach and, upon missing her prey, Julia fell forward and came into contact with someone else entirely.

Wolversley caught Julia's flailing arm and righted her before she could fall headfirst into his chest. It took Julia a few seconds to recognise who had saved her from her imprudent grab at Annabelle. She felt her mouth open and shut, but no words were kind enough to come out. She desperately wanted to say something, but the cold fear that was creeping into her limbs had already made its way to her throat.

Regaining her balance, Julia looked up at the man still holding onto her arm. The Earl's dress this evening was polished but worn with a careless air, speaking loudly of the wearer's disdain for the general public's opinion of him. He wore a jacket of dark blue, beneath which lay a waistcoat embroidered with silver. His shirt points were high without being vulgar, and his cravat, wrapped around his neck and folded in a plain design became him very well. Julia had caught a look at his legs and feet when she had almost lost her balance. His silk stockings barely masked a set of very athletic calves, and his feet were encased in fine dancing pumps. All in all, he looked rather dashing this evening, especially, as she noticed, he had had his hair shorn back into a crop that showed off his well sculpted chin to perfection and framed a pair of gray eyes whose fierceness could not be ignored.

"Good evening." Wolversley's deep voice sounded. He released her and performed a stiff bow.

Words eluded Julia for a few seconds. She took a swift glance around the room to reassure herself that the feeling she was completely alone with him was all in her mind. Then she inhaled and swallowed.

"My lord, I...I am afraid I am needed by my father."

She wished the words back as soon as she said them. For the first time since she had seen him again, she had let him hear the vulnerability in her voice. She was not acting the headstrong woman, determined not to be hurt. She was afraid, and she had let him see it.

Julia made to turn away, but Wolversley took hold of the arm he had released just moments earlier. His grip was not painful, but neither was it weak—it was an absolute refusal to let go of her.

"Miss Rotherham, I must speak with you immediately."

"I am sorry, but I...." She was trying to make excuses but her voice was faint and the words wavered.

"I must insist." Her eyes showed him that he had won. "Privacy will be necessary." He released his hold upon her arm, his hand slipping across her lower back to guide her.

She shot him a look which dared him to touch her again on pain of death, but he ignored it. They began their walk through the ballroom together. She flicked open her fan, making slow movements with it, acknowledging the greetings of fellow attendees. By the time they had reached the far side, no one was watching them. They would be safe to disappear together, but only for a short time.

"Oh, I say, made up have you?" A foxed Courtenay pounced upon them suddenly.

"Why, I—" Julia started in embarrassment.

"Well, go ahead and dance with this chap then," continued Courtenay, "though I shall be wanting a dance with you later, pretty girl!"

Courtenay flicked a finger on her cheek, and Julia ached to swat him with her fan. Instead, she schooled a look of affability onto her countenance. "Perhaps later, my lord. For now I am much too warm, and a turn about the room is all that answers it."

Julia could sense that Wolversley admired her quick-witted reply.

"Alas, I shall miss you whilst you are gone," Courtenay called out.

"Of course you will," said Wolversley, taking no pains to hide his patronizing tones from the drunk. "Now if you'll excuse us, Courtenay." He smiled at the gentleman, pushing him gently aside and walking on.

"Course, course, old chap." Courtenay gave a complimentary wink to Julia before stepping off to annoy someone else with his high spirits.

Wolversley muttered something about Courtenay having had too much wine. "We would do well without such attention. Tell me, I have not been to this house before, is there anywhere we can speak in private?"

Julia peered down a corridor and saw a side room with a door ajar. "Over here," she said, without thinking any further than her wish to escape the obnoxious presence of oafs like Lord Courtenay.

She walked into the room and heard the click of the door shutting. A feeling of alarm surged through her. She swung round, the fear intensifying when she saw Wolversley turning from the door he had just closed. They were secluded, shut in a room together. She breathed in, choosing to turn her fear into defensive readiness. She looked him in his face, prepared for whatever verbal attack he had planned.

What she saw when she looked in his face was not at all what she expected. Instead of the forcefully composed man in the ballroom just five minutes since, he was now a man fraught with emotion and about to lose control. His face was all agitation, and his body, unable to stand still, was pacing the room like a lion. One hand drew up his jacket and rested on his hip, the other raked its fingers through his newly cropped hair.

Julia was silent for as long as she could stand, the impropriety of the situation falling in on her like a crushing weight. "You spoke of immediacy, my lord, and I am keen that we should not be missed."

Julia's pragmatic tones forced Wolversley to look at her. His hand, fresh from running through his hair, was now rubbing his chin. But though she had gained his attention, he did not reply and instead, resumed his pacing.

This is ridiculous, thought Julia. She looked to the door handle, determining how to effect her escape. "My lord!" she spoke with force and was relieved to feel the loud words bring courage flooding back through her.

The thudding of his feet ceased. Slowly and deliberately he placed both hands behind his back, squared his shoulders and looked her directly in the eye.

Then, just as surely as he had gained his courage, she lost hers, leveled by the piercing gray gaze. She could hear her heartbeat replace the thudding his feet had made a few moments before. Her breath hissed in and out past her teeth. She blinked.

"Some distressing information has come to my attention," he blurted out. "It concerns both yourself and Mr. Highsmith whom, I understand, you...wish to marry." His jaw clenched convulsively upon the last word. "Please, understand, I approached him first, but he refused to listen. Therefore, I am come to you. I feel bound by honour to warn you that your intended has been regularly enjoying the attentions of…certain females…." His gaze faltered, but only for a moment. "I could not be at ease until you were apprised of the truth."

Julia sucked in a gust of air. So, *that* was what he needed to say to her? Had her nerves not been so shattered, she would have found much hilarity in Wolversley's sombreness over Highsmith's cavorting. He wasn't her betrothed. It really was no concern of hers. But Wolversley did not know that.

"Indeed?" she said haughtily. "And where exactly did you come upon this information?" Her eyes drifted, as if disinterested, towards areas of the room not contaminated by his presence.

"A reliable source. I wished to spare you pain."

"Spare me pain? Ha!" It was the lady's turn to pace the room.

Julia's sudden outburst caused Wolversley's eyes to widen. "Yes," he sighed. "I did…I still do wish to spare you pain."

"And what is a wish? Good intentions are nothing without actions to validate them, and neither of those things have ever been your strong suit, my lord."

"You wish to bring up the past in the midst of the present circumstances? We are talking of the here, the now—of Highsmith, not myself. I could not stand by as a trusted friend of the family and say nothing."

"Trusted?" Her hands flew up in the air, and her eyes blazed with anger. "The one thing that I can solemnly swear, most noble Earl, is that I have no trust in you whatsoever—no matter the ignorance of my family."

"I am sorry for it. But whatever your feelings towards me, the warning I am giving you is not to be dismissed lightly."

His calm response only served to enrage Julia further. "Indeed?" she spat out. She paced the room again, agitation marking her every move.

"Julia…I mean Miss Rotherham. You are being difficult

about an event from the past while I am talking of the present."

"I do not believe your words, Lord Wolversley." She could not even bear to look at him—the pain and humiliation were too great.

"If happiness is your true desire, then you must believe them. Lay aside the past—it does not matter now—and look to this present situation. The rest is unimportant." His face was a mass of frustrated lines. She could see that there was something underlying them, a deep affliction driving his words.

All of a sudden he strode towards her. The candles in the room flickered, irritated at the disturbance. Outside the room, the music was playing and people's laughter could be heard in stark contrast to this room's tense interior.

"Unimportant?" Her voice became little more than a whisper. "It was unimportant?"

He took a step back, as though he had trodden on someone's foot by accident. Julia turned, allowing him to see the tears falling freely down her cheeks. He moved forward, as if by instinct, his hand raised to caress her cheek.

"Stop!" Julia put up her own hand in protest; the little whisper of anguish in her last words billowed up again into a gale of anger. "How dare you even speak to me after what happened! I cannot believe I have been able to converse with you, even look upon you—you who took everything away from me." She was a hairsbreadth from him, her chest rising and falling a fraction of space from his own. "You promised. You promised and you took it away, all of it. You took away a life you had promised, a security a....a..."—she faltered her eyes dropping to his lapels—"a love."

It was whispered so low that he could have missed it, but she could tell from his eyes that he had not.

The vulnerability was gone in an instant, the sorrow

replaced by anger as she felt the last ounce of her restraint desert her completely. "You took everything from me!" She could feel her hands clenching into fists and starting to shake. "I was seventeen, Lucius! I was a girl, merely a girl, but"—she paused, her rage dissolving as the next words came—"did you not care at all for my heart?"

Tears brimmed and tumbled over her cheeks again. Her deep brown eyes finally found his with a levelness in them despite her grief. "You broke it. You broke it without a care and walked on with no backward glance. You broke me. I am broken." Her gaze dropped to the floor. She turned and walked away from him, her arms wrapped around herself and her shoulders slumped in defeat.

"I...." He began after a few moments, but he could not complete the sentence. He tried again. "Yes." He offered no apology, no explanation.

He did not care, and with the final truth out, she felt the last bit of ground beneath her feet crumbling away. Everything she had built around herself, believed in, hoped for, was fading away.

"But I wish to keep you from such a pain again," he said, "in your new plans."

"New plans? What new plans?" If she had not been so overcome with sorrow, she would have noticed the enormous amount of control it was taking for him to speak at all.

"Your future engagement to Mr. Peter Highsmith. You must listen—"

"Do not waste your breath." The tears had stopped for the moment. She wiped her face with a handkerchief, feeling the sore puffiness of her eyes. She rested her hand on a chair back and spoke with a tired, frustrated voice. "It was all a pretence."

She watched him as she said it, and it was clear that the full force of this admission hit him like a blow to the gut. He swallowed. His jaw clenched, unclenched, and clenched again convulsively. A muscle under his right eye twitched. His lips pursed and his eyes clouded.

"What?" he uttered, his voice dark and unpredictable.

She said nothing in answer and that was a mistake. He bounded over to her, seizing the tops of her arms in a vise-like grip. She should have been scared, she should have struggled, she should have screamed. She did nothing; she simply waited in his arms, allowing her emotionless gaze to meet his own blazing eyes.

She had lied. She had lowered herself to manipulate and play games with him, just as he had done to her in their youth. But she did not care anymore. Let him be angry with her—let him flog her for all she cared.

His grip on her arms did not relent. His face was mere inches from her own, his breathing heavy, his body tense. He did not repeat himself, although questions were pouring from his eyes as they bored into her.

Finally, the scrutiny becoming too much, she spoke, her voice holding a tone of defeat only too recognizable. "Why did you re-acquaint yourself? Why did you come back and make me face you when you gave me no such opportunity before? Do you like to cause me pain? Am I sport, my lord?"

In the silence that followed, the sound of a door handle clicking echoed through the room. Both their heads turned. Caught up in the emotions of the moment, neither fully realised the situation they were in.

As the door swung wide, Julia felt Wolversley's grip become unbearably tighter. Realisation dawned. They looked on each other with horror, acutely aware of the hell that was about to break loose.

In the open doorway stood Courtenay, his face flushed, his frame barely vertical. Despite his drunken state however, his next words were disturbingly coherent and devastatingly loud. "Oh, I say! Making love to the delightful Miss Rotherham, are we?" He stumbled forward, tipping his glass to the apparent lovers. "I knew it! I dashed well knew it!"

After that drunken entrance, the evening collapsed like a house of cards. Before Julia could disengage herself, Wolversley had thrown her away from him, their seeming embrace now only too obviously something they were trying to hide. Julia stumbled away, pressing her kerchief to her face, trying to calm her emotions enough to think clearly.

"Blast it!" Wolversley cursed.

When Julia looked back to the door she saw why. After hearing Courtenay's exclamation, a variety of spectators had crammed into the doorway for a better view. There was no escaping it now. When she caught the eyes of her supposed lover, she saw a reflection of her own thoughts there. They were caught like rabbits in a poacher's snare. They had been found in one another's arms, and—what was much worse— they had been found entirely alone.

Wolversley raked a hand through his hair, uttering a few more expletives and looking back to the doorway. There was no time to waste. He knew exactly what propriety bade him do, and he must do it now!

"Miss Rotherham, I must find your father." He left her, pushing through the crowds now gathered.

She wanted to cry out, she wanted to stop him. But as she stood alone on the carpet in the centre of the small room, she found herself incapable of speech.

What had just happened? There was a ringing in her ears. Her hand flew to her head as she felt suddenly unsteady. Her shaking hands found a table, and she perched in a most unla- dylike fashion upon the edge.

More people crowded into the room, but not to speak to her. She could hear their murmurs. She could feel their looks as they whispered behind thin fans. She was going to faint. She was going to allow herself to succumb to that feminine affliction she despised—but in this scenario, she would not be scolding herself afterwards.

Then, just as suddenly as Wolversley had left her alone, her father came in. His hand was firm on her arm as he assisted her to stand and accompanied her through the house. The ball was still going on, many of the revelers still oblivious of the scandalous excitement, or else just being informed of it. There had been enough at the door, however, to see what had happened and to place Julia Rotherham's reputation on the teetering edge of destruction. No amount of explanation, no amount of evidence to the contrary could change the appearance of what had occurred. Soon all the guests at the Merriweather home would be gasping about it, and soon every member of the ton would be telling the story over tea.

The Rotherham family gathered posthaste, and as the carriage rolled to the door, Julia's father placed her inside. She did not remember the sea of faces she had walked past but five minutes since, not even Highsmith's, and she did not realise she was crying until her sister secretly stuffed her own lace handkerchief into Julia's hand. As for her supposed lover, the man who had destroyed her honourable reputation, the man who had just now spoken to her father, she did not see him at all.

CHAPTER NINE

"...a scandalous woman of questionable virtue..."

THE DARK NIGHT ENVELOPED WOLVERSLEY. HE stumbled several times as he wandered over the cobbled streets. Catching his balance, he wandered on, a sorry sight in rumpled clothes, his cravat stuffed into a coat pocket and his shirt tails escaping his silk breeches.

White's was no sanctuary for Wolversley tonight. The club would be teeming with the happenings of this evening, every gentleman present feeding off the scandal that had burst into the world at the Merriweathers' ball. The Earl's favourite watering hole and their supply of Burgundy would have been welcome, especially at such a time as this, but with that haven out of bounds, the Earl was wandering slowly home, trying his best to forget the events of this evening and the part he had played in them.

He *had* managed to obtain a bottle of Burgundy, the cheap vintage he had a particular liking for, from an indecent place he had passed during his meandering route home. During the transaction which had supplied him with solace for his mind, there had been a rather friendly doxy, but the wench had been put off by his brusque manner. He had no interest in fleshly solace.

Clutching the bottle with his left hand, he lifted it to his lips and drained the remainder. He cursed the emptiness, rubbing his red lips upon his shirt cuff. The liquid left blood-like smears upon the once pristine material—his valet would weep to see it. Leaning against a wall, he let the bottle slip from his fingers and smash across the cobbles, thousands of tiny fragments reflecting the light from a lone street lamp like a pool of water.

"Blast." His cloudy eyes looked up to see a phantom-like figure scurry close by him. "Gerroff! You cursed bung nipper!" His shouted words were barely intelligible as he struck out to cuff the pickpocket, but with his vision impaired by drink he merely swatted the air, missing the street urchin by a foot or more. He cursed again but sighed loudly when he felt his pockets untouched, the contents undisturbed.

Continuing his walk home, his mind skittered over the details of the evening, refusing to recall the truth of what had happened. Snippets of conversation filtered through his mind.

I must speak with you immediately....

His errand that evening had been urgent.

And where exactly did you come upon this information?

It had been Courtenay who had told him about High-smith, but he could not have admitted that to her.

Trusted?

She was right—what reason could their past have given her to trust anything he said.

Do not waste your breath. It was all a pretence.

A pretence. A falsehood. She had allowed those words to slip off her tongue without a care where they landed. And they had fallen like embers from a smouldering fire, burning the recipient with shame and a heap of other impassioned feelings that he could not pull apart to identify. She had lied to him about Highsmith—she had lied to him, and he had believed her. He had been forced to act the fool, and for what?

Why did you re-acquaint yourself?

Did he even know the answer to that question? It had all been an accident to start with, an accident authored by that blundering fool Courtenay. But the surprise of seeing her again had left him bedazzled, bewitched. He had tried desperately to keep away as he had vowed to himself he would do years ago, but she had been there, right before him, and he could not help but stay in her presence.

Then he had felt that burning desire to tell her the whole, to bring into the open the events which had torn them apart so many years ago, with no detail left unsaid. But, alas, she had been too hurt to listen.

Why had she even felt the need to lie about Highsmith? Was it to keep him away? Or was it to make him jealous?

Well, it certainly did not matter now. The pretence she had played so well was the source of the prison which now surrounded them both. There was no way out.

Wolversley leant his head against the brick wall of a darkened shop, his thoughts crystallizing and clarifying in the truth that wine brings. They were trapped, yes, but was it a trap he wished to escape?

He had not seen Julia after they had been caught alone together, after he had gone to seek her father as propriety demanded. He had no notion of her feelings, but if they were as undecided as his own, perhaps....

No, he must not think upon these things—he must not jump to conclusions. There was still so much broken past in need of repair. He must start to think of how to go about mending the damage.

The effects of the cheap drink he had swallowed were starting to wear off. The cold was closing in upon him, forcing sobriety far quicker than he would have liked. The night air pinched at his cheeks and lips and pricked the end of his nose. Half an hour later, the cold had worked so well upon him that he was able to walk in a fairly straight line and no longer cursed at every London carriage driver who passed him.

After a journey involving heavy feet and heavier thoughts, he reached the steps of his own Town house. Pausing, he leant back to look up at the large, cold structure which imposed itself onto the street of smaller dwellings. His top lip curled back into a scowl, his eyes narrowing at the severe building his uncle had once inhabited. How differently he might have felt about this house had different choices been made by others. Foolish decisions which had not been his had tainted all mental associations with his London home—if he could call it that.

It was too late to pity himself. There was no changing it now. Besides, the feelings of self-pity disgusted him. He snorted, brushing a hand down his coat. Fitz would still be up, awaiting his master.

Sure enough, upon reaching the top step, he found his loyal servant there to open the door and look down his nose at his beloved master. Wolversley stepped into the hall noisily, his evening pumps slapping against the hard floor with a gait hardly that of a polished gentleman.

Fitz, adept at handling his master when somewhat indisposed, was agile enough to sidestep the haphazard movements of the Earl. He bowed. "My lord, would you be wishing to retire straight away?" He asked as though it were a normal question, ignoring the disheveled state of his master and the impolite time of night.

"Of course, you jackanapes!" snapped Wolversley. He threw his hat across the entryway at Fitz whose dependable hands caught it without a hint of surprise.

"Very well, my lord. Am I to warn your valet before he sees

your lordship?" Despite the very improper question, the white-haired Fitz looked the picture of innocence. He ran meaningful eyes over Wolversley's attire, pausing pointedly at the stained cuff protruding from his jacket.

"Barker will fit if he is not warned. Tell him if you wish, Fitz," replied Wolversley. Under the scrutinizing eye of his long-serving and longsuffering retainer he was beginning to feel the hour and the excesses of his drinking.

Fitz, although exhibiting no human feeling, an action most appropriate in a servant, was not unobservant of others' exhibitions of feeling. The years he had spent in service to his lordship, a man whom he admired for his perseverance and sheer determination, had left him wise as to his master's mood. He could hear a strain in his lordship's voice and could see a tired defeat in his eyes. Having already estimated the amount of the Earl's alcohol consumption, he did all he could to help alleviate the effects—or at least postpone them.

"Would my lord wish for brandy to be sent up?"

Wolversley allowed a broken smile onto his lips and shook his head a little. "God bless you, Fitz. I will not refuse." He paused, deciding whether to divulge the evening's events. "You must partake in some too, for your master has this night become engaged to be married."

Even Fitz's eyes boggled at this, and his jaw struggled against the overwhelming urge to drop several inches.

But his lordship was in no state to notice Fitz's first ever lapse in facial control. "Send it up to my room."

The butler recovered his countenance and offered his felicitations to his master. The Earl responded with a snort. More perplexed than ever, Fitz took his lordship's coat, ushering him upstairs with an abnormal amount of deference. Upon entering his chambers, Wolversley shared a glass of brandy with Fitz who was so bowled over by the honour, that his usually frank words were lost to him.

The moon was in full reign over the heavens, although shielded from view by a veil of newly-formed rain clouds, when Fitz and Barker finally left their master. It was closer to morning than evening, but Wolversley was still not asleep. Dressed for bed, the Earl sat beside the fire, his silk dressing gown's rumpled folds catching the newly-banked fire's light. A lone candle perched near his elbow and, combining with the fire, cast a warm, dim light throughout the room. He ran his fingers over the arm of his chair, the faded brocade a little comforting. His other hand swilled the amber liquid inside the glass. God bless Fitz for ordering up the good brandy.

Wolversley allowed the drink to run through his mind, softly clouding the events of the evening. This worked for a short while, but soon his mind was assailed with long ago summers, with love, with loss, and with the feelings of shame and hurt that he had worked so hard to forget.

"THE WEDDING IS set for Tuesday the second," said the Earl.

Julia could see that Wolversley was watching her profile most carefully. She showed no obvious reaction. She said nothing.

It was the following day, and as duty bade him, the Earl had come to call on his bride-to-be. It was barely nine o'clock and yet Julia had been ready to see him when he had arrived. The night had not been kind, and she had risen from her bed little more rested than when she lay down. From the dark circles beneath Wolversley's eyes, she guessed that he had not slept either.

"Oh, really? That is such a shame as I already have an engagement to ride that day." She was quite aware of the fact she sounded missish. She had to make a decision—break down before him or cover her pain with anger. The latter seemed more attractive.

"Madam, have a care to remember I am protecting your honour."

Apparently, it was not just her that felt anger at their joint predicament.

Huffing, Julia batted at her skirts, irritated that her mother had left her alone with this man. She had heard the bell when he had arrived—her heart leaping into her throat at the sound—but it had taken him some time to find her.

Lucy, who was playing the reluctant spy, told her that he had gone to speak with her father in the library first. That hallowed ground was now off limits to Julia whilst her father was in it, for since the incident last night at the Merriweathers' ball, he had imposed a silence on his eldest daughter, refusing to make eye contact, to share in the private jokes they usually would have enjoyed together, or even to sit in amicable silence. If she entered the library today, the space between them would be full of tension and from her father's side, Julia knew, full of so much disappointment it made her heart ache.

Thankfully, Julia had Lucy, and though the maid heard little of what went on between Wolversley and Mr. Rotherham, she heard enough to know that Mr. Rotherham's placid, usually humorous character had been replaced by that of a protective father, angry at a man for besmirching his daughter's name and eager to force right to be done. What Lucy had not been able to see was the confusion Mr. Rotherham felt and the look he cast heavenwards on the Earl's exit. Nor did she hear the exasperated words, "Those two!" emitted by Julia's father when the door had closed. Lucy barely had time to recount the results of her mission when the Earl descended upon her mistress in the morning room.

Julia, who since the Earl's entrance had refused to afford him any view besides her profile, finally decided to face him.

After all, she would have to look him in the eye for a good many days more. Her heart sank at the thought. She had always believed in marrying for love, at best, or for a little affection, at worst. Instead, she had been cursed to become betrothed to...she had no name for him.

She turned an agitated, mostly angry, countenance upon him, but he was no longer looking at her. He had walked over to the tall morning room window. He stared out of it, apparently intent on the activities of carriages and shop boys beyond the pane of glass.

She hated that he seemed so calm. She wanted him to be angry like her. His anger would have justified her own temper. The matter-of-fact tones he spoke in were not the tones of frustration she wished to hear. How could he be so composed? Serene, even?

She would settle for coldness if it was not to be anger. If he could only be rude, she would know how to react. After all, she had caught him quite unfairly, and she was not oblivious to that fact.

"Perhaps I do not wish for my honour to be protected."

He looked round at her sharply.

"Would that not be the better path to take? After all, we neither of us wish for this. I could just brave out the damage our...our private conversation has done." She carried on, trying to reassure herself that this was a course she could actually follow. "I would perhaps be shunned for a little while, but eventually I might be able to re-enter polite Society. I suppose I might never be able to marry now, but—"

"Stop talking."

The abrupt command made her bridle, but he carried on before she could say anything. "You know as well as I that 'braving it out,' as you put it, is not an option. You would be shunned from all Society with no guarantee of setting foot back inside those circles. Your family would suffer for your ruined reputation, your sister's prospects would be tainted, your brother would find the mamas of those he courted turning a cold stare towards him—afraid that he would do something scandalous like his elder sister—and your parents... you know they would be devastated if you decided not to accept my help."

He paused for breath, and she was too shocked by what he was saying to respond in the gap he left. "Having all Society's eyes looking unkindly upon you is not something to be taken lightly. It affects everything." He spoke as though he knew of this first hand. "Marriage is the only way forward."

The way he had described her current circumstances and the potential outcomes of them was too horrible. Would all of that really happen? Of course it would—she knew it would, otherwise she would not have had to try so hard to justify *not* marrying him even in her own head. It was all too awful to imagine. She would ruin her family's lives if she did not marry Wolversley. And now *her* life must be ruined for the protection of those she loved.

"I suppose I had best pretend to be excited," she said at last, wishing to break the painful silence but too horrified to address the things he had said.

"I am sure you can contrive to act so." His voice was hard. "I have seen that acting ability of yours displayed to full advantage."

So he *was* angry. His tones were undeniably clipped. He was angry with her for her deception with Highsmith. She had to admit that now she felt sorry for her part in the lie. She had been foolish, and she realised with a certain irony that her father had been right. Her hurt had caused her to act rashly, and this farcical engagement was the result.

"Yes, quite," was all she managed at first. Then, her anger kindling, she burst out with something stronger. "My skill at deception is something I was reticent to use. I would not have, if you had not—"

"Not what?" His gray eyes were disconcertingly intense, boring their way into her.

"You know very well. I asked why you renewed your acquaintance—you gave me no answer. I simply have no idea why you would wish to see again the woman you jilted, for that is what I am." Her chin had risen challengingly.

"I had no notion that your sister's coming-out ball was in fact that. Courtenay brought me along in a closed carriage, and I had no idea it was the Rotherham household to which I was going until it was too late."

For some unfathomable reason, the tiny fleeting hope which had been hovering inside Julia Rotherham plummeted like a stone. He had not desired their re-acquaintance.

"Now, to the particulars...."

And so he carried on like clockwork, as though all of what was happening was normal. As though he had never jilted her. As though they had not been caught alone and caused a scandal. As though this sham of a betrothal was not some half-hearted attempt to save her honour, which to be completely frank, she was not overly bothered about saving if this was how salvation would come. He was indifferent. Nothing was affecting him. He behaved like some statue, immune to the feelings the events around him should by all rights create.

She had heard nothing of what he had said in the last few minutes, and she could not stand to be in his presence any longer. A bout of tears in her room would set her to rights— anything to relieve the heaviness she felt within her. She turned without saying good morning, and her hand was on the door handle before his speech stopped her.

"Julia—I can call you that now. I think we are well enough acquainted, don't you?"

"I am not your wife yet, my lord," she snapped back, her

patience fraying like a ripped hemline. "I am still Miss Rotherham until you speak your vows."

"Julia." His voice was sterner; she did not answer back.

She was cross with herself for her behaviour, for her missishness, and his tone brooked no disobedience.

"We are both of us quite knowledgeable of one another. I merely wish to say that in the forthcoming actions I take in defending your honour, we might as well make peace. Do you not think that would be better than a lifetime of bickering?"

She wanted to slap him, to say something cutting and clever, to give him a withering look, anything! "Yes, why not, for we have been engaged before. I think I remember the part I play. Just make sure not to run off again, and I'm almost certain we'll get along famously."

She gave him a beaming smile that belied the coldness in her eyes and in her throat, and then she curtseyed so low it was mocking and said her farewell.

Once she had tripped gaily up the stairs, leaving Wolversley grinding his teeth in the morning room, she entered her bedroom. With the door firmly closed behind her, she crumpled to the floor and let the tears that had been building up flow freely down her face.

"THERE Y'ARE MISS, an' here y'go." The stable master tried to hand Julia her whip after she was safely mounted. Her mare shied away, sidestepping some droppings and banging her quarters into a stable door.

"Now, now you fuss-pot!" said Julia. "I'll have none of that." Julia swung Sheba's head over, digging her heel into the mare's side to straighten her up. As soon as the horse responded, Julia relaxed the reins. "Thank you, James." She seized the whip before Sheba could take exception a second time. The sharp movement caused a pain in her injured shoulder. Although it was mostly healed, it was still stiff and could ache on occasion. "Kindly tell my mother that I intend to go for a long ride."

"Yes, Miss Rotherham." The stable master tipped his hat, noticing the clipped tone in his mistress' voice and the tense expression on her face. He, along with the rest of the servants, had heard of Miss Rotherham's engagement, but unlike many of the other retainers, he had been in this family for so many years that he remembered Lucius Wolversley. He did not know the ins and outs of his mistress' relationship with the Earl, but it was clear she was not awaiting her nuptials with excitement or anticipation.

"You are sure you want no groom, miss?"

Julia could think of nothing worse than company. Dear Highsmith had sent a note a few days ago to say he was obliged to depart for Bath to visit a relative, leaving her bereft of the only company she could stand, and to make matters worse, every morning since the ball the Earl had found some reason to visit. After this morning's visit to discuss her removal to his countryseat, all she wished to do was ride.

"Quite sure. And if my mother says anything, you direct her scolding to me—you understand, James?"

"Yes, Miss Rotherham. Enjoy the ride."

"I always do, James." She let slip a small grin, and though it was forced, the stable master appreciated it.

As soon as she had nodded in farewell, Julia kicked Sheba a little harder than usual, and the mare sprang into a high-stepping trot. The cobbles sounded under the horse's hooves. The steady clip-clop as well as the fresh air was already having the desired soothing effect on Julia's emotions. She did not give a backward glance to the house. She needed to clear her head, and a morning ride was going to do just that.

She had not gone two hundred yards when she felt Sheba

gathering beneath her like a coiled spring. The mare was building so much energy she was certain to explode before too long—and it was all Julia's fault. Not only had she kicked the sensitive mare hard enough to cause her to gallop but she had chosen to ride with all the tension of the past few days emanating from her. Even now, Julia was nudging Sheba to go faster, almost subconsciously, as though she could run away from everything.

The end of the road intersected with another where riders were passing, carriages turning, and street sellers hawking their wares. Julia had difficulty holding Sheba and almost trampled a seller of Seville oranges who was chanting near a corner. She apologised whilst trying to rein in the skittering horse. Saliva was foaming at the mare's mouth. Her neck arched as she tried to have her own way and bolt.

Although Julia was an accomplished horsewoman, she could not help feeling a little anxious, and she was thankful to see the entrance to the park up ahead. The trot had turned into prancing, and the horse turned sideways as she tried to evade the bit again. Julia giggled nervously as she entered the park at a sideways canter. She squeezed and released the reins gently, her posterior seated firmly back in the saddle.

"Oh, Queen of Sheba, you shall not have me off today! I quite fancy keeping my dignity, thank you very much." Julia gave the mare a sharp tweak of the right rein, bringing her back into a steady trot.

"Good morning, Miss Rotherham!" said a sickly sweet voice.

Julia turned in the saddle as much as her riding habit would allow. The owner of the voice was none other than Lily Merriweather, taking a drive in the park with her mother. She sat in a landau stopped across the other side of the wide path, pulled by a pair of calm bays. How Julia wished she could be atop one of those sleepy animals at this moment!

Julia saluted Miss Merriweather with her whip, hoping to make a quick getaway, but apparently the other woman was in the mood for chatting. She motioned Julia over to her, and Julia felt she could do nothing but obey, seeing as her reputation was already in tatters. She could not go gallivanting around being rude to everyone, however much she would like that. She must be thankful that Miss Merriweather was even acknowledging her. The realisation that she should be thankful was rather vexing.

"Hallo!" she called as she manoeuvered Sheba closer. Her riding salute had been many years in perfecting, and she was happy to hear it was not failing her even in this moment of awkwardness.

"Well met, Miss Rotherham," said Miss Merriweather, still oozing with pretend politeness. "I am sorry I had no chance to bid you good evening before you left my ball four days since." The girl was looking charming in a pale pink promenading dress complete with a straw bonnet trimmed with matching flowers and ribbon. She was the perfect example of a young woman recently come up from the country, embracing her rural heritage to display innocence as well as fashion—except for the fact that she had not recently come up from the country. She had already seen a Season in Town, and no one who knew her would fall for that feigned innocence.

"I was called away quite suddenly," replied Julia, running her free hand down Sheba's neck to soothe the agitated mare. She herself needed soothing—she could still remember the look her father had given her this morning when they had crossed paths in the hall. It was only a brief look, but it contained all the disappointment she had occasioned by her folly, and there was nothing she could do to right it.

Lily Merriweather's mother, who was a quiet, retiring lady, quite the opposite of her high-strung daughter, bid good day to Julia before hiding beneath her parasol once again. This left

Miss Merriweather free to send another pointed comment towards Julia. "I heard your exit from my ball was rather impromptu. You have caused quite a stir—I hardly think anyone remembers whose ball it was at which such exciting events took place."

Julia felt a mixture of pleasure that the girl was put out and guilt that she should have made her unhappy. Although why her conscience should bother itself over a minx like Lily Merriweather was more than she could fathom!

"I am sure that is not true. You were very becoming, and every gentleman's eye was upon you."

"Not everyone's." Miss Merriweather said it too quietly and too quickly for Julia to acknowledge and challenge. She carried on rapidly. "No groom today, I see?" She placed an elegant hand, gloved in blue kid, upon the cushions of the carriage and leaned over the side of the vehicle. "That is most daring of you!"

Julia, having comprehended all of what she had said, chose not to rise to her words. She could justify herself, explain that all the grooms had been busy, but she honestly felt no point in it.

"Tell me," Miss Merriweather said, ignoring Julia's silence and deciding to draw out the conversation on purpose, "is it true that your marriage to the Earl is to be very soon? I suppose that is why it does not matter after what happened— you riding without a groom and being quite scandalous, I mean."

Julia's mouth tightened, and as the tension spread throughout her body, Sheba decided she wanted to throw a tantrum. Before Julia could answer Miss Merriweather, she had to sit a few playful bucks and smack her mare twice with her whip to get her to be sensible again.

"I do apologise for that," Julia called out after the excited mare had come under control. She ground her teeth a little against the pain in her shoulder which had flared up at the jolting movements. "To own the truth, I have promised to tell no one the date of the wedding. The Earl is just so romantic, you see. He says he wants it to be a vision of loveliness."

Julia was a little surprised at herself for lying. A few moments ago she had felt sorry for Miss Merriweather, but her prying and the pain in Julia's shoulder had annoyed her. Apparently, these days her ability to spin falsehoods was nothing short of expert. She simply could not allow this preening girl to lord it over her, and so she had stooped to untruths.

"Oh, how interesting." Miss Merriweather was, to Julia's satisfaction, not enjoying the conversation anymore. "Well, I look forward to it, whenever it is...you are sure you cannot tell me?"

"Quite sure!" Julia smiled sweetly while making a vow in her head not to invite Lily Merriweather to the wedding.

"I shall bid you good day then." Miss Merriweather commanded the driver to depart, and Julia was left alone, watching the landau pull away.

Finally able to ride in peace, Julia ought to have been happy, but peace was not the feeling that occupied her mind. Her conversation with Miss Merriweather had alerted her to the fact that this was no longer a small family problem of scandal to be hushed up. It was out in the open. Her life had been irrevocably changed, and this marriage, however much she hated the idea of it, was going to take place.

The Earl is just so romantic. Julia shuddered to remember her bald-faced lie to Lily Merriweather. Yes, the Earl was romantic enough to jilt a woman without cause and romantic enough to wed the same woman six years later only because Society dictated it must be so. No matter how much she might try to deny it to herself, Julia had spent the last six years with a heart broken for love of Lucius Wolversley. And now that

Lucius Wolversley was finally to wed her, that heartbreak would only worsen—for it was painfully obvious that the Earl did not love her in return.

The first section of the park, which was interlaced with flowerbeds and promenades, had given way to a longer stretch of open land. Sheba knew where she was, and after waiting so patiently she did not need to be asked twice when her mistress gave her her head. The horse suddenly sprang forward and bounded into a beautiful gallop. Her long legs ate up the ground, and the frustration and excitement the horse had been feeling bled away.

Julia's own emotions faded away in a similar fashion. The feelings waging war inside her gave way to nothingness and to wholeness at the same time. The wind roared past her ears, her hair flared out behind her, and her hands ran with Sheba's head. She felt at peace in this moment. Nothing could touch her here, nothing could affect her here—with this feeling she could conquer anything.

Her eyes shut, giving her the sense of being in a time of her own. She could feel Sheba moving beneath her, every limb stretching and working together to bound forward. The air snorted in and out of Sheba's nostrils. Every pound of the hooves on the ground vibrated through Julia, and there was that brief moment between strides of what felt like flying.

In that time that was all Julia's, she prayed. She prayed she would be spared from the impending marriage, she prayed that her family would not suffer for her actions, and she prayed that somehow the pain that was becoming so much a part of her would disappear.

Sheba's hooves were kicking up great pellets of mud, and it was not long before her chestnut sides were stained with sweat. The end of the green came faster than Julia would have liked. Her mare, filled with the elation and relaxation of a good gallop, pricked her ears and slowed her pace. She fell into a regular canter, and Julia came back to the world.

She was by a group of trees now. Tall oaks faced her, their gnarled trunks forming what could be comical faces. Sheba slowed to a happy, lolloping walk, her ears now flopping to the side with each bob of her head. Julia sighed and looked up to see thousands of green leaves forming a moving, living ceiling above her. This is where she wanted to stay.

Leaning down, she rubbed and patted her mare's neck. "Good girl, Sheba. You liked that didn't you? Eh, girl? You needed that run, eh?" She could see steam rising off the mare's neck—she would have to walk Sheba back to cool her off.

Julia's return journey took some time, and when she turned into the Rotherham stable yard she was just beginning to feel herself again. Unfortunately, the sight of a visitor's carriage with a familiar crest upon the door gave her an immediate sinking feeling, destroying the calm she had cultivated with such effort.

"Fiddlesticks!" Julia muttered under her breath. Dismounting, she dropped her whip to the ground and pulled from her pocket a carrot that she had swiped from the kitchen. Sheba's gentle lips picked the carrot off her mistress' hand, and her teeth made a satisfied, crunching noise. Pieces of the shredded vegetable fell from her mouth onto the cobblestones. Having had a good gallop and now eating a carrot, Sheba was in blissful heaven. James, who had been attending to the carriage horses, came over to his mistress.

"An' 'ow was she today, miss?"

"Oh, splendid! She always is though, James. Have you been feeding her oats by any chance?"

"Well, yes, miss, though you can't tell the master. I feed her the 'alf scoop afore you rides 'er just like you asked. Was she too strong for you today then, miss?"

"No, don't be silly, James. She was perfect—nothing like a bit of energy to spice up a morning ride."

"Only, beggin' your pardon, miss, but I knows you 'ad that fall t'other week, an' though I knows you for a sticky-seater, I don't wanna be causin' you no injury, miss."

"Nonsense, James. That fall was nothing but silliness and shall *never* happen again."

James' soft brown eyes peered at her, eyebrows raised—a look that made Julia suspect he knew the truth. "I should 'ope not, miss. Most unlike you. Me and your father never taught you to fall from a little 'igh-spirited cantering."

"Exactly. So keep giving her the oats—it makes her a brilliant ride." Julia grinned impishly at the stable master. "But don't tell Father. He would be decidedly put out."

A crooked smile worked upon the stable master's mouth, the soft spot he held for Miss Rotherham always winning out over his other loyalties. He had taught her to ride when she was naught but a child. And when she was not much older, he had found her alone in a loose box, singing to a sick horse to "make him better." The little girl's doctoring had been proven effective a few days later when the gelding recovered, and Julia had never been far from the stables since. In all James' time as stable master, and before that as a groom in various establishments, he had seen many a child grow up and learn to ride, but there had been something different about Miss Rotherham. She had horses in the blood.

"Oh, aye, I'm sure 'e would. 'E don't like you to ride out without a groom either, but you likes to bend the rules, miss, in more than 'orse riding, I think." There was a twinkle in James' eyes.

"Of course, James. I suspect the servants have been speaking of my shocking engagement to Earl Wolversley? Apparently, I am quite adept at breaking rules, more so than I thought. I am sure that an oat-crazed horse in comparison to that scandal would not worry Father too much."

Julia picked up her whip from the ground and threw a wicked grin back at the stable master before skipping up the steps to the house. She knew the servants below stairs must be reveling in the gossip surrounding her scandal, but James would not be the same. She trusted him, ever since he had picked her up after her first fall from a stout Shetland pony. She could joke with him however she liked and be sure no word of it would cross his lips in the servants' quarters. Besides, it did not much matter now—she was already a scandalous woman of questionable virtue, and she might as well learn to be honest about it.

Just before entering the house, Julia cast her eyes back to the carriage in the stable yard. He had already been here once this morning—was that not enough? What was he doing back again? She toyed with the idea of sitting in Sheba's stable until he went away but decided that it would anger Mama. She sighed and, placing a hand on the door, resigned herself to her fate and entered the house.

CHAPTER TEN

"...brief reigniting of kinship..."

As one of the servants announced Julia's return, Wolversley, who had been waiting a full hour already, rose quickly. When she entered the room, the late morning light that shone through the window poured itself over her, catching the shine of her brown curls and making her entire countenance look striking. The brisk morning air had splashed her cheeks with red, and on her left cheek was a small spatter of mud. This mud spatter was mimicked on the hemline of her dress, and as she looked down to lay her whip on the table, a thick lock of hair loosed itself and fell about her face. She looked altogether untidy and altogether appealing. Best of all was the gleam in her eye, one gained by some mischief committed, this time involving the lack of a groom and far too many oats.

"Ah, there you are, Julia," said her mother in a tone of rebuke. "You have been quite naughty keeping the poor Earl waiting."

The man of whom Julia's mother spoke was oblivious to

the reprimand delivered on his behalf. He had risen and bowed, but could not help but be arrested by the appearance of Miss Julia Rotherham. Deep within him a sudden desire, long smothered, stirred. He felt a warmth creeping through his limbs and a strong inclination to reach out and kiss this woman.

"My apologies, I am sure," said Julia, without bothering to imbue her words with the smallest amount of sincerity. "Though to what I owe the pleasure of a second visit I have no idea."

The tart words forced Wolversley to recover himself and disguise what he was feeling. What was he thinking being attracted to his soon-to-be wife?

"Well, you shall soon hear," clucked Julia's mother. "But a moment in your ear, my dear. Am I to understand that you went out without a groom? Quite on your own?"

"Yes, indeed, most daring of me. But I can ride so much faster on my own."

"Pray don't make jokes, girl! What if you fell with no one to help? I am sure you should have waited longer before riding with that shoulder."

"How is the shoulder?" asked the Earl, not pleased to hear of Julia's escapade but still eager to save her from more of her mother's censure.

"A little stiff," Julia replied. Wolversley felt the indifference in her words keenly. "But not too stiff to ride, and I certainly would not have anyone stop me." She shot him a challenging stare.

"I doubt anyone could." His quick wit earned him a brief smile, but then Julia's countenance reverted to its former implacable frown.

Mr. Rotherham, secluded in a corner armchair with an open book on his lap, watched the couple's interchange with some interest.

"One of these days you will get yourself into trouble with your disreputable behaviour, my child," Mrs. Rotherham said in admonishing tones.

"I think it is a little late for that, Mother," her daughter shot back.

"Julia!" Mr. Rotherham said with a considerable degree of firmness. His daughter, who had missed seeing him since he was sitting in the corner behind her, jumped at the sudden exclamation. "Do not speak so crassly, and not in that tone to your mother. You may decide to speak so under your own roof, but you are not there yet, and I highly doubt your betrothed would condone it."

Julia turned red and glared at Wolversley. He sensed that she was laying the blame for her irritability at his own door.

"I am sorry, Mama. That was very rude and improper of me."

"And most unlike you, my dear. It is usually your sister who uses such tones with me." Mrs. Rotherham turned sympathetic as she received her daughter's apology."

"Tones?" shrilled Annabelle, who had been standing on the threshold for the very end of this exchange. A dark-haired girl stood beside her. "I declare, I use no such thing. I am most sensible in my emotions, unlike some." She cast a pointed glance at her older sister. "Anyway, I've finished showing Selina the house—"

"Good gracious, Lucius!" Julia exclaimed, looking at the black-haired beauty to Annabelle's left. "It is your sister!"

Wolversley watched as Julia's jaw dropped a few inches. He noted with happy surprise that Julia's own surprise had caused her to accidentally use his Christian name.

Selina smiled and stepped forward to embrace Julia. Although her looks were similar to her brother's, she differed in one particular that made her all the more striking—her eyes were green, not gray. The contrast of those bright emerald eyes with her raven hair was immensely appealing, and the delicate form of her facial features made her a rare beauty.

Wolversley looked on with pride as his betrothed took Selina's hands and drank in the changes that time had wrought. Selina had outgrown the chubby cheeks that Julia doubtless remembered from six summers ago. She was now a tall, slender woman, standing at her brother's brow in height.

"Oh, Lady Selina, it is so wonderful to see you again!" Julia beamed at the girl.

"The same to you, Miss Rotherham! It has been an age."

"I will say yes to that!" Annabelle joined in. "Indeed, the last time I saw you, you were being packed off to that ghastly boarding school. Do you remember our plan of escape?"

"Oh yes!" Lady Selina laughed, the sound like the tinkling of bells. "We made it as far as West Dean before my brother found us."

"And how grown you are!" Julia shook her head in pleasure. "You have become a charming young woman."

"Oh, do stop patronizing her!" snapped Annabelle.

Selina's green eyes flicked between the two sisters, and despite her youth a gleam of amusement was evident in them.

"Thank you, Miss Rotherham."

"Call me Julia—I insist."

"A high honour," Wolversley murmured, taking a pinch of snuff. He had hoped that Julia would receive his sister with warmth, and matters had not disappointed him.

"Well then, Julia," said Selina with a smile, "I suppose I must call you that, for according to what my brother tells me, I am to be your sister-in-law."

Wolversley watched as Julia's cheeks coloured with embarrassment. She could not hold Selina's gaze. He had never known her to be the least self-conscious and was curious to see her headstrong nature acting so subdued.

"Lady Selina arrived while I was paying my morning visit

here," he explained to Julia. "When I returned to my house to find her, she was most excited by the news of our re-acquaintance and betrothal and demanded to be brought hither at once." As Wolversley filled in the gaps of the story, he thought wistfully that at least *someone* was excited about the impending marriage.

"Excited indeed!" replied Selina, beaming with pride at her brother and then shooting Julia a look of mock surprise. "Though why you have accepted him is quite beyond my understanding."

The room fell into a tense silence, no one quite knowing what to say. It was broken by another tinkling of Selina's appealing laughter, and Julia was more than thankful when Wolversley continued the conversation. "My sister is only recently out of the schoolroom and, as such, has not yet been launched into Society. Whilst she resides in Town, I am afraid her social engagements will be significantly limited."

"Oh, what a shame!" cried Annabelle.

"Indeed." Wolversley sounded less than convinced. "But a necessary evil, Miss Annabelle, until next Season when I intend to bring her out in full style."

"Oh, wonderful," said Mrs. Rotherham, "and Julia can no doubt help as your wife. I don't doubt you will hold some of the most fashionable balls in Town."

Julia had no words. She was sure that by this time next year she would have died from the affliction her dire circumstances would cause. Perhaps that was too dramatic—maybe she would simply have become a lunatic, or just an eccentric... yes, she could be an eccentric.

"Miss Rotherham?" Wolversley turned to address her. "Perhaps I might entrust my sister to your care whilst she is in Town? She needs new dresses, or so she tells me."

"And so every woman will tell you," chimed in Mr.

Rotherham from the corner, without looking up from the book he was reading. "Take no notice."

Wolversley's mouth cracked into a smile, making his brooding face look a good deal more attractive. "Unfortunately, my sister is hard to take no notice of, sir, and I was wondering if Miss Rotherham would be so good as to accompany her to the modiste tomorrow?"

Julia seemed a little taken by surprise at this request, but she also appeared flattered to have been asked. "I would be delighted to escort Lady Selina. I shall take you to our modiste. She is one of the finest dressmakers in London. She is French and came over when the Revolution took her shop in Paris. Shall I call upon you tomorrow at ten?"

"With me, of course!" Annabelle jumped in. "Mama, may we have the carriage?"

"Oh yes, my dears, by all means." Mrs. Rotherham smiled indulgently, happy that her children were not squabbling and even happier that her eldest daughter seemed to be resigning herself to her forthcoming wedding.

George Rotherham had spoken to his wife frequently over the last few days about how shocked and ashamed he had been by Julia's behaviour. Mrs. Rotherham had watched her husband pacing and lecturing, knowing that beneath the bluster, beneath the indignant countenance, was a worry for his eldest daughter. And now, as the young people gathered closer together at one end of the room, their conversation full of lighthearted jokes, Mrs. Rotherham leant back in her chair and slipped a sly, and very rare, wink at her husband. George Rotherham cleared his throat in turn and gave his wife a severe, unconvinced look, which only made her laugh and shake her head.

THE ROTHERHAM CARRIAGE drew up to Earl Wolversley's London home at a quarter to ten. Annabelle proclaimed herself to be "abominably cold"—which Julia interpreted as meaning that she was slightly chilly and enjoying the hot brick beneath her feet—and refused to leave the carriage. As a result, Julia had to descend from the carriage alone and knock on the door of the London Town house. When the great oak door swung open, a familiar face greeted her.

"Fitz!" she exclaimed, her hands flying upward.

"Miss Rotherham!" the butler replied in equally shocked accents. It was true, all of the servants had heard of their master's betrothal—the whole of London had—but to see Miss Rotherham again after so many years! "It is a pleasure to see you again, Miss Rotherham." And for once, the retainer's face showed it. The unreadable countenance he had perfected over many years peeled away as he smiled gently at the woman before him. "And my best wishes on your engagement."

"Ah,"—she had been waiting for that—"I remember you saying that before." She smiled mischievously, for Fitz, out of all of Wolversley's servants, had been the only one to guess the secret of their first unannounced betrothal.

The retainer's mask returned, and he showed nothing of the flavour he felt at hearing her words. "Lady Selina is at her toilette but will be ready shortly. His lordship said to invite you to join him in his study."

"Oh, no." Julia put up a hand. "I would not wish to intrude." She had never visited Wolversley's London house and now she looked past the butler to the rest of the hall, she saw that it was a sombre residence, not home-like but rather a monument to the past. From the looks of the outdated furniture, it seemed that it was little used or cared for. "I can wait just as well in the morning room."

"His lordship was hoping you would join him. He has been waiting for you." Fitz began to lead her away without any more ado, and all Julia could do was follow. He brought her out of the main hall and into a narrower passage that was not any lighter in character than the depressing hall had been. Was the whole house this bleak?

Opening a door to the right, Fitz showed Julia into a room that was altogether different in feel. The library, although it was as outdated as the rest of the house, was somewhat more comfortable. Sunlight poured in through a tall window and refreshing signs of life, a desk littered with papers and an inkwell lately filled, dotted the room. There were several jars of snuff too, sitting on a shelf on the wall behind the desk. Julia could see the pearl snuffbox belonging to Wolversley lying open and empty upon the desk, waiting to be refilled, and standing next to it, the one who would refill it.

Fitz bowed himself out of the room, leaving Julia facing her betrothed.

"Good morning." His voice was deep, and despite her best efforts at ignoring it, the husky tones were somewhat attractive.

"It is never a good morning when you have committed an atrocious scandal. Papa still will not talk to me." Julia said it without thinking, then realised it was almost as if she were confiding in Wolversley. "But the weather, I grant you, is fine." Her sharp tones were her only defence against the fluttering in her stomach.

The corner of Wolversley's mouth threatened to pull upwards into a smile. "I believe this is only the second time we have been alone since...everything happened."

"No doubt you are right. I have kept no such score." She was lying, again.

"How are you?" He had skirted the desk, and his gray eyes were no longer amused—they were piercing in their intensity.

"I beg your pardon?" Her voice wavered.

"How are you? You have been dealt a bad hand far faster than anyone should be."

"A gamester, are you?" She tried to joke.

"Jules."

It was funny, because although Peter and sometimes her family called her by that nickname, Wolversley had been the first to do so, a long time ago. When she heard it, she suddenly felt as though she were underwater. Sights, sounds, and smells blurred and faded.

Wolversley leant forward, and for a moment she thought that his hand might touch her. "I am sorry for...for this situation."

She sighed, pulled out of her reverie reluctantly. "As am I, but there is nothing to be done. We are each other's devil for the foreseeable future."

"Is that how you see me? A devil?"

"Well, I...." She didn't know what to say. "Oh, don't listen to me." She cast her hands up in the gesture of a spent temper. "I am always saying the wrong thing."

There was another wry curling of the corner of his mouth. "I remember."

She caught his gaze. "Of course you do." Then she stepped away from him, looking at the objects in the room. "Tell me, do you remember why you left me?" She spoke the words with such calm assurance, as though she were asking him some commonplace question.

He did not answer straight away.

"You might as well tell me. Honesty—is that not key to a successful marriage? Give me at least the truth so that I do not have to go on in ignorance."

Again Wolversley paused.

"I am sure I can hear whatever it is. If I am not attractive to you, or if there is another woman...I can bear it."

"Jules...." But his words were cut off.

Selina had entered the room bidding good morning to them both and excited for the promised trip to the modiste. With a few words of farewell, the two women departed. Julia was the last to leave. She paused on the threshold, a hand on the door frame. She looked at Wolversley, his eyes still trained on her and his lips half-parted to speak, but she turned away before anything else could be said, desperate to get away from his presence and the truths he could reveal.

JULIA WAS NOT much for conversation when they entered the carriage. When her mind finally came together enough to pay attention to the other two occupants, she found Annabelle in the midst of describing her latest beau.

"Oh, Lady Selina, wait until you see him! He is just so very charming!" Annabelle clasped her hands to her bosom and performed a mock swoon, falling upon the carriage cushions.

Julia smiled at the bemused look on Selina's face. "She is infatuated I am afraid, Lady Selina. Our only hope to survive this carriage journey, however short it is, is to gag her. It's extreme, I know, but trust me, it is most essential. I shall stop the carriage and ask James to do it before she can go on."

Selina's pleasant laughter flooded the carriage. Annabelle shot her sister a poisonous stare.

"Oh, Miss Rotherham, you always were amusing—my brother says that since your re-acquaintance he has been reminded of your flavour. He always used to love to joke, but now he is grown up he is so serious. You will be good for each other, I think."

The honest statement left Julia quite unusually speechless.

"Never mind them." Annabelle flapped a dismissive hand at her sister and turned herself towards Selina so that she could engage her whole vision. "They are done-up already, but we, well, Lady Selina, we must find our own matches before the Season is out." The blue eyes sparkled with mischief.

"You must call me Selina. It sounds such fun, dear Miss Annabelle, but I am not yet out!"

"Oh, fudge! It matters not one jot, and do call me Belle. You will be allowed to card parties and small gatherings, and you may rely on me when I say that there will be plenty of gentlemen present. I will be able to tell you all about them because I have been searching them out since my coming out."

"And who, out of the masses, is the gentleman over whom you were just swooning?" asked Julia. Unlike Selina, who would no doubt be privy to every secret of Annabelle's, Julia as her elder and most repugnant sister, would not be allowed to hear any of them.

"Mr. Sylvester—I declare, of all the gentlemen, he is by far the most handsome and the most charming. He constantly praises me. I swear he is ready to cast himself at my feet already."

The shamelessness of her speech made Julia grimace a little. When had her younger sister become so brazen?

"So he is your beau?" Selina asked, her innocence of Town making Annabelle the fount of all Societal wisdom concerning courtship.

"My beau?" Annabelle tapped an elegant finger, gloved in kid, against her delicate chin. "Oh, I would not say that...yet." She smiled wickedly.

"But you must love him if you speak of him so?" Again Selina's innocence betrayed her.

"Love!" Annabelle laughed. "Oh, what a strong emotion, to be sure. I cannot commit myself to declaring my heart is feeling such an emotion, but he is delightfully handsome and his words are very pretty."

Julia disliked the tone Annabelle continued to use. Now

she sounded all arrogance. Didn't she understand that love was not a game? She could be hurt. Did she not know that?

"I suppose every gentleman in Town is handsome and charming. But I should like it if I could meet Mr. Sylvester." Selina now seemed to be under the same spell as Annabelle, her eyes filled with the same dreamy look as she imagined her own creation of Mr. Sylvester.

Julia frowned at them both, though neither saw the rebuking look. Annabelle was over-excited on her own, and adding Selina's naïve company was bound to bring trouble. Handsome and charming indeed! Julia sighed. How little Wolversley's sister knew of the world, to be thinking such happy things about everyone's character. Trouble felt likely, and Julia knew Wolversley would not be happy if his sister came near anything remotely related to trouble.

"Mr. Sylvester," Annabelle whispered in rapt tones.

"And he is untitled?" wondered Selina.

Her words made Julia think for the first time of the disparity in positions between herself and Earl Wolversley. She had never considered it before, though she knew he stood in a superior station. They had grown up as neighbours, and Julia's father's fortune had meant that their lifestyles were hardly different. That being said, for the first time Julia realised that she was an untitled maiden marrying a peer of the realm. The only reason that it would be considered acceptable, though that was hardly an object because of the scandal, was because of the dowry she would bring to the match.

Was that why Wolversley had not fought the circum-stances? Was he looking forward to the fortune she would surely bring? Was he in financial straits? Perhaps that's why he had cried off six years ago, because he had not needed the money—and now that he was in financial need he was back. The thought made Julia feel sick.

But just now, in his study, he had seemed kind. She could

almost believe that even if he did not love her, he did not hate her. He had seemed so solicitous, obviously caring about her feelings. Did she care for his?

"Yes," returned Annabelle, "a just consideration, for I wish to marry to my utmost advantage. However, he is to be inordinately rich one day through inheritance, and as I say, he is dashingly handsome, so perhaps I could be persuaded...." Annabelle looked coquettishly at Selina. "I am sure if you were to be introduced to Mr. Sylvester by my brother that you would see his virtues for yourself and find my interest quite justified."

"Now, wait a moment," Julia interjected. "Lady Selina has not come out yet, Annabelle. There is very little chance of her meeting Mr. Sylvester. And seeing as we know little of his character, I think it is perhaps for the best."

"Oh, *do* you!" That last opinion was too far for Annabelle. She was the picture of pique, and as the carriage rocked over a set of particularly uneven cobbles she became even angrier.

Then, all of a sudden, she smiled. It was not the genuine smile she sometimes bestowed but the suspicious one which Julia did not trust.

"Well, so be it," Annabelle said in false sweetness.

Julia's eyes narrowed. Now she was sure there was something amiss. Never was her sister so quiet and sweet unless she had her own way. Irritatingly, Annabelle gave nothing away during the rest of the carriage journey, nor did she spill the machinations of her mind during the time they spent at the modiste. Julia watched as Annabelle whispered and giggled with Selina in a way that made her think they were conspiring. This really was not good.

Despite her misgivings, Julia succeeded in ordering two new dresses for Selina as her brother had requested. Madame Trouleux was most helpful in the selection of the fabrics which would best display the raven-haired beauty of the young woman. Julia even gave in to her obstinate sister's demands for a new shawl.

When they came away from the modiste, Julia was sure of two things—that Selina was as innocent as the driven snow and that her association with Annabelle was sure to lead to no good. The heavy weight of responsibility for Selina was beginning to bear down on Julia. She could not let Lucius down, no matter the circumstances between them. She would have to watch Selina like a hawk.

She glanced across the carriage; they certainly were two beauties, opposites in colouring but both attractive. More than that, they were sly, and whatever Julia did, she would not allow herself to be left one step behind.

A FEW DAYS later, upon attending a small card party, Julia saw the full extent of her sister's plotting. Lady Selina had been granted permission to attend the small gathering by her brother as it was mostly attended by those who would soon be her family. The dark-haired girl arrived on Wolversley's arm only a few moments after Julia's own arrival.

The Earl made quick work of the space between the door and Miss Rotherham, as did his sister who possessed the same long legs. Julia turned to see them descending upon her. They bid her good evening, Selina's eyes wide with excitement as she looked about her at the strange faces present. Wolversley's sister was not with the betrothed couple long, however, as Annabelle, seeing her new bosom-friend arrive, rushed in like a wave, her golden curls bouncing with her light steps, and stole Selina away on a tide of whispering and giggling. Watching them disappear, Julia rolled her eyes but refrained from voicing her displeasure.

She looked up at Wolversley and realised, with a feeling akin to anxiety, that the tension between them had only grown and evolved since their last meeting in his library. The anger that had so characterised her first re-acquaintance with him had faded somewhat, and it had been replaced by an intolerable fluttering in her stomach. When precisely this change had occurred, she could not tell. Perhaps it had been when they had become engaged, when the prospect of intimacy between them had gone from incredibly unlikely to inevitably certain. Whenever the transformation had begun, whether with their betrothal or with the little sparks of flavour and concern he had shown, her feelings were changing.

She saw that he was wearing another new jacket. The cut bid no correction. He looked—how dare her mind think it!—he looked handsome.

But that austere expression that he wore so often was still there. Was he was angry with her? "How serious you seem this evening, my dear." She spoke the endearment with light mockery. "Whatever has put you in this mood?"

"Serious? I am no such thing." And with that, his gray eyes transformed from ominous to cheerful. His mouth broke into a generous smile, and he offered his arm to Julia. "You are looking very beautiful tonight, my dear." He used the same inflection of mockery, but the compliment seemed quite genuine.

Julia felt her insides leap a little. Drat that disobedient stomach!

"And your jacket is a great improvement. It shows off your…"

"Yes?"

"…your shoulders to great advantage." She chose not to return his gaze as they turned about the room together.

"I thank you for the unprecedented compliment." He stopped and bowed towards her, dimples appearing on either side of his mouth. She remembered those dimples.

"You are a cad." She slapped a hand lightly on his arm.

"Aye."

The confidence and quickness of his replies were making small invisible hands pull at the corners of her mouth. Goodness, was he making her smile?

"I am to marry a cad—how very dashing of me."

"And I am to marry an impetuous and headstrong woman. How very foolhardy of me."

He actually grinned at her, just like a youth. And she returned the grin with one of her own. What could this mean? Was she resigning herself to her fate?

"Just as my sister is headstrong," said Wolversley. "She wanted to come tonight, and I could do little to stop her."

"I wish you had."

"What's this?" He frowned, the wistful tone arresting him.

"Oh, merely a jest," said Julia, not wanting to burden him with her premonitions regarding Annabelle's poor influence on Selina. "She is very beautiful," she said, turning the conversation so as not to alarm him.

There were clear signs of brotherly affection in Wolversley's voice when he spoke of Selina. She was his only family now that his uncle was dead, and Julia did not wish to upset him. Startled, she realised that she was moulding her conversation out of care for *his* feelings. It was a familiar action long unused.

"So you find her much changed?"

"Yes and no. In appearance, she has blossomed. In friendships...it is as though my sister and Selina have never been apart."

Wolversley nodded. "She has grown more beautiful, but she is still very innocent."

As he shared this confidence, Julia reflected that it was

almost as if she and *Wolversley* had never been apart. Could those six years of pain really disappear so easily?

Wolversley cast a glance over at the two girls who were whispering to each other behind their fans. "We shall see whether that friendship proves to be a blessing," he said, with a trace of flavour still in his voice.

"I fear it will not," replied Julia, unable to completely stifle her misgivings.

"There you are again with your serious tones. It is not *I* who should be accused of excessive gravity tonight. I swear, I shall be wanting the angry words or the coldness back again if you continue."

She looked at him archly. "You shall have them back. Do not worry."

But would he? She was thawing, melting as old feelings warmed and came back to life once again. She was not sure that she could continue as she had been doing. "They were plotting together at the modiste's today. I could not find out what they were conspiring to do, but now I see the object of their plan."

"And what do you foresee?"

"It will all end in tears."

"And what do you prescribe?"

"A sound whipping."

"A remedy that suits all."

"Yes...." Her eyes focused on the scene unfolding, her ears no longer paying attention to what Wolversley was saying.

"But the object of their plan—what is it?" The Earl stared at her, confused by her word-sparring.

She did not answer. Without a care for politeness, she walked away from the Earl, her eyes fixed intently upon the object she had been speaking of. In this case, however, the object happened to be a person.

Positioning herself discreetly behind a servant who stood

to attention near the wall, Julia observed her brother presenting Sylvester to both Annabelle and Selina. "Fiddlesticks!" she whispered.

"Yes." Wolversley had followed her and now stood at her elbow. His whispering tickled her ear and made her jump a little. She shot him a quick glare, to which he paid no heed and only continued his observation.

"I see what you meant," he whispered again. "There is something about that particular gentleman that one cannot quite like."

"That is exactly how I feel!" exclaimed Julia in an excited whisper, delighted to hear someone finally agreeing with her on that score. She turned her wide green eyes upon his lordship, and it was not until she rested them full on his face that she remembered to whom she was speaking.

Wolversley's eyes gleamed in return. He leaned closer, his head adjacent to her own and so close that his short cropped hair nearly brushed against her own hair.

"Now, now, my lord." She turned, waggling her fan at him warningly. "Such proximity is bordering on indecent."

"Judging by our most recent endeavors, I would gauge this to be a step closer to decency."

Julia's eyes narrowed into a scowl, but it took a good deal of effort to suppress the smile that was lurking at the corners of her mouth.

Wolversley took an obliging step backward. "Better?"

"Much." Julia fanned herself, suddenly feeling hot, though it was rather draughty in the card room. The heat she was feeling came from an entirely different quarter.

"I have a proposal," said Wolversley, looking over to their congregated siblings.

"Another? How romantic." Julia's smile had struggled free and had now captured her face, holding it hostage with dimpled cheeks and curving lips.

"This time it concerns those two ladies." Julia could feel Wolversley's eyes on her lips, before he jerked his head back in his sister's direction.

"A proposal to two more ladies? Really, I should be shocked. You are almost a...libertine." Julia said the rude word with a slight cringe. For all she knew, he *was* a libertine. Had that not been one of her suspicions as to why he broke off their engagement six years ago?

"One of my many faults." Wolversley gave his rejoinder with a boyish grin. "My proposal is that we should keep a watch over that gentleman's activities. Not only is there something not to like in that man"—he once again gestured to the group—"but I am sure I have heard the name Sylvester before. I cannot place it yet, but I shall!"

"Whether you do or not, there seems little action we can take. I tend to think the headstrong character you ascribe to your sister is far outmatched by Annabelle's own. I cannot reason with her, though I have tried. If I say to take one way, she will undoubtedly take the other."

"That sounds like a familiar Rotherham trait."

"Oh, does it now?"

"One I have missed." Wolversley's words hung in the air for a moment as a slight shyness descended upon the two of them.

The Earl coughed. "We can at least watch, and discourage their interest in him—if they will listen."

"Discourage? It will take a little more than discouragement to ward off young affection." As soon as the words had run over her lips, Julia faltered, retracting her eyes from his. She recalled the countless letters she had penned to him, demanding to know why he had left her. None of them had been answered.

Those thoughts were too painful, and she jumped back into the conversation to change the subject. "Have you noticed the attention we draw? It seemed as though I was destined to be an indifferent debutante, but I see now that I shall be an infamous wife!"

It was not a statement well-equipped to stop the painful thoughts. Julia put on a smile again, but this time it was obviously forced.

WOLVERSLEY SAID NOTHING. Julia's use of the word *wife* was sobering. Despite her best efforts, he could see the pinching of her lips and the tired anxious look of her eyes. Her bravado was something he admired, but it was also something he could see through. There were times amidst her impetuous words and actions where he could glimpse the vulnerable girl he had known. The old Julia was so clearly evident, mixed in with the knowledgeable woman of Town she had become. Did she still have the same hopes and fears she had had before, when they had shared them, when they had known each other through and through? Now they were changed, they were grown, and the world had left its scars upon them, but the root of their characters was still there. Her bravery still hid a fragile woman with a courageous spirit, just as it had always done.

"A glass of ratafia?" Wolversley asked.

She seemed grateful for the offer. Wolversley received the beverage from one of the servants, placed it in her hand, and took up a glass of his favourite liquid in his own.

Julia put the glass to her lips. "I swear you are conspiring to make me act with even less decorum—you intend to make me drink far too much, just as you did at my sister's ball."

"*I* did that?"

Wolversley watched a flush come over her cheeks. She had

admitted her vulnerability, and her only refuge was to drink her ratafia.

"I doubt I could force you to do anything." It was circumstance, not he, that was forcing her into marrying him.

"A toast." Wolversley raised his half-drained glass.

"To what?"

"To the protection of fair maidens from unsavoury characters, by any means necessary."

She smiled. "To spying on them, to commanding them, and to making them thoroughly resentful."

They both drank. Julia tossed off half a glass, and Wolversley watched as a brilliant smile came over her face.

"Now that we have fortified ourselves," the Earl said, "shall we begin ruining their lives?"

"With pleasure." Julia placed a hand in the crook of his arm.

Wolversley breathed in with silent satisfaction. It was the first time since he had been forced to ask her father for her hand that she had seemed herself. Her wit had always been something he had loved about her, and he had just been reminded of it. In this moment, as they walked together, a truce seemed to have sprung up between them, and the marriage did not seem like the worst evil. If she could be happy —even if she could never love him—he could be content.

Or at least, *almost* content.

He breathed in again. Ever since he had seen her come back from her unaccompanied ride, he had wanted to kiss her, an action which he feared would be rebuffed. He stole a glance down at her profile, the cheeky upturn of her nose and the outline of her lips visible. Would she stop him if he tried?

They discarded their empty glasses on the tray held by a nearby servant and moved off towards the group. "The elder brother and the elder sister," said Wolversley. "What a strong front we must present."

"I only hope it is strong enough," Julia replied.

"Hallo!" the Earl hailed the others, and the betrothed couple took their place in the gathering, wreathed in smiles and effusing good cheer. "May I wish a good evening to all," cried the Earl in joyful greeting. It was the most excitement he had shown since being in Town.

"The happy couple!" Sylvester was the first to speak. "A good evening to you both!"

"Oh, you look delightfully sweet together." Selina rubbed her hands together, smiling with happiness. "I am so pleased you are to be married."

Julia put up a hand to stop her outpourings. "I am the one who is pleased that I shall be gaining such a wonderful sister-in-law."

"Oh, I say! All this female sentiment is too much for me." Freddy Rotherham pulled a face of disgust.

"You are so vulgar, Freddy," said Annabelle. "You ought to be happy that Julia is *finally* to wed."

The barbed comment directed at Julia's age did not miss its mark, but Wolversley noticed that, for once, Julia did not respond. She had her eyes focused on a far more important goal. It seemed that her sister would go unpunished...for now.

"Well, yes, of course! I am dem' happy for you Julia. But stap me if I didn't think it was Highsmith who had taken your fancy."

An awkwardness descended upon the gathering as quickly as frost on a winter morn.

"Oh, blast! I didn't mean it like that," Freddy blurted out.

Wolversley's arm tensed at the comment, an action that Julia, with her hand resting on his forearm, must surely have felt, but if she had, she gave no sign. Wolversley looked at her, but she refused to meet his eye.

"At least you have found love," Sylvester cut in, "and how in love you look! Love is something many strive for and few find." But he was not looking at Julia and Wolversley. Instead his gaze had crept over to Selina and Annabelle who both blushed at the attention.

"And do you know much of love, Mr. Sylvester?" Julia asked, the blunt question taking Sylvester aback.

He regained himself remarkably quickly, however, and replied with aplomb. "As much as any man on its trail. I look forward to the day I can call a woman, as beautiful as these two ladies present, my love."

Annabelle and Selina responded as they should—they giggled and hid behind their fans.

"Perhaps a little less time at the tables with my brother would help you find your ladylove." Julia was all amicable tones and easy smiles. Wolversley relaxed and enjoyed watching her work. She was spinning some sort of web, he could tell, and any minute their quarry was certain to bumble into it.

Sylvester, mistakenly thinking himself sailing in safe waters, answered gaily. "Oh, we certainly do enjoy playing together, do we not, Mr. Rotherham?"

"I'll say," said Freddy.

"And I'll say you mean a gaming hell. Is that where you have been frequenting the tables?" Julia spoke theatrically, brandishing her fan at the powdered face.

At this, even the thick mist of infatuation that was clouding Selina and Annabelle's eyes lifted a little. Their innocence was enough to make this conversation shocking indeed.

"No, Miss Rotherham! I do assure you—"

"Enough! You are leading my brother into most improper ways, I declare!"

"Never you mind where I spend my blunt, Julia!" Freddy reprimanded her.

"Oh, but I mind very much. However, we are here for

amusement, are we not? I shall lay aside your questionable leisure activities, Mr. Sylvester."

"I beg thanks for that, and may I say, my lord, that your betrothed is looking very fine this evening?"

"You may, and I could not agree more," replied Wolversley. It was taking a great deal of his self-control not to laugh at Julia's behaviour. However, his agreement with Sylvester's comment was made with the utmost sincerity. He caught sight of her lips again, full and appealing. He must have looked for a little too long for Julia caught his eye.

Fanning herself quickly in order to hide what Wolversley thought was a blush, she then smiled sweetly back at Sylvester. "Perhaps you are not all bad, Mr. Sylvester."

"I hope not, Miss Rotherham," replied Sylvester. He seemed very unsure of this woman now—as well he should be, thought Wolversley. Julia had been cold as ice to him in the last couple of weeks, but she had never been as outright poisonous as she had just been to Sylvester. She was a formidable woman, one to be reckoned with.

"Tell me, how are you enjoying the Season so far, Mr. Sylvester?" Julia asked.

"Oh, immensely, I can assure you. I have not ventured out to many social engagements as of yet. However, I believe I can say with certainty that you three ladies must be by far the most beautiful at any such events."

His words set Annabelle and Selina to the blush, but Wolversley was glad to note that Julia would not give him any such satisfaction. This sort of fellow thought he could overcome anyone with his honeyed words, but Julia saw through that nonsense.

"You must have been the toast of your Season, Miss Rotherham." Sylvester had seen her silence at his last comment and was now trying something more direct. He smiled, making the rouge on his cheeks stand out even more.

"Do you imply I am old?" she asked, eyebrows raised in mock horror. Wolversley stifled a laugh, his arm shaking beneath Julia's firm grip.

Sylvester floundered a little before coming about. "No, no, Miss Rotherham. I meant nothing of the kind."

"Am I to take that answer on faith?" She sighed. "Oh, do not worry. I shall forgive you the insult."

"Most certainly it was not meant to be an insult. I only meant to praise your beauty. I expect you have had many suitors?"

"Indeed, but the suitors I had did not take to insulting me as part of their courtship." Julia fanned herself with an air of dignity that only made Wolversley's amusement increase and Sylvester's bewilderment grow. "Perhaps it is better you do not attempt any courtship here—I am worried you will insult my sister, or his lordship's."

"I think that would be best," the Earl concurred.

"I assure you," said Sylvester, taking umbrage at last and intent on preserving his good standing in Annabelle and Selina's eyes, "I mean every word I say with the best intentions and truest sincerity."

"What? Every trifling piece of flattery? Surely you would be betrothed to a cohort of women if that were the case?"

"Steady on, Julia!" said Freddy, coming to the defence of his friend. "You are being very hard on ol' Sylvester."

"Yes," agreed Annabelle with a glare. "He has been nothing but agreeable to Lady Selina and me. He has said some very pretty things."

"Oh, Mr. Sylvester, you must be careful whom you flatter."

Where there had been confusion, there was now perfect clarity. Wolversley watched as Julia held Mr. Sylvester with a level gaze, and though the youngsters in the group could not know the full meaning of her stare, Mr. Sylvester certainly did.

He had seen that stare many times before, although usually from fathers or women much older than this one. It was a warning.

"One cannot control one's heart." His words were carefully chosen for his audience, and his gaze did not waver from Julia's.

Wolversley felt a shiver run through Julia. She seemed hypnotized by those cold black eyes. The Earl supposed that what Sylvester had said was true, but only true if the person in question had a heart—a matter entirely open to debate where this slippery man was concerned.

The powdered dandy excused himself to obtain a drink but returned a few moments later, doubtless to prove to the group that the scandalous Miss Rotherham had not scared him off. Despite Julia's warning, he spent at least an hour charming the young ladies before taking them both to a table to play whist with Freddy Rotherham.

Never having been much for cards, Julia retired to a sofa in an adjacent room which still allowed a good view of the party of four through the open door. Wolversley accompanied her and sat beside her on the sofa. After a short while, the other occupants of the side room filtered off to the card room to find a game to suit their taste.

"You are not for cards?" asked Wolversley, determined to stop her from brooding.

"I never liked playing—you know that," she replied missishly.

"So the angry words are back. What have I done to deserve them, may I ask?"

"Well!" She threw her hands up in exasperation. "I must say you were not much help before! You barely said a thing. It was up to me to be quite rude in an attempt to put him off. I would much rather you make a fool of yourself in the future than I!"

"I will make a note of that, but I must say you do it so well." As he spoke, Wolversley braced himself for the attack that he knew would come. He had forgotten how much enjoyment there was to be gained from tormenting this beautiful woman.

Julia gasped, swatting him with her fan several times, but the Earl only chuckled and snatched her fan away to make her cease.

"I only jest—you needn't take it so seriously."

"Well, it is most difficult. As your sister says, you are very serious now you are old—it is hard to know when you are jesting."

"I thought you were the one who is old, according to Mr. Sylvester."

That comment did make her smile impishly.

"I needed to get the measure of him. That is why I left you to...ruffle his feathers." Wolversley put it delicately, fearing she would snatch the fan back and begin batting him with it again.

"And do you have the measure of him?"

"Not entirely," he confessed.

"Do you know, apart from your rousing toast, you are utterly useless?"

"No, I have actually made a plan while you have been berating me. I intend to scour London for information of him on the morrow. He could well be harmless, but if we were to find proof of some darkness in his past, then our warnings might hold more sway over our charges."

"It is your sister I worry for. She is so very innocent."

Wolversley's brows lifted. Julia had been innocent when he had last seen her, and now here she was in all her worldly wisdom.

"Yes, I shall speak to her."

"No, do not, for she will simply do the opposite of your bidding." Julia's brows furrowed.

"That is true." Wolversley had dealt with his sister enough times to concede this point. "Is there anything else troubling you?" The puckering of her brows, however serious she thought she looked, made her look sweet, like a child confused by a mathematical sum. He wished he could embrace her, to tell her it would all be well. But as much as he wanted to, he knew she needed to give him permission for such intimacy, and she certainly had not done so yet.

"Only that I fear I may have been too rude. Though he may well deserve it, it was most improper of me. If we do find out he is of good character, what then? Though from his eyes I would say he is no good."

Wolversley smiled as she voiced her train of thought.

"I shall explain all to Mr. Highsmith when he returns. He may be of some assistance."

The Earl's smile disappeared. Despite the knowledge of Julia and Highsmith's pretence, he could not help feeling discomfort at their spending time together. The man still had feelings for Julia—he would swear it! And Julia? Perhaps there was more to her own feelings for Highsmith than she let on. It was not as if she had said yes to Wolversley of her own free will.

"If you indeed told him the whole of our past, I fear he will never forgive me for what I have done to you." Wolversley's tone begged an answer.

Her gaze was direct and unwavering. "I am not entirely sure *I* shall forgive you. And until I do, there is certainly no point in wondering whether others will."

The bluntness of the reply was something he undoubtedly deserved. How many times had he had the chance to tell her now and failed? He must, he *must* tell her. The kiss he had felt his lips yearning for just a short time ago seemed as remote as ever. He remembered when they had first become betrothed— he remembered kissing her, the scent of her skin, running his hands through her hair. How much he wanted that now, but alas, his dream of intimacy was as remote as the moon from the earth.

Then a sickening feeling spread through his body. Had Highsmith kissed her? Had someone else kissed the lips of the woman he had loved since his youth? The woman he.... He needed to tell her, but the timing had to be right, and with Sylvester's presence there were more troubling matters to be dealt with.

All the while his thoughts had been running backwards and forwards in time, Julia had remained silent. What was she thinking? How much did she hate him for what he had done? He yearned for her forgiveness, but it would not be given tonight.

And so with the cold finality of Julia's words still ringing in Wolversley's ears, they left each other, their brief reigniting of kinship and the closeness Wolversley had hoped for snuffed out in the moment of reality's reappearance.

CHAPTER ELEVEN

"WOLVERSLEY HAS BEEN AWAY FOR SEVERAL days attempting to glean information," Julia said, walking beside Highsmith in the park, her arm in his.

The sun had risen unhindered by the clouds this morning making London a pleasant place to be. The Rotherham household had also risen full of cheer despite the tumultuousness of recent days. Someone had suggested at the breakfast table that they go out walking, and upon Highsmith's calling later in the day, the idea had been put to him. He had acquiesced with pleasure, and now he, Mrs. Rotherham, her two daughters, her son, and Lady Selina were taking the air in Hyde Park.

With Wolversley absent, Selina had gone to stay with the Dowager Countess of Grasmere, one of their few relations. It had not, however, stopped the Rotherhams from inviting Selina on their outing today. It was the fashionable hour, and the park was filled with a host of the most dashing persons in

Society who were also eager to take advantage of the fine weather.

Julia and Highsmith walked behind the rest of their party. In front of them, the two younger women assailed Mrs. Rotherham with tales of Mr. Sylvester's charm, and Freddy joined in every now and then to give a vote in his friend's favour. This had left no one to bother with the things Julia and Highsmith had to discuss.

Highsmith had not seen Julia since that awful moment when her father escorted her out of the Merriweathers' ball, under the judging scrutiny of a thousand eyes. As he had been away in Bath for over a week, he had not had a chance to speak with her concerning it. It was the subject he most dearly wished to converse with her about, but Julia had been too intent upon explaining the new situation with that odious Sylvester.

"Surely he will not turn up anything too bad?" said Highsmith, dismissing her concerns. "It is very good of the Earl to put himself out so much for your sister—admirable even." He allowed himself that one compliment before falling back into his dislike of the Earl.

"It is his sister he works for, not mine. I doubt his concern would be so zealous if it were only Annabelle who ran the risk of trouble."

Highsmith did not respond to her comment. He had allowed one sprig of admiration for the Earl to grow in him— he did not wish to allow another. The man was cursed commanding, and he disliked the way he had ordered him about in White's. And now he was engaged to Julia. Engaged! He still could not believe it.

Julia's comment allowed Highsmith to turn the conversation toward the subject he most wanted to touch upon. "I have not seen you for some days, thanks to my uncle's illness. Bath is duller and duller these days, so I am happy to be back in London and happier to see you—I was very worried after what happened at the Merriweathers' ball, especially when I was called away so suddenly. You and Wolversley seem to be sorting well, though—I trust you are not at dagger drawing just yet?"

"Not yet."

The little smile playing on her lips was not lost on Highsmith. Exactly how long had he been gone? It was scarcely two weeks ago that he and Julia had been making their own subterfuges to fool the Earl, and now Julia and Wolversley were companionable enough to be making their own subterfuges to undermine Sylvester. Highsmith's jaw clenched, giving a firmness to his boyish face.

"You are both sure that Sylvester does not have honourable intentions for either of the girls? They are quite smitten with him. Can you not trust their judgment of his character?"

Highsmith certainly did not trust Julia's judgment of the *Earl's* character. He had had several days to think about it, and the more he did, the more he wondered about the Earl's real intentions during his private interview with Julia at the Merriweathers' ball. Was the improper situation really an accident? The Earl had reacted so quickly, seemingly without the need to think, and if he had been a minute slower in addressing Julia's father, Highsmith might have offered for her in his place.

"Certainly not!" Julia's outcry brought Highsmith back to the predicament at hand. "Are you so foolish, dear Peter? Trust the judgment of two girls just out of the schoolroom? I had rather trust the judgment of my mare Sheba. It is not for young women as it is for young men. You are subjected to pretty women early in whatever forms."

Highsmith noted her veiled allusion to a knowledge of

men's activities that was most improper for her to possess—it was not for nothing that God had given her a brother.

"It is different for us," continued Julia. "We are confined to the company of females for the majority of our youth before we are suddenly thrust into a sea of men. We are taught accomplishments and given some education, but we receive very few tools to navigate the complicated realm of the other sex. To our untrained eyes, most are handsome, and one word of flattery is to us an utterance of deep devotion. We have no experience of true love or the falseness infatuation creates. Those girls simply do not understand love yet."

"And do *you*?" Highsmith spoke the words like an accusation. Was he right? Was her anger towards Wolversley fading?

She did not answer.

He *was* right! Her silence only proved her guilt. How could she love a man who had shunned her and shown her no affection or care for six years and ignore the gentleman who stood before her, whose proposal had not only been flattering but sincere? Highsmith's boyish face looked angrier and suddenly older.

Julia seemed not to notice, her eyes on the path, aware only of her own thoughts.

"You realise you do not have to marry the Earl to save your reputation."

Julia looked up, surprise changing her face. "But I do, Peter. My family will suffer if I do not. Papa, he would...." She stopped short, her face filled with pain.

"There are other gentlemen besides Lord Wolversley." Highsmith said nothing more, partly because no words came to mind and partly because he had laid his heart before her once and she had spurned it.

Julia stopped and, unhooking her arm from his, turned to face him. Highsmith watched as she bit one of her perfectly full lips.

"Oh, Peter...."

They stood there for a few moments, the breeze pushing against them both and urging them to move on down the path.

Finally Highsmith spoke. "No more words—I understand." A hint of bitterness lay beneath his words which he could ill conceal. But he took her hand back in his arm and gently patted it as they set off once more shoulder to shoulder.

"Giving you up is the most difficult thing I have ever done, Jules. And I never had you to start with, so I don't understand how that cursed fool ever let you go!" His language was appalling. He should not have used it, and if he had been more himself he would not have. He sighed. "My heart is an open book written with a clear hand, but yours, Jules?"

A sideways glance showed the puckering of her brow. Such indecision showed in her face.

"I know you do not wish to speak or even think of your engagement. It has been hard to have any conversation with you about it, but...do you not think you should at least try to decipher the feelings you have for your soon-to-be husband?" The words bit at his heart even as he spoke them.

"Oh!" cried Julia, squeezing his arm tighter and leaning on him, a very sisterly squeeze thought Highsmith with frustration. If only she could love him.

"I suppose they should be feelings of love, should they not?"

Highsmith said nothing, his eyes firmly on the path ahead.

"I don't know," said Julia with confusion. "One moment I wish to kill him, the next I...I..."

"...know that you're deeply and irrevocably in love with him." Highsmith struggled against what he was about to say. "I do not know why I am about to advise this, considering how badly it has gone for me in the past—today being another confirmation of my ill-luck—but...." All of his heart cried out to silence him, but his head told him to push on. "Prudence bids you tell him."

Even as he said it and cast another look at her, it all became clear to him. Julia's heart had always been out of his reach. It had never been free for him to win.

She looked at him as if he had thrown a pail of cold water on her and turned her out in the cold to freeze. "And…what if…what if he responds by mocking me? I could not bear ridicule. Or he could be indifferent? That would be worse. Besides,"—she threw up her free hand—"I am not certain that I love him. I feel I can never forgive or trust him."

Highsmith waited out the painful pause.

"I find myself loathing him for waking up these feelings in me once again. But the feelings are altogether…oh, why do you remind me that they are unrequited? You are a poor friend today, Peter."

Highsmith bit back a harsh retort. Unrequited love was not something she could complain to him about. For once his cheery demeanour failed him. "Do not come to me for advice then if it is so unwelcome!" He kicked at the grass by the side of the path.

Julia turned large, apologetic eyes towards him, "I do not mean to cause you pain, dear Peter. I am sorry. If you wish to leave me, I can find my own way back to the others."

Highsmith was half tempted by the offer, but the honourable man still hidden inside of him bid him stay. He coughed away the sentiment that had blue-deviled him and said in a remarkably quiet voice, "I only wish you to be happy, Jules. You know that."

Hearing such love in his voice melted her resistance.

"I know," she whispered, patting his arm.

They walked on in amicable silence for some time before Julia began to chuckle. "Do you know, my father gave me some advice on marriage years ago."

"That must have been quite something." Highsmith, despite his heartache, was relieved to be speaking of something else. "Considering how ardently he tries to hide away from your mother behind the pages of his books."

"I know." Julia smiled. "He spoke to me about marriage being a series of compromises—it seems Wolversley and I have both had to compromise with our choice, so I suppose we are off to an excellent start!"

It was meant as a joke, but it grated upon Highsmith. It was too soon to joke about her marrying another man. He said nothing, however, and thankfully Julia turned the conversation in another direction. "I am fully settled, but these young girls, they are in much more dire circumstances than I, for I am to marry an Earl, and they have no match besides a man I cannot trust. It is all very hard." Julia spoke the last sentence with an audible waver in her voice, and Highsmith looked at her to see tears forming in her eyes.

"Oh, my dear," he said, his hardness from the hurt crumbling away. He took the hand she had placed back in his arm and squeezed it, the only physical expression that they were allowed as friends. "Nothing is as dire as all that. Sylvester doesn't deserve your tears." Neither did Wolversley in his opinion, but Highsmith didn't mention that. "You are quite right—best to focus on these young ladies instead of on yourself. Are we in high hopes of Wolversley finding something of relevance?"

"I suppose so. I do not know how these inquiries take shape."

"And what of us? What do we do in the meantime?" He would take any task to distract him from the darkness of his disappointment.

"Watch and discourage. Nothing may come of it, but if he is up to no good then I am afraid for the girls. A lady's virtue is far too easily lost, and I do not think they yet understand that."

"Have you spoken to your father and mother?"

"Briefly, but Mama says she has heard nothing to make her think Mr. Sylvester is anything but a most agreeable gentleman. Papa will not listen to me—he will not even look at me —so no words past my lips, no matter how well-meant, will fall on fertile ground. I think Mama believes I am being impetuous and somewhat of a hypocrite. I cannot deny it—I am in their black books."

"Well, at least you gave a warning at that card party I missed, and you said he understood it. He would be foolhardy indeed to attempt anything now. The danger is in the secrecy."

They had caught up with the others on the path, and Highsmith's voice gave way to the sound of a carriage somewhere behind them. At first ignored, the group turned as the hooves grew louder, rapping out a two-time beat upon the pathway. They saw a curricle speeding toward them, a dashing pair of dark bays striking out in front of it. The horses were trotting at a spanking pace, their heads held high, saliva flecking their chests and the stain of sweat upon their coats.

"It is my brother!" cried Selina joyfully.

JULIA RECOGNISED THE Earl's dark hair beneath his hat and saw the concentration in his gray eyes. He handled the reins with dexterity in well-practised movements, and despite the obvious flightiness of the pair, he had them well under control. He leaned forward, willing his team onwards, and watching him made Julia wish she were driving the pair.

Despite her best efforts, her father had refused to let her learn to drive a pair. He considered the art too dashing for a woman and had rejected Julia's proposal for the family to buy a curricle.

Unbeknownst to Mr. Rotherham, however, the youthful Julia had convinced Wolversley to secretly teach her to handle a pair—but since the dissolution of their engagement, she had had to content herself with a single pony and trap when at home in the country. As she watched Wolversley driving, she recognised the old, familiar way that he looped the reins and moved the curricle over, preparing to stop.

The vehicle came to an abrupt halt beside the party, the horses even more impressive now they stood before them. They could have been mistaken for black if not for a few stray bay hairs around their stifles and underbellies. They were both big and powerfully built, the veins bulging along their necks as they pulled to have their head. The holder of the reins allowed the leather to slip between his fingers in response to their excellent work.

Swiveling in his seat, the Earl removed his hat and bowed to the gathering. "Good morning, all! Mrs. Rotherham, may I say you look in fine fettle today." His cheery exterior masked a seriousness that Julia could only imagine resulted from his mission. It had been a success then—or not, depending on which way one looked at it. She longed and feared for the moment when he would pull her aside and tell her all about it.

"Oh, my lord, you talk such flummery," replied Mrs. Rotherham, "though I will not deny I enjoy it." She smiled coyly at the Earl and glowed from the compliment, any misgivings about gaining Wolversley as a son-in-law having apparently disappeared.

"Only truth, madam. I trust my sister behaves herself?"

"Oh, yes, telling me stories of the many handsome gentlemen she has met since coming to Town."

The two younger ladies exchanged worried looks but were put at ease by Wolversley's next words. "I wonder, madam, might I solicit the hand of your elder daughter for a short drive, that is, if it is agreeable to all?" He looked at Highsmith, a challenge in his eyes. The gentleman matched his gaze.

"Yes, I am sure she would be delighted as long as Mr. Highsmith can bear to lose her company?" Mrs. Rotherham was most cheery and determined to see Julia's forthcoming marriage not as a scandal snuffer but as a triumph.

Highsmith looked to Julia and voiced his acceptance when he saw the look in her eyes. Wolversley sprang down from the carriage as she approached and handed her up onto the high-seat before taking his place once again. He put his hat back upon his head and gathered up the reins.

"I bid you all good morning! I shall return her to you in half an hour, unscathed I promise." He let a charming smile onto his lips and then set forth.

With a low swoop of the whip and a play with the reins, he urged the horses forward with a leap, a feeling Julia had been preparing herself for. He had always driven like this, and even now in spite of herself she found it exhilarating.

"Fitz told me where Selina was. I came at once. I have news." Whatever else the others might have thought, Julia could see that this tête-à-tête in the carriage was to contain no romantic pleasantries.

"Pray, do not keep me in suspense."

"I made inquiries at some of the clubs and hells, but it was not until I went a little farther afield I heard of him."

"Did you travel outside of London?"

"Yes."

Julia saw dark shadows beneath his eyes. As she watched his profile, she saw his face was tense and set.

"It was in Bath I heard of him."

"Bath? You cannot have missed Mr. Highsmith by much."

"I didn't, but I hardly thought to call upon him when I was on such an errand."

Was that irritation in his voice?

"I have friends staying there," he carried on, not waiting for her to offer a rejoinder. "The news they told me does not bode well for us."

"I see." So he was a fortune hunter—that is what they had been fearing, and that is what Wolversley had gone to find out. Julia was to see, however, that the worst was yet to come.

"After a deal of time spent in the Pump Rooms gleaning the gossip and speaking to friends, I came across the story of a...."

"Yes."

"This may shock you. I know you think yourself strong and used to the ways of the world, but there are things no woman should be exposed to." She did not answer. He continued. "I heard of Sylvester's dealings with a certain woman. She is less than genteel now, but from her manners and air I gather she was not always low. She spoke of Sylvester's promising her marriage. They eloped, but he left her destitute when he found she had an insufficient dowry. With no money, she could not find lodgings, nor had she references to find work. She was forced to support herself by...." Wolversley trailed off, but Julia could very well guess what sort of employment he was referring to. "Her employers were less than kind...they threw her out when they found out she was already pregnant by Sylvester. She spoke of the babe...with tears...he was lost to hunger when she had no money to feed him. In truth, I do not know how she still lives."

Julia gasped.

"He left her ruined." Wolversley was driving the horses ever more forward and Julia now understood the harsh look to his face.

"Cursed fiend!" He whipped up the horses once again.

It took several minutes for his anger to cool. Julia said nothing. She was still grasping the information she had just been given. She felt sick to her stomach for the woman. All she could wonder was what would become of her? Besmirched, fallen, friendless, alone. And that man, he was walking and talking as if such actions were nothing to him, as if he had disowned that past. He was a cruel man with no punishment afforded him.

"We must tell the girls," she said, realizing the dangerous nature of the situation.

"Yes, and soon. There is no telling what his plans are." The Earl's voice was more level now, the carriage's movement seeming to have done much to calm his temper.

"Could you or my brother warn him off?"

"Not without causing talk. He will demand proof, and the lady has refused to come forward. I doubt he knows she still lives."

"I understand her wishes. I had no idea someone could be capable of such cruelty and absence of feeling."

"I have heard of such things, but I have never encountered them as I have now." He slowed the horses to a bouncing walk. "You must promise me to watch over the girls and have nothing more to do with that gentleman. I fear your brother has fallen under his spell."

"Freddy never did have much sense." She avoided his direct gaze.

"Do you wish me to talk to him?"

"No, I think my brother bears you ill will for compromising my virtue. I shall get Peter—rather, Mr. Highsmith— to speak to him." She could see him wince as she slipped in using Highsmith's Christian name. "We are bound for Vauxhall Gardens tonight—both Annabelle and Selina are dizzy with excitement."

"A curse on that place!" said Wolversley. "Sylvester is bound to appear. We must warn the girls before we go."

"In that case you must set me down, for I can already feel

Annabelle's towering rage coming on, and I must talk her out of it before Vauxhall."

"A moment, Miss Rotherham!" Wolversley called out to the overzealous girl who was already trying to jump from the moving curricle. He stopped the horses and reached down to retrieve a package from between his legs. "I purchased this for you as an engagement present."

Julia received the present tenderly, sitting back down and placing it on her lap. She stared at it, too surprised for the moment to open it.

"I was not expecting—"

"I know," he cut in, his voice gentle, "but I thought of you when I saw it."

She began to unwrap the present and soon felt the softness of cashmere against her fingertips and saw the pattern of an Indian shawl.

"I...thank you, my lord."

He nodded but did not make eye contact.

"But I cannot wear it. It would seem...." she could not finish her words. What would it seem? Too much like a real betrothal? She did not know how she felt about him—how could she accept a token of...was it affection?

"It would please me if you did."

There was a silence that could not be described as anything other than awkward. It was only broken when Julia saw the party ahead.

"There they are. I must go that I might speak to Annabelle as soon as possible." She rose again and attempted to step down from the carriage.

Before she could do so, he whipped up his pair and set them toward the party. Julia hit the seat with a thump and shot the Earl a venomous yet reluctantly humorous look.

He soon set her down properly beside her mother and sister and took up Selina in her place. Then, both having separate missions, they went to their work, with the almost certain guarantee that the recipients of their admonishments would have no appreciation for them.

"You evil witch!" Annabelle leapt off the bed, angry limbs scrambling as quickly as they could to get away from her sister. "I cannot believe you would say such horrid lies! Simply because he has not even looked in your direction!"

Annabelle's reaction was far more severe than Julia had been anticipating. She had expected some anger, perhaps a raised voice, but not nearly so much fury as she saw before her now. "Why would I care if he looked in my direction? I am engaged!" Her pitch rivaled Annabelle's own.

"Only because you threw yourself at the Earl. You caught him quite unfairly, and do not attempt to deny it!"

Julia gasped. Reeling in shock, she took a few seconds to gain her composure. "Annabelle, I am only trying to protect you."

"Protect me? Pah! Do you want to know what I think you are really doing?" The girl's eyes were bright, her smooth cheeks flushed a violent red, and her delicate figure poised in a fighting stance.

Julia wondered how on earth her sister managed to look so beautiful in the midst of such a temper tantrum. Sighing, she resigned herself to answering the question. "What do you think?"

"I think that your only reason for telling me this about Mr. Sylvester is to keep me unmarried so that you may triumph over me! You have always been jealous of me. Even before I came out you were desperate to spend all your time in my company, to make sure that you were shining brighter than I was. Now you are trapped and forced to marry a man you loathe, and still you must make it a triumph over my own conquests."

"Annabelle, you are being ridiculous!" As soon as the patronizing words came out of Julia's mouth, she knew she had made a deadly mistake. In a desperate attempt to salvage her position before her sister reacted to the comment, she continued. "I want nothing more than for you to be happy. If I did not truly want that, I would not bother telling you the truth about that man."

"Truth? Truth? What fiddle-faddle! I expect Mama and Papa have not believed you, and why should they, for it is such nonsense! You tell me these things to ruin my chances."

"I tell you them to better your chances." It was true that Julia's parents had dismissed her concerns about Sylvester, claiming she was too highly strung in her present situation to be thinking clearly. Her father had refused outright to speak to her as he had continued to do since she had caused the scandal at the Merriweathers' ball. Her mother had just patted her hand and told her she had been just as nervous before her own wedding.

"Mr. Sylvester has never done anything to make any of the things you have said remotely plausible. He is the epitome of charm and gentlemanly character."

"That is what he seems, but you can never know the truth of someone when you have known them for so short a time."

"Short a time it may be, but I do know him—my heart does. And Selina agrees with me! He is one of the most wonderful men I have ever met."

Julia wondered if Selina's infatuation with Sylvester was as extreme as Annabelle's. "I just do not want you to get yourself into an uncomfortable position. I do not want you to get hurt." If Sylvester ended up deciding that the heiress with a title was more to his liking, then Annabelle would be hurt indeed.

"Why can you not simply content yourself with your horrible Earl and leave me alone? You know that Papa is furious, disappointed even, with you."

Julia was beginning to feel sick. She clung to the bedpost for support.

"Yes, you should feel awful," said Annabelle, happy that her words had found their mark. "In fact, it's quite comical— you stopping me from causing a scandal when you have already ruined your own family. I am amazed Mr. Sylvester even wants to converse with me. If that does not show the genuine virtues of his character, I do not know what will."

Julia realised with a sinking feeling that she had done much to make this situation come about. After all, though Sylvester was after money which both the Rotherhams and Lady Selina did have, it was Julia who had made him think he could get it. She was the one with the loose morals, the one who had caused a scandal herself and compromised her own virtue. Knowing that, why would he not think that the entire family was fast?

"Please, Annabelle, I know I have not been perfect, and I am far from the best sister, but please, just promise me you will do nothing foolish?"

"More foolish than your actions?" her sister spat back before turning to her dressing table and screaming for Lucy to come and dress her hair.

Julia watched the maid enter and set about her task, her skillful fingers finding a way to pin Annabelle's curls back with room for the Venetian mask she intended to wear. Lucy said nothing to give away the fact she had heard the entire argument. As much as she might like to lecture Miss Rotherham in private, she knew when a family squabble was beyond her help.

Julia sat watching Lucy work, a glazed expression taking over her face. She had failed in her mission more fully than she could have foreseen. Rather than following her advice, Annabelle would now be bolting like a frantic filly down the completely wrong path. If anything, she had put her sister in more danger. She feared for Selina and Annabelle and for what Highsmith had said about the dangers of secrecy. She was a failure. She could not keep her own life in order, let alone her sister's.

Julia slid from the bed, making towards the door to leave the room. As she crossed over the threshold she sent a prayer up to heaven. Though God had not been listening to her recently, perhaps he would listen to her now on Annabelle's behalf.

CHAPTER TWELVE

"...a chaperone's most horrifying nightmare."

VAUXHALL GARDENS WAS FILLED WITH THE same level of passion and excitement as Annabelle's bedroom had been only a few hours before, the only difference being that the excitement evident in the Gardens was one of frivolity not rage. Crowds of costumed bodies and masked faces were flooding through the entrance to take their places in the booths around the dance floor or else walk the grounds and admire the amusements on display.

The dense gathering did nothing to detract from the general splendour of the place. Amid the well-kept shrubberies and blooming flowers, coloured lanterns lit the way with warm, inviting hues. Wide paved walkways gave room for larger parties in the central areas. Off these branched shadowy paths, winding away from the general populace to provide secluded walks and small arbors for the more ardent lovers.

Chinese-inspired buildings, looking the worse for their age in daylight but still quite attractive in the dim light of dusk, enticed visitors away from the trees that lined the main promenade. The Chinese rooftop curls were tipped by stars in the clear night, and those torches in the sky were reflected in the ornamental ponds below. The whole place had a magical feel and a beauty which proved intoxicating to the revelers.

The London night was already preparing to cast anchor on the horizon, leaving in its wake the perfect half-darkness for romantic trysts to take place in the sheltered walks of the Gardens. While dowagers fanned themselves, admiring the acrobatic antics of the tightrope walker Madame Saqui, their masked daughters were making eyes at gentlemen and signaling their intention to tryst with a flick of their fans.

The Rotherham family had travelled together in the carriage, all but Mr. Rotherham who had stayed home to "look over the accounts." In truth, he was indulging in some very good brandy and falling asleep over a botanical book before the fire. His family hardly fell for his falsehood about the accounts needing going over. George Rotherham had never been fond of parties. Though he had stomached and sometimes enjoyed the rollicking fun of balls and gatherings—especially when chasing the young Miss Kingley who would become Mrs. Rotherham—he was now far more satisfied with the comforts of home. Society could spend its time waiting on those rare occasions when he deigned to immerse himself in it. He had been to two balls this Season—his daughter Annabelle's and Miss Merriweather's—and that was quite enough for the near future. He still could not bring himself to talk to his eldest daughter since that last ball, and he thought it best to refrain from any other social engagements in order to preserve the familial relationships he still had. And so it was that his family left him unhindered at home.

Sans Mr. Rotherham, the party, including a recently joined Mr. Highsmith, entered the pulsating atmosphere of the Vauxhall Gardens. Annabelle had never been to Vauxhall and even Freddy betrayed his ignorance where the famous Gardens were concerned. As they walked the promenade, the two youngest Rotherhams looked about themselves, awestruck by the majesty of such a place. Annabelle was entranced by the jugglers, and Freddy had caught sight of Madame Saqui up ahead. Before long they reached the central area and were led by Simpson, the master of ceremonies, to the booth they had hired.

Now seated, Julia looked about her, using her fan for a screen as she scrutinised her surroundings. Several gaudy looking women walked past their box. Her eyes followed their progress to a gathering of well-dressed people all engaged in flirtatious conversation. A cursory glance could see that each of the individuals had wine in hand…and mischief in mind.

Julia's eyes moved on to spy out the other booths in their proximity, but she saw nothing to alarm her. There was no sign of Sylvester, although in this crowd it would be hard to spot him—the masks made it virtually impossible! It was quite simply a chaperone's most horrifying nightmare.

She had her own irritating mask in place, a beaded wonder which was already making her nose itch. She glanced at Annabelle who was refusing to speak to or even look at her elder sister. Julia sighed. It was not as if Annabelle had never acted this way before. It seemed that she was engaged in a fit of temper as often as not these days. Perhaps Julia had been wrong and there would be no trouble over Sylvester—but even as the thought popped into her head, Julia knew it would be too much to hope for.

Removing her eyes from her sister, Julia sensed Highsmith's presence at her side. His colourful mask concealed his face, but he was close enough for his arm to press against hers, and she would have recognised his figure anywhere.

"I have seen no sign of him so far."

"Nor I," she replied, not needing to ask if it was Sylvester of whom he spoke. They were both aware of the dangers this evening. "I must pay close attention to my sister. She would have none of my warnings earlier today."

"Unfortunate—"

"Come, come!" called Mrs. Rotherham, breaking into their tête-à-tête. "We must all be seated, for if we do not sup now we may miss the fireworks!" Despite her age, she looked like a girl fresh from the schoolroom on her first outing. "I know your father is no devotee of Vauxhall, but I declare I have always loved the Gardens! There are so many amusements and such fun to be had."

"Shall we not wait for the Earl and Lady Selina?"

"Ah, my dear." Julia's mother turned to her. "I should have known you would be thinking of your love! And to think you saw him only earlier—you will be quite inseparable after you marry!"

Julia pondered the truth of her mother's words. Yes, they would be inseparable, for better or for worse.

The Earl had made most of the wedding arrangements. The event was only days away and yet Julia had barely thought of it. Her fears over Sylvester had obliterated the melancholy she should be feeling at the loss of her own freedom. She must keep her head—her sister and Selina's safety depended upon her.

Reminded of her sister, she looked across at Annabelle who was exclaiming at every colourful attraction about her. Her excitement bubbled over, and Freddy could not help joining in. Around them swirled a crowd of other figures, their identities concealed by the ubiquitous masks.

"Peter?" Julia's voice caught in her throat.

"I am already on my way." She could see that he had read her thoughts, and she had no need to ask him to go to her sister and act as a well-meaning shadow.

A little of Julia's tension left her, and she took a deep breath to rid herself of the rest. At least she could be confident in Highsmith's chaperonage. Watching her volatile younger sister sent a shiver of foreboding running through her body. Youth was such a fragile thing. It would take a minor tip of the scales for everything to be overturned and ruined. She thought with bittersweet feeling that at least her heart had been too broken for her to be susceptible to any fall from grace. At least until now.

She pulled her shawl farther up her arms when the night-time breeze picked up and pushed a windswept curl away from her face. It was the Indian shawl that the Earl had given to her as a betrothal gift. She had worn it. Rubbing the soft material between her fingertips, she thought of him. Her husband. That is what he would be—her husband.

Highsmith was entertaining Annabelle, pointing out the many amusements around the Gardens whilst always maintaining a guiding hand upon her arm. Julia smiled. He was just the sort of husband Annabelle would need, understanding but worldly. If Julia could see Annabelle happily and safely settled, then perhaps she herself would not be too unhappy in her own scandalous marriage.

The wedding would be a gray shadow of the bright day she had always hoped for, but she knew that at least she would be comfortably taken care of. It would not be a love match, but at least it would be a bearable one, one which would give her both a title and all the things she could ever want or need. Somehow that seemed a hollow victory when she thought of what she and Lucius had once had. Perhaps it would be a love match of sorts, but unless she followed Highsmith's advice, she would be the only one to know there was love involved at all.

She had obtained the one thing she had sighed, groaned, and grieved over, the thing she had hoped for during the passage of so many years. She had Wolversley, but the circumstances were a cruel twist of fate. Her hopes had come true but in a distorted form barely recognizable as the desires she had held before. The love that they had once shared was gone, at least on his side.

She turned away from her party to school her face into submission and shoo away these thoughts of the future. But however much she tried to dispel them, they still surfaced in her mind. She felt a restriction in her chest, as though she were unable to take a full breath. He must never know. She could not expose herself again—rejection a second time was something she would never recover from.

As Julia gazed away from her own family, her eyes passed over the many masked faces laughing in the light cast by hundreds of lanterns. She worked her fan in quick motions as she sat in the booth, but despite the night breeze she had felt only a moment ago, she still struggled to breathe freely.

Then suddenly, out of the blur of masked faces before her, she saw him—Sylvester! All thoughts of her own fate dissolved. He was in the midst of pulling his mask down to cover his face, and she could see from the flicker in his eyes that he had just been watching *her*. A shiver passed through her, and as all thoughts focused on the present danger, her breathing came back quick and fast. She had felt the cold calculation in that gaze. She had seen the evil that dwelt there.

Julia rose from her seat in the booth and walked out onto the dance floor. She did not take a direct line to the man—she skirted the floor, always keeping him in sight. Then, as if some malevolent forces were at work, several revelers passed before her, and when they were gone the man had disappeared. Her eyes cast about to the left and the right, but she could not see him.

Clutching an arm about herself to ward off the feeling of anxiety that overwhelmed her, she spun round, now desperate to get back to the safety of her own party. She crashed into another reveler and was in the midst of mumbling an apology when she felt a firm hand beneath her right elbow. She would have snatched herself away, but she could feel it was steadying her, not spiriting her away to God knows where. The voice that whispered itself into her ear flooded her with a relief she did not know she had the capacity for.

"I saw him too."

She turned to the tall, dark man who stood beside her, the man who was to be her husband. The plain design of the Earl's black mask suited him perfectly, and his gray eyes were all the more piercing set off by the dark material.

"He's here! He's here! I must go to Annabelle. Where is your sister? Is she safe?" The cool command she praised herself for was lost as the demands came out in panicked succession.

"They are both safe." Wolversley moved his hand from her elbow to the small of her back, pressing her closer to his side. "Highsmith is watching over them both. There they are." He pointed to the two girls who stood in matching dominos, obviously a plan of theirs. Both their masks were gold and purple with feathers decorating their edges. "They will come to no harm for the time being."

"We must go to them." She tried to push past him, but he sidestepped into her path.

"In a moment," he murmured. "Be calm, Miss Rotherham. There will be no mischief tonight."

His words quelled her rising anxieties a little, but a frown remained on her brow, the lines in her forehead just evident above her mask. "I am not so sure of that." She peered at the groups of revelers again, trying to gain another glimpse of Sylvester. She could not see him. The spot where he had stood moments ago was still vacant, and there were no other signs of him nearby.

"Are you all right, Jules?"

This question regarding her wellbeing spoken with clear tones of concern surprised Julia somewhat. There was no coldness, no mockery there, and she found herself thankful for his care. It was then that she realised Wolversley's arm was around her waist and his hand pressing her towards him.

"Yes...yes, I am quite well, thank you." She pulled away from him, a sudden shyness forcing her voice to waver and her eyes to avert themselves from his gaze. She could already feel the warmth that flooded her cheeks stealing higher and higher up her face, her green mask doing little to conceal the redness.

Wolversley acknowledged her rebuff by clearing his throat and dropping the arm he had been giving in support. "Miss Rotherham, whilst Highsmith takes our places in watching over our sisters, I feel we must talk a moment." His eyes gestured toward one of the side paths that led away from the main area of the Gardens.

The thought of them alone together was too much for Julia. They were supposed to be watching over their charges, not planning their own secret assignation. She could not say yes. Her head was a whirl—she had no idea where her heart stood at this moment.

"I cannot," she managed. "It would be...."

"Improper?" he finished her sentence with a tone of irony. "As you have quite rightly pointed out before, we are hardly models of propriety. Besides, we are already betrothed, and you know as well as I, these Gardens are notorious for their trysts—surely it would be remiss of us not to take advantage of one of these secluded walks? I wish to talk to you without interruption."

Why? Why on earth did he wish to talk to her? "You are adamant?"

"Quite."

"In that case I hardly have a choice. Do you know, as much

as you like to lecture me on my own inflexible attitudes, I believe you are just as stubborn as I am."

"Are you pointing out one of my many flaws? How ungenerous of you." Wolversley spoke candidly, a smile resting lightly on his lips.

Julia tried her best not to give in to the grin that begged for display. "I know—a fault of my own. Now come, if you think it so important that you have my private ear, we must be quick. The fireworks will surely be soon and Mama will miss us if we are not back in time." Not that it mattered much, for as he had said, they were already engaged and could take a few more liberties than girls just come out into Society.

Wolversley took her arm in his. "You do like to order me around."

"Well, I had better start my practice now." The joke fell flat on the ear of both parties, and upon uttering it, Julia decided that for the rest of the evening she had best mimic a mute.

The Earl guided her through the crowds, past the laughter of jostling plebeians that only grated on her anxious nerves. She had known that he would eventually wish to speak to her. The nuptials were drawing near, and he no doubt wished to explain his particular distaste for the day and how the marriage would work out most conveniently for them both. After all, if he had jilted her once on account of the pleasures the world had to offer, it was safe to suppose that he intended to keep enjoying those pleasures even after propriety coerced him into marrying her.

The Earl drew Julia off the main promenade and down a narrow winding path that branched away from the main throng of revelers. The bright lights of Vauxhall began to fade as they were obscured by shrubs, and soon even the booths and fire-eating performers were hidden by the small trees that entwined themselves together.

As the vision of Vauxhall's amusements faded, miraculously, so did the noise. Music, singing, and conversation all dwindled down to silence the farther they walked. The quiet of the night replaced the sounds, and the darkness drew in around them.

Wolversley halted abruptly, forcing Julia to do the same. He turned and surprised her by reaching up to release the ribbons of his mask. As it fell to the ground, she could make out the features of his bare face in the dim light. He was watching her intently, and the look made her body quiver. Must she remove her mask too? But then there would be nothing for her to hide behind.

She looked into those penetrating eyes and knew, in that instant, that he would be able to read her thoughts, mask or no. *No fear, no fear, no fear.* If she kept repeating it to herself then maybe the fear really would go.

"You are looking very beautiful this evening, Jules." Wolversley's voice was husky, his eyes roving over her.

Was that...desire? She could not reply. What was the meaning of his words? Had he not jilted her six years earlier? Had they not been caught in this coil unwillingly? Was there some possibility that his heart had changed?

They had not come here to make love, she told herself. They had come to discuss the arrangements for their marriage of convenience in a business-like fashion.

But as he said her name, she was too enthralled to be indignant. She had not seen that look in his eyes, nor heard that tone in his voice, since he had bestowed both upon her years ago. That fierce intensity was something she had not understood when she was young. Now, as a grown woman, she understood it well, the raw desire restrained and controlled by that one compliment he paid her.

"Is that what you brought me here to say?" She could not help the guarded tones. She had been hurt before, and her heart had defences which bristled like a palisade even when she did not bid them come forth.

He did not answer but instead moved closer. The space grew smaller. Her breathing came shallow, sharp, and fast. She was not ready for this. Why could he not be clear? Why must she be guessing at his motives?

"What did you wish to say?"

"I wish to say so many things, to explain so many things." But in this moment, it seemed like explaining was the last thing on his mind, that all he wanted to do was....

He traced a finger down her face, turning his hand over, hooking her mask, and tugging it gently upwards. The satin ribbons gave way. Julia felt the relief of a nose no longer tickled by the mask, and then inwardly scolded herself for thinking of something so trivial at a time like this.

With the green mask now resting atop her brown hair, she was exposed. The pale moonlight that filtered through the trees fell upon her upturned face. She could feel the warmth of his breath upon her cheek.

"You wore it," he said, his hand running up the side of her dress to feel the soft material of the shawl.

"Yes," she almost panted the word, her body coming alive with the faintest of his touches. "If you have nothing to say, we have no need for discussion. Let us return to the others." Yet, despite her words she was not moving. Her feet had rooted themselves to the spot.

"The wedding is mere days away."

"I know."

"I have to tell you...." But he did not continue. His eyes were transfixed by her face. He leant his head down.

She felt the softest flutter of his lips upon hers. His arm wound its way around her back, drawing her to him. She would have been helpless in his arms had she closed her eyes a second sooner.

But that single second allowed her to catch a glimpse of another couple stealing away into the darkness. They ran along a path parallel to Julia and Wolversley's own, and she could hear the sound of stifled laughter. The two lovers paused nearby, the man swinging the woman around and into his arms. It was simple for them in their requited love. Julia caught a glimpse of the lover's face as he pushed his mask away, preparing to lean in for a kiss.

At the sight of that pale skin set with two black eyes she knew instantly who he was.

"Sylvester!" The words died on her lips as she looked on in horror. As she pulled away from the Earl's kiss, the nearby gentleman kissed the maiden in the gold and purple mask. Even though the hood of the girl's cloak covered her hair, Julia knew instinctively that it must be Selina. She had arrived at Vauxhall at the very time Sylvester had disappeared from sight. And she was so naïve—it would be easy for her to have been seduced into this dark pathway.

"No!" Julia let out a cry, snatching herself away from the Earl and running towards the lovers. She pulled at branches, desperate to make a way through to the parallel path. She stepped over flowerbeds where freshly laid dew stained her slippers. Even before she reached the other path, the man, who had heard her outburst, was urging his ladylove to flee. He glanced back at Julia, struggling through the bushes, and whispered something in the ear of the masked woman before escaping with her into the darkness.

"Julia!" Recovering from Julia's untimely outburst, Wolversley had followed her through the flowerbeds. He was by her side in moments, but the lovers had already vanished.

"You said Sylvester. Did you see him? What happened?"

"He was here, with your sister, I am sure of it. Oh, she is so young, so innocent." She was wringing her hands, her face a picture of worry.

"By God, I shall kill him!"

Julia could not help but cower from the wrath in Wolversley's voice. She believed he would do it.

"It is my fault, entirely my fault! I should never have left them with Highsmith."

"It's too late for regret. We must decide our next move." The Earl was pacing now, his anger tangible. Julia noticed that he said nothing to alleviate her guilt. No doubt he agreed with her—that she had failed to take care of his sister.

"He will cover his tracks well. Now they have met in secret we are in dangerous waters. We must be vigilant. He may have spoken of elopement."

"Oh, this could not be worse."

"There is no use in theatrics!" barked the Earl, losing his temper.

Julia flinched. "What would you have me do?"

"The best way to keep vigilant is to ensure he cannot contact Selina. Clearly, my words did nothing to get through to her. She has no idea of the man she is dealing with." He swung round to look at Julia. "Can you take my sister on? There is no telling whether a servant will be paid off to deliver secret messages to her. I am but rarely in Town and have recently hired new servants. I cannot guarantee their loyalty as I'm sure your father can his."

"I can, if you wish it, but there is no way to warn the servants about secret missives without spreading word of scandal."

"That is true." He paced again. "But you can intercept anything she receives, if your servants' loyalties are swayed by blunt, can you not? You will have access to her rooms."

"I suppose." Everything was so terrible. Julia hated theatrics, but she could not help wanting to burst into tears. Everything was going wrong, and it was all happening at once.

Now the Earl was relying on her to protect his sister. She only hoped and prayed she could do it.

"Come," he commanded. "We must go and see it done." With that he left her to follow. No arm was offered, and the feelings that had been growing between them, that had come so close to fruition, were dashed amongst the shrubbery of Vauxhall.

CHAPTER THIRTEEN

"...the end to the pleasant weather."

THE FOLLOWING DAY SAW SELINA INSTALLED in the Rotherham household. Wolversley had told some cock and bull story about his wanting her to enjoy some pleasant female company rather than being restricted to the company of her unsociable brother, and Mrs. Rotherham had welcomed the lovely Selina with open arms.

"Lucy, have Lady Selina put in the room adjacent to Miss Annabelle. It has an adjoining door, my dear," said Mrs. Rotherham, patting Selina's hand. "No doubt you and Annabelle will like that."

"Thank you, Mrs. Rotherham, I am so pleased my brother thought of letting me stay." She smiled sweetly. "We shall all be family soon!"

"Yes, and this will have to be a regular occurrence." Annabelle skipped toward her friend, bore her away from her mother, and attempted to whisk her upstairs where they could revel in last night's adventure, but Julia, coming through from the morning room, stopped their progress.

"Welcome, Lady Selina." Julia held out her hands to clasp Selina's own. "I am sure you will have far more fun here with us ladies than with your brother." Her bright eyes looked over Selina's shoulder at Wolversley who had just entered the hall.

"More fun with me, you mean," hissed Annabelle. She still had not forgiven Julia for her interference yesterday. Julia wondered if Annabelle knew about the secret tryst her friend had shared with the man that she herself admired. Sylvester took pleasure in flirting with them both, but it seemed that when it came to making a decision, the heiress with the title had won out. Would Annabelle welcome Selina with such open arms if she knew Sylvester was whispering plans of elopement in her ears? Julia thought not.

But instead of using her own knowledge maliciously, Julia bore her sister's cutting comment without retaliation. "If there is anything you need or wish to talk about, you know where you can find me." She smiled gently at Selina, hoping that the girl would confide in her and allow her some influence in the situation with Sylvester.

"Thank you, Miss Rotherham. My brother thinks I shall act more properly here—he threatened to send me home if I do not behave."

Julia thought, with some misgivings, that it would be better to send her home anyway.

"That I did," said Wolversley, "as any respectable brother should. Behave yourself, sister." He kissed Selina's cheek before losing her to Annabelle who tugged her upstairs.

"Thank you, Mrs. Rotherham and Miss Rotherham," Selina called over her shoulder. "I am sure this stay will be wonderful." The two young women disappeared from view on the staircase, their girlish titters echoing off the floor and walls of the hall.

"Ah, well I must go and see George," said Mrs. Rotherham. "He was in the kitchen intent upon disrupting my menu earlier today. I have told him more than once that he may not have pheasant twice in a week. It is so expensive to bring it up from the country." Mrs. Rotherham disappeared through a servants' door, leaving the betrothed couple alone.

"She will be safe in your care, I am sure," the Earl said after a few moments of silence.

"I shall do my utmost to guard her. I only hope no bad comes of this."

"It shall not. I am going to find Sylvester's lodgings tomorrow. I intend to deliver a message he will not wish to ignore. It is high time he realises who protects Selina...and your sister as well."

Julia nodded. She remembered the half-kiss Wolversley had laid upon her lips last night and felt suddenly self-conscious about being alone with him once again. Would he try to kiss her again? Should she stay and let him make the attempt? "I think I shall leave you now, my lord. After my mother has scolded my father, she will no doubt wish to take me on another shopping trip for wedding finery."

"It is only a few days until we are man and wife," the Earl stated in a level tone, as though trying to comprehend it. He walked over to the window and stared out into the distance.

The small hope Julia had been harbouring since last evening of a marriage of mutual affection was flitting away. He made no attempt to reignite the interest he had shown last night. His actions had no doubt been a lapse in his judgment. Even now, she saw he had not removed his hat or gloves. He had no intention of staying and renewing those sentiments. It was simply a dream born of the magical lights of Vauxhall.

"At least the preparations will keep the girls occupied. Now I really must go. Good morning to you, my lord."

"Good morning, Miss Rotherham." He bowed stiffly and took his leave.

WOLVERSLEY CHOSE TO walk home, sending his carriage on without him. He had no wish to get back to the business of the day any quicker than he needed to, not when his mind was so preoccupied. He had thought about Julia's lips long after Sylvester's intrusion upon their tryst. They had been so close to his—he had felt them upon his own—before she had snatched them away.

He thought with a certain degree of anxiety that perhaps she had not wished for him to kiss her. She had been apprehensive—he had known that—and he did not blame her for it, but he had taken the opportunity that was afforded him. He had chosen actions over words, and now he regretted it. How could he have pushed intimacy on her like that without offering the explanation she so deserved? Curse it! He turned a corner and smothered the urge to kick out at a lamppost he passed.

Up ahead the street grew busier. There was a young couple exiting a house, kissing fondly before climbing into their waiting carriage. Man and wife, no doubt, in the first months of matrimony before the rose-coloured view of each other wore off. Wolversley thought grimly that he would never have to wait for his wife's rose-coloured view of him to wear off since it would not be there to begin with.

What must she think of him? Trapped as she was, she had had no choice in the affections he chose to bestow upon her. Perhaps that was why she had escaped from his arms so rapidly. He felt sick as he realised that she may have merely been accepting his amorous advances as part of the role she was forced to play as his betrothed.

The young couple in the carriage sped past him, no doubt on the way to another gay engagement after having spent the morning in each other's arms.

What would happen when they were married? As he thought of the marriage bed, he vowed he would not force himself upon her, no matter the need for a son. The estate that Wolversley had laboured so hard on recovering needed an heir to continue his work, but he would not obtain one if it was against Julia's will.

If only he had taken the chance that had presented itself and told her the truth. She might, even now, be forgiving him a little, or at least be coming to terms with what had happened six years ago. Instead, they were further apart than ever, and the moment for truth had passed. He could not tell her now, not after the way he had tried to kiss her.

He thought back to the way she had looked at him just a quarter of an hour since. There had been fear in her eyes, an anxiety about her movements. Had she been afraid he would renew his amorous attentions? Well, he would not, not until the time she asked him to...and that might well be never.

He was making good headway now, his long legs carrying him home of their own accord while his mind was elsewhere.

Upon his arrival home he was greeted by his most faithful servant. "My lord." Fitz bowed his master in. "Lord Courtenay awaits your pleasure in the library."

"Indeed?" Wolversley's tone was sharper than he meant it to be, and he immediately repented that his private thoughts had provoked him to rudeness towards his butler.

"He has been waiting some half an hour for you," replied Fitz. "I installed him with some of your lordship's brandy."

Wolversley took off his hat and gloves, handed them to Fitz, and reluctantly walked in the direction of the library to perform the duties of a host. He opened the door to quite a sight, one which would have set him to chuckling if he had been in better spirits. Courtenay, his brandy glass forgotten on top of the paper-covered desk, had put one arm into Wolversley's dressing gown, which the Earl had left upon the back of his chair, and was eyeing the material through a quizzing glass.

Without looking up he called, "Fantastic stuff! Indian no doubt, or Chinese? It looks rather fine against my wrist I must say—quite sets off my fair complexion. Where'd you get it?" And then Courtenay's head popped up, the quizzing glass still over one eye giving it a grotesquely large look.

"I forget," replied Wolversley, wandering over to the table upon which sat the crystal decanter of brandy. He had no wish to hold grudges, his emotions spent in other quarters. Besides, Courtenay was a good friend; his loyalty in Wolversley's years at university proved that.

"Listen," said Courtenay, his voice, suddenly serious, breaking into Wolversley's thoughts. Before going on, Courtenay plucked the dressing gown sleeve off his arm most conscientiously, laid the dressing gown gently back over the chair from whence it had come, and then replaced his quizzing glass in his pocket. "You have no doubt wondered at the lack of my company, and in truth I have missed you." He paused. "But I felt I could not come into your presence again after my hideous faux pas which has led to such a travesty befalling you."

A travesty. It had not seemed a travesty last night, thought Wolversley. This morning it was so different.

"I am come"—Courtenay's voice rose to some kind of crescendo, his ring-covered hand rising in a flourish and then falling before him as he bowed—"to beg forgiveness."

The shock on Wolversley's face dissipated, and the look of weariness, which had stolen over his features during his solitary walk home, returned. He waved a hand weakly and muttered, "It is no matter, Courtenay." And then, with slightly more fervour, he said, "Now pour me a glass of that blasted brandy before I collapse."

"Oh! You are the best of men! Hallelujah, I say! Brandy, of

course." Courtenay attacked his task with as much speed and efficiency as the venerable Fitz, and before long the two friends were seated in amicable silence, each partaking of the good brandy Fitz had provided.

"I am grateful to be so freely forgiven," said Courtenay, breaking the silence that his friend seemed intent upon keeping. "But I did…"—he trailed off, as if unsure whether to proceed—"I did provide you with a wife, did I not?"

The joke met with no laughter; not even the flicker of a smile passed over Wolversley's lips.

"You are not happy to be wedding Miss Rotherham?" he asked, evidently trying a different tack to compel his friend into conversation.

That question, however, was hardly one Wolversley felt he could answer. Happy? How could he be happy when he had forced a kiss—and was about to force marriage—upon the woman he had wronged so deeply.

"I fear happiness will not be a blessing our marriage enjoys," said the Earl flatly.

Courtenay, embarrassed by the part he had played in this debacle, shifted awkwardly in his seat.

"But, I mean, she is a handsome girl, there is no doubt about it, and she will bring an equally handsome fortune to your estate. I know how you have worked hard to bring your estate about, so you're not exactly flying without a feather, but such a blessing is hardly something to turn one's nose up at."

Her fortune? Wolversley sighed, pinched the bridge of his nose, and then pushed his fingers over his eyes, massaging the skin. Could he bring himself to use such ill-gotten gains?

"Surely," said Courtenay, still trying his best to cheer his friend, "all these things taken together must make this match at least a little bit desirable?"

But as with all the other questions running through his mind, Wolversley simply had no answer.

As Julia suspected, Mrs. Rotherham had arranged another trip to the modiste. Her eldest daughter must have the finest wedding wardrobe no matter the cloud hanging over her match. The younger girls took rather more persuading than Julia had anticipated to join her and her mother on the trip. Considering Annabelle usually required no second bidding where clothing was concerned, Annabelle and Selina's resistance only increased Julia's anxiety over them. The fact that they could not come into contact with Sylvester at the modiste's was exactly the reason she wished them to join the excursion. When they finally agreed, she felt a wave of relief wash over her, but she was still acutely aware that she had been left in the dark as to the reason for their initial reluctance.

The trip did not take long. Madame Trouleux had made up the gowns that they had ordered on a previous trip in a miraculously short time. She was a wonderful modiste and, in spite of the turmoil in her homeland, she was still able to obtain the latest designs from friends across the Channel who dressed the most fashionable women of Paris. She could perform miracles with muslin, satin, and silk, and her French wiles could undo the purse strings of the most miserly Society mother. Mrs. Rotherham was no exception to this tradition.

"Ah, Madame Rotherham, you are well, yes?" The dressmaker greeted her customer with kisses on either cheek.

"Yes, Madame Trouleux, I am delightfully well, thank you. My eldest's wedding day draws nearer, and soon she will be comfortably settled. After that, I shall only have to think about Miss Annabelle's future happiness. A mother's burden will grow lighter!"

"And everybody knows that a mother's burden is weightier than a father's. You have done well to see your daughter so suitably matched. I congratulate you again,

Madame Rotherham. It will not be long, I think, before Mademoiselle Annabelle finds her love—she is *si très jolie.*"

Annabelle beamed at the Frenchwoman and then glanced at Selina, a secret understanding passing between the two. No, Julia thought, Selina could not have told her friend that Sylvester, instead of paying common court to them both, had begun making love secretly to *her*. For a moment, Julia felt sorry for Annabelle and the pain of betrayal that she would certainly feel later if all should be revealed.

"Welcome to all you mademoiselles and, ah, and you have brought back the beautiful Lady Selina." The Frenchwoman's large inquisitive eyes fell upon the dark beauty with pleasure. The young girl blushed under the scrutiny. "I think you will be the toast of your Season along with Miss Annabelle, yes?"

"Oh, bless you, Madame Trouleux, for your kind words," said Mrs. Rotherham, "but Lady Selina is not yet out. This is her first time in Town, and so her engagements, as you can understand, are restricted."

"Ah, I see, but of course, that is why you blush so—you are new to compliments, yes?" The modiste pinched Selina's cheek affectionately. "You will soon become accustomed, such a beauty as you are."

"You are too kind, Madame Trouleux," replied Selina.

The greetings taken care of, the tall, statuesque woman led them through to a room at the back of the establishment where dresses already made up hung upon mannequins awaiting their owners to come and claim them. She spoke as she walked, asking Mrs. Rotherham the latest news, explaining the newest intricacies of fashion, and offering plenty of compliments.

"And your wedding," she said, turning to Julia. "How wonderful! It is to be so soon. I am, as you English say, over the moon for you!" She clapped her hands together before seating the customers on a chaise lounge and offering them refreshments.

Julia did as she always did when she came to the modiste. She admired Madame Trouleux whose height and angular features could be called striking rather than beautiful. She was enigmatic not only in her looks but also in the way she moved and carried herself. There was no doubt that she turned heads wherever she ventured in London. Even Julia's brother knew of Madame Trouleux.

The Frenchwoman's hair was as dark as Selina's, though it was laced here and there with mature lines of silver. Her dress was very modish, as was to be expected in her profession. The drapes of the muslin and the luxurious gold and red of her wrap could have been called theatrical, had they not suited the remarkable appearance of the wearer so well. Her dress billowed about her and then swung to the side as she sat down dramatically.

"Now, I am to show you my work, no, it is more than that—they should be called my masterpieces! I have never created *si rapidement!* You will look radiant, Mademoiselle Rotherham—nothing but the most beautiful dresses for you."

Julia, usually hating flattery, forgave Madame Trouleux for it, for she had known her since her debut into Society and could not dislike a woman who had helped in so many ways. "Thank you, Madame."

"No need!" The lady put up a hand in protest. "Now, I think you must choose the wedding dress. I have barely time, but I wish to make it as a gift, *pour vous.*"

But receiving a new dress free of charge was a step too far. Julia simply could not accept so lavish a gift. "No...no surely, I can just wear the dress you have made for me already, the one of dove gray silk."

"Absolutely not!" cried Mrs. Rotherham.

"*Absolument pas!*" echoed the modiste.

"You are to be a countess, my dear. You will not wear just any dress and you must not insult Madame by denying her the gift she wishes to bestow!"

"Mama, really! I need no such thing. I do not wish to cause Madame any trouble."

"Trouble? It is no trouble! A gift. You have always been a favourite of mine, Mademoiselle Rotherham. I do wish to gift the dress to you."

With another bout of persuasion from her mother, Julia gave in, allowing herself to be led into another room where Madame Trouleux had laid out bolts of material beautiful enough to tantalize any bride.

Julia's eyes were automatically drawn upwards to the bolts of material in bright colours. She had never before chosen a dress of pale fabric, apart from the patterned muslin day dresses that every young woman wore, and she found herself looking anywhere besides the pale satins and silks on the lower shelves. Eventually, she was forced to pull herself away from the more vibrant fabrics to look at the whites and creams Madame had laid out for her, and when she did, she saw they were just as beautifully crafted as their brighter counterparts.

"I can make up the dress in relatively little time, Mademoiselle. I have already shown your mother the fashion plates I have, but I will give you time to make your own mind up, yes?"

Julia thought gratefully that once again her faith in the modiste had not been misplaced. She had known the Rotherham ladies long enough to understand that Julia's taste differed substantially from her mother's.

"Thank you, Madame Trouleux, you are too kind."

"Bah!" The Frenchwoman shook a hand at her. "Now, I have many beautiful materials here as you can see."

Julia slid the back of her hand across the most beautiful ivories her modiste could offer.

"Here is silk, satin, taffeta, gossamer, and the laces they are over there." She pointed to yet another table with the most intricate point-work Julia had ever seen. "I had such beautiful lace when I married Henri." The Madame's eyes went misty in an instant as she gazed back over time. "Ah! You will be so happy, I declare, for to be married is a great gift, *n'est-ce pas*? I was so happy with Henri before *la Révolution*. But, enough of me! What is your idea of the perfect wedding dress, *ma chère?*" Madame Trouleux placed her fingertips together two at a time and then stared at Julia over the pyramid they made.

Her idea of the perfect wedding dress? Had she ever really thought about it? No. Julia dropped her fingers onto the soft fabrics. Now she had to make the choice in the little time she had—yet another forced decision precipitated by the unfortunate circumstances.

As she felt the smoothness of a bolt of silk, Julia thought back to last night, when the shawl the Earl had given her was the only thing that lay between her shoulders and his hands— to last night, when his lips had met hers as lightly as a butterfly flitting over the surface of a lake. She pushed down the feeling of anxiety she was trying to keep buried within herself. She must remain calm and impervious to everything.

"Perhaps a large portion of the lace? Patterned trim on the sleeves, yes? And...." The Madame was forcing Julia's hand purposefully. She knew her customer better than Julia realised.

"No," cut in Julia. She paused, hesitating, and then continued with more certainty. "No, I think I like that silk, the plain one." She moved over and pulled out a smaller bolt to examine it. "Yes, I like this one."

"Ah, the dupioni silk! With the natural imperfections, yes?" Madame Trouleux nodded in a sage way. She pulled a ream of the material free from the bolt and, flying it high, allowed it to fall in a swathe about Julia. "Yes, it suits you well,

I think." A warm smile spread across her angular countenance, and she dropped a wink on her customer in a knowing way.

Julia realised ruefully that the Madame had been playing with her with the suggestions of an intricate wedding dress. Madame Trouleux knew Julia's taste for the simple and the elegant. A look of understanding passed between the two before the modiste swiftly whipped the material away, rolling the bolt back up and carrying it with her as she ushered Julia back to the room which housed the rest of their party.

"The decision has been made," proclaimed the modiste in majestic tones. "Now I must work. I will say good day to you ladies!" Madame Trouleux immediately started waving her hands at the four women, trying to shoo them out of her shop as though they were mischievous street urchins.

"But, wait!" protested Mrs. Rotherham. "We have not discussed the pattern! I have not told you the design." Her shocked cries resounded through the room. "My daughter's dress, I want it to be covered in the finest silver lace, like that of Princess Charlotte's, and she must have the most elaborate headdress. She is to be a countess, you know, the Countess Wolversley."

At the description of her mother's ideal wedding dress for her, Julia's mouth puckered up as though she had sucked upon a lemon slice.

"I know what is to be done!" declared the modiste, continuing to wave them out with her hands and veritably chasing the party through her shop. "Mademoiselle Rotherham has spoken. I know her desires. I need nothing more to create the most beautiful of bridal gowns apart from an empty shop!"

"I have told you nothing of designs, though! Surely I am to have a say?"

Madame Trouleux paused, looking over to Julia. "Mademoiselle Rotherham has had her say. I know exactly what Mademoiselle will need, and better, I know what she will like!"

Julia found all these theatrics rather humorous. The two other girls would have as well had they not been looking between each other nervously and trying to make their way unmolested to the door of the establishment.

"What about the other dresses you have already made for my daughter?" The question was a last attempt by Mrs. Rotherham to hold her ground.

"They will be sent over, of course. I know my customer well enough that they will fit *parfaitement*. I send them to the Rotherham house or to Lord Wolversley?"

"Rotherham!" Julia said curtly, quite incapable of coming to terms with the idea that her clothes, her belongings, and herself would be under Wolversley's roof in just a few days. She was not ready to become a part of his life yet.

"*Très bien!*" No sooner had this positive expletive passed the Madame's lips than she began to brandish the silk bolt she was still holding in order to herd them out like sheep. The weapon worked exceedingly well, thought Julia, as the party poured out onto the street.

The Madame bid them good morning before slamming the door of her establishment shut. Her *au revoir* had barely been heard over the fellow shoppers and street sellers who thronged the street calling out to friends or purchasers alike. The women did not spend long amongst the masses but looked for the Rotherham carriage straightway. James had been walking the horses, but upon seeing the ladies he slowed them to a halt and assisted the party into the carriage.

When they reached the house, both Annabelle and Selina stepped down from the carriage, but Julia was fated to remain a captive a little longer. Mrs. Rotherham directed James to continue on to the first of the morning calls she had arranged. She might have a daughter who had disgraced herself, but as George had said to her, disgrace was only as powerful as one let it be. If she brought her daughter with her on these morning calls, then perhaps it would do a little to repair the damage that had been done. She said as much to Julia who was resenting the need for her attendance.

Julia heard the wise words and dutifully did as her mother bade, stopping at what felt like a dozen houses for visits filled with boring gossip and the latest on-dits. None of this could begin to touch the turmoil of Julia's preoccupied mind, however much she tried to accept the distraction.

After what seemed an age, they finally began to make their way back to the Rotherham home. Their homeward journey heralded the end to the pleasant weather. Outside the smudged panes of the carriage windows, rain clouds gathered. The sky took on a sickly yellow tinge, as though it were suffering an illness, and the clouds thickened in the heavens. By the time mother and daughter arrived home, there were dark droplets gathered in heavy plumes above, ready to flood the earth below. The air hung thick and close, and rather than the freshness a shower promised, the sky was angry above them, a storm threatening. Julia observed, upon stepping down from the carriage, that it did not feel like a normal bout of bad weather.

Before she could enter the house, a single heavy drop of rain fell on her forehead. Usually she would welcome a storm. As a child she had loved the rolls of thunder and the bright flashes of lightning. She would stand outside their house in Sussex on the well-kept lawns, and watch as the precious water poured forth from the heavens and quenched all living things in sight. Her mother would scold her and warn her of fever; her father would just smile. He would already be planning to hunt for butterflies when the storm had rolled away.

Julia stood before her London home, knowing with sadness that her father would not smile at her now. Worse than that, as she looked up at the heavens, she realised she would not be watching storms from her parents' West Sussex house in the future. She would be watching them from another's. That is where all her clothes would now be sent, that is where all her books would sit on dusty shelves, and that is where she would be. It was a bleak prospect. She was losing her family for another that held no deep-rooted affection for her. She would be quite lost in another's world, and though everything would be the same—the same lightning and thunder flashing and rolling over Wolversley's house—everything would be entirely different. She felt the throb of grief at all that she was about to lose.

"Come, my child," her mother held out a hand to her. "You will not be mine much longer, and I have a mind to sit with you alone a while before dinner. Will you come dress with me?"

Julia smiled at the affection in her mother's voice and pressed her two hands over her mother's. "I would love to, Mama." As the carriage rolled away, mother and daughter entered the house arm in arm, leaving the gathering clouds to do their worst.

"Mama," Julia whispered, a quarter of an hour before they were to go down the staircase and join the others.

"Yes, child." Her mother was already dressed for dinner. She held a brush in her hands and was running it down the length of Julia's loose hair.

"I am sorry. I am sorry I have brought such shame upon us."

"Hush, my child. What's done is done."

Julia sighed. "Is Father still very angry with me?"

"Your father is not angry. He is only upset."

"I am marrying an Earl, and my father is upset." It was comical, but Julia said it with such sadness upon her face. Her father upset was far worse than her father angry. She was such a disappointment to him.

"It is not the suitor, nor the circumstances, my dear." Mrs. Rotherham pulled apart a knot at the base of Julia's neck.

"I have not shamed him into unloving me?"

"Foolish child. Your father and I will always love you—that is why he is worried over this wedding. I see it will all be quite well when it is worked out, but your father, he is worried that you will not be happy, my child."

Julia bit her lip and hated the tear that rolled down her cheek. "Is it so very hard to be married, Mama?"

Mrs. Rotherham hummed. "Yes, it is hard. A partnership is always hard when both parties are infallibly right in all things. Your father and I have learned that." The older woman smiled as she turned her daughter to face her. "Such pretty hair," she said, stroking the length of it and cupping her daughter's face.

"Marriage, my child, is the noblest institution, and it would not be so worth having if it were not some little work to have. I know you will be happy with his lordship—I remember when you were young together and I could hardly separate you, and I remember when you courted and were betrothed, though you think I have forgotten it. I did not want to bring it up and hurt you, my child—that is why I have not mentioned it—but I will now. Have you not perhaps wondered why the Earl has taken such an interest in you since coming to Town? Perhaps a little of what you two once had is still there, and a little can be made into a larger amount with hard work.

"I love your father, but love is a choice more often than a flippant feeling—I am sure he would say it of me when I am boring him with little on-dits. And I should certainly say it of him when he is intent on disrupting my dinner plans in the kitchen, or striding out of the house in the wet to catch butterflies when we are about to receive visitors." She chuckled. "I choose to love your father then, as I always will." She patted her daughter's cheek and rose. "I shall fetch Lucy to do your hair."

Lucy came and dressed Julia's hair in silence, for once omitting her customary remonstrations. She curtseyed out of the room when she was finished, and Julia sat a moment longer, staring at herself in the reflection before sighing and rising. When she had left her mother's boudoir, she was met by her father. Julia wondered if her mother had told him to fetch her.

Mr. Rotherham said nothing but offered his arm to his daughter, something he had not done since her betrothal. They walked down to dinner together, and just before they entered the dining room Julia whispered, "I love you, Papa."

"I love you too, my child," he murmured back. Without pausing, he led her through the door.

CHAPTER FOURTEEN

"...looking for the truth..."

DINNER HAD BEEN A QUIET AFFAIR, and with no evening engagements—a turn of events that Julia was very thankful for—Annabelle and Selina were confined to the house along with the rest of the Rotherhams. The girls, still whispering and conspiring, retired early. Julia was sure they had feigned their headaches, especially because they were so obviously simultaneous, but she did not murmur any dissent, merely watching them go with some relief. Selina was safe from Sylvester tonight at least. Julia retired not long afterwards, worn out by the events of the day and ready for sleep.

It was midnight when Julia woke, an unfamiliar noise bringing her out of her slumber. She had not been sleeping heavily, her fitful slumber interrupted by strange and anxious dreams. When she finally came fully to consciousness, she felt disoriented. It was difficult for her to distinguish exactly what it was that had brought her out of sleep. Her eyelids fluttered open, warring against the weariness that threatened to retake her mind. What had woken her? She was on the verge of turning over and falling back to sleep when the worries of recent days jarred her fully awake.

Facing the canopy above her bed, she scraped several curls from her face and opened her eyes wider. The fire had long since grown cold and dark. Outside, the rain was drumming against window ledges and smattering against the panes of glass. Perhaps it was the rain that had woken her—the rain, and nothing more. The rhythmical patter led her in and out of consciousness for a time, her eyelids rising and falling slowly until they barely opened at all.

Julia had no idea how much time had passed when another noise sounded. All the trappings of sleep fell from her instantly, and she sat bolt upright in the bed. Her tired eyes strove to see in the dark room. It had been a door closing. A high whining creak and the click of the handle had given it away. However quietly the action had been intended, she was certain about what she had heard. She ran the possibilities through her mind. Perhaps it was her brother, home after a night of gaming. Perhaps it was a lone servant going to bed late. There were many possibilities that she could think of that would mean nothing amiss, but even as they ran through her mind, one after the other, a sense of misgiving was building. She had to investigate.

Climbing out of bed, Julia padded over to where she knew the window lay and threw open the curtains to let the moonlight, which kept intermittently escaping the rainclouds, fill the room. The exit from her bed and the rapid movement to the window had made her lightheaded. She swayed a little by the window casement before regaining her balancing. The air was cold outside her bed, and soon her toes were numb. Pulling a wrapper from a nearby chair, she covered herself to ward off the chill and put an inquiring ear to the wooden door of her room.

Julia waited a few moments. Hearing nothing, she rested

her weight on the door handle and heard it click beneath her hand. All was silence and darkness as far as she could see into the hall. For the first time since she was small, she realised how absurdly terrifying her own home could be when plunged in deep darkness. Irrational fear gripped her, but it could not stifle the greater fear of what might be occurring elsewhere in the house. Taking a deep breath and telling herself to stop acting like a child in shortcoats, she stepped out.

Still Julia heard nothing. She left her bedroom door ajar and began to make her way down the dim corridor. First, and most importantly, she must check on Selina. Once again, she felt the weighty responsibility she had been given bear down upon her. She paused outside their guest's door. Just a little farther down the hall was her sister's room. Both doors were tightly shut. She listened for any sound of slumbering within —sounds that would ensure her intrusion was unwarranted. But however much she strained her ears, she encountered only disappointment. Silence reigned.

Julia's hand rested on the door handle, pressing down, ready to ease it open so she could assure herself that the sleeping beauty was still in her bed. That assurance never came.

Up until this moment, when she opened the wooden door and found an empty bedchamber, Julia had not known the depth of horror she was capable of feeling. Fear paralysed her at first, and then she sprang forward in a panic. Even from the door she could make out that the bed hangings were not drawn and that the bed was still made up as it would have been yesterday morning. Running into the room, she threw up the bed covers in some wild attempt at uncovering a tiny Selina still here, still sleeping peacefully. It was of no avail. Lady Selina had gone.

Wait! thought Julia. She must stop and think. Selina had been her responsibility and a terrible thing had just occurred, but only ill logic would result if she did not calm her nerves. Besides, she must stop flinging bed covers here, there, and everywhere if she did not want Lucy to hear. That woman had ears like a bat.

Where could Selina have gone? It must be past midnight, and there was no sign of her in her room. Was she still in the house? Julia could not wake anyone until she was sure that Selina had actually disappeared—there would be a scandal in it if she breathed a word before necessary. Or maybe it would be more accurate to say she could not wake anyone apart from her sister. Those girls had been hatching some plan for days. Surely, Annabelle would know what was afoot!

Julia ran nimbly across the room, reached the door to the adjoining chamber, and flung it open. Casting a glance around the darkness of the room, she soon caught sight of another empty bed. What hijinks were these? Where on earth had the two girls gone?

Turning on her heel, Julia was about to flee the room and sound the alarm when she caught sight of something on Annabelle's desk. The damask curtains above the desk were slightly parted, as if someone had wished to watch the street below, and by the dim beams of a street lamp, Julia saw a crumpled piece of paper upon the desk. She snatched it up, unfolding it as she walked, and took it straight to the embers of Annabelle's dying fire in an attempt to read it.

It was no good. There was not enough light. She left the room in frustration, sure that she already knew what was going on, but determined not to believe it until she read the proof.

Coming out to the hall once again, Julia slipped quickly into one of the servants' passages, knowing they would have a candle burning. Lucy always asked for one to be left in the hall should there be any trouble. Julia stood beneath the brass holder in which the solitary candle flickered and tried again to read the note.

Dearest Love,

If what you said to me is true and you do love me, then the only way for us to be together is to elope. You yourself have explained the obstacles in your family. No one will allow us to marry if we stay. Our only hope is to flee. If you truly love me, as you declared at Vauxhall, then meet me at midnight. I shall be waiting for you outside your house with a carriage prepared for our flight. We are star-crossed lovers, you and I, and if you fly with me, it will not be long before we are joined together forever.

Hope and prayer are all that sustain me as I wish, most fervently, that you will come with me. You carry my heart, my love. Be gentle with it, and do not let it die. Bring it back to me tonight, and from there I shall give it to you forever.

My love already speaks as I write this to tell me that you will not fail to come. Farewell until tonight.

The one whose heart and hopes you hold,
S.

Julia could hardly believe what she had read. Elopement? Running away? A carriage at midnight? Burning with a sudden fury, her eyes narrowed and she screwed up the paper in one hand. How dare he! How dare he assume to elope with Selina! But wait, was it Selina? The note had been found in Annabelle's room. Which one of the girls could it be?

Julia thought of her sister's headstrong nature, but surely even Annabelle would stop short of elopement! Selina's innocence sprang to mind. She had never been in Town before. She had never experienced the compliments of a skilled flatterer. And she did not have the guidance of a mother or a sister to warn her about such things. A note like this could easily persuade her of Sylvester's love and that she ought to love him in return. Julia paled. If it was indeed Selina, then she had failed to protect Wolversley's sister.

But if it was Selina, then why was Annabelle missing too? Had her sister helped Selina escape? That seemed too strange to be believed. And yet, what else could she suppose? Perhaps Annabelle had spotted the lovers escaping and was even now chasing after them, trying to thwart their plan out of jealousy.

Fear gave way to shaking as Julia was filled once again with incandescent rage. She snatched the candle from its holder and left the servants' passage for the hall where she stood in the flickering darkness, panting out her fury.

Think! Think! He would have had a chaise and four, no doubt. That would be the quickest way to leave London, though surely he would have to change horses before long? If it was Lady Selina, was he truly taking her to Gretna Green? Surely he would not use and cast off an Earl's sister as he had that woman in Bath? Unless the whole thing was some sort of malicious sport on his part?

Julia began to feel sick with the possibilities. She still held the note in her hand. It quivered as her whole body shook. Taking a deep breath, she calmed herself. Midnight, the letter had said. The time was not long past. She knew what she needed to do.

In the half-light she nodded to herself and, with a final deep breath for the last of the resolution she needed, went back to her room. Once inside, Julia discarded the note in a drawer. There was no use leaving it on display. If all went to plan, her mother and father would never see it, would never know. Then she left her room.

Instead of returning to Selina's room, she made quick work of the hallway and journeyed to her brother's. She opened the door with care, but her guess had been right—he was not yet home from his nocturnal activities. All was safe.

Julia slipped into the room, closing the door quietly behind her. She placed the candle in the holder her brother had beside his bed. For once, instead of fighting it, she allowed that most problematic of her vices, her impetuosity, to take over. She gave herself no time to think before ransacking her brother's wardrobe.

A shirt, cravat, waistcoat, jacket, breeches, stockings—all went flying over Julia's head into a pile on the floor. When the pile was as complete as she could make it, she turned to face it and slipped out of her wrapper. Keeping on the chemise she had worn to bed, she attempted to dress. It took more time than she had expected. She had no experience of men's clothing, for obvious reasons, and though they seemed perfectly simple when on someone else, they were completely alien to her fingers as she tried to fasten them on. She was not even used to dressing herself in her own clothes without Lucy's help—now she had to put on these ridiculously complicated garments if she had any hope of getting Selina back unscathed.

The cool air of her brother's bedroom was at least some encouragement to get dressed rapidly. She managed the shirt, breeches, and stockings in a little less than ten minutes, and from there it seemed easier. She was thankful, as she pulled on the waistcoat, that her brother had not yet grown into his full maturity. Though the clothes were cut for a man, they were not absurdly big on Julia. All she needed was to pass for a boy, and she could do so in these garments, though not with any degree of fashionableness. The buckskins were appallingly baggy on her legs, something Highsmith would abhor, but it was the cravat that really caused problems. Her brother, who had had a few years of practice, still could not quite get his head around the art of the folds, and she was a woman. What did she know about the intricacies of tying a cravat? Three lengths of linen were discarded, crumpled and ruined, on the floor before she gave up. She would have to make do with an awful knot.

Shrugging into Freddy's jacket, one of Weston's creations, she completed the desired illusion. To any passerby she would appear a boy, if not a young man. She felt completely peculiar, and had the situation been less urgent, she would probably have pranced about her brother's bedroom for some minutes observing herself in the looking glass. As it was, she frantically went for one last rummage in her brother's wardrobe and found a pair of top boots. Pulling on the leather footwear which was several sizes too big for her, she stood up, her hair in complete disarray.

Hair! What was she going to do about all this hair? James' hat—that's what she would wear! The stable master always left his large hat hanging on one of the hooks in the yard, and it would cover her hair well enough.

This was it. She was ready. She left her brother's room, blowing out the candle before she went, and made her way through the silent house to the back door which would lead her to the stable yard. A single lantern, hanging from a hook beside the door, shed light on the steps. She scurried down them on the balls of her feet, the leather of the boots making far less noise than the wooden heel would.

A new rush of anxiety hit Julia as she walked across the cobbles of the stable yard. She had to get Selina back before any more damage could be done. Her despair over failing Wolversley again was almost overwhelming.

The other side of the stable yard housed a number of loose boxes. Julia knew exactly which one to go to. "Sheba, hello there, we have to go on a ride." She stroked the mare's velvet nose. "You must be good for me tonight. Everything depends on us." The mare snorted, obviously not approving of the smell of Freddy Rotherham's clothing.

Next, Julia needed to find Sheba's bridle and saddle and waste no time about it. Jogging along the stable row, she stopped by a hook on which rested, as she had known it would, James' hat. At least this small thing was going as she had planned.

Julia reached up to take it off the hook. As she did so, a hand flew out of the darkness, clamping down on her wrist like a vise. Gasping from fright, Julia almost jumped out of her skin.

"Right, sonny," a voice sounded from her side. "You've got two choices—run off now or stay and play wi' me. There's only trouble for you 'ere." The voice was all too familiar, but the tone was downright terrifying.

"James!" exclaimed Julia in a whisper that was a mixture of terror and relief.

As the supposed boy turned towards him, James' jaw dropped several inches, his hand unclamping her wrist and slapping against his forehead.

"Miss Rotherham! What 'n earth are you doin' 'ere at this hour?" His eyes which had been fixed to Julia's face now ran over her dress choice with a growing look of disbelief.

"Thank heavens it is only you!" Julia pulled the hat down from the hook. "I must borrow your hat—it is a matter of life and death!"

James' disbelief turned to comedy after that explanation, and he tried his best to stifle chuckling.

"James, please! You'll wake the grooms."

"Sorry, miss." He was most certainly *not* sorry, his laughter still trumping his bewilderment.

Ignoring him for a moment, Julia gathered up her hair and twisted it into a tight pile. "Are you quite finished?" She asked imperiously as she pulled the hat in place. "If you are going to be here, you may as well help saddle Sheba. Be quick about it!"

She ordered him about as though it was a morning ride she was organizing.

"And will it be th' bridle you're wantin' too, Miss Rotherham?" James asked, not moving an inch and still surveying her, a gleam of amusement in his eyes.

"James, please, just do as I say."

"Now, now, Miss Rotherham. I'm sorry, but I don't see 'ows I can 'elp you to go off gallivantin' into the night dressed as a...a lad. Mr. Rotherham wouldn't 'ave any of it, an' not sure I will either."

"Galloping," corrected Julia. "I shall be galloping into the night." She pulled the first bridle she saw off the wall and walked away from James and back towards Sheba.

"Whoa! Miss! Now, slow down. You can't go out alone."

"Funny, I say *whoa* to horses," she replied, not slowing her pace, her hand already on the bolt of Sheba's box.

"Well, you're actin' like a right mad un', miss—"

"James!" She swung round to face him with eyes ablaze. "I'm going with or without you. I have a young girl to save, so if you want to watch over me then, for goodness' sake, tack up your own horse!"

James' expression changed at the mention of a young girl in trouble.

"I knew somethin' was amiss, I 'eard a carriage nearby a short while ago. That's why I was awake to catch you stealin' my 'at." He scratched his chin.

"Carriage? Did you see which direction it went?"

He shook his head.

"In that case we have even more ground to catch up. James, help me if you will or go to bed."

James' misgivings were still apparent, but he had known Miss Rotherham almost her whole life, and though she had an impetuous temper, she was no fool. If she said a girl was in need of saving, it was most probably Miss Annabelle, and it was most certain that he needed to help.

"Well, you won't be able to ride Sheba in your usual saddle, miss, not wi' them breeches you 'ave on."

"Oh, fiddlesticks! Does Sheba have another?"

"Yes, miss, but you don't know 'ow—"

"I'll learn!" Julia snapped.

Both knowing their missions, the two set to work. Julia saddled Sheba with surprising efficiency, due to the many hours she had spent with the horses, and James saddled Rufus, the heavy-set, trusty chestnut.

The rain had picked up, dulling the sound of the horses' hooves on the cobbles when they led them out. James tried to help Julia into the unfamiliar saddle. She swatted away his hand. She had seen her brother and father mount a thousand times—she could do this! She dropped the left stirrup several holes and threw her foot into it. Her boot slipped out twice, but she was finally able to gain a grip and swing herself up into the saddle.

Exhilarated, Julia shifted in her seat to get used to the entirely new feel. She noticed that Sheba was unusually calm, considering the upset to her normal routine. The mare felt the sense of purpose driving her mistress tonight and stood obediently while Julia tightened her girth and adjusted the stirrups. She had no idea of the best way to ride astride, but James had told her to shorten the stirrups if she really did intend to spend the night galloping. The rain was falling heavily, and before they had even left the yard the pair were soaked through atop their horses. Julia was thankful for the grip of her plaited reins as she drew the wet leather through her fingers.

They were out on the street in front of the house in no time. Julia glanced in either direction, droplets of rain gathering on the brim of her hat and dripping across her vision. All she saw were sheets of rain in either direction and the dull glow of the street lamps.

"James?"

"S'all right, miss. If'n you meant some sort of runaway with a gent was 'appenin', then I got a fair notion where they could be 'eaded." The stable master's mind was already working ahead of hers. "They'll go out the north ways, and I know the posting inn they'll change at. When we get there, we can ask after 'em. I'm sure no innkeeper worth his salt will have ignored an unmarried couple comin' through."

"Excellent, now let's move!" Julia shouted, kicking Sheba forward. The mare needed no second bidding to bound forward into the night, and Rufus' heavy hooves clattered not far behind.

As the hoof beats faded into the distance, the Rotherham house fell back into a peaceful slumber. At least, it was almost peaceful. All was quiet except for the entrance hall—a room Julia had left undisturbed as she left through the back of the house. In the hall, the muffled sounds of crying escaped from behind a locked cupboard door. The rattle of the handle sounded, and the occupant prayed for deliverance from her prison.

"WHERE IS YOUR friend Sylvester tonight then, Rotherham?" asked Highsmith, placing another bet and directing his gaze towards Julia's brother.

More ears than Freddy's heard Highsmith's question. Courtenay was playing cards with the two of them, and Wolversley had been wallowing in his thoughts when Highsmith's words roused him. He sat up straight in the chair he had been lounging in and came over to the table upon which the gentlemen played. He too had noticed the slippery

Sylvester's absence, and he would rather hear more about that then sit brooding over his own affairs.

It was two in the morning, early still, but Wolversley had already drunk a fair amount. In mere days he would be a married man, and he still had found no way to tell Julia the real reason he had broken off their first engagement. The matter was suspended between them like a sword on a string.

As Wolversley waited, Freddy gave a shrug. "Visiting some relation or other—an aunt, I think. Says if he pays his dues he'll be rich someday. You know how it goes." Freddy laid another card.

Highsmith directed a loaded glance towards the Earl who noted it with one raised brow. Wolversley could well believe Sylvester had said those exact words. He tipped another dose of Burgundy into his mouth. The red liquid brightened the stains already upon his lips and found its way to the corners of his mouth.

Tonight had been slow, and all that had played upon his mind was Julia's upturned face at Vauxhall—that innocent, beautiful face that was only ever revealed when she discarded the mask she wore. Last night, it had come off with the masquerade mask, and she had stood before him as she once had long ago. All he could think of was her. He had been so close to telling her the truth.

"Wolversley!"

Freddy's hail dragged the Earl from his reverie.

"Wolversley, come! You must play at least one hand. Highsmith and Courtenay are beating me most unfairly."

Despite Freddy's good-natured invitation, Wolversley still shook his head. "No, I—"

His excuse was cut short as another voice, a familiar one that grated on every fibre of his being, chimed in, unbidden, to the conversation. "Oh, Rotherham, you are a young pup! Do you not know that Wolversley does not play that game, nor any other game, in fact?"

Jonathan Oldsburg-Windlesham had swaggered into the gaming room from the corridor of the club. He sniffed at a lace handkerchief he held at his nose. The upper half of his body swivelled in an odd fashion so that he could see around the ludicrously high shirt collar he wore which acted like blinkers would on a hackney.

"Windlesham, pleasure!" cried Freddy Rotherham, looking with admiration on the apparel the dandy wore. He was, however, quite oblivious to the cold feeling that had entered the room with the foppish gentleman.

"Jonny Odd, what an unpleasant meeting." Courtenay greeted the newcomer with a look of distaste. It was his turn to play in the game with Highsmith and Rotherham, but he would not allow a trifling thing like cards stop him from standing to his friend's defence. "Deal me out," he said flatly.

Once the deed was done, he came to stand beside Wolversley. The Earl's long legs and broad shoulders gave him the advantage not only of height but also weight against the pernicious Windlesham. Of course, he had no intention of using those advantages physically, unless his hand was forced, but it gave him a good deal of satisfaction to straighten himself up to his full height and watch Jonny Odd step back a little.

"How sickeningly sweet you two are," Windlesham jeered. "It's just as if we were at university all over again." And just as at university, he had his own coterie of friends sailing in on his coattails. Two other gentlemen, with a similar predilection for foppishness, sidled up to join with Windlesham in synchronized sneering.

Wolversley rolled his eyes at the immaturity on parade before him.

Courtenay took it upon himself to answer back. "Yes, and you look just as though you are still at school, Jonny Odd.

Always were a baby face, weren't you? That's why we called you Jonny Odd. Well,"—Courtenay paused to examine his fingernails—"for that and other reasons." He flicked an invisible particle of dust from his jacket cuff.

"Oh, and the taunt still stings!" The smooth-faced Windlesham mocked the attempt at insult. Done with his direct assault, he turned to Freddy Rotherham who was looking quite baffled by the recent interchange. "I am surprised your sister accepted him even in her spinsterhood." He flourished his handkerchief at the Earl. "For he lost his fortune years ago. Don't you know that's why he doesn't gamble?"

Wolversley stepped forward, seeming to double in size. His eyes darkened, and even Windlesham could not help but cower at the menace in them. "Get back to your doxy, Windlesham."

The lethal tones made both Highsmith and Freddy Rotherham sit back in their chairs. Courtenay remained unmoved, standing resolutely at his friend's shoulder.

"Why should I leave? I shall miss the utter pleasure of watching as you have to refuse this gentleman's offer of a game." Windlesham gestured at Freddy Rotherham, as if bidding him to ask Wolversley again to join them at cards.

Freddy's mouth hung open like a panting dog on a hot July day. He had realised he was caught in something quite beyond him and was now merely resigned to watch the to and fro of the conversation.

"No." Wolversley leant back on one foot and drained his glass before continuing. "You should leave because you are dishonouring me in front of my future family. I shall see you pay for it if you do not leave my presence immediately." His steady gaze took a little of the sneer off of Windlesham's face.

"It will be your loss of fine company."

"I'm sure your definition of *fine* differs quite dramatically from mine," replied the Earl, his harrowing gaze chasing the despicable man back.

Windlesham grumbled something inaudible, his face translating it as a complaint, before signaling to his lackeys and leaving the room.

There were a few moments' silence where no one knew quite what to say.

"You all right, old boy?" asked Courtenay eventually, placing a supportive hand on Wolversley's shoulder.

"Just fine." Wolversley reserved that reply for Courtenay but then turned to the rest of the gentlemen. "I believe I shall end the evening here, gentlemen." He executed a swift bow and left with no more words.

"DON'T LISTEN TO Windlesham," said Courtenay to the other two gentlemen after the Earl had left. "Load of clap-trap he's spouting—always was a devil."

"I say! Wolversley's not flying without a feather, is he?" asked Freddy Rotherham incredulously.

Highsmith's own thoughts were echoing the question, a sharp concern for Julia surfacing. What if Windlesham's claims were true and Wolversley had nary a penny to his name? Was the "compromising situation" at the Merriweather ball actually an underhanded scheme? Had he entrapped Julia into this engagement solely for the sake of her fortune?

"Good gracious, no!" Courtenay shot back. "Well, that is to say he was, years ago, not his fault either. Happened while he was at Oxford with the rest of us and Windlesham's not let him forget it. The man's a cad, the way he picks on the weaker —though that's not to say Wolversley is weaker. He proved himself strong when he dragged his estate out of dun territory. No doubt I could take some tips from him about estate management. Anyway, Jonny Odd's always been a devil to him —jealousy, I think."

"I say," was all Freddy could reply to that saga.

"When exactly was this then?" asked Highsmith, his brows creased with suspicion. "That he lost his fortune, I mean." His mind was working rapidly, trying to piece together the time-line of Wolversley's life.

"When he came of age, I believe. Some dastardly uncle of his squandered everything he was supposed to be holding in trust for Wolversley and Lady Selina. Caused the devil of a falling out and a fine mess for Wolversley to clear up. Though don't tell him I told you so."

When he came of age? Highsmith wondered how long ago that was. Could it be? Were his guesses right? Or was it willful imagining for Julia's sake? He didn't know, but he had to find out.

"I say, did you hear me, Highsmith?" Freddy Rotherham asked.

"What? Beg your pardon?"

"I said do you want another hand dealt you?"

"Er, no, thank you, I...er...." Highsmith stood. "I think I will call it a night as well. Nothing like a good night's sleep to restore one." His tone rallied at the end of his excuse. He had a mission to fulfil. He wanted to find out the truth to satisfy his own curiosity. He needed to find out the truth for dear Julia's sake.

Bidding the other two good night and thanking them for their company, Highsmith left the club, but instead of returning home, he walked in another direction entirely. He set out looking for the truth in the direction of Earl Wolversley's London home.

CHAPTER FIFTEEN

"...ruin was imminent..."

THE ROAD HAD DISINTEGRATED INTO MIRE. The rain had liquefied all the dust on the highways, and now a slick surface squelched and sucked at the feet of every passerby. The mud made travelling hard on the horses, and the incessant rain proved a source of constant irritation for the riders. The horses' coats were soaked, their underbellies covered in mud. Julia's borrowed jacket was already soaked through, the wool stiff and difficult to move in, her skin wet and cold beneath. She slowed Sheba occasionally, afraid the deeper mud would lame her mare. Julia could not help but wonder how the coach had made it through this if Sylvester and Selina had indeed come this way.

Julia and James had had no luck to the north and had now turned west in hopes that the weather had slowed the escapers as it was slowing the rescuers. Perhaps they still had a chance of catching up with them.

"They're sure to have chosen west if not the north. There's plenty o' land to get lost in those ways, and Kent would be too easy a place to get found in." James' words did much to restore Julia's low spirits.

They began trotting as the low mire gave way to a higher track. Julia had just about mastered a rather clumsy rising trot. Despite the unusual position of her legs, she was enjoying the security and freedom that riding astride was giving her. At this rate, she would never want to go back to sidesaddle.

As she concentrated on the up and forward motion, her mind raced ahead. If they had not gone north, but rather west, then what was Sylvester's intention? Surely they would have gone north if he had wanted to reach Gretna Green in the shortest amount of time? This did not bode well.

Half an hour later, the heavy pellets of rain eased a little and then thinned to a steady drizzle. The fine moisture found its way just as quickly through her brother's clothing, if not quicker. She was thankful for the greatcoat that James had lent her—at least it kept the wind at bay if not the wet. The capes flapped out behind her, and the long side panels that were intended to protect her legs from the weather failed miserably as they too were carried backwards by the wind. Her legs were nearly numb from the cold, and she knew that when she needed to dismount the leather of the buckskins would be stuck to her skin.

Despite the hope that James was displaying, Julia was falling deeper into despair. Even Sheba's forward-going strides, which defied the mare's hatred of rain, did nothing to ease Julia's fears. The time they were spending travelling was giving her time to think, to run through all the possible scenarios. Not one of them was good.

What would Wolversley say when he found out she had let his sister run away? He would jilt her again, she was sure, and she would be left once more, this time with her reputation in tatters.

It was not so long ago that she had wished that she could

escape this forced marriage. But now, the idea of the betrothal failing to come to fruition did not fill her with the relief she had expected. It left her instead with a pile of indecipherable feelings pulling her in every direction. Amongst them was the growing anxiety about the path she had taken, dressing as a boy and riding out in the middle of the night with none but her stable master. This time she really had gone too far, and if they could not find the runaways, then she would be in far more trouble than could be fixed by a speedy marriage to an Earl. Her ruin was imminent, as was the ruin of another young girl not yet out.

What if they could not find Selina? What if her fate was to be the same as that of Sylvester's other known lover, mother of a dead bastard child, with no fortune, no hope?

"Up ahead, miss!" called James from behind her.

She looked up from the path and saw the dim, flickering lights of a posting inn.

"That's the inn we're lookin' for." James brought Rufus alongside Sheba. "Now remember, miss, you're a lad. Can't go squealin' if they know nothin' 'ere, not like before. They looked at you mighty strange at the last inn when you screeched to make 'em tell you the truth. If you're not careful, word'll spread of odd goings on. You needs to try and talk like me, deep, and remember your name's David Salt."

Julia nodded, accepting the name James had given her— an insignificant first name but the stable master's own surname. Gathering their reins, they pushed forward into a careful canter and were upon the inn in minutes, the bulky Rufus slightly behind, unable to move with as much agility as Sheba. Julia was still belting forward when she heard James call her to slow. She had been leaning forward, just as she had seen her brother do, and the excitement of the chase and the lights representing her goal up ahead had overtaken her sense.

"Slow, miss. None of 'em will want to talk with us if we look 'alf mad."

Julia did as she was bid, and they both came into the yard adjacent to the inn at a respectable trot. Sodden hay and straw mixed together on the floor, giving texture to the paste of mud that had been brought in by all the other horses that evening. A miserable-looking stable lad stood in the shadows of a stall warming his cold, wet hands on the neck of a cart horse. He came reluctantly out of his sheltered position in order to greet the new arrivals.

"Sirs." He tugged at his forelock looking over both the gentlemen who appeared very much the worse for wear. His gaze paused upon Julia, and she shifted uncomfortably in her saddle.

"Lotta mud on the road?" The boy had already ascertained from the look of James that there were no lords or ladies to be worried about here, and his respectful tone had changed to the one with which he addressed his peers.

"Oi! Less o' the cheek!" barked James, used to dealing with young grooms. "My master ain't in no mood for your nonsense. He wants to know somethin'."

"Aye! Aye! No offence meant, sirs, no offence. Best make your question quick afore we gets more soaked than we already are." Though he had spoken more respectfully, he seemed unimpressed by James' reprimand.

Julia looked down at him with a little compassion. He did not even have a thick coat on and was visibly shivering.

"Answer my question, and I'll buy you a drink to warm your bones."

Even James was impressed by the masculine voice Julia had adopted.

The boy's ears pricked at the promise of a warm beverage.

"I wish to know about a particular set of persons—whether they have come through here."

"What a question! We gets a lot of *particular persons* through 'ere."

"Here." Julia tossed him a coin she had found in one of her brother's pockets. "See if that doesn't help. A gentleman and lady—"

"With no weddin' bands and not a single servant. Would they be the ones you're after?" As he finished the sentence for Julia, his face softened and his mouth broke into a broad, gap-toothed smile.

Thank the Lord for nosy servants, thought Julia ecstatically. "That'd be them. They've come through here already?"

"Better." The lad bit the coin, checking its value before giving away his last piece of information. "They're still 'ere!"

"Here? Still?" Julia threw the tails of her greatcoat over one side of Sheba and leapt off the horse, her legs almost crumpling beneath her after the hard ride.

The boy had only just pocketed his payment when Julia threw the reins at him. She steadied herself, leaning on Sheba's neck while she spoke, both horse and rider heaving with exhaustion. "Take my mare and see her stabled."

"Master!" cried James aghast. "We cannot go in alone. Now we know where they are we must fetch 'elp." He dismounted.

"No, *you* must do that. Fetch Lord Wolversley as quick as you can. I shall stay. Now they are found I cannot let them out of my sight." She came closer to James so that the stable boy would not overhear. "Tell him it is his sister and a man by the name of Sylvester. He will come."

Julia's accomplice frowned and planted his feet where he stood.

"James, please trust me. I shall do nothing if I do not need to. All that needs doing is to keep a lookout and make sure they stay until help can arrive."

"But 'ow will you do it? What will you do?"

"Only enough to keep them here. Do you have any coins?"

He tossed her a small leather coin purse that had been tucked in his coat.

"Thank you, I shall see you have double back. Now go!"

She watched him turn a tired Rufus homeward and disappear out of the stable yard into the night once more. She hoped beyond hope that Wolversley could be found and that he would somehow forgive her for this. At least she could be sure he would come for his sister's sake. That is what she was relying on. She would keep them here as long as she could without being seen and then leave the handling of Sylvester to Wolversley when he arrived. He would know what to do; he had already been ready to warn off the gentleman tomorrow. Julia thought how ironic it was that Wolversley had planned to run off the fortune hunter the day after the fortune hunter had planned to run off with his sister. Why was life never straightforward?

Turning towards the inn's back door, Julia realised in that moment that she had never been so alone in all her life. What would Lily Merriweather say if she could see her now, in a sopping wet jacket and buckskins covered with mud? Well, all was lost anyway. She might as well enjoy the scandals she was so good at creating.

Making sure the stable boy was out of sight, Julia pulled off the hat and put up the hair that had escaped during the ride. She threw off her anxieties and embraced an air of confidence as she strode across the yard and walked into the taproom. A brusque, gruff-looking innkeeper handed her the tankard of ale that she ordered. It was nearing half past two in the morning, but the innkeeper had not turned in for the night, doubtless because so many late travellers would be turning to the inn in the face of such terrible weather.

Julia surveyed the taproom, seeing more people still awake than she would have guessed. Many of them looked like her, weather-beaten and exhausted, resorting to this inn as the only alternative to the difficult travelling conditions. She chose a table in the corner by the fire, hoping to encourage warmth to return to her bones and maybe even manage to dry her clothes a little.

Ordering the tankard was a feat that she had found surprisingly easy, but drinking it was another matter. She ogled the huge flagon filled with amber liquid. She contemplated how much she *could* manage and how much would be *wise* to manage. She eventually swallowed a few bitter sips, wondering after the first one why gentlemen liked this brew so much. She owned that it was probably the same as when a debutante gingerly sipped her first champagne, until six years later she became like Julia, finishing every punch bowl in sight and swigging down champagne at every opportunity.

Across the room from Julia were two gentlemen, both dressed in fashionable, though wet, garments. She focused on her tankard but stole a few surreptitious glances in their direction, suddenly anxious that she could be recognised. She was thankful to see she did not know the gentlemen. One was eyeing her with a certain amount of inquisitiveness. She leant her elbow on the table, an action she would have been raked over the coals for at home, and attempted to cover half her face with her hand. She smiled in relief when she felt the mud smeared across her cheeks from the ride. At least they would not be able to see her smooth chin. She pulled the hat lower on her forehead and tucked in a tendril of hair that had escaped. Pretending to be a boy really was quite a lot of work.

She then looked to the other occupants in the room. Seated at the table beside her was a man she guessed was the stable master of the inn. It was not so much the appearance but rather the smell that tipped her off. He was a lean-looking fellow, fair hair poking out from beneath a cap and laughter lines showing at the corners of his eyes. You would think it was the middle of the day he looked so awake. Next to the man, on a three-legged stool, a white terrier perched, looking inquiringly at her owner with her head cocked on one side. The fair-haired man saw Julia admiring the animal. "Good for rattin', my little 'un." He winked at Julia, ruffling the black and tan ears of his ratter. The bitch wagged her tail in appreciation.

Julia smiled in return and then turned back to her tankard. She must not attract any more attention, not even pleasantries from a stranger; she was here to do a job. After twenty minutes at the table and still no sign of her quarry, she pushed back her chair and stood. Leaving her barely touched tankard, she weaved between the tables, hunching her shoulders and attempting to walk like a member of the opposite sex. She would go back to the stables and check on Sheba—and maybe while she was there, the stable boy would tell her the situation with Sylvester's carriage.

Out in the stables Sheba was happily installed in a dry box with a fresh bed of straw banked up at the sides. The mare had been rubbed down with a straw wisp, and a woolen blanket was lying over her back, soaking the rain away from her skin. She munched contentedly on hay, and if Julia had not known any better, she would not have supposed that the horse had been on a punishing midnight ride and was a few miles from home.

"She's a mighty fine 'orse. Don't see many like that comin' through 'ere."

Julia spun round, surprised by the voice intruding on her silence. She relaxed a little as she saw it was only the stable lad from earlier.

"Aye, she's a good 'un," replied Julia, using the accent she had just heard from the terrier's owner in the taproom.

The stable boy was not going away. He stood there staring at her. Perhaps he could see right through her disguise. Maybe he already knew she was a woman and was just waiting for her to admit it. After all, she had a lady's mount, and she was hardly the normal height for a man. Blast! She really could do without being found out.

"Fancy earning some money?" she asked, deflecting the attention from herself and stopping the curious stare. She needed to turn her mind back to the matter at hand.

"Always." He bestowed another gap-toothed smile on Julia.

"Excellent," she said, managing to sound both masculine and in control. "The gentleman and lady we spoke of earlier—I need you to inform me when they intend to leave, and I can't ask the innkeeper. You seem like the sort of fellow who understands the need for discretion." She played to his ego.

"O' course, sir, o' course. Well, if'n that's what you've been waitin' for, then you'd best know they asked for their carriage to be ready just a moment ago. Came for a change of 'orses, but had to wait when the lady complained of feelin' ill."

Clever, thought Julia, delighted that Selina had the sense to delay their progress. Perhaps she had already realised her mistake, which would certainly make it easier to extract her when the time came.

"We must delay them! You cannot let the carriage leave. I must wait for my man to return before they go."

"Well,"—the boy rubbed the back of his neck with a grimy hand—"I suppose I could delay 'em." He smiled wickedly, tipping his cap back to expose more of his grubby, grinning face. "After all, the stable master put me in charge of the 'orses tonight. He won't be out o' the taproom again." He puffed his chest out proudly like a cockerel.

"Good. You'll be rewarded handsomely, but for now...." Julia flicked another coin over to him, this time from the purse James had lent her.

"Thank'ee kindly. Though, I best warn you, the gent's mighty bad tempered. Already been shoutin' 'bout leavin' and been ignorin' the lady's illness. 'E only gave in 'cos the innkeeper offered food to the woman to make 'er feel better. So's I don't think 'e'll stand to be kept waitin' for long."

Julia understood the warning. All she could do now was wait, and that's what she did. She returned to the taproom, and she prayed over her tankard of ale.

HIGHSMITH WAS ALMOST upon Wolversley. His chase had commenced as soon as he left the club, and he was closing in upon his quarry at last. The Earl was just mounting the steps of his London home when Highsmith came within speaking range. Finally, he could get the answers that he wanted to know—that Julia sorely *needed* to know. Highsmith raised his hand, intending to hail Wolversley, but a great commotion behind him stopped the salute.

The Earl heard it too. He paused on the steps and turned in the direction of the noise. The clattering was getting louder. Hooves were striking cobblestones in rapid motion. A man's voice was urging his horse forward. Highsmith and Wolversley both strained their eyes. The drizzle and mist had formed a curtain across the road, and neither gentleman could see the approaching beast and rider.

It did not take long, however, for the curtain to be ripped in two and for a madman on a horse to appear. Metal shoes clashed and slid against the stone of the road, and Highsmith was sure he saw sparks flash from the collisions. The clattering reverberated off the walls of the surrounding buildings until the rider began to slow his mount, coming to an abrupt and grateful halt between Highsmith, who still stood on the pavement, and the Earl who stood on his steps.

Highsmith watched the man, who was soaked and muddied, drop from his saddle and approach his lordship.

The fellow's legs were shaking as he walked, a clear sign of exhaustion, but even so, he broke out into a jog in order that he might meet the object of his journey more swiftly.

"What the devil?" muttered Wolversley under his breath. His long legs took him back down the stairs with a single step. "What in blue hell is going on here?"

Highsmith, standing not ten yards away, shifted where he stood, and Wolversley, looking past the groom, caught sight of the motion. "And what the devil are *you* doing here?"

Highsmith hurried over to the steps. "I was wanting an interview with your lordship—but who is this gentleman?"

"Lord Wolversley?" questioned James, pulling off his sopping hat, a spare since Julia had his usual one. He twisted it with his fingers, wringing out a small cascade of water.

"Yes? Out with it! What do you want from me?"

"I say, James?" said Highsmith, finally recognizing the man through all the mud. "Is that you?

"Oh, Mr. Highsmith, thank the Lord in heaven! Miss Rotherham sent me to his lordship. She says a man by the name of Sylvester has run off with a girl. Your sister, my lord." James did not meet Wolversley's eye. "They're stopped for a while and she asks your help."

He panted a little and then, catching his breath, gave the address to the Earl. He seemed eager to explain all the events of his waterlogged ride—how they had stopped at a posting inn north of London, failed to find their quarry, and then struck out again to the west. That is what had taken them so long to catch up with the runaways, but thankfully, they had still been at the posting inn. The return trip had taken James far less time, now that he knew where he was going.

"Good heavens!" declared Highsmith.

"Apt words," Wolversley responded. He made no response to the stable master but instead leapt up the steps two at a time and rapped on the door.

Fitz cracked the door open, shocked by the thunderous knocking and barely able to maintain his composure. He was relieved to see his master.

"A horse, and be quick about it!" Wolversley bellowed.

The butler needed no other encouragement than the wild light in his master's eyes. He scurried off to rouse the stable boy without so much as a questioning glance.

"Lend me a horse, Wolversley!" cried Highsmith. "I'm coming too, darn it!" It sounded like the worst kind of trouble, and he was not about to go quietly home and lie in bed wondering if Wolversley had been able to sort it out.

"Make it two horses!" Wolversley shouted to the back of his retreating servant, not bothering to argue with Highsmith.

"An' what shall I do?" asked James looking back and forth between the two men.

Highsmith shrugged. Wolversley surveyed the big red horse and the stable master. Both looked exhausted.

"Go home, but stay awake. We will be bringing back my sister before first light and may need you. Not a word to any of the other servants, understood?"

"Yes, my lord, and Miss Rotherham, what about 'er?" he asked.

The question was simple enough, but it rocked both gentlemen to their foundations.

"Miss Rotherham?" exclaimed Highsmith. "You mean to tell me she is at the posting inn too?"

"Yes, sir, she would not be stopped from goin', no matter 'ow much I argued with 'er. Once we found 'em she sent me back. She wouldn't come back without Lady Selina, sir."

Highsmith turned to look at Wolversley and saw the Earl's well-schooled jaw fall open in shock. If anything, he seemed even more upset at the news that Julia was at the inn than the first revelation that his sister had run off with Sylvester.

"Very well," said the Earl, recovering command of his

voice, his face, and his feelings. "We will be bringing back Miss Rotherham too."

Highsmith was glad of the certainty in Wolversley's voice and glad that the weight of this expedition had not fallen solely on *him*.

While they waited for the horses, Wolversley ascertained the best route to take from the Rotherham groom. "You've done well, James, and I know you are spent. But may I ask you to stay awake a little longer? We will need to get into the house again without the other servants knowing. I suppose Mr. and Mrs. Rotherham are still abed?"

"Yes, my lord."

Highsmith snorted. It was just like Julia to go running off without telling her parents.

Wolversley seemed to have expected as much. "Rouse them when you get back. They will have to know of this—there is no way to hide it from them, for I am sure they will wake when we arrive. I will need their counsel as to how to keep this hushed up."

James nodded. He bid the gentlemen good night before turning back to an exhausted Rufus who looked ready to drop. The gelding had carried on even when he had turned lame upon hitting the cobbled London streets once again. James stroked his nose gently as they walked and then ran a hand along his neck and kept it resting there as the animal plodded homeward.

Wolversley watched him for a moment, thinking how much he would like a stable master like James tending his own horses. "We'll need to change," he said abruptly.

Highsmith looked down at his pumps and satin breeches. Changing clothes might seem like a waste of time in the face of such urgency, but he acknowledged that he could never bring himself to ride a horse in the clothes he was wearing.

"You can borrow buckskins and a pair of riding boots

from me." Wolversley was already walking into the house, casting that last sentence over his shoulder as he went.

By the time they had dressed and come back downstairs, the horses were ready. Highsmith looked rather ridiculous in an evening jacket, buckskins and top boots, but he had a greatcoat, also borrowed from Wolversley, to cover the whole and somewhat salvage his dignity. The Earl himself was looking even more gauche. He had discarded his evening attire entirely and carelessly thrown on a pair of buckskins, shirt sans cravat, and a greatcoat. He pulled his boots on and snatched up his riding whip.

"We must be quick!" said Wolversley, flinging himself into the saddle. His horse responded to his urgency, half-rearing at the pressure of the Earl's legs and bounding forward into a canter. Highsmith followed in quick pursuit, and when the two had left the narrower streets behind, they faced the open road that led out of London and toward what might prove a most interesting situation.

CHAPTER SIXTEEN

"...that odd time just before sunrise."

"They won't stay no longer," Julia's spy whispered to her across the table. "The gent's tryin' to get the lady to leave now."

Julia had hoped and prayed Wolversley would arrive before Sylvester decided to leave, but the moment was upon her and all that stood between Selina and her ruin was Julia. She nodded to the lad in thanks for the information.

"You want 'elp, sir?"

"No." Julia managed the faintest of grateful smiles. She could not let anyone see Selina properly. That would risk the gossip-mongers' wagging tongues, and that would be the end of her ladyship's reputation. Julia had to keep this matter secret and arrange things as quietly as possible. "Thank you for the help you've already given me." She flashed a brief smile.

"O' course. We don't gets a lot of this 'eighty-flighty stuff. It's quite fun." He gave another gap-toothed smile.

"Saddle my mare, will you?" Julia asked. Best to be prepared in case she needed to make a quick getaway with

Selina. She wasted no time thinking about the fact she had never ridden astride with another person on the same horse before!

"Are you goin' to drink that?" asked the boy, eyeing the tankard of ale.

"No, you can have it after you direct me to their room."

"S'the private parlour—through there." The boy waved a grubby hand towards a corridor off the taproom and then brought the hand back to rest on the handle of the tankard. By the time Julia had risen, the boy had already swigged half the liquid down.

The taproom was quieter now. It was nearly half past three in the morning. The innkeeper was out the back, probably snoozing propped up between the barrels of ale. The two gentlemen who had been watching Julia with interest had moved on, and the stable master was dozing, his head laid across the table, his white dog laid out like a slug at his feet.

Julia breathed. What exactly was she going to do? What if Selina didn't want to come home? Surely she would if Sylvester was being a brute, but what if they had made up since they had been here? What if that was why they were now leaving?

Focus! Focus!

"Have you finished with that?" Julia asked the stable boy.

The stable boy, who had guzzled the ale with what seemed like supernatural speed, nodded, the amber liquid still lining his lips. Julia picked up the tankard and walked through the taproom.

Her boot heels clicked on the wooden floor. She focused on putting one foot in front of the other. She clutched the metal tankard. It could prove useful...as an excuse, or as a weapon. The control she exercised over her breathing stilled the shaking of her hands. She drew her shoulders back and headed down the corridor, readying herself for confrontation.

Half candles flickered in the wall holders, burning low at this hour. Black soot stains ran up behind the wax obelisks like permanent shadows on the wattle and daub walls, stretching all the way to the roof of the ancient building. A floorboard squeaked underfoot, a lone sound in the sleeping establishment.

Julia paused before the parlour door, her hand upon the handle. She took one last breath to gather her courage. In that instant, she heard the sound of hooves far off. The boy was getting the carriage ready. She must act now.

Turning the handle, she threw the door open and stepped into the well-lit room. From the corner of her eye, she caught sight of a slender, cloaked figure seated in a chair in the corner. There was no time to look more closely, however, to see if the girl was happy or distressed, for directly in front of Julia was Sylvester, pacing the room like an angry lion.

He turned his cold and merciless eyes upon the intruder. "Is the carriage ready yet, brat?" he demanded of the mud-spattered boy before him. "I've been waiting a cursed long while!" His coat was flared open, and his bony hands were resting on his hips, his fingers curved like talons.

Julia faltered a little before the sneering menace in his face.

"Come!" He spun round without waiting for an answer, gesturing to the girl in the corner. Despite his command, she did not turn. From the shaking of her shoulders, Julia could see that she was probably crying.

The sight of Selina in such distress filled Julia with the courage she needed. Indignation broke out inside her like a wildfire, and she stepped into the room and shut the door.

"What the blazes is the meaning of this?" demanded Sylvester, shock and anger heightening the pitch of his voice.

"Sir." Julia lifted her hand from the door handle and bestowed an unflinching gaze upon the gentleman. "I know who you are and what it is you intend. But that girl"—she pointed to the cloaked and hooded creature—"is in my safe-keeping, and you shall release her to me now."

"You cheeky young upstart! Who do you think you are?"

"Her safekeeper, as I have already said. Release her."

"I shall do no such thing! You think I am abducting her? She came with me of her own volition. I have never seen you before. Who are you to interfere?"

"Please, Mr. Sylvester! Please let me go!" The girl turned her teary, reddened face towards her lover-turned-captor.

Julia gasped, arrested by first the voice and then the face. "Annabelle?" she cried, watching the hood of the girl's cloak drop and the golden curls of her own sister's hair fall out about her shoulders.

"What's going on?" shouted Sylvester, looking from the muddy stable boy to Annabelle, trying to discern both the reason for the boy's bewilderment and for his knowledge of the lady's name.

Annabelle looked even more puzzled than Sylvester. She stared at the boy who was coming to her rescue, her eyes slowly narrowing. Julia could see the truth was not far from her grasp.

"Leave the lady and be gone!" commanded Julia, but the theatrics did nothing to promote her cause.

"You cannot stop me, boy. Annabelle, we're leaving! Now!"

"I don't want to!" whimpered Annabelle. "Oh, please, just leave me, Mr. Sylvester. This has all been a terrible mistake." Her bosom heaved with sobs as she turned to Julia. "He has been so cruel. Please take me home." Her blue eyes pleaded with Julia, fresh tears coating her pale cheeks.

"Well, quite frankly, Annabelle, I did warn you!" snapped Julia, her motherly tendencies getting the better of her common sense. "I mean, I only came thinking it was Selina! Honestly, I expected better from you, you silly girl!"

"Selina? What?" Sylvester was becoming more and more confused by this stable boy who had taken it upon himself to scold his captive.

"Do not let me begin with you!" Julia turned her muddy face on Sylvester. "I warned you off, you awful crusty beau! I know all of your evil misdeeds. Did you think it would be easy the second time you tried to ruin a lady of quality?"

"Ruin me?" whispered Annabelle. "But you promised me marriage—you said you loved me!"

"Oh, you are so naïve, Annabelle!" exclaimed Julia in exasperation. "He is after the fortune that will be bestowed on you when you are wed. And now that he has stolen you away, he no longer has to make any pretence of loving you."

Annabelle, starting to understand, turned furious blue eyes towards Sylvester. "So that is why you have been asking all those questions and have been so cruel and angry when I have not answered. You awful man!" A flicker of defiance was finally visible through Annabelle's wet-goose exterior.

"Silence, you fool!" cried Sylvester, frustrated with the strange turn of events. "Who are you, you cretin?" He turned his evil gaze on Julia. "When did you warn me off?"

She was standing firm at the door, waiting for Sylvester to make a move. The handle of the tankard she held behind her back was digging into her palm. She was clutching it so tightly her knuckles were turning white. Her eyes darted to Annabelle, warning her to stay where she was. If Sylvester did anything, Julia would attempt to bash him over the head.

Sylvester was just about to make a lunge for Annabelle— doubtless to drag her out of the parlour kicking and screaming —when the sound of raised voices in the hall made all three of the room's occupants pause and prick up their ears.

"At last!" Julia whispered in relief.

Sylvester began to panic. Whoever this boy was and whatever the noise was outside, it did not bode well for his schemes.

He was caught in the devil of a bind. He did the only thing he could, and snatching at Annabelle's arm, he hauled her towards the door.

"Stop!" cried Julia, raising the tankard, ready to hit him.

Sylvester was too fast for her. He brought his free arm up and delivered a blow to Julia's mouth. It sent her reeling backwards towards the door just as it swung open.

WOLVERSLEY, WHO HAD woken the innkeeper from his snooze in the larder, threatened him with a harsh thrashing if he did not tell him where the lady and gentleman without wedding bands were. The innkeeper complied and pointed down the hallway where the Earl could find his quarry.

Wolversley flung open the door, ready to charge in and attack. He was put a little out of kilter by a young man reeling backwards towards him. Thinking him a lackey of Sylvester's, Wolversley stuck out his leg to trip the lad. It did the trick, and the boy hit the floor in a crumpled mess. He looked up from the lad only to be confronted with the fleeing form of Sylvester.

Now it was Highsmith's turn. As the fortune hunter barged past the Earl, Highsmith greeted him with a hard right facer, followed by a smart uppercut that sent him down to the floor out cold. A moment of stillness descended after the rapid confrontation, and the two gentlemen stood together looking about the desecrated room.

Highsmith was the first to locate the origin of the shrieking. "Annabelle, kindly shut your bone box!"

The girl obliged, minimizing her screams to a pathetic sniveling.

"Better." He walked over to her stunned person. "Now,

we understood it was Lady Selina, not you, who eloped with Sylvester."

"No." Annabelle gulped and sniffed. "She begged me not to go. At first she helped by letting me have the same mask as hers at Vauxhall to trick you all, but after she realised her brother was telling the truth, she begged me not to carry on with him. She... she knew I had a message from Sylvester and I was to run away, but when I showed it to her she threatened to tell Mama and Papa. I told her not to tell, or I would be beastly to her, so then she followed me to the door." She sniveled again. "I *was* beastly to her." Another bout of tears ensued. "I locked her in a cupboard."

Highsmith's eyebrows shot up at that—locked her up? Well, he hoped that Selina had been liberated by now. Instead of reprimanding Annabelle, however, he chose to calm her as she seemed to be nearing hysterics. "Now, now," he said, patting her shoulder. "You are safe and I'm sure Lady Selina will forgive you." There were more important things to sort out. "But, Annabelle, you must tell me, where is your sister? We were given to understand she was here."

"Where is she?" Wolversley's voice, harsh and panicked, echoed Highsmith's.

Annabelle raised a shaking finger to point at the unconscious heap of boy on the floor. "I...I think *he's* Julia."

"What madness?" Highsmith stared at Annabelle as though the affair had addled her senses.

Meanwhile, Wolversley bent down to examine the boy. He made a choking noise when he turned the lad's face into view. "Julia!" he shouted, pulling her boy-clad form into his arms and frantically checking for breathing.

"What?" cried Highsmith.

"It's Julia," said Annabelle. "She must have disguised herself to come and find me." Her explanation was surprisingly coherent, considering her tearful state.

Highsmith, who by now understood, felt rage boiling inside him. "You bloody fool!" he shouted at Wolversley who was still trying to revive Julia by pouring the contents of his hip flask down her throat. "I'll give you a drubbing you won't recover from, you insolent dog!" He ran over to Wolversley, yanking him to his feet and striking him hard across the face. The Earl staggered backwards but made sure not to tread on Julia who was still lying on the floor.

Annabelle slid from her chair and, avoiding the cockfight, crawled along the floor to her sister's side. Once there she began crying over her sister, moaning about how she had caused Julia's death.

"How dare you!" shouted Highsmith. "You've always caused her harm. I'll send you to Old Scratch, mark my words!" He was flinging blows wildly now, but the Earl was not fighting back.

"And the devil may have me, but first, let me attend to—" Another hard blow knocked Wolversley almost off his feet.

"And you were to marry her with no fortune to keep her? Planning on battening off her inheritance? You're no better than Sylvester!"

"What?" Wolversley blocked the next blow, skirting a table and crossing over to the other side of the room.

"First you jilt her, and then, not content with trampling on her heart, you throw her on the floor and trample her!" Highsmith lunged.

"I had no idea it was her," said Wolversley, dodging, "and neither did you."

"You never did care for her." In came another right hook.

Wolversley caught Highsmith's arm this time and threw him backwards with it. Whilst his opponent was off balance, the Earl used the opportunity to answer the charge. "I forbid you to speak of what you don't understand." His voice rang clear and strong through the room.

As this battle was raging across the parlour of the old inn, Julia's eyes fluttered open under the refreshing shower of her sister's tears.

"Oh, thank goodness, I didn't kill you." Annabelle threw her arms around Julia sobbing into her brother's clothes.

It took a few moments for Julia to gather her wits, but once she did, she immediately shrugged out of Annabelle's embrace and rose unsteadily to her feet. After the blow she had suffered, the warm brandy Wolversley had dosed her with must have been doing a good deal to keep her vertical—that and her downright indignation. Despite the purple bruise on her jaw, she still managed to shout at the sparring pair. "For goodness sake! Stop fighting like children!"

Both gentlemen instantly forgot each other and turned to the voice of authority. Julia was, needless to say, quite a sight, and fists were quickly forgotten. With drying blood staining a line from her nose to chin, mud mingling with the scarlet, and her hair finally escaping from James' hat, she was the strangest looking boy that ever existed.

"Now that I have your attention," said Julia, directing the gentlemen's gaze to Annabelle whose mouth hung open like a goldfish's, "I believe there is a young girl here who needs to be returned home before morning dawns on this fiasco of an elopement."

"Yes," agreed Highsmith, his sense finally returning to him. Whatever disagreements he had with Wolversley could be resolved later, once Julia and Annabelle were safe.

"And I trust you gentlemen know what to do with that creature?" Julia pointed disgustedly at Sylvester who had not yet regained consciousness.

Wolversley and Highsmith, still stunned by Julia's sudden resurrection from unconsciousness, looked at each other and then back to Julia, nodding.

"Good," she said. "Excellent." Highsmith watched her put

a hand to her head and had a premonition that she was about to topple. "Hmm." She grasped at the wall to steady herself. "Yes, good...."

The adrenaline that had been coursing through her body since midnight, the hard blows she had taken upon coming here, and now the brandy all merged together. Her legs crumpled beneath her, and she slid quietly to the floor. Highsmith nearly raced to catch her, but somebody was before him. Before she fell, the Earl was at her side again. He caught hold of her and laid her head gently against his arm.

Highsmith could see Wolversley murmuring into Julia's ear and then stroking the wild hair from her face. With her legs tucked beneath her like that and her body at such a queer angle, it could not be comfortable. Highsmith cast about for a soft, flat surface.

"Here, lay her here." He pulled cushions to one end of an old, battered window seat to create a makeshift bed for the invalid.

Wolversley already had a hand beneath Julia's head; he slipped his other arm under her knees and raised her small frame with little effort from the floor. He walked to the bay window of the old parlour and placed her gingerly on the bench, kneeling beside her to check her breathing and feel her forehead.

"Is she bad?" asked Highsmith, filled with concern and a little jealousy. He was reminded of another fall that Julia had had, although that time *he* had been the one at her side and Wolversley the onlooker.

Wolversley did not answer straight away and paused a moment to massage her temples. "I do not think so. When she fell to the floor, she must have hit her head. If she wakes soon, we will have no need to worry."

"For Annabelle's sake, and her own, I hope she does. We cannot take her back in this state."

"I will fetch some water and rags to wash the mud from her face," said Annabelle, for the first time in many days deciding to be a help rather than a hindrance.

Highsmith watched as Annabelle took a last look at Julia's sleeping face before she rose from her side to search for the innkeeper. It was painfully comical how much the two girls could bicker and fight, but the moment one of them was in trouble, all hatred melted away as if it had never been there. Annabelle's golden curls fell forward as she rose, the perfect contrast to Julia's dark tresses, and Highsmith realised with a start that Annabelle—pesky, annoying little Annabelle—had become quite a beauty.

Wolversley had not turned from Julia, nor would he. The mud and the blood caking her face seemed no deterrent to him, and Highsmith speculated that the hounds of hell could not drag him from her side now. He had been murmuring to her constantly, too low for Highsmith to hear, but loud enough for the sleeping Julia.

What could he be saying to her? A recitation of stories from their shared youth? A declaration of how his heart stood?

"You still love her." Highsmith spoke quietly to the Earl's back.

Wolversley did not answer aloud. He nodded, short and quick, without moving from his station.

"I loved her too," Highsmith offered, not truly understanding why he did so.

"I know," replied Wolversley.

"But she loves you." It took Highsmith all of his pride to acknowledge it, but the truth had to be said.

The men remained silent after this exchange. Highsmith watched the Earl continue to speak to Julia and stroke her hair. He was a man clearly distraught. When Highsmith had first met the Earl, he would never have imagined him like this—he would have detested him outright if he had known. Seeing him now, he could not help but admire the man. His love for Julia was unquestionable. They loved each other, though each was unsure of the other's feelings, and there was nothing Highsmith could do to come between them. She was not Highsmith's love to claim. He knew that she never had been. And despite the fact that any remnants of his own hopes for a future with Julia were now dashed, he only wished that Julia could waken now to realise that her feelings for the Earl were reciprocated.

Annabelle came back then, having regained her composure and chattering nineteen to the dozen. "The innkeeper's wife was most helpful. She had woken and heard the shouting and was sure someone would be shot, so she had already put some water on to heat. Fancy that? Very sensible of her. She was ever so nice to me. She gave me these fresh rags, torn from an old sheet, and has sent the other guests back to bed."

"Well done, Annabelle," Highsmith responded, making the girl glow after her night of failures. "You did not mention anything about...?"

"Do not be absurd! I may have been silly enough to run away, but I said nothing of who we were. In fact, I made her believe we were a feuding family with star-crossed lovers who had run away from Kent and were caught this side of London."

Highsmith's eyebrows rose in surprise at Annabelle's ingenuity, but he was still sceptical. "That will only raise her suspicions."

"Well, I thought of that, but asking for hot water and rags does raise the suspicions anyway, as well as all that shouting, so I thought the best thing was to offer her an explanation and even better if it weren't the true one."

"You are a minx!" Highsmith said smiling. He took the pot of hot water and carried it over to Julia for her.

At first, Wolversley refused to move. He motioned for Annabelle to hand him the rags and water, but Annabelle shook her head. She had caused her sister all this trouble, and she would be the one to clean her up. Wolversley eventually gave in but directed Annabelle to be careful around Julia's jaw which was already swelling into a dark bruise where Sylvester had struck her.

As the men looked on, Annabelle dipped one of the rags into the steaming water, wrung it out, and then ever so gently began to dab and rub away the mud. She was careful, Highsmith observed, to change the cloth often, saving Julia's skin from being rubbed raw by the grit in the dirt. Slowly, a small section at a time, Julia's face was revealed, and the brown colour was transferred from her skin to the water in the pot.

When Annabelle was close to finishing, Wolversley finally looked away as if he could stand it no longer. He paced around the room, bringing his hands up to rake them through his hair. Highsmith could see the thought in his wild eyes—what if she did not wake up?

He had his own thought that he had been mulling over—ever since his conversation with Courtenay at White's. He had seen that Wolversley truly did love Julia, but there were other considerations besides love that counted for something.

"Wolversley, a word?"

The Earl was in no mood for words.

"Please, my lord?" Highsmith pushed him. "Just one question."

Wolversley acquiesced, and Highsmith drew him to the far side of the room away from the two women.

"The interview I sought this evening—the reason I was at your house when James rode up—I would not feel I had done my duty in protecting Julia if I did not seek the answer I came for. You clearly love her, so why did you jilt her in the first place? And then, later, did you purposely contrive matters to become betrothed to her again? Are you marrying her, in part, because of your lack of fortune?"

"That is three questions."

"I push my luck, but I must know. Julia must know."

Wolversley rubbed his chin. "My uncle...." He paused. Highsmith could tell how difficult this was for him to say. "My uncle was entrusted with my inheritance after my father died. It was not just mine, it was also Selina's wedding dowry—all was in his care. When I came of age, I found that my uncle had abused the trust my father had placed in him. He had found a clause in the will that allowed him to access the bulk of our inheritances, and he had done it to great effect. Selina's wedding dowry and most of my fortune had been squandered on his gambling habits and wild living.

"I found this out shortly after we had become engaged, and I had left her for a time to pursue my studies at Oxford. I could not marry Julia with no way to support her, and—you seem to know her character well—do you really think she would have agreed to break off the engagement if I had told her why? No, she would have insisted on accompanying me into my poverty, my ruin. I had to protect her from my own shame, my own disgrace."

The resentment Highsmith had been fostering against the Earl now disappeared completely. In its place a respect for the man which he had not thought possible was forming.

"I spent years building my fortune back up," continued Wolversley. "I never stopped thinking of Julia, but I knew that until I recovered my standing in the world's eyes, I could not speak, and once I did that, it would almost certainly be too late. I did not expect to be welcomed back. I assumed she would marry someone else.

"When I attended the Rotherhams' ball on coming back to Town, the truth is, I had no idea who the host was. I came as Courtenay's friend. I had no way of knowing I would see

Julia there, and when I did, I saw the marks of the pain I had caused her, the scar left upon her by my own hand. I wanted to tell her the truth—I tried so many times—but she would not listen. I did not deserve that she should.

"Then she hatched that plan with you, and everything began to go wrong. I never meant to compromise her—I never meant for us to be betrothed. But circumstances conspired against us, and I was forced to offer for her, just as she was forced to accept me. Before, I had her love but no fortune to support her with. Now, I have my fortune, but I am afraid that love is gone. I will have wronged her twice now, once by jilting her and once by marrying her. But no, to answer your question, I am no fortune hunter, at least, not for one that does not belong to me."

WOLVERSLEY'S TONE WAS incredibly bleak as the truth that had been pent up so long finally burst out into the open. He felt relief that someone finally knew—even though that someone was not Julia—but at the same time, an overwhelming sense of sorrow. "Does that satisfy you?" he asked Highsmith.

The other had no time to reply, for at that moment, Annabelle turned joyfully towards them and announced that Julia was awake. Both Wolversley and Highsmith rushed to her side, but Wolversley noted that her eyes were fixed on his face alone. Had she heard what he had said?

A sudden shyness sprang up inside him. "Are you all right, Miss Rotherham?" he said, using her proper name and then realizing how ridiculous that was, considering the circumstances.

Julia tried to sit up, and six hands reached out to help her. "Thank you! Thank you! I am quite all right," she said, shooing away the assistance they offered. Despite her words, her hand flew to her forehead, and she wavered a moment. "Annabelle, are *you* all right?"

The younger sister clutched Julia's hand, tears rimming her eyes. "I am all right, thanks to you, dear sister."

Julia smiled, and Wolversley noted that now, without the mud and blood covering her face, she looked quite like her old self again, albeit somewhat pale and dressed in boy's clothes.

"Where's Sylvester?" she asked.

The question caused the other three occupants of the room to whip round in alarm and give a collective sigh when they realised the man still lay unconscious on the floor. They had not spared him a thought in the commotion surrounding Julia.

"A very good point, Jules," said Highsmith. "We must decide what to do with Sylvester before he comes to and tries to hop the twig."

"I have a fair idea of my own," said Wolversley, "but we need a way to wake him."

"I have just the thing," Annabelle chimed in, picking up the pot of muddy water that had now turned lukewarm. She beamed a devilish smile at the two gentlemen and passed them the pot. "After you."

"Excellent." Wolversley returned her smile as he took the pot from her, and with a quick, jerky movement he dashed the contents over the sleeping Sylvester.

It was with a great deal of pleasure that the two gentlemen and two ladies watched the victim wake, shocked and dazed and half-soaked in the muddy water.

"What the...!" Sylvester cursed, and coughed, and spluttered, the powder on his face streaking into the rouge.

"Glad to see you have decided to join us in the land of the conscious once again." Highsmith's cheerful tones were at odds with the freezing look he was bestowing on the man.

"Sylvester,"—Wolversley looked down at the blinking victim who was struggling to sit up and continued with Highsmith's train of thought—"it seems you have underestimated the protection which this lady enjoys." The Earl's eyes turned dark and his voice hard. "I give you fair warning—if I ever see your face again or hear that you have spoken of tonight's events to anyone, my pistol will have found its next target, and I shall offer no mercy."

"And do not think Lord Wolversley stands alone," Highsmith added, broadening his shoulders as he stood beside the Earl. Wolversley heard Highsmith's words with satisfaction. There was a distinct possibility that this fellow and he were becoming...friends?

Sylvester froze at the Earl's menacing words. Droplets of water dripped down his long, thin face depositing his face powder on his dark jacket. Comprehension dawned in his eyes. He had supposed the Rotherham family an easy mark, assuming it would only be Freddy Rotherham with whom he would have to contend, but at the sight of Wolversley's inescapable, fury-filled gaze, fear began creeping its way into every part of his body.

"Now, Sylvester," Wolversley barked. "I believe that is your cue to leave."

The fortune hunter scrambled to his feet, and Highsmith's last words followed him out—"I shall be round to your lodgings in the morning. You'd best have gone."

As Sylvester's loathsome figure disappeared, the remaining four realised that they would need to depart as well, and as soon as possible. The parlour of the inn was in a state; there was a chair knocked over, an empty tankard on the floor, and muddy water spattering the rug.

"I must pay off the innkeeper," said Wolversley, certain that that was the best thing to be done.

"I'll come with you," said Annabelle, wishing to return

the pot and the rags to the innkeeper's wife, and Wolversley marched from the room with her in tow.

As she scurried down the corridor beside the striding Earl, Annabelle spilled out her gratitude. "I want to thank you for rescuing me—for rescuing us both. I know you probably thought it was Selina, as Julia did, but thank you anyway."

"Your servant," said Wolversley, without abating his step.

"I know you love her."

The Earl's step faltered.

"It's clear."

"To everyone but her," said Wolversley dryly.

"That's because she thinks she knows best. Well, she did tonight, but she doesn't always."

Wolversley did not reply but thought on Annabelle's words as he paid the innkeeper and asked for their horses to be made ready.

The young stable boy, who was still awake, came belting over to the taproom bar. "I 'eard the barney. Is the mister all right?"

Wolversley looked puzzled for a moment.

"'E told me to make you wait,"—he gestured to Annabelle—"an' then 'e said 'e would go in an' 'andle it, but 'e was tiny— no match for that nasty gent."

"Aye," said Wolversley, cottoning on. "The young man is fine. Took a bash to the chin, but that was all."

The stable boy grinned. "'E gave me 'is ale 'e did. I'll get your 'orses ready in a jiff!" With that he bounded off.

On returning to the parlour, Wolversley and Annabelle saw that Julia was up on her feet but was having to be heavily supported by Highsmith.

"Blast this dizziness!" she said in an unladylike manner. "How am I to sit on Sheba if I feel like I am constantly at sea?"

Wolversley came to her side and took her weight from Highsmith, putting one arm firmly about her waist. "The horses are being readied. Miss Annabelle, gather anything you brought with you. We must leave nothing which can be identified. Then, Highsmith, you take her outside. She can ride on your horse, and I'll take Miss Rotherham."

Highsmith nodded, leaving Julia in Wolversley's care without any reluctance now that he finally knew the truth.

Wolversley began to help Julia to the door. Her chin lifted as she argued with him for the sake of arguing. "I probably could ride Sheba, you know."

"I don't doubt you'd try, but this time you will do as I tell you."

Surprisingly, Julia made no complaint at being ordered about so brusquely. Perhaps it was nice to have someone else making the decisions after such a long night of making them herself.

The horses were standing saddled in the yard by the time Wolversley and Julia made it outside. The innkeeper, patting the coin purse next to his breast, was happy to maintain his silence on the night's events, and his wife was just happy the inn had not been the site of some casualty in an illegal duel.

It took Highsmith only half a minute to lift Annabelle up onto his borrowed horse and climb up behind her. The stable boy threw him Sheba's reins, the mare now irritated at being tossed out of bed twice in one night, and Highsmith caught them, ready to lead the riderless mare home.

Wolversley and Julia took a little longer to mount. The stable boy was helping with the Earl's horse when he caught sight of Julia's freshly washed face and the bruise purpling her jawline. The boy's eyes widened.

"I knew it!" he exclaimed in undertones.

Julia managed to wink at the boy as Wolversley hoisted her onto his pommel. She pushed her first finger to her lips, and the stable boy nodded. The admiration in his eyes would linger for a while after the riders departed, admiration for the strangest, bravest woman he had ever met.

Wolversley mounted up behind Julia, placing his arms either side of her to hold the reins. He thought on Highsmith and Annabelle's words. They had both said it—surely they could not both be wrong. Julia loved him. The thought of it, and the feel of her body snug between his arms felt right. He would not let her get away again.

Dawn was not far away, and it was imperative that they returned before it broke over the London rooftops. Highsmith tipped his hat to the innkeeper, and then Wolversley followed suit as they turned their horses homewards.

The ride home was marginally slower due to the doubling up of riders, but they still moved at a fair pace. The rain had stopped now, and though the road was muddy, the surroundings were quiet in that odd time just before sunrise when nature stills itself, as though poised in readiness for the next day. Julia sighed and, finally allowing her exhaustion to overtake her, leaned back onto Wolversley's chest and slept.

CHAPTER SEVENTEEN

"...impetuous and headstrong."

THE LATE HOURS OF THE EARLY morning had been a series of tearful reunions and halfhearted reprimands. Even Mr. Rotherham's eyes had become misty, though he later denied it fervently. Highsmith and Wolversley had been thanked and thanked and thanked again. Mrs. Rotherham embraced them, Mr. Rotherham shook their hands, and Annabelle laid a tearful kiss upon their cheeks.

The gentlemen had not been able to stay long, however, since the dawn light was hastening to break over the horizon, and they could not be seen here if the scandal was to be snuffed out. They had left, each for their own bed, Wolversley sending a lingering gaze back at Julia who was being supported up the stairs by her maid Lucy.

"Tomorrow," Mr. Rotherham had said to him, patting him on the shoulder. "Come back tomorrow and see us, my lord."

The following morning in the Rotherham household was a slow one. Since most of the occupants of the house had been awake at some point during the night, none were overly keen to rise from their beds when the sun finally came up. Even Mr. and Mrs. Rotherham, who had waited up with Lady Selina for the return of the rescuers and rescued, had deigned to stay in bed until late. James had been as good as his word and roused the necessary parties when he had returned last night, though it had taken some time to find Lady Selina, whom Annabelle had locked in a hall cupboard during her escape. James had released her, and when she saw Mr. and Mrs. Rotherham and the truth was revealed, they assured her that she was not to blame for what had transpired and that Annabelle would be roundly reprimanded for her horrid behaviour. This promised action had not been necessary, however, as Annabelle, upon her return, had tearfully apologised and begged forgiveness from her friend. With enough dramatic events having taken place to last him the rest of the year, James had retired, and for his troubles, he had been given the day off.

Most of the occupants of the house gathered in the morning room after breakfast, though the Rotherham daughters were still abed. Mrs. Rotherham and Selina sat side by side, the former frequently turning to smile and pat the hand of the latter in motherly affection.

Mr. Rotherham was also feeling the effects of yesterday's events. Behind his customary book he was still marveling at the tenacity of his eldest daughter and the good fortune they had all enjoyed in having everyone back at the house, safe and without the breath of scandal. It was a miracle. It was not just Julia who had worked wonders last night—they could never repay what Wolversley, or Highsmith, had done for the family. Mr. Rotherham had been looking on his daughter's upcoming nuptials as a worrisome event, unsure whether the marriage would make her happy—now he was looking on them as a blessing. There was no doubt in his mind as to the couple's feelings for each other. Now if only they would tell one another! He sighed and flattened his pages in an attempt to concentrate on the book once again.

Whilst these three enjoyed their reflective occupations, Freddy, who had joined them, was utterly bewildered by their behaviour.

"You are all acting dashed odd this morning!" he declared, after Selina yawned for the seventeenth time and Mrs. Rotherham looked up over her embroidery to make another comment about the weather. "How can you all be so cursed tired when I'm in fine fettle and was not even home until dawn?"

"Language, Freddy," his father reprimanded him from behind his book.

"Well, it really is above and beyond, all of you tired and not talkative. Belle fawning over Julia upstairs, who is still asleep I might add. Mama, you are going soft, I say. And this morning I wished to go for a ride only to be told James had a day of leisure given him and the horses were all resting. Ridiculous!"

"Let me understand you," Mr. Rotherham said, putting down his book. "You are complaining of our lack of energy in the morning, our quiet reflection and contemplation, your younger sister's affection for her elder, my caring for our servants well, and the horses needing a day off from your wild riding?"

Freddy looked sulky at that summary of his woes. "It sounds appallingly foolish when you put it like that."

"Yes, it does, doesn't it?"

At that moment a knock sounded on the door downstairs, and Mrs. Rotherham looked over to her husband. Mr. Rotherham rose and put a gentle hand on her shoulder, and Selina, who had been sitting at Mrs. Rotherham's elbow passing her skeins of thread, also placed a hand over her hostess'.

Freddy rolled his eyes at the continuing odd behaviour but was pleased when Lord Wolversley, Lord Courtenay, and Mr. Highsmith were announced. His surprise at this morning's events was increased when he saw the exhaustion written across two of the gentlemen's bodies and the battered look of Wolversley's face!

"My lord, my lord, and Mr. Highsmith." Mr. Rotherham shook Wolversley and Highsmith's hands warmly and bowed to Lord Courtenay.

"Good morning, Mr. Rotherham," Highsmith responded.

"A *very* good morning," replied Mr. Rotherham. He turned to greet Wolversley, but the Earl was far more interested in searching out the rest of the room. There was only one person he wished to see this morning.

"Oh, Lucius!" Selina leapt up from her seat, upsetting the embroidery thread, and came to embrace her brother. She buried her head in his chest and hugged him until he thought he might burst. He kissed the girl on the head, gently prying her away from him. "Now, now, pet. No need for any more tears." He gave her his handkerchief. "You knew I was well last night."

She took the offered fabric and dabbed delicately at her cheeks. "I know, oh, I am being silly, but it is so good that everything is well again."

"I concur," said Courtenay who had already been apprised of last night's events by Wolversley, as any best friend should be. The delicate matter had been conveyed to him under the strictest confidence and directly afterwards, Wolversley had told him of his intentions for this morning and asked his advice. The baron had replied that he only knew love was a gamble and that the Earl should simply play his hand. After what had happened with his uncle, Wolversley had sworn off gambling...but this was a different sort of wager entirely.

"It is a miracle," added Mr. Rotherham.

"What on earth happened in this house last night?" exploded Freddy.

All six of the others turned to him with a look of conspiratorial amusement and said almost in unison, "Nothing."

At that moment Annabelle and Julia entered the morning room, Annabelle taking Julia's hand in her arm. The blow Julia had received from last night had left her jaw a little swollen with a large purple bruise mottling the skin tones.

The younger sister guided the elder farther into the room and then looked over sheepishly to Selina. They had had their reconciliation last night, but when one locks one's friend in a cupboard, good feeling is never instantaneous. Luckily for Annabelle, however, Selina had a forgiving nature, and soon Selina's eyes softened as she looked to her friend and a little shy smile passed between the two. This little interchange was another of the many things that Freddy Rotherham missed.

He took one look at Julia and threw his arms up in the air. "And I suppose that plum-coloured mark on Julia's chin is nothing? I demand to know what has happened. Nothing makes sense here at home, and I called upon Sylvester on my way home this morning and he is gone from Town. What the devil is going on?"

"That saves me one task," Highsmith whispered to Annabelle who returned a mischievous smile.

Wolversley had moved away from Selina as Julia entered on the arm of her sister. He was standing almost in the centre of the room and despite the other persons present, the Earl and Julia just stood there staring at each other.

"I think," said Mr. Rotherham, sizing up the situation, "that we should all go to the library to tell Freddy about the secret of last night."

Mrs. Rotherham had already risen to her feet, knowing her husband's thoughts. "Yes, I quite agree. Come now, Lady

Selina. You too, Annabelle, Mr. Highsmith, and Lord Courtenay."

"Right away, Mrs. Rotherham." Courtenay flourished a hand and escorted the two young ladies through the doors alongside Mr. Highsmith.

"Freddy," his father said sternly, commanding the boy away from the two who still stood staring at one another.

"Dashed odd! Dashed odd, I say!" he muttered before following his father out of the room and closing the door behind him.

Mr. Rotherham sent Annabelle, Selina, Courtenay, Highsmith and Freddy towards the library, with instructions to Highsmith to tell the whole of last night's adventures. Then he and Mrs. Rotherham walked toward the staircase.

"You know, my dear, I believe I owe you some sort of apology." Mr. Rotherham placed a loving hand in the small of his wife's back as they took the stairs together.

"You often do, but I have to be honest, George, I am unsure as to which wrong this particular apology is for." A coy smile fell into the well-worn lines on either side of Mrs. Rotherham's mouth as she looked up at her husband.

"I believe you said on the night of Annabelle's coming-out ball when we first saw Wolversley again, that you thought enough time had passed that there was hope for the two of them. And now there they stand, confessing their love for each other in our morning room—or at least, I hope that's what they are doing."

"Why, yes," Mrs. Rotherham exclaimed with much satisfaction, "I believe I did say that."

They had reached the next floor now and they paused. Mr. Rotherham faced his wife and, with a flair quite unusual for his normally quiet self, performed the most extravagant bow. "I bow before your superior knowledge of the marriage mart and your matchmaking ways."

Mrs. Rotherham laughed, taking hold of her husband's arm and dragging him upright. "Do you know, George?" she said, guiding him towards her sitting room. "If I did not know better, I would think you were jesting at my expense."

"Me? Never!" His eyes twinkled down at her.

"Well, I do know better, for if you were, you know I would be most displeased—one might even say, wrathful."

"Oh no, my Wrathful One! We can't have that, can we?" He closed the door of the sitting room and bent down to place a kiss on his wife's lips. "You were quite right, my dear," he said, drawing away from her a moment, "and I only hope they can be as happy as we are."

"I am sure they will be," she replied. "And as we both know, I have a superior knowledge of these sorts of things." Smiling, she tipped her head upwards and kissed her husband again.

THE TWO DOWNSTAIRS in the morning room had not moved since the departure of the others. They still stood looking at each other. It felt as though the air had left the room.

Julia finally spoke. "I heard you last night."

Wolversley's face tensed. "I thought you might have. I wanted to tell you—I tried—but I had already done so much damage to you. I could not bear to cause you any more hurt."

His words raked at her wound, cleaning it so that it could now stop festering and heal. But despite the freedom the cleansing brought, the pain still caused tears to come to her eyes. "Why did I have no say in the decision that broke our engagement? You could have told me."

"Would you have listened?" He came forward, running

gentle fingers down her face and over the swelling on her jaw. "I'll kill him if I ever see him again."

"We won't," she replied, the protectiveness of his words and the look in his eyes sending quivering warmth through her. She returned to the subject of their past that lay, so intimately, between them. "Do you think you know me so well that you could have guessed my answer all those years ago?"

"Yes," he said, cupping her face with both hands and stepping closer still.

"You are incorrigible."

"And you are impetuous and headstrong."

"You tripped me up at the inn."

"I did," he said ruefully. "And I feel terrible about it. You made a very convincing boy. Although, I must say, your information on which of our sisters eloped was rather off." He chuckled.

"Yes, I was as shocked as you to see Annabelle there."

"I will say this for you—this time your impetuousness did some good and saved your sister from ruin." As he gazed down at her, all the severity in his countenance disappeared, and the face of her young love returned. She smiled and then followed his gaze down to his jacket pocket. She saw him pick an object out of it, and as he did so, he looked up to catch her eyes. It was a string of irregularly-shaped freshwater pearls.

"These were going to be my wedding gift to you," he explained. "I should not let you see them yet, but—"

"You remembered," she cut in, in a hoarse whisper. "I knew you remembered that morning when you called on us after the ball."

"Yes."

It was that simple. Yes, he remembered when they had found a pearl from one of her mother's necklaces and stolen it away together that Julia might have it. Yes, he had remembered her love of the jewel, of its pure and unique nature—the same jewel that Julia had treasured ever since, the same jewel that he had seen her drop the morning after their first meeting. Yes, he remembered everything about their young love.

A tear slipped from her eye.

"Julia." Wolversley's voice had also turned to a whisper. He tipped her chin up and looked directly into her eyes. "Julia, I will not force this marriage upon you. If I can find a way to give you your freedom, if that is what you really want, I will do it. I will make sure you can make your own decision."

She placed a tentative hand on his cheek. "Lucius, for someone who claims to know me so well, you fall down a little. Like a trained hawk, you may set me free, but I will always,"—another tear slipped down her cheek—"always return to you. I love you, Lucius."

With that admission, he swept her up into his arms and kissed her as ruthlessly as her bruised jaw would allow. Everything they felt was familiar. The sweetness of their lips, the hands that ran through each other's hair, the hunger that had not abated in all these six years—it all came back in full force.

After a few moments had passed, Wolversley pulled away to look at her. "I have been waiting to do that since I first saw you at your sister's ball." He pressed his body closer to hers. "If only we were married. Tomorrow is much too far away!"

Julia giggled. "Now who's being impetuous?"

The End

REVIEW THIS BOOK

Thank you for reading *The Unexpected Earl*.

If you enjoyed it, please share your review on Amazon, BookBub or Goodreads to help other readers find my book.

FREE CHAPTER
THE WIDOW'S REDEEMER

Chapter 1

Everything has beauty, but not everyone sees it.
– Confucius

"I don't understand your meaning, sir." A little crinkle appeared between Letty's brows. She folded and unfolded her stitchery, her hands becoming more agitated with every second that passed.

She cast the sewing onto a small side table and began teasing the frayed cuffs of her muslin day dress before standing abruptly. Leaving the doctor behind, she walked over to the small window set deeply into the farmhouse wall. Silence followed. She stared at the rugged slabs of stone that made up the thick wall and kept the winter winds at bay.

The beginning of the week had brought her husband back from the gaming hells of London. He had been sickening from exposure to rain and cold on his journey home and had fallen from his horse. Could life be so ready to change? Were the cards being dealt as she stood here?

The physician was packing up instruments into his old leather bag. There was the clink of draught bottles as they slotted into place, the creak of un-oiled leather, and the click of a stiff clasp.

Letty swung back round to face the retreating doctor. "But surely there is something more that may be done?"

His small white head shook in a well-acted sadness. Perhaps he had given this news a dozen times, perhaps he had given it a hundred times over. His headshake was so perfected and his eyes so full of sympathy. It was a slow and definite last retreat.

"It is merely a matter of nursing him until his time comes." He paused, wetting his bottom lip before taking a long breath. "Has he drawn up a will?"

Letty's thoughts scattered everywhere at once. She had not thought about a will. Even the mention of one but two days ago would have seemed unwarranted, almost absurd. Yet here John lay, with waxy skin and red-rimmed eyes, the smell of fever on him. The scent was curious; body odours were mingling with the wood smoke and damp, producing a rank and stale smell.

A will, was that what the doctor had said? John had been in charge of business matters, and he would not have had the forethought to write a will at seven and twenty, or at least not the care.

"I am not sure." She reached a hand up, unconsciously checking her hair. These were not things she had expected to confront in her second year of marriage.

"I suggest you summon your lawyer as soon as possible. It is hard to estimate how much time your husband has left."

She nodded dumbly, blinking quickly in a last, vain attempt to understand the enormity of what was happening. A sad smile marked his lips, as though that settled the business. With no more to be done, he took up his case and descended the tight spiral staircase.

Letty followed behind, grappling with the feeling of shock but still aware of her obligation to see the doctor out. In front of the house, the small boy who looked after the farm's horses waited with the doctor's animal. Letty watched the physician mount the small Dartmoor pony. The animal shook his head in impatience for his hay and stable and was only happy once his hooves were falling in a steady beat. John's wife waited at the door until the creature disappeared from sight.

For a moment she stood silently, contemplating the sentence which had just this evening been hung over her life. The gathering gloom descended upon her still figure, leaving her a lonesome silhouette in the evening farmyard. Dew settled unbidden upon the landscape, the droplets disturbed a little by a sea breeze. The sky was dark—hues of blue, grey, red, and purple all slowly merging into one as night formed above her. In a far off pasture the soft lowing of a cow could be heard. The familiar sound brought her back to the problems at hand. She shook off the desire to sleep and, turning on her wooden heel, walked hastily inside.

A small fire, which had been lit early in the evening, was glowing sluggishly in the grate. The scent of it had gradually penetrated everything in the room. Objects surrounding the bed were cast in an unusual light. Several rapidly drawn up letters scattered a small desk in the corner of the room, the wax on each one looking like a small arachnid in the dim light. A bowl of tepid water reflected a little of the firelight, giving the depths an eerie luminescence. A rag hung over the side of the basin, like a lone shipwreck survivor crawling to safety.

The moonlight was firmly in control of the rugged landscape outside the window when she finally drifted off. The large winged armchair in her husband's room had become her home in the past week, ever since he had been taken ill. The heavy woollen blanket, which was now draped across her unconscious frame, had become the roof over her head.

Letty was awakened by nightmares only half an hour after she fell asleep. Too many worries consumed her mind which, until settled, would prevent her from further rest. Soon, realizing the cold had frozen her aching joints, she rose to dab her husband's brow. He made no indication of consciousness.

The farmhands had brought John back after finding him unhorsed and drenched on one of the farm tracks. After all, a drunk man was no horseman. Letty had not heard from him while he had been in Town and even his return had been a surprise.

Pausing a moment, she watched the knitting and un-knitting of his feverish brow before turning and making her way to the desk. She shuffled the letters that lay there into some kind of order and gingerly placed another log on the fire.

"Lettice?"

She spun on her heel at the sound of the rasping voice. Small feet bore her swiftly from the fireplace to John's side. She knelt on the wooden floor to better look into his weary eyes. He was groggy, his eyes roving about the room, though Letty could see lucidness as they settled upon her.

"Yes, John? How do you feel?" She dunked the cloth in the basin and made to wipe his beaded brow.

"No, no more of that. You have made me cold enough." He turned his head from her.

She nodded slightly, placing the rag back into the basin.

"Why has this come upon me?" he cried out suddenly. "I am in such pain!" He writhed on the bed and upset the soiled bed linens.

"How can I make you more comfortable? Your pillows, do you wish to sit up?"

"That's the last thing I want to do, Lettice. My back, it aches terribly." He paused. So little strength was left to him; it was an exertion even to speak a single sentence—especially a sentence filled with anger. "My mother was right. We should never have left Town. None of this would have come upon us."

Her eyes dropped to the disordered bedcovers. "We would never have met."

He made no response and turned his head away once

again. Letty could not stand the feeling of ineptness. She stood up, pausing by the chair, and then made her way to the fire. There was an old loaf of bread left on a cutting board by its side. She was hungry; it was early morning, a long time since she had had her frugal dinner. She started sawing off a piece to toast over the fire.

"Will you not ask if your sick husband wants something to eat?"

"Do you?"

"No, but you could at least act the caring wife."

Letty did not answer. It was best she refrained while John was in this mood. Then, with a sobering feeling, she realised that perhaps there would not be many more of his moods to bear.

"The doctor said...well, he said the fever is not abating. He was worried. You are weakening rather than strengthening."

"And so I expect he thinks I should call the lawyer." John coughed, a wracking sound that clawed at his lungs and rattled his core.

"He did mention it, yes." She did not mean it as an attack, but John took it to be one.

"So quick to make me sign over my fortune. I have been ill but a week." The well-known scowl lines of his face deepened in a sneer.

"John?" She turned to face him. Despite their differences, to tell a man he was dying could never be an easy thing. How could she approach it? How could she say it?

As it was, she would not have to bear the discomfort of speaking it. He had turned his head away again, and he would not turn it back now. He had read it in her anxious eyes all too clearly. Death was inevitable to all men, and to him it would come sooner than to most.

She stayed by his bed, quiet, trying hard to clear her mind of all the thoughts that clamoured for attention. It was still dark beyond the walls of the house, dark like her mind which was filled with a hundred worries. She would go on through the night worrying, waiting by his side and watching his pain.

Dawn came slowly. She rose from the chair she had been waiting in and walked round the bed to face him. As her gaze fell on his face, the cockerel crowed. His eyes were cold, distant, and lifeless. His body was pale and hard, the worries of a lifetime written in the lines of his harsh, heavy face. She left him there. She did not close his eyes but walked through the cold house in search of her shawl so that she could go to the village and fetch the funeral men. The lawyer never came and neither did her tears.

John's body was made ready for burial, and the farm's tenants were duly informed. Letty would be the only one following the coffin to the graveyard on that bleak walk. No friends came; even family, it appeared, were unable to attend. Letty wondered that John's mother did not come to bury her son, to see the last trace of his earthly self disappear into the ground. It would not be until later that she would receive a letter explaining that, upon hearing of her son's death, the mother had locked herself in her room and was refusing to eat or come out. To lose a husband had been the first trial for that mother to overcome, but now a son also within two years was more than she could bear. So Letty was left to walk behind her husband's coffin alone.

The last of the rich brown earth was tossed carelessly by the gravedigger. The soil sprayed across the grave that contained a body that was once a man. Feeling a cold northerly breeze spring up, Letty clasped the material of her thin pelisse closer. She looked around the deserted graveyard, sighed quietly, and then turned to make the lonely walk home.

Letty's mind was absent. Her body, however, was seated in a large leather armchair, the springs of which were becoming rather too obtrusive, while the stuffing was half there and half missing. The chair was in a tiny room at the back of a building that constituted the solicitors' offices. The rambling structure was situated in the village, a little set back from the other buildings, and was condemned by many to be in a worse state of repair than the infamous blacksmith's. This was partly due to the age and personality of the main law-working occupants, but it was also because their clientele possessed a low standing and, therefore, a deficient income.

Despite the building's exterior and the general tattiness of the objects within, it was a tidy little office. Nothing seemed out of place, and, unlike most solicitors' desks, this one did not have paperwork scattered across it. Letty was alone in the room for a long while. The faint mutterings and voices, muffled by the wall, floated in to her. The noises all washed over her, and she did not pay them much attention. How could she be interested in the chit-chat of persons she had never met when her future was being located, shuffled, and glanced over?

The man who would be the bearer of all news concerning her future eventually opened the door. He paused on the threshold. Letty could hear his steady breathing though she did not look round. Her head remained perfectly still, her eyes forward, and she had a politeness about her carriage. She clasped her hands loosely in her lap, ready for whatever would be thrown into them. She may not have had a governess who had taught her fine languages or clever mathematics but, thanks to her parson scholar of a father, she was no fool. That pause upon the threshold was one small thing which warned her of what was to come.

Why would a solicitor pause on the threshold, run a hand-kerchief over the perspiration that had suddenly beaded on his brow, give four brisk sniffs, and then straighten his plain cravat before facing his client? The answer was plain and it was simple. It whispered itself into Letty's mind. It said: fear.

She smiled faintly as the solicitor took his seat. He was a short, wiry old man and rather outmatched by the much too large wooden desk. He managed a small, polite smile before he placed his stack of papers carefully out before him. With all of them equally spaced and perfectly straight, he cleared his throat and began.

"Now, Mrs. Burton, ah, here we are, ah, yes. Now I have drawn up and put together all the estate's values and assets including the farm and the house." He refrained from using the term "your house", and that was when she began to realise her true predicament. "I have then compared them to repayments needing to be made, yes, um, now...." He readjusted his wire-rimmed spectacles while the small tuft of white hair in the centre of his head quivered. "Yes, ah...."

Letty's heart was tugged a little by the awkward situation this man had been placed in. She rested a tentative hand on the desk but took care to distance it from the solicitor's own hands. She captured his gaze with her frank brown eyes. "Mr. Glenville, I am led to believe that sometimes husbands have little to leave to their wives due to unfortunate business circumstances leading up to a sudden death. I understand that this cannot be helped." She kept her eyes on his, speaking far more with them than with her mouth.

"Yes, yes, of course. So glad you understand, Mrs. Burton. It can cause such upset, you see, when the value of the estate and assets comparative to various debts is read out. That is why—well, never mind that." He reshuffled the papers then took them up again and read on in a calm, precise voice. When he had finished, Letty remained poised for a few moments longer, allowing the information to take its rightful place in her mind. She had been completely unaware of the debts and the precarious position John had been in before he died.

"I see," she said finally, with far more firmness than Mr. Glenville had expected. "And now, tell me truthfully, can the assets fulfil the repayments in their entirety with anything left over?" Her eyes fell back into focus as she spoke, containing a hardness that had not been there before.

"Well, Mrs. Burton, this is where it gets rather more complex. You see, your husband's affairs had fallen into, well, how shall I say? Difficult times. Therefore, through my calculations of his estate and the debts he accrued from purchases, as well as the debts from ah…several respectable establishments in London."

Letty's neck could not help but tense at the reference to her husband's regular appearance at some of London's most fashionable gaming hells. It had not been unusual for him to be away from Cornwall for weeks at a time while he entertained himself in London. She remembered the look of disgust and the lack of farewell as he journeyed away from their house each time he went to the metropolis. How could he, a bred gentlemen, stand to be in the country with little or no entertainment? Coupled with this was the severe lack of society that had attended him ever since his marriage to Letty. So severe were the consequences of his disadvantageous marriage that to spend only moments in his wife's presence was too much for him to bear.

He would be off, of course, entertaining himself in some club or another, chasing days of past glory in the far-gone Seasons. He met his friends, the ones she was never permitted to see, the ones in front of whom she could only prove an embarrassment. She had often wondered what those friends had heard of her. If it were spoken from John's lips, then it would not be praise. There had been a few times when his words had stung more than his hand upon her—not many, but a few.

"Oh, I beg your pardon, Mr. Glenville. Could you please repeat what you just said?" Letty's back straightened and her mind returned from that far off place.

"Have no fear, Mrs. Burton." Mr. Glenville smiled slightly. He liked Lettice Burton, even if she had married above her station. She seemed a sweet girl, and yet, as he saw her sitting there, he reflected that she was much changed from the girl he had seen on her wedding day. She no longer looked an innocent, fresh-faced child; she was a woman now, at least about the eyes. There was a sort of wisdom there, a lack of that childlike naivety she had once borne. "I understand this is a difficult time. Losing a spouse is a terrible thing, especially at so young an age."

Letty bowed her head in assent, but behind the eyes that Mr. Glenville had deemed wise, there was no grieving heart. Was that wrong? Letty felt pangs of guilt, and yet, as she raised her head again and felt the slight bruising at the back of her neck, the guilt bled away.

"What I was beginning to explain was the financial plan for Highfield. In order to cover the debts owed, I am afraid that the only way is to sell the house and the farm along with it."

Letty, after several days of widowhood, felt the first tears pricking her eyes. The guilt came back, but it was overcome with sadness. She thought with fondness—and bitterness—of the home she had shared with John and for a moment could not bear the thought of its inevitable loss.

"I understand, Mr. Glenville. I give you all the authority to see to the matter. I shall prepare the house and farm for a new owner and take my leave of the tenants."

"Madam, I know this is outside of my authority, but I just

wish to inquire—have you anywhere to go? I would not go about selling this property for you if you have no safety."

Letty smiled at him, his kindness a surprise yet fitting with his winsome face. "It is quite all right, Mr. Glenville. I am sure that my family will take me in." She said it with a certainty she was far from feeling. "In the meantime, the debts must be paid. Please sell Highfield, and before other debts are settled, take your own wages out of the sum. I do not wish to see you underpaid."

Mr. Glenville looked down at the desk, shuffling papers in a brisk fashion. He pulled a handkerchief out of his pocket and fluffed it about his nose. He was trying his hardest to smile his thanks without seeming impertinent. When he looked up, he saw a large smile brightening Letty's mouth, and it instantly put him at his ease. The smile remained, covering the anxiety inhabiting her mind and protecting her from further sentiment or questions. She rose to exit.

Mr. Glenville came out from behind his desk and made to take her hand. The sudden movement caused Letty to shrink back instinctively, her arms moving to protect her body. Mr. Glenville's owl-like eyebrows rose and crinkled in confusion. Letty, her wide eyes taking in what she had just done unconsciously and the harmless gesture of the man which she had misread, dropped her hands to her sides in embarrassment.

"Thank you, Mr. Glenville," she said, trying to speak as though nothing unusual had just occurred. "You have been exceedingly helpful. If you could send me a missive here and there, to update me on the sale's progress and debt repayments, I would greatly appreciate it." She made no move to give him her hand.

The small man, willing to ignore the strange episode, bowed deeply before straightening again. Something flashed in his eyes, but Letty missed the look of admiration he bestowed upon her. She was already crossing the threshold, planning in her mind what needed to be done next.

Letty had barely eaten a thing at lunch, and now, as she was walking to the farm tenants' houses, a feeling of weakness came over her. She would not be eating until the leave-taking was done, however long it took. The sky was overcast though it was not likely to rain. Letty observed the sun-whitened clouds that threw everything into an oddly naked light.

The dirt track, which she had walked down so many times to oversee the farm work while John was away, was slightly damp thanks to last night's rain. Her black widow's garb had been bought at the cheapest price, so if a little mud spattered the hemline she did not much care. She was too used to walking in the country to be bothered about hemlines or complexion.

Her small figure went in and out of the few cottages on the farm. She bade farewell to the many families, the familiar smell of animals and earth in her nose. She was touched by the few words of condolences that were uttered, even if the tenants cared little for the loss of John. She saw their many concerned eyes and knew their feelings were for her.

To them she was the kindly parson's daughter who came and asked after each and every one of them, never forgetting a name. Yes, they would be sorry to see her go, yet the promise of a new master who might not be as tyrannical as the last was something that gave them hope. Why had the gentleman come from Town to a small piece of Cornwall in the first place? It was a piece of the country scorned by the modish, and clearly it had been scorned by him as well.

Letty knew of the many questions that her union with John had raised. They had been worlds apart in station, and they would never have married had it not been for one indiscretion. That one incident, which had been so easily misread, was the reason she had been married for two years to a man who did not love her. If only John had not led her into a compromising situation because of his own desires; if only she had not so easily mistaken his lust for love. He had been a man whom she had thought she loved, and it had taken time for that naivety to fade after their hasty marriage. She had slowly realised his resentment of her, and it was a resentment that had in two years grown savage.

Yet, as she spoke to each tenant she felt a slight loss, a slight sense of pain at the parting she was making from the place that had been her home, no matter the circumstances. She remembered that she needed to write a letter to her parents asking their shelter. Would they be able to take her back into their parsonage? Somehow, it seemed impossible to go back to her childhood home—that place where her father had once tutored John, where they had met, where the unfortunate incident had happened which forced them to marry.

Too much had happened to her, had been inflicted upon her, for her to return to that place where she had once been so innocent. She felt as though the innocence she had worn in her youth had become polluted. She could not return to live the life of someone she would never be again. As the last tenant closed the door behind her, she turned toward her home, and as she walked back in the twilight, she knew that tonight, at least, it was too late to think upon the future.

The following morning brought a letter from Theodora Burton, Letty's sister-in-law, who resided in Truro. The small, pretty hand, familiar to Letty, brought a little smile to the young widow's lips. What had her relative been up to now?

17 October 1815

Dearest Lettice,

How are you? I am so sad to hear of John's passing away. It was such a dreadful shock! I actually said to Mrs. Grockel, my housekeeper, how sudden it was. I even dropped my paintbrush when I read the letter you sent me about it. (I was in the midst of decorating a small cabinet and now it is totally ruined as I dropped a black paintbrush right in the middle. I have no idea what to do about it. Mrs. Grockel said to paint it one colour again. I told her if she wished to spend hours repainting the pattern she is welcome to it!)

Anyway, I am getting quite beside the point! Mr. Burton— well, David to you, I suppose, since you are family—has become quite ill, and as I thought you may be in need of some company and so shall I, I am inviting you to come and stay with us a while. Would you like to? Please say yes, for if I only have Mrs. Grockel to speak to I may fall ill myself, though I do not wish to exaggerate, of course.

I hope everything is well with you, dear sister, and I look forward to seeing you soon. I send my love—

Your dearest sister-in-law,

Theodora Burton

Letty folded the letter and laid it in her lap. She turned to gaze out of the parlour window onto green fields that heaved up and fell away outside. Her thumb stroked the thick paper; perhaps it would be good to visit Theo. It had been a long time since she had seen her, and it would be a way to save her parents any expense. Her father had been graced with a decent parish, but that did not mean money had ever been plentiful.

The thought of her father only brought her mind back to John. If only money had not been so scarce when she had been young! Her father would not have had to take on gentlemen to tutor. She would never have met John, and they would never have married in a desperate attempt to avert the scandal.

She suddenly shook herself. What was she doing? Self-pity would help nothing. The past was set in stone and ultimately unchangeable. She must think of the future. If she could not change past actions, she could at least try to survive the present. She reprimanded herself and then, flicking the long plait of hair she had been fiddling with back over her shoulder, she rose, clasping the letter. She sat in John's old chair at the large wooden desk, the high back overshadowing her, and took out a sheet of paper. Once the letter to Theo was finished, sealed, and sent, Letty went about packing the few dresses she owned into a small trunk. She saw to the business of the farm, and finally coming back to Highfield, she began saying goodbye to her home.

And so the farm, the house, and all the possessions therein were left to the debt collectors. Letty took her final leave with only a small trunk and a portmanteau to her widowed name. She removed to her sister-in-law's house in Truro. While Theodora's husband remained sick, Letty would be the young wife's comforter and companion.

The widow remembered with such clarity the day on which she left: the crisp morning air that pinched at her cheeks before she stepped up into the carriage; the sweet smell of earth that was laced with traces of briny sea air; the wind that flung her long hair back and forth, loosing it from the contraptions imprisoning it; the sky that was thick shades of iron grey and layers of towering clouds building above; the heath and shrub- covered landscape in all its unruly beauty she knew so well—all was left to the elements behind her. The animals were hidden away in warm homes together, the only farewell being the natural blow of westerly winds.

The harshly sprung carriage afforded a small view through a murky pane of glass of the country which she loved. This view she engraved in her mind's eye. She would keep it for a time when she needed to know there was a place like heaven, a paradise somewhere.

philippajanekeyworth.com/TWR

WANT TO BE IN THE KNOW?

Be the first to know about freebies, sales and when Philippa's next book releases by signing up to her newsletter.

Sign up below:

philippajanekeyworth.com/newsletter

ALSO BY
PHILIPPA JANE KEYWORTH

LADIES OF WORTH

From the gaming hells of 18th century London to Bath's fashionable
Pump Room, the Ladies of Worth series opens up a world of
romance, wit and scandal to its readers. With formidable heroines
and honourable heroes who match each other wit for wit you'll find
yourself falling in love with the Ladies of Worth.

philippajanekeyworth.com/FMT

philippajanekeyworth.com/ADD

philippajanekeyworth.com/LOW

philippajanekeyworth.com/DOD

REGENCY ROMANCES

philippajanekeyworth.com/TWR

philippajanekeyworth.com/TUE

FANTASY

philippajanekeyworth.com/TE

ABOUT THE AUTHOR

Philippa Jane Keyworth, also known as P. J. Keyworth, writes historical romance and fantasy novels you'll want to escape into.

She loves strong heroines, challenging heroes and backdrops that read like you're watching a movie. She creates complex, believable characters you want to get to know and worlds that are as dramatic as they are beautiful.

Keyworth's historical romance novels include Regency and Georgian romances that trace the steps of indomitable heroes and heroines through historic British streets. From London's glittering ballrooms to its dark gaming hells, characters experience the hopes and joys of love while avoiding a coil or two! Travel with them through London, Bath, Cornwall and beyond and you'll find yourself falling in love.

Keyworth's fantasy series The Emrilion Trilogy follows strong love stories and epic adventure. Unveiling a world of nomadic warrior tribes and peaceful forest-dwelling folk, you can explore the hills, deserts and cities of Emrilion and the history that is woven through them. With so many different races in the same kingdom it's become a melting pot of drama and intrigue where the ultimate struggle between good and evil will bring it all to the brink of destruction.

f facebook.com/philippajane.keyworth

y twitter.com/PJKeyworth

instagram.com/pjkeyworth

a amazon.com/author/philippakeyworth

BB bookbub.com/authors/philippa-jane-keyworth

g goodreads.com/philippajanekeyworth